THE BIG HIT

THE
BIG HIT

A Novel

JAMES NEAL HARVEY

MYSTERIOUSPRESS.COM

OPEN ROAD

INTEGRATED MEDIA

NEW YORK

Copyright © 2014 by James Neal Harvey

Cover design by Tracey Dunham

ISBN 978-1-4804-8580-8

Published in 2014 by MysteriousPress.com/
Open Road Integrated Media, Inc.
345 Hudson Street
New York, NY 10014
www.mysteriouspress.com
www.openroadmedia.com

To Ursula, with all my love

THE BIG HIT

1.

The girl had class.

Mongo had seen that right off. She was tall and slender with dark red hair and big jugs, and there was a beautiful tattoo of a butterfly on her ass. She'd cost him two thousand bucks for the night.

The tab was worth it. When he woke up this morning he had another helping, and now he was totally relaxed and ready for the day. He fluffed up the pillows and lay back on the bed, watching her get dressed.

Her clothes were classy, too. Frilly white panties, a gauzy bra. Tight-fitting dress with a short skirt, green to match the color of her eyes. She put on pumps with four-inch heels that showed off her legs, and when she saw him looking she gave him a friendly smile.

Mongo liked hookers. When you hired one, it was such a straightforward deal. You didn't have to buy her drinks or dinner, you didn't have to waste time getting down to business. You didn't even have to talk to her, if you didn't want to.

Best of all, she wouldn't know your name. You just paid her and played your favorite games and sent her on her way.

Of course, if you did want to talk, you might hear some interesting stories. This girl had told him she was only working until she earned her law degree from NYU. Once she had the degree and was admitted to the Bar, she'd become a public defender and stand up for all the poor people who were getting shafted by the system.

Not bad, but Mongo had heard better. Every girl had a tale, and he had yet to run into one who said she was in the life because she liked it and the money was good.

This girl's name was Darlene. That probably wasn't what it said on her birth certificate, but so what? She could call herself Mother Teresa, for all he gave a shit. What counted was performance, and she'd delivered.

She put on fresh lipstick and eyeliner and flicked her hair with a brush, checking her image in the mirror. Then she came over to the bed and squeezed his hand.

Her voice was soft. "'Bye. You were wonderful."

It was so phony he had to laugh. "So were you," he said.

"Hope I'll see you again."

He knew what she was really hoping for, but that was okay too. He got up from the bed and went over to the desk, dialed the combination on his attaché case and swung back the lid. His wallet was inside, along with a tape recorder and some other stuff.

He'd already paid her when she first arrived last night, but now he took another hundred-dollar bill from the wallet and handed that to her as well. "Little extra for you," he said. "Thanks for the ride."

She batted her eyes. "Oh, gee, thank *you*."

After she left, he went into the john and pissed forever. Then he brushed his teeth to get rid of the lousy taste, and when he finished he stepped into the shower and hosed himself down. As the hot water pounded his skin, he thought about what he was going to do today, and excitement kicked in.

This would be a big hit, one of the biggest ever. And, if it went as planned, a clean one. Afterward, he'd leave New York and go back to LA, where he'd receive part of his fee in cash. The rest would be deposited in his account in the Caymans.

Once that was settled he'd be off to Vegas, where he'd get in some action at the tables, buy himself a few more Darlenes, and wait for another job. Talk about the good life.

He shaved carefully, lathering and relathering his face before slicing off the whiskers. He knew most guys hated to shave, but he enjoyed it. The practice helped him look his best, and that was important to him. Not just because his work called for it, but also because he was proud of his strong, lean features.

Checking his appearance, he noticed that there was a bit of stubble on his head. Hardly enough to say so, but better to get rid of it. He lathered his skull and ran the razor over that too, using the same deliberate technique as he had with his cheeks and jaw. There now—smooth as a baby's ass.

Next he trimmed his mustache. It was thick and bushy, and he clipped the ragged ends with scissors until they were perfectly neat. When he finished, he splashed on cologne and swiped his armpits with deodorant.

Then came the most important parts, starting with the hair. From the attaché case he dug out the mop of reddish-blond curls and carefully placed it on his head. It was the work of one of LA's best wigmakers, meticulously constructed of human hair and custom fitted. Last, he opened the tiny case that contained his contacts and slipped the lenses into place.

The result, he decided, was dynamite. The image staring back at him from the mirror was that of a handsome, athletic young dude with a confident, casual air.

Turning away from the mirror, he caught sight of the tattoo on his left shoulder. It wasn't nearly as fine as the butterfly on the girl's tush. While hers had been perfectly drawn in delicate shades of coral and purple and pink, his was a small, crude fishhook he'd created himself with a pin and indelible black ink, back when he was in Q.

But if the tattoo wasn't the best in the world, it had meaning to him, reminding him how far he'd come since those days.

The suit he chose was a tan Armani. It draped smoothly and looked great with the cream silk shirt and the red Ferragamo tie. His shoes were brown suede Guccis.

Mongo loved clothes, always had. Nowadays he could afford to spend a fortune on his wardrobe, buying only the finest and most expensive things. It was another reminder of how he'd brought himself up from nothing. The key was that he'd never stopped improving his professional skills, while still making sure to enjoy himself along the way.

Once he was dressed, he glanced at the gold Rolex on his left wrist. Ten past ten; time to get moving. He was hungry, but he wouldn't stop to eat.

Instead he'd come back to the hotel afterward, pick up his luggage and then take a cab to JFK. He already had his ticket, and there would be lunch on the plane. For now, there were other things to take care of.

A packet of blow lay on the dresser. It was a wonder there was any left. He and Darlene had snorted most of it the night before, when they were flying over the moon.

Rolling up another crisp new bill, he drew powder into each nostril until he'd finished the last of it. This was good shit; the rush came fast.

Returning to the desk he got out his notes, along with the materials he'd had printed in LA. He studied the papers once more and then glanced through the story in yesterday's *New York Post* that said the actress Catherine Delure was in town to promote her new movie, *Hot Cargo*.

There was nothing useful in the article. He'd been given everything he had to know before he left the West Coast. He dropped the newspaper into the wastebasket.

Next he lifted the tape recorder out of the attaché case. The device appeared to be no different from a million others, black and with a row of buttons on top, the Sony logo in white.

But this was no ordinary tape recorder.

He touched one of the buttons, and the top popped open. Mounted inside was a compact unit with two short steel barrels and two metal cylinders, all of it welded together smoothly.

Each of the barrels held a fléchette that was two inches long and a half inch in diameter. One for the job, the other as backup. Each of the cylinders contained a powerful charge of compressed air.

The guy in South Central who'd built the piece had haggled with him over the price, finally settling for six grand. That was a bargain. If necessary, Mongo would have paid twice as much. He checked the fléchettes one last time and closed the top of the recorder.

Next he dug into the case for a tube of toluene-based glue. He coated each fingertip with the fast-drying adhesive so that he'd leave no prints on anything he touched. The stuff always felt a little strange at first, but he knew that after a few minutes he'd get used to it.

As soon as the glue was dry he tore up his notes and went into the bathroom and flushed them down the toilet. The tube of glue he tossed into the wastebasket. Finally, he set the tape recorder back into the attaché case and snapped shut the locks.

Everything was in order, he was set to go. He put on a pair of tinted aviator glasses and left the room carrying the case.

As he walked along the corridor toward the elevators, he felt as if he was floating. It wasn't the coke high; it was knowing what he was about to do, knowing how smoothly he'd carry it out.

When it came to killing somebody, Mongo figured he was the best there was.

2.

The outside air was balmy. The sun was shining, puffy white clouds were drifting across the sky, and the trees were wreathed in pale green leaves. Altogether a beautiful spring morning, and Mongo was enjoying it. He walked along Central Park South at a steady pace.

As usual, the hotels were busy. Taxis and limos were pulling up in front of them, disgorging passengers while bellmen grabbed the luggage. The visitors seemed excited to be in the city.

There was also plenty of action. The sidewalk was thronged with pedestrians, the majority of them female. Some were dogs, but now and then Mongo spotted an eight or better.

As he passed the Park Lane Hotel, he saw a real knockout. This one was a brunette in a beige suit, standing with a guy while a doorman whistled for a taxi. Mongo smiled at her and was pleased when she smiled back. It made him feel good as he went by.

Not that he needed to feel any better than he did. The blow had worn off by now, but he was in a great mood anyway. He was on a job, and that was the best high of all.

Besides, he'd learned from experience to stay sober when he was working. Once when he was a kid, he and his buddy Art Ruiz were bombed out on speed when they robbed a gas station. They were happily scooping bills from the register when the guy who owned the station came up with a sawed-off twelve and shot Ruiz in the face.

Mongo ran like a madman, and the cops never connected him to the case. Later on he'd laughed about how Art had looked with most of his head gone.

But Mongo remembered the lesson. Since then he'd never used anything when he went out on an assignment. No booze, no dope of any kind. You had to be as sharp as you possibly could be. The way he was now.

At the corner he waited for the light to change and glanced at the Plaza. People were going in and out of the entrance, and more limos were lined up at the curb.

Across the way was a little park with flowers and shrubs and a statue of a guy on a horse. The statue was gold-plated and streaked with bird shit. Mongo wondered who the guy was and why he rated a statue, sitting there with the pigeons crapping on his head.

When the light said *walk*, he crossed Fifth and waited again as the traffic whizzed by, finally turning left and going up another block to the Sherry-Netherland. As he approached the entrance a doorman saluted, and Mongo went inside.

This was supposed to be a first-rate hotel, but Mongo didn't think much of what he was seeing so far. The lobby was small and old-fashioned, with a lot of polished wood and marble. It probably hadn't been updated in fifty years, maybe longer.

He picked up a house phone and asked the operator to connect him with Catherine Delure's suite. After a couple of rings, a female voice said, "Yes?"

"Jack Thompson," Mongo said. "From WNEW Radio. Here for my appointment."

There was a pause, and the voice said, "What appointment?"

"The interview with Miss Delure. We got a call yesterday from

Sandra Rosen at Galaxy Films in LA, asking us to set it up. Who is this, please?"

"My name is Dana Laramie. I'm Miss Delure's secretary. Are you sure you're on the agenda?"

"Yes, of course. I'm supposed to ask Miss Delure about her new movie, *Hot Cargo*. The interview goes on the air later today, and it'll run again tomorrow and the next day."

"I'm sorry, but I didn't know anything had been scheduled for this morning."

"Maybe you ought to call Rosen. You want her number?"

"No, it's too early to reach anyone out there."

Exactly, Mongo thought. He feigned exasperation. "Okay, it's all right with me. I'll tell the program director she didn't want to do it."

"Wait a minute. How long would this take?"

"About twenty minutes."

"No more than that?"

"It shouldn't. I ask her a few questions, and that's it."

"Hold on, I'll check." There was another, longer pause, and then Laramie came back on. "Okay, you can come up."

"Thanks. Where are you?"

She gave him the number of the suite, and he put the phone down. She'd sounded okay, her tone low pitched and smooth. He wondered if her looks went with the voice and decided they probably did.

He took an elevator up to the floor where the suite was.

As he approached the entrance, a guy wearing a maroon jacket with the hotel's logo on it appeared from around the corner and said, "Can I help you?"

"I've got an appointment here," Mongo replied, and reached out to press the buzzer.

"Excuse me," the guy said. "I'm with security, and I'll have to check on that. Your name, please?"

Mongo looked him over. The guard had thinning hair and sagging jowls and the aura of an ex-cop. "It's Thompson," Mongo told him. "Jack Thompson, from WNEW Radio."

"Just a minute, please." The guard pressed the buzzer, and the door opened. But instead of the good-looking woman Mongo had expected, a very large man was standing there.

"This gentleman says he has an appointment," the guard said. "His name is Jack Thompson."

Mongo said, "I called from downstairs."

The big man nodded. "Yeah, come on in."

The security guy backed off, and Mongo stepped inside.

After closing the door the big man said, "My name's Chuck Diggs. I'm Miss Delure's bodyguard."

"Hello, Chuck." Mongo dug a business card out of a jacket pocket and handed it to him. While the guy examined the card, Mongo examined him.

He'd known some big men, but this one was something else. Mongo himself was an inch over six feet, yet he found himself looking up at him. Diggs had wide shoulders, and instead of a neck, the shoulders just flowed up into the sides of his head. His hair was cut close to his scalp. He had on a light-gray sport coat and a checked shirt, open at the collar. Mongo made him for around three hundred pounds.

Diggs stuck the card into his jacket pocket and said, "Got anything else? Anything official?"

Mongo took out his wallet and opened it. Behind a clear plastic window was a New York driver's license with his picture and the name Jack Thompson on it. The license was as phony as the business card.

But it satisfied Diggs. "Okay," he said. "Now open the case. I have to see what's in there."

"Sure, no problem."

Against the nearest wall was a table with a vase of flowers on it. Mongo pushed the vase aside and laid his case flat, thumbing the combination and popping the locks. He raised the lid and said, "Be my guest."

The bodyguard peered at the contents. Besides the tape recorder, there were some blank sheets of paper and a spiral notebook and a couple of ballpoints. Also a small package of Kleenex.

Diggs lifted out the tape recorder, looked at it, and put it back in the case. Then he closed the lid and snapped the locks shut.

"One more thing," he said. "Sorry, but I have to do it."

"Whatever you say."

Diggs began patting him down, and Mongo said, "Careful, Chuck. I'm ticklish."

No response. The guy apparently had no sense of humor.

When he finished, Diggs stepped back. "Wait here a minute."

The big man turned and went through a door on the far side of the foyer. As Mongo stood there, he admired the flowers in the vase. The bouquet had at least a dozen different kinds of blossoms in it. He brought his nose closer and found they smelled as good as they looked.

The door opened again, and a woman came out into the foyer, heels clicking on the marble floor. She had dark hair and blue eyes and was well built, filling out the front of her blue cardigan nicely.

She stuck out her hand as she approached. "Hello, Jack. I'm Dana Laramie."

"Hi, Dana." Mongo shook her hand. Not bad, he thought. He'd guessed right.

"Miss Delure has agreed to do the interview," Laramie said, "provided you really do keep it to twenty minutes. We've been busy since we arrived, and she's very tired. So promise me you won't take more than that."

"I promise."

"All right, please follow me."

She led him back the way she'd come, Mongo studying her rear end. She knocked once on another door and opened it, and he stepped past her. She closed the door behind him.

The space was a large sitting room decked out in what he thought might be real antique furniture. A bank of windows gave a view of Central Park.

Two women were in the room, and it wasn't hard to tell which one was the star. The blond hair and the great body made Delure unmistakable. She was sitting on a sofa with her legs crossed.

The other woman looked like a rodent. Short and pudgy, she wore a blouse and baggy slacks. Some contrast between her and Delure.

The actress flashed a smile he figured had taken her years of practice to perfect, exposing snow-white teeth. "Hi, I'm Catherine Delure." She didn't offer to shake hands.

"Hi, Catherine," Mongo said. "Welcome to New York. You look sensational." She did, too. The dress she had on was a silvery color, cut tight across the hips and low in front. Her boobs, he thought, were world class.

She flashed the same smile once more, as if it was controlled by a switch. "Thank you."

The pudgy one said, "I'm Penny Ellis, Miss Delure's assistant." She waved a hand toward the far end of the room. "We'll work at the desk, okay?" Without waiting for an answer, she went over there and began arranging chairs.

We? Mongo hadn't anticipated that. He'd assumed the interview would be one-on-one, just him and Delure. But apparently the rodent was inviting herself to the party. Okay, so he'd just have to accommodate her.

Ellis said, "Would you like something to drink? We have Pellegrino and diet soda."

Mongo declined, and he and Delure went to the desk. The two women sat on one side, and Mongo took a chair across from them. Opening his attaché case, he took out the tape recorder and placed it on the desk. He set the case on the floor.

"How was the weather in LA?" he asked, fiddling with the buttons on the recorder.

"Smoggy," Delure said. "And it's been hot the last few days."

"Which is only normal for this time of year," Ellis added.

Mongo wondered whether they were lesbians. Be a shame if Delure was wasting all that talent. Although maybe she swung both ways. He'd known a number of women like that, including two he'd hired in Chicago for the weekend last time he was there. The three of them had a ball. Something for everybody.

"All set," he said, looking up at them. "Let's just take it nice and easy, okay? Make it real conversational."

"Sure, go ahead," Delure said.

He spoke in a strong clear voice, like the shitbirds you heard on the radio. "Catherine, it's great to have you here in New York."

"Nice to be here. I love this city."

"And the fans here love you. We hear your new movie's sure to be a big hit."

"It's a very good picture. We had a sneak showing in Westwood, and the audience went wild."

"It's called *Hot Cargo*, is that right?" He was getting a kick out of this.

"Yes. It's a thriller, and full of very exciting action. It was directed by Tony Gregarian, who's just about the best there is."

Mongo adjusted the position of the tape recorder. "What's the story about?"

"The dope scene in LA. Smugglers try to bring a shipload of cocaine into Long Beach, and I mess up their plans by shooting some of the bad guys."

Should have used me as a consultant, Mongo thought.

"So then the others turn on me," she went on, "and there's a marvelous chase sequence with cars on the Santa Monica Freeway. Tony had four cameras going, one of them in a helicopter."

"How about the male star—who's he?"

"That's Terry Falcon, a fine actor."

"He's the love angle?"

"Right."

"They say he's queer. Or is that just a rumor?"

She looked startled but recovered quickly. "Terry is very talented."

"Uh-huh. Are there other beautiful women in the movie?"

"There are some in supporting roles, but those are minor parts."

Mongo had to swallow a laugh. "I see. By the way, here's something I've always wondered about: When you do a sex scene, do you really get it on?"

She frowned. "No, nothing like that happens."

"Honest? I've heard they just keep a sheet over you so the camera doesn't show you're actually doing it."

The frown deepened. "Those are just stupid stories. Like what you find in trashy magazines, or the supermarket tabloids. But they're certainly not true."

"Is that so? I remember seeing one of your movies one time, I forget the title. There was this scene where you and some guy were in bed, and he was pumping away. I could swear he had his dick in you. And you sure convinced me you liked it."

Her face again registered surprise, and then anger. She darted a glance at Ellis, who seemed astonished. Then her gaze swung back to Mongo. In a tightly controlled voice she said, "As I told you, nothing like that ever happens."

"No? You probably waited for a break, right? And then you did it in the dressing room. Anyhow, I had a hard-on that wouldn't quit, just watching you."

Delure leaned forward. "Turn that thing off," she snapped. "This interview is over."

"Fine with me," Mongo said. He touched a button on the tape recorder, and the cover snapped open. "Just one more question. "How about dry-humping—can you come that way? Bet you can."

She showed the teeth again and glared at him. "Penny, go get Chuck. Tell him to throw this asshole out."

"Damn right I will." Ellis rose from her chair and looked at Mongo. "You insolent bastard."

He touched another button and shot her.

The report was a low-pitched *chug* as a charge of compressed air drove a fléchette deep into her chest. The impact slammed her back against the wall, an expression of pain and horror contorting her features.

Delure's mouth dropped open, but before she could scream, Mongo shot her as well.

There could be no doubt he'd nailed them both. Each woman had been struck dead center, a fléchette punching straight into her heart. The steel projectiles were bigger and heavier than .45 slugs, and he knew nobody could survive taking a well-placed hit from one. The shock alone could kill you.

He sat motionless, watching them. Ellis had slid to the floor in a crumpled heap, and Delure lay sprawled in the chair. Their bodies were twitching, their sightless eyes staring and glassy. Crimson pools were rapidly soaking the women's clothing.

After a moment he stood and reached over, holding his finger against the artery on the side of Delure's neck. Even with the coating of glue on his fingertip he could tell there was no pulse. He did the same thing with Ellis and got the same result.

There was another door in there, one he surmised led into a bedroom. He went to the door and opened it cautiously. A king-size bed was in the room, along with tables and lamps and a dresser and a chaise longue and an armchair. Closets lining one wall were packed with women's clothing. Other garments were strewn about, draped over the chaise and on the bed. A bath was at the far end of the room, its door ajar.

None of that interested him. On the dresser, however, he spotted two things he'd hoped to find. One was a black leather handbag with a clasp of interlocking Cs that identified it as a Chanel. The second object was a large jewelry box, also of leather, its color dark brown.

Stepping over to the dresser, he opened the handbag and found a fat alligator wallet inside. Not bothering to check what it contained, he thrust the wallet into his pants pocket.

Next he opened the jewelry box and scooped up handfuls of rings and necklaces and other pieces, jamming the loot into the pockets of his jacket. After cleaning out the box, he went back into the sitting room.

He put the wallet and jewelry into his attaché case, along with the tape recorder. He closed and locked the case and took a deep breath, making sure he was calm and unruffled. When he was satisfied, he picked up the case and went to the door that led into the foyer.

He opened the door and stepped out, saying over his shoulder, "Thanks again, Miss Delure. Enjoy your stay in New York." Then he closed the door behind him.

Laramie and Diggs were sitting in the foyer. Diggs was reading a newspaper, and Laramie was working with a laptop. Both got up as they saw Mongo.

"All done?" Laramie asked.

"All done," he said. "And right on schedule. Even had a minute or two left over."

She smiled. "That's fine. How did it go?"

"Perfect, I'd say. Miss Delure said to tell you not to disturb her for a while. I think she wants to take a nap."

"Oh, okay."

He nodded to Diggs. "See you, Chuck."

Diggs waved a massive paw. "Later, man."

Laramie walked with him to the entrance. As he left the suite she said, "I'll look forward to hearing your interview on the radio."

"Best I've ever done," he said.

3.

NYPD Detective Jeb Barker was in an apartment on Twenty-Eighth Street, interviewing a woman with long black hair and puffy lips. She wore a sleeveless top that was unbuttoned to her navel, and she was trying to charm him. According to a tip, she'd been the girlfriend of a dealer of smuggled cigarettes brought up from North Carolina by the truckload.

The dealer had operated out of a basement in Murray Hill, and in addition to the smuggling rap, he was wanted for beating a rival's head in and dumping the body into the East River. When the cops homed in on him, he disappeared.

The girlfriend was playing dumb, answering each of Barker's questions by saying she didn't know. Or else she didn't remember. As to the departed lover's whereabouts, she didn't have the faintest idea.

Barker handed her his card. He told her to give her memory a jog and to call him. If she didn't cooperate, he said, she could be in a lot of trouble.

The threat was bullshit, of course, but sometimes it worked. Whether it would in this instance remained to be seen. Although judging from the smirk on her face, she wasn't buying it.

As he was leaving he glanced at the TV set, which she hadn't bothered to turn off while they spoke. It was tuned to a soap opera, and at that moment, the show was interrupted suddenly by an announcer who spouted news of a double murder in the Sherry-Netherland Hotel.

One of the victims, the announcer reported breathlessly, was purported to be the movie star Catherine Delure. Apparently, the murders had taken place in the course of a robbery.

Barker didn't wait to hear more. He bounded out of the apartment and took the elevator to the ground floor. From there, he ran to the street, where he'd parked his beat-up green Mustang hardtop.

He jumped into the car, slapped the flasher onto the roof, started the engine, turned on the siren and both radios, and hit the gas. With the lights and the noise going, he pulled out into the eastbound traffic and began jinking his way through the river of cars, taxis, and trucks, pushing the Mustang as hard as he could.

At Park he ran a red light and swung north, figuring the broad avenue would be the fastest route to the hotel. Other drivers showed little interest in moving over, even for an official vehicle.

At one point he couldn't get past a large black Mercedes that was hogging the left lane. Finally he nudged its rear end, and the schmuck at the wheel reluctantly moved over. When Barker went by, the guy glared at him and flipped him the bird.

As he drove, Barker listened to the police radio with one ear and to WINS with the other. A dispatcher was giving units only the name and address of the hotel and a code 10-10, but the AM radio went on squawking news of the murder. Like the guy on TV, the radio announcer sounded excited enough to wet his pants. He probably had.

And for once, Barker wouldn't blame him. If the report was accurate, this would be big. Very big. A movie star killed in one of Manhattan's most prestigious hotels? That was shocking news, on a national and even on an international level. Not only would the NYPD be in an uproar, right up to the police commissioner, but so would the mayor.

Especially the mayor. His Honor would see the crime as a blot on the city's reputation, and therefore politically damaging.

And costly. Tourism was a huge source of income, and the case would surely put a dent in it. With the fears of terrorism and the memory of 9/11 still in people's minds, who'd want to come to New York and be vulnerable to an attack?

Also, a lot of money poured into the city from fees and other expenditures by entertainment companies using the city for locations. In fact, the NYPD had a special movie/TV unit to assist them. Seen from any angle, stars getting murdered here would not be a positive development.

So the shit would indeed hit the fan, and the pressure from the top down would be intense. A good reason for Barker to reach the scene as quickly as he could.

His cell phone buzzed. He dug it out of his pocket. "Yeah?"

The caller was his partner, Joe Spinelli. "Did you get word on the homicides in the Sherry?"

"Yeah, I'm going there now. You still at the lab?"

"No, I just got to the hotel. What a ratfuck. You wouldn't believe what's going on."

"Yes, I would. See you in a few minutes." He stuck the phone back into his pocket and continued to maneuver his way through the mass of northbound vehicles. He and Spinelli had worked together for the past year, and Barker was the senior partner. They got along well, although they had little in common. Spinelli was married with two kids, and often tweaked Barker about his swinging bachelor lifestyle.

Barker was navigating the Grand Central bypass when another call reached him. This one was put through on his police radio by a dispatcher. It was from his boss, Lieutenant Frank Kelly, commander of the Seventeenth Precinct Detective Squad. "You at the scene?" Kelly asked.

"On my way, Lieu. Is it true the victim's Catherine Delure?"

"Yeah, that's been confirmed. She was shot, and so was another female who was with her. Apparently the other one was her manager."

"Radio said they were robbed?"

"Yes. The perp stole Delure's jewelry."

"Any witnesses?"

"Some of the people who work for her saw the guy. I sent detectives, but Homicide arrived and took over. Lieutenant Hogan's in charge. You know him?"

"Yeah. A double-barrel prick."

"Keep that opinion to yourself," Kelly said. "Hogan might not even want you there."

"Maybe. Although I figure he'll need all the help he can get."

"True enough. But I don't want to hear him complaining you got out of line."

"That mean I have to take orders from him?"

"Of course. I just told you, he's in charge of the case. So cooperate."

"Okay, okay."

"Pick up everything you can," Kelly said, "and then fill me in." The call ended.

Barker slipped the Mustang through a hole in the traffic and trod the accelerator. Park was a bit wider up here, and he could make better time. Asshole drivers or not.

So the radio guy had it right: the famous Catherine Delure had been killed. And so had the other woman. But why? Had they resisted the robber?

He tried to picture Delure, but the best he could come up with was an image of blond hair and a zaftig body. He'd probably seen her photo someplace, maybe on a magazine cover. He didn't think he'd ever seen one of her movies.

But then, the only films he watched were on late-night TV, and he only watched those if they were thrillers. He couldn't stand the cop shows, pretending to be authentic and instead coming off as silly. And he didn't know one actor from another.

Gloria, his now-and-then girlfriend, was the opposite. She was familiar with every star and could tell you every movie they'd each appeared in. And like millions of other people, she was fascinated by details of their personal lives.

When he reached East Sixtieth Barker turned left, thinking he'd get as close to the Sherry as possible. But he could see that there was already a jam-up at the corner of Fifth ahead of him. He pulled the Mustang into a no-parking space and shut it down. Picking the police plate off the floor, he dropped it onto the dash and got out of the car.

Barker was six feet tall and powerfully built. He had a thatch of black hair and a square jaw that made him look aggressive, even when he wasn't. His nose was slightly off-kilter and there was a jagged scar on his left cheek, keepsakes from an argument with a drug dealer back in his undercover days.

He had on his work clothes: a navy blazer and gray pants, a white button-down and a vaguely figured red tie. It was the same outfit he usually wore, in the belief that it made him look like a businessman. He was wrong; one glance and you'd make him for a cop.

As he walked toward Fifth he took out his gold shield and clipped it to the pocket of his blazer. He saw that along with the throngs of civilians and uniformed police officers, there were patrol cars and an ambulance and an NYPD van in front of the hotel. Also two TV trucks.

In the street, a line of taxis apparently had been caught in the backed-up stream of traffic and was now stuck in it. Some of the cabbies were blowing their horns and leaning out their windows and shouting. As if that would somehow extricate them from the mess.

Shoving his way through the mob of civilians, Barker noted that the crowd was similar to what you encountered at most crime scenes, only much bigger. The rubbernecks were packed together, wide-eyed and openmouthed, many of them babbling eagerly as they stared at the hotel entrance. More were arriving each moment.

What did they expect to see—a mad killer running out the

doors with a gun in each hand? Or maybe Catherine Delure herself? Dripping blood and waving to her fans?

At the entrance, TV cameramen were shooting the scene, red lights glowing on their cameras, and reporters were shouting questions at the cops who were holding back the crowd. One of the reporters was in an officer's face, yelling that he should be allowed to go inside because the people had a right to know. The cop was not persuaded.

Barker stepped past them and gave his name and rank to another uniform who was keeping the log. The guy scribbled on his clipboard, and Barker went into the lobby.

There was a crowd in here as well, apparently hotel guests who wanted to leave but were being held in place by a cop while a detective questioned them. The guests were all well dressed, and some were obviously pissed off. Barker asked another cop for directions and went up in an elevator.

A uniform was guarding the door of the suite. He looked at Barker's shield and nodded, and Barker walked past him into a foyer. From there he went into a large living room filled with plainclothes detectives. Of the many people in the room, one of the first he recognized was his partner.

"How'd you get here so fast?" Barker asked him.

Spinelli was shorter than Barker by several inches. He looked up and grinned. "Subway. You drove?"

"Uh-huh."

"The mayor frowns on people like you. But welcome to the circus." He waved a hand at the swarm in the room. "You ever see one like this?"

Barker hadn't. Both male and female detectives were present, and the NYPD's finest were doing everything they shouldn't— walking about and touching various objects—as if they too were googly-eyed movie fans. One guy was smoking, which was strictly forbidden by the regs. What was next, picking up souvenirs?

"They're over here," Spinelli said. He led the way to the far side of the room, where detectives were watching an assistant medical examiner make a preliminary check of the victims.

Catherine Delure's body was sprawled in a chair, next to a table. Her head was thrown back, her face pale and contorted in an expression of agony. The ME had opened her blood-drenched dress and her bra, revealing a blue hole in the flesh between her ample breasts.

The second female was on the floor, half sitting against the wall. Unlike Delure, that one was short, fat, and homely. But her features wore the same look of shock and pain. Her blouse was unbuttoned, exposing a similar type of wound in the center of her chest.

Barker noticed there was no blood spatter on the wall behind the victims. That was odd, he thought. Especially considering the size of the bullet holes in the two women.

The ME was a young guy wearing latex gloves and peering owl-like through thick glasses as he photographed the bodies with a tiny digital camera. When he finished he got out an iPhone and punched the buttons, apparently making notes, or perhaps sending them. Detectives were tossing out questions but he paid no attention, continuing to fiddle with his gadget.

One of the detectives was Dan Hogan, the lieutenant who headed Manhattan Homicide. He was balding and had a nose like a prow. Ordinarily, someone of his rank would not take direct charge at a crime scene. But this was no ordinary crime.

Hogan obviously didn't like having his questions ignored. "Must've been high caliber," he said. "At least a .357, maybe bigger. Right, Doc?"

The ME scowled. "You know I'm not supposed to say anything here. Autopsy will tell you, and you'll get a complete report from the pathologist."

Hogan's voice rose. "Hey, I'm running an investigation. I need all the information you can give me, and I need it now."

Letting everybody know who's in charge, Barker thought.

"So let's have an answer," Hogan said.

"Okay," the ME said. "All I can tell you is they were shot. But I have no idea what caliber the weapon might have been."

"What about the exit wounds?"

"There aren't any. And that's all I'm gonna say."

Hogan reddened. "Jesus Christ."

But the ME had gone back to pushing buttons on the iPhone.

The Crime Scene Unit arrived, its members carrying equipment cases. The unit's chief was a sergeant who complained that the site had been badly compromised. He shooed people out of the room so that the forensics crew could start combing it for fingerprints and fibers and take photos. Hogan grumbled, but he and the others left.

In the foyer, Barker drew Spinelli aside. "The second victim was her manager?"

"Yeah, name's Penny Ellis."

"I understand there were witnesses."

"Three people saw the perp and talked to him: a hotel security guy, Delure's secretary, and a bodyguard. But nobody saw the shootings. Apparently, the hotel guy didn't know anything, but the other two might. They're in adjoining rooms. Secretary is Dana Laramie. Bodyguard's Chuck Diggs."

"You question them?"

"No, Hogan did. He gave me a stiff-arm, said I should stick with the robbery."

"And?"

"The perp cleaned out her jewelry box. The secretary wasn't too sure what was in it. Box is in the bedroom."

"Let's have a look." Barker went back into the living room, Spinelli following, and from there into the bedroom. The CSI sergeant wore an expression of disapproval, but he didn't try to stop them.

The bedroom was littered with articles of women's clothing, some of them draped over chairs, others lying on the king-size bed. A rollaway table covered with a white cloth bore a vase filled with spring flowers and an array of soiled breakfast dishes.

The jewelry box was on a dresser. It was about eighteen inches square and made of dark brown leather. A tray had been taken out of it and tossed aside, and both the tray and the box appeared to be empty.

"You could put a lot of stuff in that thing," Spinelli said. "But look at this." He pointed to the interior of the box, which was lined with tan suede.

Barker looked and saw that one object remained. It was a gold ring set with sapphires.

"So he was in a hurry," Spinelli said. "Killed the two of them, and then he grabbed the jewelry and hauled ass."

A handbag was also on the tabletop, black leather adorned with a gold logo of interlocking Cs. The flap was unfastened. Barker took out a ballpoint and lifted the flap with it.

The handbag was filled with an assortment that included a lipstick and a compact and a small hairbrush and a few other odds and ends. Nothing unusual about the contents, except that one thing seemed to be missing.

"No wallet," he said.

Spinelli shrugged. "Maybe in one of the drawers. Or maybe the guy got that too."

The two men rifled through the drawers and found nothing but more pieces of clothing.

"You can comb the room later," Barker said. "Right now I want to talk with the witnesses."

Spinelli's eyebrows rose. "Think you ought to let Hogan know?"

"Yeah, I'll ask him for permission. After I talk to them."

The pair left the suite and went to an adjoining room. A young woman was sitting in a chair, dabbing her nose with a tissue. Her eyes were red from crying.

Barker was mildly surprised. He realized he'd been expecting her to be on the flashy side, but instead she was low-key, dark haired and wearing a blue cardigan and a gray skirt. Even with the red-rimmed eyes, she had a lot going for her.

"I'm Detective Barker," he said. "You were Miss Delure's secretary?"

"Yes."

"I need to ask you a few questions."

"I've already told the other detective everything I could."

"Yes, but tell me."

"I don't know whether I . . ." She shuddered, and then with an effort got hold of herself. "All right. I'll give you any help I can."

"Go through it from the beginning, if you would, please. From the time you got to New York."

She took a deep breath and exhaled. Delure and the others had arrived two nights ago, she said. They stayed in, and ordered room service for dinner. Miss Delure wanted to go to bed early, so she'd look her best for a number of interviews that had been scheduled. Yesterday, she had been a guest on the *Today Show*, and later on *Good Morning America*. Also there were a couple of magazine interviews, which were done at the hotel.

"Dinner in again last night?" Barker asked.

"No. She and Penny joined Terry Falcon and Len Zarkov for dinner at the Four Seasons."

"They're also in the movie?"

"Terry is. He's the male lead. Zarkov's the producer."

"Did the bodyguard go with them?"

"He rode with them in the limo to the restaurant, but he wouldn't have been at their table for dinner."

"They go anywhere else afterward?"

"I don't believe so. They were back here by eleven."

"And what happened this morning?"

"A man called me from the lobby. Said his name was Jack Thompson and he was from WNEW Radio and was here for an interview. I didn't have it on the schedule, but he said it'd been arranged by Sandra Rosen at Galaxy Films in LA." She paused.

"And?"

Laramie looked as though she was about to cry again, but she pulled herself up once more. "And then I spoke to Penny, who said it would be okay. So I told him to come up." Her lip trembled. "How could I have been so stupid?"

"Can you describe him?"

"Tall, with curly reddish-blond hair and a mustache. I think his eyes were blue. He was well dressed, had on a tan suit. And he was carrying an attaché case."

"Did you see what was in the case?"

"No, but Chuck did. Apparently there was nothing unusual."

"Notice anything else about him?"

"Just that he was friendly and sort of casual. Seemed very sure of himself."

"Joe," Barker said, "get Diggs in here, will you?"

Spinelli left the room, and Laramie pulled a tissue from a box on a nearby table and blew her nose.

"Sorry to put you through this," Barker said.

"It's okay. I just . . . never should have let him in."

"Don't blame yourself. Instead, try to concentrate. Any small detail might help. So if anything occurs to you, let me know."

"I will."

Spinelli was back, and with him was a hulk of a man whose shoulders threatened to burst the seams of his sport jacket.

"Chuck Diggs," the big man said, and thrust out his hand.

Barker shook it. "Detective Barker. You were Miss Delure's bodyguard?"

"Yes, and I want you to know I'm goddamn mad about how that guy conned us. Wish I could get my hands on the son of a bitch."

"You notice anything suspicious or odd about him?"

"No, or I never would have let him in."

"Did you talk to him when he came into the suite?"

"Just to ask him for his ID. He gave me his business card and showed me his driver's license."

"Was it a New York license?"

"Yeah, it was."

"Where is the business card? Do you have it?"

"No, the other detective took it."

"Lieutenant Hogan?"

"Right."

"After you looked at the man's ID, did you frisk him for a weapon?"

"Absolutely. I patted him down top to bottom. Even his legs. He was completely clean. I made sure of it."

"And you looked into his attaché case?"

"Yeah, I did. Nothing in it but a tape recorder and some paper and pens."

"You check out the tape recorder?"

Diggs's eyes narrowed. "Of course. There wasn't anything unusual about it."

"While he was in the other room with Miss Delure and Miss Ellis, did either of you hear any strange noises?"

Laramie shook her head, and Diggs said, "Didn't hear a thing. He must've used a silencer. Although Christ only knows how he could have hidden the gun. Like I said, I went over every inch of him."

"How long was he in there?"

"About twenty minutes."

"When did you discover Delure and Ellis had been attacked?"

"Not until about an hour afterward," Diggs said. "Maybe a little longer."

"When the man came out of the living room," Laramie said, "he told us Miss Delure wanted to take a nap and not to disturb her for a while. Then after some time went by, I knocked on the door and got no answer. So I opened it, and oh God."

"I knew as soon as I looked at them they were both dead," Diggs said.

"What did you do then?"

"I had the hotel security guy come in, and he called down for help. Told them to get the police over here fast."

Barker turned to Spinelli. "You got questions?"

"Yeah, I do," the detective said. "How long had you two worked for Miss Delure?"

Laramie said, "I was hired a little over a year ago."

"And you?" Spinelli asked Diggs.

"I've been on board seven months."

Barker said, "How much jewelry was in that box in the bedroom?"

"Quite a bit," Laramie said. "Rings, necklaces, watches, and so on. Miss Delure always took a lot of things with her whenever she traveled."

"Could you make out an inventory?"

"I could try, I suppose. Although I don't know how accurate it would be."

"Do your best. We'll get it from you later. And another thing: Was Miss Delure married?"

"Divorced. Her ex-husband is Ron Apperson. He owns an investment company in Beverly Hills."

"Kids?"

"No."

"When did they split up?"

"A couple of years ago. They weren't married very long."

"Was the divorce amicable?"

"Yes, as far as I know."

"Did they stay in touch afterward?"

"I suppose so. I know they talked on the phone once in a while. And they had lunch a few weeks back."

"Any other family?"

"Her father lives in Connecticut. In Greenwich, where she grew up. He's in poor health, and she wanted to go out there and see him while she was here."

"There was a brother, too," Diggs put in. "Here in New York."

"His name is Roger Delaney," Laramie said. "Delaney was Miss Delure's real name. Her brother runs the family business."

"What kind of business?"

"Something to do with mining. The company is called Delaney Industries."

"Okay, that's enough for the moment," Barker said. "But there'll be more questions for you as time goes on." He dug out his wallet and handed a card to each of them. "If you think of anything that could help us, anything at all, be sure to call."

Both said they would.

"Good. Come on, Joe."

4.

The next stop was the observation center, in the bowels of the hotel. It was a large room, with one wall covered by TV monitors that showed every public area in the building. The monitors were controlled by a visibly nervous older man who was sitting at a console. A tag on his jacket said he was Walter Krachik.

This space was also swarming with detectives. Barker recognized several of them. One was a sergeant named Charley Coyle, who worked under Hogan in Homicide.

Hogan was talking with a guy who was apparently in charge of security for the hotel. Another security man, the one who'd encountered the shooter at the door of Delure's suite, was standing off to one side. When Barker introduced Spinelli and himself, the man said his name was Ed Dougherty and that he was an ex-cop.

"I was in the job twenty-five years," Dougherty said. "Came to work here right after I retired."

"You spoke to the perp?"

"Yeah, but just to ask what he wanted. He said he was from

WNEW and he had an appointment. When I asked the bodyguard, he said to let him in. After a while he came out of the suite and got into an elevator, and that was it."

"Did he seem tense, or in a hurry, when he left?"

"No, the opposite. He was laid-back, almost like what I'd call jaunty. Told me to have a nice day."

Barker nodded his head toward the monitors. "The cameras pick him up?"

"Yeah, two of them. One in the lobby and the other when he went from the elevator to the suite. Got him leaving, too."

"Let's see what he looks like," Barker said. He and Spinelli stepped over to the console, and Barker asked the operator to show the tapes.

Hogan shot a suspicious glance at Barker. "You won't get much. I already had them run a couple of times."

Barker ignored him. He told the operator to go ahead.

"Watch the number seven monitor," Krachik said. "That shows him in the lobby."

The camera's perspective was from above, and there was no sound track. The tape revealed a man carrying an attaché case entering through the front doors and walking past other people to one of the hotel's house phones. He picked up the phone and spoke into it, hung up, and went into an elevator.

Hogan had a point, Barker thought. The images on the monitor were in black and white, and slightly blurred. He could make out the man's form well enough, but not much in the way of details. Dana Laramie had said the intruder had curly reddish-blond hair, but if she hadn't told him that, Barker wouldn't have known it from looking at the grainy picture.

He had Krachik run the footage four times. The subject was tall and trim and carried a case, but the tape showed nothing more definitive than that.

"Okay," he said. "Let's see the next one."

The operator punched up the tape on an adjoining monitor. The images had the same lack of clarity as the others and revealed no additional details. The elevator door opened; then the man stepped out and made his way along the corridor to the door of the suite. There he spoke to Dougherty for a moment. The door opened, revealing Chuck Diggs, who stepped aside to permit the man to enter. The door then closed.

So maybe Hogan had it right, Barker thought. Not much help from this stuff.

But the next tape contained a tantalizing detail. The intruder left the suite and walked past Dougherty toward the elevator. As he did, he glanced up at the camera and grinned. Barker still couldn't see his features clearly, although the flash of white teeth was unmistakable. The man got into the elevator and the doors drew shut.

"You see that?" Spinelli said. "He was telling us 'fuck you.' The nerve of that creep."

A final shot depicted the subject leaving the lobby. As before, he seemed in no hurry, strolling to the entrance and disappearing.

Barker asked Krachik to make copies of the tapes. "All of them. We'll want to send them to the lab and have them enhanced."

"I already told him to do that," Hogan said.

Again Barker ignored him. With luck, the enhancement just might give them a sharper impression of the guy's features. The result would be better than nothing, certainly.

Finally, Barker thanked Krachik and stepped away from the console. He told Spinelli to wait for a set of tapes, and to be sure to get the inventory of the victim's jewelry from Dana Laramie. He then left the room.

"Barker."

He turned to see Hogan approach.

"Does Kelly know you're here?"

"Sure he does. You need help, so here I am."

Hogan seemed to think that over. As Barker had expected, the lieutenant wasn't likely to turn away an experienced detective. Even one with Barker's reputation.

"I understand you talked with the secretary and the bodyguard," Hogan said.

"Yeah, so?"

"So you should have cleared that with me first. I'm leading this investigation, and it doesn't help to have people running off in all directions."

Barker told himself to stay cool. "I was just doing what I could, Lieutenant."

"Then keep in mind that this case is the biggest thing the department has had in years, and it's my responsibility to see it's run properly. The only reason I'd let you and Spinelli work on it is because I need extra hands. I want the two of you to concentrate on the robbery angle."

"The robbery angle?"

"Correct. What we have here is a double homicide, but the motive was obviously robbery."

"How can you be sure of that?"

Hogan's upper lip curled. "Look, Barker, I been working homicide a long time. One thing I learned is, if a motive isn't sex or jealousy, it's money. The jewelry in that box could've been worth as much as a million bucks. And that's enough to give any mutt a hard-on. You follow me?"

"Sure. But this guy was a lot more sophisticated than the average booster. He had to be, if he could pass himself off as a legitimate employee of WNEW."

"No question. So what I want you and Spinelli to do is see if you can turn up something about him from fences or street sources."

"Isn't that a job for the Robbery Squad?"

"They'll be working on it too. I'm setting up a task force, and like I said, I'll take all the help I can get. Even you two."

"Okay, but—"

"No buts. I've got the videotape and three eyewitnesses, and that'll make it easy to get a real good rendering of the perp's face. When that goes out in an APB, I expect to have plenty of leads. Meantime, get going. Anything you come up with, even if it doesn't seem like it's important, you report it to me. That goes for both you and Spinelli. You got that?"

"Uh-huh."

"Don't try to be a hero, Barker. I wouldn't want to have to complain to Kelly. You've already got a couple strikes against you. One more and you could be walking a beat in the Lincoln Tunnel."

Barker clamped his jaw shut.

Apparently Hogan misread the silence. As if satisfied that he'd made his point, he nodded and strode away.

Barker watched him go, thinking, Christ, the shit you have to put up with.

He took an elevator to the lobby, where the situation was just as chaotic as it had been earlier. Angry guests, and police trying to keep order.

Several of the cops were peering out through the entrance doors, craning their necks. Moving closer, Barker saw they were looking at a trio of men who were standing outside, conducting an impromptu press conference for the benefit of the reporters and TV cameramen.

The men were the NYPD's top brass. The commissioner himself was in the center, doing the talking. Flanking him were the chief of police on one side and the chief of detectives on the other. The media were sucking up every word, holding out microphones and shooting footage.

Behind the reporters and the camera operators was the crowd of spectators, held back by cops manning sawhorses. The gawkers were pressing and pushing for position, and there seemed to be even more of them now than when Barker had entered the hotel. People and official vehicles had turned the area into a mob scene.

The PC was blathering on, but with all the ambient noise it was hard to understand what he was saying. Still, the gist was clear enough: ". . . shocking and horrendous crime . . . cannot be allowed to go unpunished . . . will do everything in our power to track down . . . this great city will not tolerate . . ."

Standard crapola, Barker thought. Still, it wasn't surprising that the three of them had shown up so quickly. They were politicians essentially as much as they were police officials. A homicide case couldn't be more high-profile than this one, and that meant they'd get face time on TV. So they'd rushed to the scene and begun spouting platitudes.

But after the speeches were over, it would be up to the guys in the trenches, the ordinary detectives, to do the grunt work. They were the ones who might clear the case. And all the while they'd have to deal with politics themselves, as people like Hogan jockeyed to take credit, to use this as a stepping-stone for advancing their careers, simultaneously making sure to cover their asses.

Nevertheless, that wasn't what stuck in Barker's craw. What bothered him most was that flicker on the security videotape, when the killer had glanced up at the camera and grinned.

Beautiful, wasn't it? Steal people's lives and their property, and then sneer at the police. It would be good to jam those shiny white teeth down the bastard's throat.

But where was he now? Still in New York, or had he gone somewhere else, now that his work was done?

5.

Mongo tooled the Toyota up the Pacific Coast Highway and turned off onto a driveway near Zuma Beach. After covering a hundred yards of the narrow, winding blacktop, he stopped before a wrought-iron gate and sent a signal from a remote. When the gate swung open, he drove through to a small building and parked beside it. Carrying his luggage, he went to the door and unlocked it.

This was a guest cottage, part of an estate whose owner lived in LA and rarely visited. Most of the time nobody came out here except the gardeners and Mongo, and even he was often away on business. The rent was expensive, but so what.

Before going inside, he looked back down toward the road. Cars and trucks were zipping along it, as they did at all hours of the day and night. Apparently he hadn't been followed, although he had no reason to think he might have been. Making sure was a habit.

As he stood there, his gaze took in the packed-together beach houses that bordered the far side of the highway with the sea just beyond them. On the horizon the sun was setting, a red ball that cast a sparkling reflection on the water. Nice picture. Malibu was a great place to live.

Once inside, he locked the door behind him and turned on the lights. The place was neat and tidy, just as he'd left it. Keeping it that way was another habit, one he'd picked up when he was a guest in Q.

It had been a busy day, but he wasn't at all tired. He took off his jacket and tie and dropped them off in the bedroom along with his bag and attaché case and then went into the kitchen. He opened the fridge and chose a joint from a plastic box.

Now for some entertainment. He flopped into his favorite chair, turned on the TV, and set fire to the weed.

CNN had the story. He inhaled deeply and watched as a blonde bimbo with big eyes babbled excitedly.

"... was one of Hollywood's most glamorous stars. Perhaps best known for her role in *Forbidden Love*, she was adored by her millions of fans. Now it's said that her new picture, *Hot Cargo*, will set attendance records."

Sure it will, Mongo thought. That's what publicity can do for you. Want big sales at the box office? Get yourself shot. Works every time.

"Later tonight," the bimbo went on, "Anderson Cooper will do a special interview with Terry Falcon, Miss Delure's costar in *Hot Cargo*. Terry is said to be in a state of shock, but he's agreed to talk about working with Catherine, and about the picture. He feels she would want him to do that."

Mongo smiled. That Terry was a noble guy, wasn't he? Of course plugging the film and getting his mug on TV wouldn't have anything to do with it.

The blonde went on flapping her mouth, but Mongo had heard enough. He took another drag and switched channels.

KCAL was covering it as well. With its own straw-head. "And now," she was saying, "we take you to the scene of the crime, the Sherry-Netherland Hotel in New York, where earlier today the city's top law enforcement officials spoke about the case."

Cut to videotape. A huge mob of people and clusters of cars

and trucks were in front of the hotel. On the steps leading to the entrance, a trio of serious-looking men stood speaking into microphones held by TV reporters.

Mongo laughed out loud. The Three Stooges, for Christ's sake. Larry, Moe, and Curly. They must have rushed to the scene like flies zooming in on a turd. And now they were taking turns telling the world how they would track down the perpetrator of this horrifying deed.

A reporter asked what steps were being taken. The one identified as the police commissioner replied: "A large task force will be assigned to the case. We won't rest until the assailant is brought to justice. He will be punished to the full extent of the law, which is what he deserves."

Wrong, Mongo thought. What I deserve is a bonus, for doing a terrific job. He turned off the set and blew out a stream of smoke.

By now he was feeling totally relaxed. The joint was Jamaican Red, and it produced a very pleasant buzz. Nowadays you could go to a head shop and find dozens of varieties, many with goofy-ass names. *Midnight Express. Wild 'n' Wicked. Mendocino Magic.* But that was just marketing. When it came to quality, the Red was as good as it got.

Mongo should know. He'd used almost everything there was at one time or another. And had done a little dealing, too. Although not in the conventional sense.

It was after he'd been sent up for killing a clerk during a convenience store robbery, when he was still young and dumb. The guy had resisted, so naturally Mongo shot him.

Unfortunately, a patrol car had been cruising by at the time, and the cops heard the shot and ran into the store. Mongo wanted to shoot it out, but his pistol had jammed. He threw it aside and tried to fight off the cops. They beat the shit out of him with their truncheons and took him to the can.

He was arraigned the next day, and under California law the killing was defined as first-degree murder because it had been committed with a firearm in the course of a robbery. That was the murder-felony rule, and it meant Mongo could get twenty-five to life if convicted—or what the prosecutors called *Nopo*, which stood for life without the possibility of parole. Shit, he could even be sentenced to death.

But he was in luck. A weasel of a lawyer named Harold Strunk took the case pro bono. From what Mongo could gather, the lawyer had volunteered his services in an effort to cast a favorable light on his own unsavory reputation.

Strunk claimed Mongo had attempted to rob the store not for money but for food. The poor boy was desperately hungry, the lawyer argued, and the shooting was an accident. A sympathetic judge bought it, and the charge was reduced to voluntary manslaughter. So even though Mongo was tried and convicted, he wound up with a sentence of only five to ten years.

"I hope," the judge had said, "this will teach you a lesson."

It did. In fact, the lesson was one Mongo would always remember: never use inferior equipment. The pistol had been cheap junk, an automatic that froze after he fired the shot that killed the clerk. He resolved that from then on, whenever he needed a piece he'd be careful to make it a good one. A Smith, say, or a Colt. Glocks and Berettas were okay, too.

After the trial he was shackled and stuffed into a bus, along with a mixed bag of white, black, and brown losers, for the long trip north. It seemed to take forever, but at last the bus reached the sprawling facility that overlooked San Francisco Bay. Mongo was processed and assigned to a cell in San Quentin's South Block.

On his first day in the yard, he was approached by an enormous black man who wore an Afro and sported gold teeth.

The spade leered down at him. "What's your name, boy?"

"Mongo. What's yours?"

"You be a wiseass, askin' me that?"

"No sir. I meant no disrespect."

"Ah, that's good. 'Cause if you diss me, I'll squash your ass like a bug. People call me the Count. That's 'cause in here, I be the one with the power. Know what I'm sayin'?"

"Yes sir."

"I like you, boy. You pretty."

"Thank you."

"You gone belong to me, hear?"

"Yes sir."

"Tonight, before chow, you meet me in the shower. Got that?"

"Yes sir."

Mongo drifted away. Later, he asked his cellmate about the Count.

The cellmate was an old man named Charley who was doing fifty to life for committing a series of sexual assaults. He chuckled. "The Count picked you out, huh?"

"I guess."

"Ain't surprising. He likes young meat. 'Specially ones like you with muscles. But you better watch yourself. Anybody don't do what he says, he cuts 'em. You seen that hair?"

"What about it?"

"He keeps a shank in it. The COs know it, but they don't do nothing about it. Anybody gives him shit, he'll make 'em bleed. So take care, sonny."

"Thanks. I'll do that."

The shower room was hot and steamy, filled with naked men who were talking and laughing and shouting as they soaped and rinsed their bodies under the pounding streams of water. Most of them had decorated their hides with homemade tattoos. On some, every square inch of skin bore mottoes or weird designs or women's names. A few also had swastikas.

The Count beckoned to Mongo. "You come over here with me, boy."

"Yes, sir."

"We gon' get acquainted. That means you suck my cock."

"Yes, sir. But would it be all right if we waited till we were alone?"

"What's a matter, you shy?"

"Yes sir. Kind of."

The big man laughed, a low rumble that came up from his belly. "Yeah, all right. Just stay right here till these mothafuckers clear out."

A few minutes later a bell rang. The bathers departed, still jabbering and carrying on as they headed for the room where they'd left their clothing.

More minutes passed, until only Mongo and the Count remained in the room. It was quiet then, except for the sound of water dripping from the showerheads and splattering on the wet floor.

A heavy hand gripped Mongo's shoulder. "Now then, boy," the Count said. He moved his feet apart. "Get on down there."

Mongo sank to his knees. There in front of his face was the biggest dick he'd ever seen. And certainly the blackest. It was standing straight up and quivering, as if it had a life of its own. Beneath the dick was a large, hairy scrotum.

The Count's voice grew hoarse. "Come on, boy. Suck that thing."

"Yes sir."

"Well, come on, goddamn it. *Suck it!*"

Mongo wrapped his left hand around the huge penis and gripped it tightly. He moved his mouth toward it and took a deep breath. Then with all his strength he drove his right fist up into the scrotum.

The Count screamed and doubled over, grabbing his crotch.

Mongo leaped to his feet and gripped the big man's head with both hands. He heaved, and at the same time kicked the other's feet out from under him. The Count went over backward, sailing through the air until his skull slammed against the cement floor. The sound when it hit was like a melon bursting.

Mongo stood over the massive body, watching it shudder convulsively. The Count's eyes had rolled back in his head, and spittle frothed on his lips. A trickle of blood flowed from an ear. A moment later, he was completely still.

Mongo felt around in the Afro and pulled out the shank. It

was a slim piece of metal, razor sharp at one end and with a taped handle at the other. Carrying it, he walked out of the shower room, toweled down, and put on his orange shirt and pants. He saw that as he'd intended, several of the cons were eyeing him curiously. Again a bell rang, and he followed the others out of the area.

When the Count's corpse was discovered, an investigation was held. The COs agreed that he'd slipped in the shower and died of a fractured skull. They wrote that in their report, and the warden signed off on it.

But the word got around, and it earned Mongo respect. The Latinos were glad to see the big man gone, and so were the whites. The blacks didn't seem to care, so they too must have had enough of him.

After that Mongo steered clear of the gangs and mostly kept to himself. He used the shank only once, when a jealous con tried to stab him with a spike made from a toothbrush handle. Mongo decked the guy and carved an M in the center of his forehead with the shank. From that point on, nobody messed with him.

As for the dealing, it worked in a roundabout way. Juanita, his girlfriend, sent him packages containing items such as toothpaste and deodorant and mints. The packages were opened and the contents inspected, and then they were passed on to Mongo. What the COs never suspected was that the wrapping paper was actually two sheets pressed together, with a C-note between them.

Mongo was always delighted to hear from her. Inmates were paid a few cents an hour for their work inside and denied the right to have money in any meaningful amount. So the packages put him way ahead of the others.

He asked Charley which of the guards was on the take, and the old man pointed out one of them. Mongo established a business relationship with the guy, paying him to bring in small quantities of meth.

That was a substance Mongo had no personal use for, knowing the damage it could do. Instead, he bartered with other inmates who couldn't get enough of the stuff. Some smoked it, heating it until it vaporized and then inhaling the fumes, while others crushed the crystals and snorted them. Some swallowed it.

Mongo was indifferent as to how they used it. They could make margaritas with it, for all he cared. What he got in return was a number of cons who would do anything he asked of them, from washing his clothes to running errands. Supplying them with meth turned them into his personal servants.

Next he used some of the money to bribe his way to a better job. At first he'd been assigned to work in the kitchen, which was a foul place, hot and smelly and dotted with rat shit. A payoff got him moved to the library, and that was where his education began.

Supposedly his work was filing and cataloging, but he wasted no time on such activities. Instead he read for hours each day. It was amazing how much he didn't know. He was eager to learn, however, and he had a good memory. Almost every book he picked up was packed with information that was new to him. The library also boasted a half-dozen computer terminals, and when he wasn't reading he explored websites. He realized that much of what he was learning could be put to practical use.

One concept hit him like a lightning bolt:

What you are doesn't matter. It's what people think you are that's important.

He tucked that away, awed by its simple truth.

Another theory that impressed him held that staying in good shape would also sharpen the mind. He was permitted an hour of exercise per day, so he devoted it to pumping iron, and his muscular body grew ever more sinewy.

Then each night he surfed the tiny TV set in his cell, looking for more slants on everything from manners to stylish clothing. Charley knew better than to complain that his cellmate was hogging the set.

Mongo also sought out cons who had brains worth picking. One was a former stockbroker from San Francisco who'd caught his wife with another man and threw her out the window of their apartment in Pacific Heights. He could rattle off facts about finance by the hour. And he knew everything worth knowing about hotels and restaurants in European cities as well as many in America.

Another was an alcoholic who'd been a movie actor, until he drove his SUV over a woman as she was crossing the street. She'd been pushing a baby carriage at the time, so the actor went up on not just one count of vehicular homicide, but two. Mongo was fascinated by what the guy explained to him about getting into a role, how you could convince an audience you were authentic.

Then there was a hustler who had made a fine living for years by marrying rich widows and fleecing them. After each success he'd assumed a new identity and married another one. His mistake had been allowing his picture to be taken with his latest bride following the wedding. The photo appeared in the *Sacramento Bee*, and a former wife saw it and blew the whistle. Mongo found him a treasure trove of knowledge on how to acquire documents that would enable him to become a different person.

You can buy social security numbers and credit cards, the guy told him. Also forged driver's licenses and fake passports. But when you get yourself a new ID, use it only a short time, and then get another one. That way nobody can catch up with you. By the time authorities start looking, you're somebody else.

All of it would be valuable, he knew, when he got out. Especially another great concept he'd come across. It was in a book by a guy named Dale Carnegie, and that one was a lightning bolt, too.

Decide what it is you're best at, and then concentrate all your energy on making the most of it.

Okay, what was it he was best at? He thought about it, and decided it was killing people. Not only did he have a talent for it, but he liked doing it. And as Carnegie also pointed out, it was important to enjoy your work.

Mongo was sure that once he was on the outside, his skill would be very much in demand. The problem was coming up with some way to market himself. What the hell, he couldn't run an ad in the *LA Times* or on Craigslist. And he wasn't about to join a gang. His ambition was bigger than that. Much bigger.

So how could he let interested parties know what he could do? He'd just have to keep working on it until he found an answer.

In all, Mongo spent five years in Q. Juanita waited for him to hook up with her after he was paroled, but he dumped her as soon as he got out. She went into a frenzied rage, screaming about all she'd done for him, but he just laughed.

It was a wise move, he decided. She'd been useful during his stretch in prison, but now he was free. Get too close to a bitch and she could be like an anchor around your neck. Besides, when you wanted a woman, it was easier to just rent one.

The solution to his marketing problem came to him one night while he and Charley were watching TV. A commercial came on, the kind placed by law firms that say something like, "Important! If you or any of your loved ones have ever had a cough or a runny nose, call this 800 number right away and we'll sue the shit out of somebody!"

"You know how that works?" the old man asked. "A lawyer tells other lawyers he can get them business. So he runs a bunch of ads on TV, and when he gets a bite, he passes along the name of the person who got sick to one of the lawyers. He gets a fee for that, and a cut of the settlement if the case goes that far."

"Where'd you pick that up?"

"Me and another guy were trying to run a scam, claiming we had asbestos poisoning. It fell apart when we couldn't prove it, even though we had a crooked doctor. But anyhow, that's when I found out how the lawyers work together."

Mongo realized that Charley might have pointed the way to a great opportunity. It could also be pie-in-the-sky, but it was worth following up on. The more he thought about it, the more he was convinced he could pull it off.

A week after he was paroled he returned to LA and looked up the address of Harold Strunk LLP, the lawyer who'd defended him. Strunk's office was in Century City, high in one of the office towers. Mongo put on his only suit and a white shirt and a tie and went there unannounced.

The lawyer's receptionist had gray hair and a frosty manner. When Mongo gave her his name, she told him Mr. Strunk was not available, and that Mongo should call or write and ask for an appointment.

"He'll see me," Mongo said. "Remind him I was a client, five years ago."

She frowned, but she picked up a phone and spoke into it.

When she hung up, she said Mr. Strunk would be tied up for quite some time.

"I'll wait," Mongo said. He sat on a Barcelona chair and leafed through a magazine.

Three hours went by as the receptionist typed on a computer and fielded a number of phone calls. At last Strunk sent word to her that he'd give Mongo a few minutes and no more.

The lawyer's office was impressive. It was spacious and elegantly furnished in rosewood and squashy leather, and the south wall was all glass. There was a hazy view of downtown Los Angeles in the distance, tall buildings wreathed in smog.

Strunk was in shirtsleeves, seated at a vast desk that was stacked with papers. He had a narrow face and thinning hair and small dark eyes that darted one way and then another. Each time Mongo saw the man, it occurred to him that Strunk didn't just act like a weasel, he looked like one.

He didn't offer Mongo a seat. "So you're out," he said. "When did that happen?"

"A few days ago."

"Okay, I'll give you some advice. Stay clean and find a job. You get in trouble again, don't expect me to wipe your nose for you. I don't make a habit of handing out freebies. I gave you one, and you were lucky I did. Wasn't for me, you'd still be inside. Now excuse me, but I've got work to do."

"I didn't come here for advice."

"No? For what then, money? I don't hand that out, either."

"I'm here," Mongo said, "to offer my services."

"What are you talking about?"

Mongo had rehearsed this in his head. He spoke carefully. "I figure now and then either you or another lawyer you know might want somebody to go away and not come back."

Strunk stared at him.

"All you'd have to do," Mongo went on, "is give me the name and the location of the mark. I'd take care of him, and you'd collect a very large fee. Then you'd pay me a share for my end, plus expenses. And that would be it, until you needed me the next time."

For several moments, Strunk continued to gape at his visitor. Then he said, "Are you out of your fucking mind?"

"Not hardly. This'd be strictly business, good for both of us. I'd be working as kind of an independent contractor. I'm very good at what I do, and I can go anywhere and fit in. There's no reason anybody should ever know who I really am, or that there's any connection between us."

The lawyer's dark eyes darted from side to side, and then once again fixed their gaze on Mongo's face. "You're on parole, aren't you?"

"Yes, but not for long. Pretty soon I'll have a whole new ID. The guy I used to be, the one who got paroled, will disappear. They'll never find him."

"Impossible. They've got your fingerprints and a mug shot on file."

"My appearance is easy to change. And I know how to fix my fingers so they don't leave prints."

The eyes darted once more. "I don't think we should be having this conversation."

"So we never had it, right?" Mongo took a scrap of paper from his pocket and placed it on the desk. "This is the number of my cell phone. Call me when you need me." He turned and left the office.

Thinking back about that visit now, Mongo smiled. He was a good judge of character. Once a weasel, always a weasel. And the arrangement had done just what he'd said it would: made a pile of money for both of them.

Suddenly, he felt a sharp pain. The roach had burned down until it scorched his fingers. He dropped it into an ashtray and yawned.

The phone rang, and he answered it. "Yeah?"

The voice was garbled, because its owner was speaking through a device that disguised it electronically. "Nice work."

"And?"

"It's on its way."

"How?"

"United Parcel. You'll like what brown can do for you."

"I'd better."

"Don't worry. There's even something extra."

"Good. I earned it."

"Yes, you did."

"And the deposit? Something extra there, too?"

"Absolutely."

"Also good."

"Will you be around, in case you're needed?"

"Not for a while. Going to Vegas. I'll be at the Crystal Palace. You can reach me there if you want."

"Have fun." A click, and the line went dead.

Mongo closed the phone and got to his feet. Another joint would be okay. And there was also a bottle of Chardonnay in the fridge. He'd have himself a little celebration.

As he'd said, he'd earned it.

6.

Jeb Barker parked his Mustang in front of Seventeenth Precinct headquarters and stepped out onto the sidewalk. As he did, the fire station next door issued a warning blast, and seconds later Ladder 2 burst out onto East Fifty-First Street and roared toward Second Avenue. The big red machine's siren was screaming and firefighters were hanging on to the rails, and on the stern an American flag was snapping in the wind. Barker watched until the truck swung right at the intersection and disappeared.

No matter how many times he'd seen it, he never failed to get a kick out of the spectacle. Once or twice he'd even wondered whether he might have been happier if he'd joined the FDNY instead of going on the cops. And then he decided he wouldn't. A cop was what he'd wanted to be all his life.

He went into the precinct house, waving to the desk sergeant as he trotted up the stairs to the detective squad room.

The place was only moderately busy. Two detectives were talking on phones, two others were tapping out DD5s on computer keyboards. Still another was interviewing an emaciated youth. The detective was trying to get answers from him, but the kid kept nodding off. The holding cage in one corner of the room was vacant.

Lieutenant Frank Kelly's office was on the far side, behind a glass wall. Barker knocked on the door, opened it, and stuck his head in.

Kelly was on the phone. He looked up and waved Barker to one of the straight-backed visitors' chairs before his desk.

Barker sat and waited for the lieutenant to finish his call. The conversation seemed to go on forever, with Kelly's end consisting of grunts and occasional one-word replies.

It occurred to Barker that the older man never changed. Ruddy cheeks, graying hair cut short, striped blue shirt freshly laundered, an execrable multicolored tie. And, as always, an air of unshakable calm.

Barker had known Kelly since boyhood, and theirs was a special relationship. It was said that every cop in the NYPD needed a rabbi if he hoped to advance, and the lieutenant was that and more to Barker. He had made detective on his own, but it was Kelly who'd gotten him out of trouble on several occasions. The most recent incident could have ended his career.

When at last he put the phone down, Kelly said, "So how did it go?"

"It was a madhouse. Cops, civilians, media, and top brass. You could barely move around."

"Only to be expected when the victim's a celebrity. You want coffee? I just made fresh."

"No thanks."

The lieutenant picked up a pot from a credenza behind his desk and poured himself a mug. As he dropped in a lump of sugar he said, "I watched some of it on TV. They had to send extra cops to handle the traffic. I also talked to Mike Levin, the squad commander in the One-Nine. He said it was mass confusion, with a lot of conflicting stories. Did you get an idea of what actually went down?"

"Yeah, I did. The perp told the victims he was with WNEW and was there to record an interview with Delure."

"Uh-huh. I heard about that part."

"He knew just how to convince them he was legitimate, had everything worked out in advance. Delure's secretary was a woman named Dana Laramie, and she told me Delure had a lot of valuable jewelry with her. Rings, bracelets, necklaces, and so on, and the guy took all of it. Except for one ring that he either overlooked or was in such a hurry he dropped it. So now Hogan's claiming robbery was the motive, and that's why he killed the two women."

Kelly pursed his lips. "Any of that strike you as strange?"

"Hell yes it does. I never heard of a heist where the perp shot people before robbing them."

"Oh, it's happened. But you're right, not with somebody as sophisticated as this character."

"Exactly. The killer was a pro. The last thing a guy like him would want is to have a murder rap hung on him. Would've been much more logical for him to just tie up the vics and then grab the loot and take off."

"You tell Hogan that?"

"I tried to, but he cut me off. Told me about how he was one of the greatest dicks of all time. Greatest dickhead would be more like it. He's gonna have a task force working on the case, and what does he want Spinelli and me to do? Check out robbery suspects."

"Okay, if that's the way he sees it, so what? The fact is, you're lucky, Jeb."

"Lucky how?"

"For one thing, because Hogan's not refusing to have you on the case. For another, because I'm willing to free you up so you can work on it."

"I guess that's true."

"You're not exactly the most popular cop in New York," Kelly said. "After you shot that guy in the park last year, a lot of people were yelling for your head. Not just citizens' groups, but some right here in the department. The media said you set back the relationship between cops and civilians by years. I had to call in a lot of markers to keep you from getting sent down in grade, or even kicked off the force."

Barker felt the heat come up into his face. "Goddamn it, I did what was right. The guy was a serial rapist who liked little girls."

"That was never proved, though, was it? And neither was the rape."

"You know what happened, Lieu. When I got there he was on top of her, and when he saw me he got up and so did the kid. There was blood all over her, and she was scared and ran away. Then he came at me."

"All he had was a knife, and they claimed it was too small to cause any harm."

"That was bullshit too. Fucking thing was a good-sized switchblade. And how convenient that it got lost a few days afterward."

"Say what you like, but shooting him was a big mistake. The guy was a leader in the Fourth Ward."

"Okay, I won't argue about that. But it was the media that turned it into a story about a cop killing an innocent man."

Kelly rubbed the bridge of his nose with his fingers and closed his eyes. When he opened them, he said, "You're a lot like your old man, you know that? He was a hothead, too. That's what got him killed."

"So you've told me."

"I was with him, you know, the night it happened. We were on patrol in the Sixth."

Barker had heard the story more times than he could count. He forced himself to be patient.

"There was this guy who knocked over a liquor store," Kelly said. "When we got there he fired a couple rounds, and one of them hit me in the leg. Then he ran in the stockroom. I was on the floor, telling your father to wait till we got backup, but he wouldn't listen to me. He went in and there was a shoot-out, and in the end they were both dead." Kelly shook his head. "Jack had some set of balls."

Barker said nothing. A picture appeared in his mind, of his

mother's face when two police officials with gold on their caps and their sleeves came to their tiny apartment on West Tenth Street and gave her the news.

"That slug shattered my leg," Kelly said. "I could have retired with a disability pension. Instead I stayed on, and I'm glad I did."

Barker wondered where this was going.

"The thing is," Kelly went on, "there are times when you're under pressure and you have to make a decision. That's when you don't lose your temper and do something dumb. Everybody makes mistakes now and then, that's only natural. But there's no excuse for blowing your cork when the right thing to do is to stay calm and make choices that are best for the circumstances. You understand?"

"Yeah, I do."

"Keep it in mind, okay?"

Barker rose to his feet. "Okay, Lieu. I'll keep it in mind."

7.

The autopsy room was in the basement of Bellevue Hospital. It was adjacent to the morgue, where it had been located for more than a century. The air inside the room was cool and damp and heavy with the acrid stink of chemicals.

The nude body of Catherine Delure lay faceup on a stainless-steel table that was slightly elevated at the head end. Water was streaming over her blond hair and down to her feet, and her blue eyes stared sightlessly at the fluorescent lights in the ceiling. A nearby table held the remains of Penny Ellis.

Dr. Myron Robbins fussed about, checking his instruments, preparing to begin the procedure on Delure. Robbins was Manhattan's chief pathologist, a cheerful man with wisps of gray hair sticking out from under his cap.

Ordinarily, Robbins would leave the work to one of his assistants, while he observed. Assistants were on hand now, but today's subject was a star, and Robbins had as keen an appreciation of PR as anyone. No doubt the media would have questions for him afterward. So he'd do this one himself.

Another reason was that Robbins was close to retirement. He was aware that a former chief pathologist could readily find work as a consultant on TV, and that seemed like a great gig. Look at Dr. Michael Baden, who was frequently seen on Fox News. That was another reason for Robbins to shine now.

Jeb Barker was among a group of cops who were gathered nearby, staring silently. All of them were gussied up in baggy, pale green hospital gear, complete with caps and masks, as if they too were medical personnel. Only their eyes were showing, but Barker had no trouble picking out Hogan. The way the lieutenant's nose poked out the front of his mask made him easy to identify.

Barker watched as Robbins arranged his tools on a table. They included a bone saw, a long slim knife, several scalpels, two large pairs of scissors, a set of forceps, something that resembled a cleaver, a hammer with a hook on the end, and various other instruments, each glinting with reflected light.

Barker then shifted his gaze to Delure's body, and a number of thoughts went through his mind. How many men must have fantasized about seeing her lying on her back, naked? How would they feel if they could see the famous body now, with its skin cold and gray-white under the stream of water? How would Delure feel if she could see herself lying there exposed and helpless while a bunch of cops gawked at her?

Barker had seen more than his share of dead bodies, a few of them dead because of violent incidents he'd been involved in. He'd also witnessed a number of autopsies. As a cop, he was supposed to look on with no more emotional involvement than he would have felt watching a butcher trim a side of beef.

But it didn't work that way with him. He knew the procedure was necessary, because it could provide information that might help solve a crime. Yet he couldn't help feeling that the lifeless pile of meat was a human being, and that this was a barbaric ritual.

A diener, whose job it was to clean corpses before autopsies, sponged off Delure's chest and belly. As he went about it, the blue hole between her breasts was clearly visible. When he finished, he dropped the sponge into a waste container and stepped back, waiting for Robbins to begin.

The pathologist took his time. With exaggerated care, he measured the cadaver, recording his findings by speaking into an overhead microphone. As he did, one of his assistants took photographs. Robbins was featured prominently in many of the shots.

Barker could sense an air of impatience among the onlookers. He was feeling some of that himself. They all knew Delure and her manager had been shot to death. The only question concerned the bullets that had killed them. The detectives were hoping the slugs would provide some clue that might lead them to the shooter.

So come on, Doc. Move it.

At last Robbins got down to the actual procedure. He chose one of his scalpels and bent over the body. After pausing for a moment, he began to cut.

The pattern was the customary Y, starting at Delure's left shoulder. Robbins sliced his way down under her left breast and stopped at the sternum. Next, he made the same type of cut from the right shoulder until the two incisions met. Last, he cut her open down to the pubic bone.

From there on it got messy. The pathologist cut through the soft tissue and muscle and peeled back the three flaps, and his assistant dropped the upper one over Delure's face. Robbins pushed the other two aside, relegating the once-glamorous breasts to the status of excess baggage.

Next the pathologist severed the sternum with the bone saw. To cut the tissues holding the ribs in place he used heavy-duty shears, and when that was completed, he pulled the ribs aside as well. Delure's vital organs were now exposed.

"Suction," Robbins said. His assistant handed him a hose that was attached to a bottle. He thrust the hose into the abdominal cavity, and the bottle filled with dark-red blood. He returned the bottle and continued his work.

The assistant then used a small electric saw to incise Delure's skull, the tool emitting a high-pitched whine that set Barker's teeth on edge. The cap of bone came away in one piece, with wet blond hair hanging from it, and the assistant set about removing the brain.

Robbins went on cutting. He freed the larynx and the esophagus and various arteries and ligaments, and last he severed the organs' attachment to the spinal cord, bladder, and rectum. That would make it possible to pull out the entire organ set as one piece.

The diener held a tray ready as Robbins gripped the slippery mass. The pathologist tugged it out of Delure's body and placed it on the tray, and the diener put the tray on a nearby counter next to a sink. The detectives moved closer, to get a better look.

Robbins continued to work at a slow, measured pace. He washed the organs in the sink and began examining them, starting with the thyroid. When he finished, he weighed it and said into the microphone, "Thyroid normal, weight twenty-two ounces." He placed it on the countertop and repeated the process with Delure's liver.

Joe Spinelli was standing beside Barker. Under his breath he said, "It's the heart we want to see, Doc. What about the heart?"

But the pathologist was in no hurry. He cut open the stomach and recorded its contents, then slit the intestines and studied them before moving on to still another organ. Twenty minutes passed before he got to the examination they were all waiting for. He picked up the heart and washed it, peering at it as if he'd never seen one before.

Robbins then laid the heart down on the counter and held his scalpel over the center of it, where the puncture was. With deft strokes he sliced it open, exposing all four chambers.

You didn't have to be a pathologist, Barker thought, to see the amount of damage it had sustained. The shot had ripped into the cardiac muscle tissue, tearing it and causing a massive hemorrhage.

Apparently, Hogan could no longer take the suspense. "She was killed instantly. Right, Doc?"

"No."

Hogan's eyes bulged. "No? Whaddaya mean, no?"

Robbins looked at him. "Penetration trauma severely damaged both atria. That prevented blood from flowing to the right ventricle, which would have sent it to the lungs for oxygenation. Cessation of blood flow also starved the subject's brain of oxygen and rendered her unconscious. I estimate she was alive for approximately twenty seconds before expiring."

Hogan exhaled audibly. As he did, several of the others suppressed snickers.

But the lieutenant wasn't to be put off. "So where's the bullet?"

Robbins didn't bother to answer. He used forceps to reach into the torn tissue, and when he found what he was after, he held it up. Clutched in the forceps' jaws was a metal object streaked with blood.

"Jesus," Hogan said. "A dart."

"A fléchette," Robbins corrected him. "The term comes from the French. It means little arrow."

"I'll be damned. Like a bullet with fins."

Barker spoke up. "The fins are to stabilize it in flight. But it still wouldn't be very accurate, unless it was fired from up close."

Hogan glared at him. "How do you know that?"

"When I was in the Marine Corps," Barker said, "there was some work done with them. But they were much smaller than this one. A bunch of them would be packed together in twelve-gauge shotgun shells."

The lieutenant was obviously annoyed at being one-upped. He turned back to Robbins. "Okay, but what kind of gun did the guy use? The bodyguard frisked him, and he was clean."

Robbins said, "Perhaps some diligent detective work would supply the answer."

That shut Hogan up, at least for the moment.

The pathologist dropped the fléchette onto a tray on the counter and spoke into the microphone, describing what he'd found. An assistant placed a ruler next to the projectile and photographed it.

Unlike the other cops, Barker had seen enough. He realized he'd just learned something valuable. And waiting for the same procedure to be performed on the body of Delure's manager wouldn't tell him any more than he knew now.

"See you later," he said to Spinelli. He turned and headed for the door, pulling off his mask and cap as he went. In the dressing area outside the autopsy room he stripped off the rest of the gear and signed out.

Once back on the street he reflected on what he'd witnessed. He no longer had any doubt that the killer had gone to the Sherry-Netherland for the express purpose of killing Catherine Delure. The Ellis woman had probably just been in the way.

So what Barker had to do now was dig into the actress's life. Who were the people closest to her? Who might have had a motive? For starters, it would be good to have another talk with Delure's pretty brunette secretary. He hoped she hadn't gone back to Los Angeles.

8.

Dana Laramie was still in a state of shock. Nothing had ever had an impact on her emotions like the murders. In a matter of a few minutes, two people close to her had suffered violent deaths, and her world had changed completely. It felt as if she'd been hit in the pit of the stomach with a hammer.

Since then, she'd ducked the media, shutting herself off from the horde of reporters eager to interview her. But she'd received a flood of phone calls, and trying to cope with them hadn't helped her nerves. The calls had come from Catherine's lawyer, from various people at the studio, from the director of *Hot Cargo*, from the picture's male lead, and of course, from members of the media, who continued to circle her like a school of sharks smelling blood.

There'd even been a call from her former boyfriend, an actor she'd once thought she was in love with. Until she'd found out he was cheating on her with at least two other women. When he called he had seemed solicitous, but she wasn't fooled. The murders were a huge story, and like a lot of people, he wanted to stick his nose into the action. What a jerk. She was lucky to be rid of him.

The police had said they'd want her to help them create a composite drawing of the killer, so she'd agreed to stay in New York long enough to do that. But she couldn't bear to remain at the Sherry-Netherland. She'd moved to the Regency, on Park Avenue at Sixty-First Street.

It didn't make much of a difference. The awful images of the bodies were engraved in her memory. She had only to close her eyes to see the gory wounds, the expressions of agony on the dead women's faces.

Creating the composite required her to spend hours with a police artist, trying to work out an accurate likeness. Chuck Diggs helped as well, and the result looked much like the man who had come to the suite that fateful morning.

Seeing the finished drawing produced another jolt. The features were strong and masculine, and to her, they were the embodiment of evil. It was as if she was looking at the devil and he was looking back at her.

For all those reasons, she couldn't wait to get out of the city. It had been announced that Catherine's funeral would be private, but she'd asked for an invitation and one was sent to her. As soon as that was over, she'd fly back to the West Coast.

She was in her room at the Regency and about to make a flight reservation when another call came in on her cell. The caller was Len Zarkov.

"I can't tell you how sorry I am," the producer said. "Catherine was a wonderful person. And I'm sure she thought a lot of Penny. I'm sorry for you too, Dana."

"Thank you. It was terrible."

"Yes, of course it was. I wanted to express my sympathy, but I also thought it would be good for us to have a talk. There are a number of things I want to go over with you."

"Such as?"

"They're matters that concern Catherine. Especially her reputation."

"Okay, go ahead."

"Not on the phone. Could you come to my apartment?"

She hesitated. "I suppose so. When?"

"Now, if you can."

Again she hesitated. The thought of being alone with him made her uncomfortable. But finally she agreed.

He gave her an address on the Upper East Side and hung up.

She had no idea what he'd been referring to, but he'd made it sound ominous. Catherine's reputation? What did that mean?

At the moment Dana had on jeans and a T-shirt. She made a quick change, into a gray top and a checked skirt, and left her room. Down on the street a doorman whistled up a cab for her, and after she told the driver where to go and settled back on the seat, she began thinking about the call and what she knew about Zarkov himself.

He was noted for his ability to raise money for his film projects, and he often had several in development at the same time. An independent, his company was called Zarstar Productions, and his movies were released through Galaxy Films.

Catherine had remarked that his pictures rarely failed to make a profit, which was an anomaly in the business. She'd said that when he was making a movie the only things he cared about were who he could get as the stars and the director, and whether he thought the premise would draw audiences. Costs would be kept under control by his line producer. Nothing else, including the quality of the script, much interested him.

As far as his personal life was concerned, he was known as a womanizer. Or as Penny Ellis had put it, a pussy hound. It was said that he'd turned the casting couch into an art form, and judging from the women Dana had seen him with on a few occasions, that was probably true. Many of them were starlets, which was a euphemism for hungry young actresses who'd do anything, and anybody, to get ahead. With Lennie, they said, you had to lay to play.

He'd also had a string of affairs with more prominent female performers, and he was often mentioned in the gossip columns. On one occasion he'd made a pass at Catherine, who brushed him off. She was a star, and if he resented being rebuffed by her, that was just too damn bad.

It wasn't that Catherine didn't like sex. The fact was that she had loved it and didn't try to hide her appetite. Or control it. Fucking, she'd once remarked to Dana with a laugh, was a glorious way to spend your free time.

Of course, she could have had just about any man she wanted, and there were plenty to choose from. But that didn't include Len Zarkov. The only thing she'd wanted from him was a fat contract.

His apartment building was one of a row of tall, elegant structures just off Fifth Avenue. When Dana arrived, the doorman saluted and opened the door for her and she went into a lobby that was illuminated by a huge crystal chandelier. The walls and the floor were clad in beige marble, and an antique table held a large bouquet of flowers.

A concierge stood at a marble-topped desk. She told him why she was there and he spoke into a telephone and then directed her to the private elevator that served the penthouse. She stepped into it and was whisked upward.

Zarkov was waiting for her in the foyer. He was heavyset and had coarse features, and his thinning black hair was brushed straight back. Behind tinted sunglasses, his eyes were unreadable. He was casually dressed: white shirt open at the throat, black pants, black loafers. Dana thought he was far from good-looking, but there was an air of power about him, and she knew some women found that irresistible.

"Thank you for coming on such short notice," he said. "I'm sure you're very distraught."

"I am," she said. "I still can't believe it happened."

He nodded, his manner grave. "I feel the same way myself. But as I said, there are matters we should discuss. So come along, and we'll sit out on the terrace and talk."

She followed him through a living room furnished with white

sofas and chairs and ankle-deep white carpeting. A Mark Rothko painting that blended horizontal bands of orange and yellow and red decorated one wall. Two of the other walls were glass and gave spectacular views of the city.

Even more extraordinary were the views from the terrace. Looking to the east Dana could see the Queensboro Bridge spanning the river, and Roosevelt Island, and in the distance jets that were taking off and landing at LaGuardia and JFK. Still farther, miles of Long Island stretched away into the haze. To the south, the skyline was punctuated by the MetLife and Chrysler and Empire State Buildings. There was even a glimpse of the harbor.

She and Zarkov sat at an awning-shaded table and he asked if she'd like a drink. She said mineral water would be fine and he buzzed for a maid, and when one appeared, he told her to bring some for both of them.

He swept an arm toward the expanse. "You like this?"

"It's marvelous," she said. "It's like being on top of the world."

The remark obviously pleased him. "That's why I bought the apartment."

"You still have your place in LA, too, don't you?"

"Yes, of course. My business is in both places. Production in California, finance in New York."

The maid returned and served them drinks in tall glasses.

When they were alone again, Zarkov asked if Dana had heard from Jay Harris, who had been Catherine's agent at CMI.

"No, not a word."

"He'll be dealing with her lawyer," Zarkov said. "Trying to get what he can from her estate."

"I suppose so."

"Believe it. He's a slimy little prick."

Dana thought so too, but she didn't reply.

Zarkov said, "What about the publicist, Sandra Rosen?"

"She called me, mostly to commiserate. Said she's been swamped by the media, wanting more information on Catherine for stories they were doing about her."

"Only what you'd expect. The irony is that Catherine knew the value of publicity as well as anyone. But she'd be horrified by what's going on now."

Dana wasn't fooled by his pious remark. "Although it's certainly had a positive effect on the box office, hasn't it?"

"Oh, yes. The numbers look very good."

"I thought they would. I saw a newscast that showed the theater in Times Square at the opening, and there was a long line of people waiting to get in."

"It's the same as when they see a car wreck and have to stop and look. But with *Hot Cargo* they'll get their money's worth. It's a good picture, and Catherine is wonderful in it. In fact, even if she hadn't been killed it still would have been a big hit."

"Uh-huh." Actually, Dana thought the movie was trash, but she wasn't about to say so. At the preview in Westwood, the members of the audience had seemed bored, even though the film contained plenty of sex and violence. The survey afterward confirmed that they weren't much impressed.

"I tried to reach you at the Sherry," Zarkov said, "but I was told you'd moved. Fortunately, I had your cell number."

"I had to get away from the reporters. So I slipped out and went to the Regency."

"What are your plans?"

"I want to go to Catherine's funeral. It's to be held in Connecticut. In Greenwich, where she grew up."

"Yes. I wanted to go too, and so did Tony Gregarian and Terry Falcon and people from the studio. But we were told it's to be private. So we'll hold a memorial service for her in LA, at some point later on. I'm surprised you were able to get an invitation."

"I think it's because her brother knew I was close to her."

"Yes, I'm sure you're right. By the way, Penny's body will be sent to Kansas City. Her family is there."

"So I understand."

"You two didn't get along very well, did you?"

The question surprised her. How would he know anything

about that? "We had a few differences. But nothing serious." That wasn't true. She'd always found Penny to be an officious bitch, jealous of her relationship with Catherine.

Zarkov didn't press it. Instead he said, "You should go back to LA right after the funeral. Otherwise you could have problems."

"Problems? With what?"

"You could be forced to stay here in New York. The district attorney could have you held as a material witness."

"He could do that?"

"Yes. I talked to my lawyer about it. He said you and Chuck Diggs could both be held here."

"But why? I told the detectives everything I knew. They kept asking me the same questions over and over again about what happened."

"Did they ask you anything else? About Catherine, for instance? About her personal life, anything like that?"

"Not really. They were mostly interested in how she'd spent her time after we got to New York. They asked if she'd had any impression that someone might be following her, and I said no."

"And that was all?"

"Pretty much, yes. They also showed me dozens of pictures of men, but none of them looked like the one who did it. I helped them make a drawing of him. Then they had me put together a list of the jewelry she had with her. I told them I couldn't be sure it was accurate. I gave them the name of her insurance company and suggested they check with them."

"So you were completely cooperative."

"Of course. And I still don't understand why they'd want to hold me here."

"My guess is that the case is so big they'd want to keep a tight grip on it. So they'd force you to stay while the police try to find the killer."

"That's ridiculous. Who knows how long that might take. Maybe they'll never catch him. Then what?"

"I'm only passing on what my lawyer said about it. He also said something else, and that's what I wanted to talk to you about. He said you should go through your files as soon as possible and take out anything you wouldn't want the authorities to see. Anything that might show Catherine in a bad light."

"I doubt there's anything like that."

"Perhaps there isn't. But something you think is perfectly innocent could be distorted. Also, once it was made public, or leaked, the tabloids would blow it all out of proportion."

"Yes, I know that's true. During the time I worked for her, they said outrageous things about her."

"You see? Look, I've had a lot of experience with that kind of thing. I'd be glad to go over what you have and advise you as to what could cause trouble."

"Thanks, that's very good of you."

"You brought your laptop with you to New York, didn't you?"

"Yes, but I'd prefer to wait till I get back to LA to go over the files. I have more stuff there, also. Personal letters, notes, that kind of thing."

"I see. In any case, I'll help you. And I'll make sure the studio plane is available to take you back to LA right after Catherine's funeral. I have some business that will keep me here for a couple of days, but then I'll go back as well."

"Okay. Was there anything else?"

He put a hand on hers. "Only that I've always found you very attractive. Why don't you stay and join me for dinner? I'd be delighted to have you."

"Sorry, but I have a lot to do."

He moved his hand down to her leg and squeezed it. "Don't be in such a rush. I think we could have a pleasant time together. A very pleasant time."

She stood up. "Gotta go, Len."

He looked annoyed, but then wiped the expression from his face. "As you wish. Just be careful. Remember my lawyer's advice."

"I will."

He followed her back to the elevator. As she stepped into it he said, "I'll look forward to spending time with you in LA. Meantime, you can count on me for anything you might want. You have my number, don't you?"

"Yes, I do." The door closed, and down she went.

Once Dana had returned to her room at the Regency she decided that after the visit with Zarkov she needed a shower. The nerve of the oily bastard. Stay for dinner? *Dinner* wasn't what he meant. He'd acted as if he'd be doing her a favor by fucking her.

She took off her clothes and got into the shower stall and turned on the hot water. As the spray pounded her skin she felt a little better, but she was still irritated by the discussion. Obviously Zarkov considered her naive, if not stupid. His offer to help her wasn't as altruistic as he wanted her to think.

And he hadn't just been horny. In fact, two points stood out, loud and clear. He wanted her to leave New York as soon as possible. And he wanted to get his hands on Catherine Delure's personal files.

9.

A few days after the autopsies of Delure and Ellis, Jeb Barker drove his Mustang up FDR Drive and over the Third Avenue Bridge, on his way to Greenwich. Because it was morning and people were coming to work in New York, most of the traffic was moving in the opposite direction, and that was a break. The weather was lousy, however, sky heavily overcast and rain falling off and on. Perfect for a funeral.

On the Major Deegan Expressway he passed the reincarnated Yankee Stadium. According to a story he'd read in the *Post*, the new park had cost $1.3 billion, with a good chunk of that provided by the city. It struck him as unfair for the owners to stick it to taxpayers, especially since they were making a shitload of money. And besides, there didn't seem to be much wrong with the old stadium, which had been right next door.

Those issues aside, it would be nice to go to a ball game—if his life ever returned to something approaching normal. As it was, the Delure case was taking over every part of his existence.

a data analyst at J.P. Morgan. Barker told her to stick
ers and stop shoving her nose into matters he was
uss with a civilian. Calling her a civilian apparently
as much as any of the rest of it. He hadn't seen or
since.

ng Barker was alone in the car. Spinelli was in the
wn yet another known jewel thief, although with
for the task. Nevertheless, Joe felt it beat going to
ated funerals.

tter, he didn't know anybody who liked them.
rtakers, of course—or funeral directors, as they
s these days.

on I-95 the traffic was somewhat lighter, mostly
along the broad concrete ribbon. The weather also
. By the time he turned off at Greenwich the rain
zzle, although the day remained dark and gloomy.
drove to the center of town. If you didn't know
ssion you got was that this was simply a charm-
But then you began to notice that the stores were
s Fifth Avenue, and Prada, and others equally
you saw gave you another hint. There were far
nd BMWs and Bentleys and Porsches than there
evys.

Greenwich was one of the richest towns in the
had been for more than a century. This was where
the Vanderbilts and many of the Rockefellers had
great sprawling properties that featured castle-
cres of meticulously manicured lawns and gar-

most of today's residents owned smaller spreads,
es were nevertheless baroque statements of sta-
siness tycoons, sports and entertainment stars,
rs, wheelers and dealers of every stripe called
ll it took was money. Lots of it.

the town had also attracted its share of rascals.

He'd never seen so much pressure within the NYPD. Everybody
from the police commissioner on down was putting the squeeze on
the cops who were actually doing the work. And for that matter,
the PC himself was catching hell from the mayor and every tinpot
politician who saw the case as an opportunity to call attention to
himself by demanding that the killer be brought to justice.

As a result, Lieutenant Hogan now had more than a hundred
detectives in what the department was calling the Catherine Delure
Task Force, and at times it seemed as though the cops were stumbling over one another. So far they'd come up with not one solid
lead.

Hogan's order that Barker and Spinelli check out known fences,
hoping they'd run across jewelry that had belonged to the actress,
had also been fruitless. In Barker's opinion, it was a waste of time.
Especially after what he'd seen at the autopsy.

To begin with, the cops didn't even know exactly what the
pieces of jewelry were. The list Dana Laramie had provided was,
by her own admission, mostly guesswork. But she'd suggested that
because the jewelry had been insured through the Fidelity National
Insurance Company, they probably had better information. Barker
had called the firm, and they said yes, they'd issued Ms. Delure a
policy. They sent a list of their own, which contained fewer than
half the items Laramie had put down.

Not only that, but the descriptions were much too broad. "Ring
with square-cut 5-carat diamond." And "Patek-Philippe ladies'
wristwatch." And "Pearl necklace." And "Bracelet set with sapphires and emeralds." Ask anybody in the jewelry business about
pinning down such pieces and they'd laugh at you.

In fact, several had. One of them, a retailer in the Diamond District on West Forty-Seventh Street, said, "What is this, a joke? I got
things here in my shop that're like all the ones you're talking about.
So?"

The guy had a point. Even though he'd had several brushes with
the law for dealing in merchandise that later had turned out to be stolen, there was no way to connect him or his goods to the Delure case.

"Listen," he said, "let's say you were looking for signature pieces, like the stuff created by Harry Winston, or Van Cleef. Then they'd be distinctive, know what I mean? You could identify them. But you're asking me about a diamond ring, or a bracelet with jewels or a pearl necklace? Get real."

Barker and Spinelli had also gone through police records and picked out known thieves, guys who'd done time for jewelry heists. None of the men in the photos much resembled the smooth character who'd sneered at the security cameras in the Sherry-Netherland, but the two detectives tracked down a number of them anyway.

One had been paroled from Sing Sing some six months earlier. He was bald and skinny and had a nervous twitch in his left eye. The only physical aspects he had in common with the Delure perp were his above-average height and a mustache. His name was Alfred Favalo, and he hung out in a bar in the Village. Barker and Spinelli found him there and showed him their shields and IDs.

Favalo was drinking a gin and tonic and was obviously not happy to see them. To take the edge off the discussion, each cop ordered vodka on the rocks. They said *salut* and drank, and then tried to question him. But except to swallow some of his booze, Favalo kept his mouth shut. And the twitch in his eye became more pronounced.

"Come on, Al," Spinelli said. "You probably got a pretty good idea of what's going down. What've you heard?"

"Nothing. If I did, I'd tell you."

"No word on the street? Nobody's been saying anything about the case?"

"People've been saying a lot about it. But that don't mean any of them know anything. It's all rumors and guesswork. Like I said, if I knew I'd tell you."

"You would?"

"Jesus, don't you ever talk to other cops?"

"What does that mean?"

Favalo dropped his voice to just above a whisper. "I'm a CI, man."

Barker looked at him. "You

"Hell yes. I'm in touch with
Wanewski. And right now you
I don't want to be seen with y

Barker and Spinelli knock
the tab. They told Favalo to h

Later, when they were dri
Spinelli said, "The guy was r
other one's doing. How were

"We weren't. That's par
operate below the radar."

"Maybe so, but you kn
spinning our wheels."

"Could be."

Other interviews they
Barker was convinced Spi
pened to come up with s
credit for it. Until then, th
busy.

Barker's problems did
girlfriend had turned int
tion about the case. She
assumed he'd attended i
have learned about Delu

Could he tell if the a
tions? Was her hair dye
there cellulite in her th

And in addition to
life? Had he found out

When Barker refus
a monumental sulk. H
interest in his work, a
said by not confiding
didn't trust her, and I
her feelings.

Gloria was
with her numb
not able to disc
pissed her off
heard from her

This morni
city running d
little enthusiasm
Greenwich. He

For that m
Except the und
called themselve

Once he was
trucks pounding
improved a little
had become a dr

From I-95 he
better, the impre
ing little village.
Tiffany, and Sak
famous. The cars
more Mercedes a
were Fords and C

The fact was
United States and
the Whitneys and
built their estates.
like houses with
dens.

And although
many of their hous
tus and wealth. Bu
hedge fund operat
Greenwich home.

Over the years,

One of the first to gain a national reputation for political thievery was Boss Tweed, the notorious head of New York's Tammany Hall back in the nineteenth century. At the height of his career, Tweed was the third largest landowner in Manhattan. He used some of the money he stole to build a vast dwelling in Greenwich, on the shore of Long Island Sound and used it as his summer home. He died in jail on April 12, 1878, after being convicted of forgery and larceny.

Like Boss Tweed, modern criminals residing in Greenwich also tended to be the white-collar type. A prime example was Martin Frankel, a financier who'd owned a mansion a few miles north of the Merritt Parkway. Frankel swiped more than $200 million from insurance companies in five states before skipping to Germany with two blondes and a satchel full of gold and diamonds. He was arrested in Hamburg and brought back to the States to face the music. A federal judge sentenced him to sixteen years.

As for crimes of the more violent sort, there had been a number of those, too. Probably the most infamous of them took place in 1975, when Michael Skakel, a nephew of Ethel Kennedy, beat fifteen-year-old Martha Moxley to death with a golf club. Not until 2002 was Skakel brought to trial, convicted, and given a life sentence. His attorneys kept pressing, and in 2013 he was released on bail to await a new trial.

Barker's own experience with crime in Greenwich had been more recent. Not long ago he'd come there when New York cops were on the trail of a mutual fund manager who was accused of running a Ponzi scheme. The suspect lived in a huge house off Round Hill, and when Barker and the others arrived, the place seemed deserted. They forced open the front door and poked around until they found the guy hanging from a beam in the basement. Anticlimactic, but what the hell. Saved everybody a lot of time and effort.

Today was an entirely different matter. The Delure murder had aroused more public interest than anything Barker had ever worked on, by far. But he had to admit that even with all the pressure, it was pleasant to be out in the country. The trees were lush and green and the leaves were glistening with raindrops.

Courtesy required a cop from another jurisdiction to check in with the local police department—which Barker had done when he came to Greenwich earlier—and he planned to do so now. He drove up North Street and from there over to Bruce Place, where GPD headquarters was located.

Critics said the Greenwich force was more interested in serving the needs of the town's rich residents than anything else. Whether or not that was true Barker didn't know, nor did he care. It was none of his business.

He parked his Mustang and went into the station. The police weren't exactly happy to see him, having been burned by other cop visitors who had later criticized their operation.

The chief wasn't in, but Barker presented ID and explained his mission to a desk sergeant who wrote out a pass for him. Barker thanked him and turned to leave.

"Hey, tell me something," the sergeant said.

"Sure, what is it?"

"You getting anywhere with the case? I heard it was an inside job, and the guy who did it used to work for the hotel. That true?"

"It's news to me," Barker said. "But anything's possible. Thanks for your help." Jesus, even the cops were circulating rumors. He left the station and went back to his car.

To get to the church where the service was scheduled, he had to retrace his route. Once back on Putnam Avenue, the old Gothic stone structure was easy to find. A hearse and a line of cars were out front, and again uniformed officers were holding back a large crowd of onlookers. Naturally, the media were on hand as well.

Barker parked some distance away and dropped his police plate onto the dash. He walked back to the church, showed his shield and the pass to a cop at the door, and went inside.

What little light there was came through the stained-glass windows and from an array of tall candles, and it took several moments for his eyes to adjust. Large floral arrangements lined the walls, and their fragrance was almost enough to make him dizzy. A closed casket of gleaming mahogany lay on a low platform before the altar. Soft organ music wafted through the air.

Barker stepped into a dark corner and stood there, looking over the attendees. All were dressed for the occasion: mostly black suits on the men, black dresses on the women. The ladies also wore hats, many with veils.

As he watched, a few more people arrived and took off raincoats as they moved into the pews. Even in their funereal garb, the women managed to look stylish. They were thin and graceful and carried themselves with an air of confidence.

He didn't recognize any of them and hadn't expected to. Until he studied the backs of three people sitting side by side in the front pew. Two, a man and a woman, were strangers to him. Probably family members, he thought, Delure's brother and his wife.

But the third person, another woman, looked familiar. At one point she turned her head slightly, and he saw that it was Dana Laramie, Delure's secretary.

Okay, that figured. Laramie had been as close to the star as anyone the family would know about, most likely, so it was no wonder that she'd joined them for the funeral, probably at their invitation.

And for Barker, her being here was a stroke of luck. After the autopsy, he'd tried to locate her for another talk, but she'd left the Sherry-Netherland and hadn't left a forwarding address. He assumed she'd returned to Los Angeles. Now he'd catch her, either here or at the cemetery, and ask more questions.

Several minutes passed, and it became clear that there would be no more attendees than were present now. Another long pause while the organ music swirled, and at last the minister got things under way.

Fortunately, the ceremony was brief. A few psalms, and a cliché-filled oratory that sounded as if it could have applied to any woman, just fill in the name. Listening to the man drone on, Barker wondered if the minister had ever known Delure. It sounded as though he hadn't. More psalms, and then it was over.

As the pallbearers lifted the casket and carried it out to the waiting hearse, people rose from the pews and followed, led by the threesome in the front pew. Barker tried to catch Dana's eye, but she kept her head down and was out the door before he could speak to her.

When he emerged from the church and went down the steps to the street, the casket had already been loaded and she was getting into a car. The couple she'd been sitting with was in a limousine directly behind the hearse. The crowd seemed larger than when he'd arrived earlier, and the TV camera people were busy shooting this part of the event as well. They even panned shots of the hearse pulling away.

Rain was falling again. Barker got back into his car, and when there was an opening in the slow-moving procession he pulled in and joined it. It took only a few minutes to reach the cemetery, which was on a tree-lined side street.

He parked and took a raincoat out of the car and shrugged into it as he walked to the entrance, where a cop was admitting only those with invitations. As at the church, many other officers were on hand, and this crowd seemed even bigger. The media were already here, red lights glowing atop their video cameras.

When he showed his pass and went through the ornate iron gates, Barker saw that many of the headstones were ancient, some so old he couldn't read the inscriptions. There were also elaborate statues here and there, and they too seemed very old. In some of the plots, bouquets of flowers lay near the graves, wilted and bedraggled by the rain.

Dana Laramie and the couple from the church were standing beside Delure's casket, which was suspended over an open grave. Barker again took a position that was on the edge of the crowd, one that would give him a good view of the goings-on. It would also enable him to keep an eye on Miss Laramie.

Like most of the others, she was wearing a raincoat, and it was buttoned up to her neck. But she was holding a small umbrella and wore no hat, and he was able to see her clearly. She really looked beautiful, he thought, even in these circumstances.

He'd never seen so much pressure within the NYPD. Everybody from the police commissioner on down was putting the squeeze on the cops who were actually doing the work. And for that matter, the PC himself was catching hell from the mayor and every tinpot politician who saw the case as an opportunity to call attention to himself by demanding that the killer be brought to justice.

As a result, Lieutenant Hogan now had more than a hundred detectives in what the department was calling the Catherine Delure Task Force, and at times it seemed as though the cops were stumbling over one another. So far they'd come up with not one solid lead.

Hogan's order that Barker and Spinelli check out known fences, hoping they'd run across jewelry that had belonged to the actress, had also been fruitless. In Barker's opinion, it was a waste of time. Especially after what he'd seen at the autopsy.

To begin with, the cops didn't even know exactly what the pieces of jewelry were. The list Dana Laramie had provided was, by her own admission, mostly guesswork. But she'd suggested that because the jewelry had been insured through the Fidelity National Insurance Company, they probably had better information. Barker had called the firm, and they said yes, they'd issued Ms. Delure a policy. They sent a list of their own, which contained fewer than half the items Laramie had put down.

Not only that, but the descriptions were much too broad. "Ring with square-cut 5-carat diamond." And "Patek-Philippe ladies' wristwatch." And "Pearl necklace." And "Bracelet set with sapphires and emeralds." Ask anybody in the jewelry business about pinning down such pieces and they'd laugh at you.

In fact, several had. One of them, a retailer in the Diamond District on West Forty-Seventh Street, said, "What is this, a joke? I got things here in my shop that're like all the ones you're talking about. So?"

The guy had a point. Even though he'd had several brushes with the law for dealing in merchandise that later had turned out to be stolen, there was no way to connect him or his goods to the Delure case.

"Listen," he said, "let's say you were looking for signature pieces, like the stuff created by Harry Winston, or Van Cleef. Then they'd be distinctive, know what I mean? You could identify them. But you're asking me about a diamond ring, or a bracelet with jewels or a pearl necklace? Get real."

Barker and Spinelli had also gone through police records and picked out known thieves, guys who'd done time for jewelry heists. None of the men in the photos much resembled the smooth character who'd sneered at the security cameras in the Sherry-Netherland, but the two detectives tracked down a number of them anyway.

One had been paroled from Sing Sing some six months earlier. He was bald and skinny and had a nervous twitch in his left eye. The only physical aspects he had in common with the Delure perp were his above-average height and a mustache. His name was Alfred Favalo, and he hung out in a bar in the Village. Barker and Spinelli found him there and showed him their shields and IDs.

Favalo was drinking a gin and tonic and was obviously not happy to see them. To take the edge off the discussion, each cop ordered vodka on the rocks. They said *salut* and drank, and then tried to question him. But except to swallow some of his booze, Favalo kept his mouth shut. And the twitch in his eye became more pronounced.

"Come on, Al," Spinelli said. "You probably got a pretty good idea of what's going down. What've you heard?"

"Nothing. If I did, I'd tell you."

"No word on the street? Nobody's been saying anything about the case?"

"People've been saying a lot about it. But that don't mean any of them know anything. It's all rumors and guesswork. Like I said, if I knew I'd tell you."

"You would?"

"Jesus, don't you ever talk to other cops?"

"What does that mean?"

Favalo dropped his voice to just above a whisper. "I'm a CI, man."

Barker looked at him. "You're a confidential informant?"

"Hell yes. I'm in touch with Robbery all the time. Ask Sergeant Wanewski. And right now you guys can get the fuck away from me. I don't want to be seen with you."

Barker and Spinelli knocked back their booze, and Barker paid the tab. They told Favalo to have a nice evening and left the place.

Later, when they were driving back uptown in Barker's Mustang, Spinelli said, "The guy was right. One hand doesn't know what the other one's doing. How were we supposed to know he's a snitch?"

"We weren't. That's part of the idea, Joe. An informant has to operate below the radar."

"Maybe so, but you know what I think? I think Hogan's got us spinning our wheels."

"Could be."

Other interviews they conducted were no more productive, and Barker was convinced Spinelli had put his finger on it. If they happened to come up with something worthwhile, Hogan could take credit for it. Until then, their bullshit assignment would keep them busy.

Barker's problems didn't stop there, either. His on-and-off-again girlfriend had turned into a real nudzh, pestering him for information about the case. She knew an autopsy had been conducted and assumed he'd attended it. Now she was eager to hear what he might have learned about Delure.

Could he tell if the actress's smooth skin was due to Botox injections? Was her hair dyed? Did she have scars from a face-lift? Was there cellulite in her thighs? Or in her ass? Were her boobs real?

And in addition to all that, what did he know about her social life? Had he found out who she'd been fucking?

When Barker refused to reply to her questions, Gloria went into a monumental sulk. Before this, she'd never expressed the faintest interest in his work, and now she seemed to think of little else. She said by not confiding in her he was being cruel, and it showed he didn't trust her, and he was a stubborn male who ought to consider her feelings.

Gloria was a data analyst at J.P. Morgan. Barker told her to stick with her numbers and stop shoving her nose into matters he was not able to discuss with a civilian. Calling her a civilian apparently pissed her off as much as any of the rest of it. He hadn't seen or heard from her since.

This morning Barker was alone in the car. Spinelli was in the city running down yet another known jewel thief, although with little enthusiasm for the task. Nevertheless, Joe felt it beat going to Greenwich. He hated funerals.

For that matter, he didn't know anybody who liked them. Except the undertakers, of course—or funeral directors, as they called themselves these days.

Once he was on I-95 the traffic was somewhat lighter, mostly trucks pounding along the broad concrete ribbon. The weather also improved a little. By the time he turned off at Greenwich the rain had become a drizzle, although the day remained dark and gloomy.

From I-95 he drove to the center of town. If you didn't know better, the impression you got was that this was simply a charming little village. But then you began to notice that the stores were Tiffany, and Saks Fifth Avenue, and Prada, and others equally famous. The cars you saw gave you another hint. There were far more Mercedes and BMWs and Bentleys and Porsches than there were Fords and Chevys.

The fact was Greenwich was one of the richest towns in the United States and had been for more than a century. This was where the Whitneys and the Vanderbilts and many of the Rockefellers had built their estates, great sprawling properties that featured castle-like houses with acres of meticulously manicured lawns and gardens.

And although most of today's residents owned smaller spreads, many of their houses were nevertheless baroque statements of status and wealth. Business tycoons, sports and entertainment stars, hedge fund operators, wheelers and dealers of every stripe called Greenwich home. All it took was money. Lots of it.

Over the years, the town had also attracted its share of rascals.

One of the first to gain a national reputation for political thievery was Boss Tweed, the notorious head of New York's Tammany Hall back in the nineteenth century. At the height of his career, Tweed was the third largest landowner in Manhattan. He used some of the money he stole to build a vast dwelling in Greenwich, on the shore of Long Island Sound and used it as his summer home. He died in jail on April 12, 1878, after being convicted of forgery and larceny.

Like Boss Tweed, modern criminals residing in Greenwich also tended to be the white-collar type. A prime example was Martin Frankel, a financier who'd owned a mansion a few miles north of the Merritt Parkway. Frankel swiped more than $200 million from insurance companies in five states before skipping to Germany with two blondes and a satchel full of gold and diamonds. He was arrested in Hamburg and brought back to the States to face the music. A federal judge sentenced him to sixteen years.

As for crimes of the more violent sort, there had been a number of those, too. Probably the most infamous of them took place in 1975, when Michael Skakel, a nephew of Ethel Kennedy, beat fifteen-year-old Martha Moxley to death with a golf club. Not until 2002 was Skakel brought to trial, convicted, and given a life sentence. His attorneys kept pressing, and in 2013 he was released on bail to await a new trial.

Barker's own experience with crime in Greenwich had been more recent. Not long ago he'd come there when New York cops were on the trail of a mutual fund manager who was accused of running a Ponzi scheme. The suspect lived in a huge house off Round Hill, and when Barker and the others arrived, the place seemed deserted. They forced open the front door and poked around until they found the guy hanging from a beam in the basement. Anticlimactic, but what the hell. Saved everybody a lot of time and effort.

Today was an entirely different matter. The Delure murder had aroused more public interest than anything Barker had ever worked on, by far. But he had to admit that even with all the pressure, it was pleasant to be out in the country. The trees were lush and green and the leaves were glistening with raindrops.

Courtesy required a cop from another jurisdiction to check in with the local police department—which Barker had done when he came to Greenwich earlier—and he planned to do so now. He drove up North Street and from there over to Bruce Place, where GPD headquarters was located.

Critics said the Greenwich force was more interested in serving the needs of the town's rich residents than anything else. Whether or not that was true Barker didn't know, nor did he care. It was none of his business.

He parked his Mustang and went into the station. The police weren't exactly happy to see him, having been burned by other cop visitors who had later criticized their operation.

The chief wasn't in, but Barker presented ID and explained his mission to a desk sergeant who wrote out a pass for him. Barker thanked him and turned to leave.

"Hey, tell me something," the sergeant said.

"Sure, what is it?"

"You getting anywhere with the case? I heard it was an inside job, and the guy who did it used to work for the hotel. That true?"

"It's news to me," Barker said. "But anything's possible. Thanks for your help." Jesus, even the cops were circulating rumors. He left the station and went back to his car.

To get to the church where the service was scheduled, he had to retrace his route. Once back on Putnam Avenue, the old Gothic stone structure was easy to find. A hearse and a line of cars were out front, and again uniformed officers were holding back a large crowd of onlookers. Naturally, the media were on hand as well.

Barker parked some distance away and dropped his police plate onto the dash. He walked back to the church, showed his shield and the pass to a cop at the door, and went inside.

What little light there was came through the stained-glass windows and from an array of tall candles, and it took several moments for his eyes to adjust. Large floral arrangements lined the walls, and their fragrance was almost enough to make him dizzy. A closed casket of gleaming mahogany lay on a low platform before the altar. Soft organ music wafted through the air.

Barker stepped into a dark corner and stood there, looking over the attendees. All were dressed for the occasion: mostly black suits on the men, black dresses on the women. The ladies also wore hats, many with veils.

As he watched, a few more people arrived and took off raincoats as they moved into the pews. Even in their funereal garb, the women managed to look stylish. They were thin and graceful and carried themselves with an air of confidence.

He didn't recognize any of them and hadn't expected to. Until he studied the backs of three people sitting side by side in the front pew. Two, a man and a woman, were strangers to him. Probably family members, he thought, Delure's brother and his wife.

But the third person, another woman, looked familiar. At one point she turned her head slightly, and he saw that it was Dana Laramie, Delure's secretary.

Okay, that figured. Laramie had been as close to the star as anyone the family would know about, most likely, so it was no wonder that she'd joined them for the funeral, probably at their invitation.

And for Barker, her being here was a stroke of luck. After the autopsy, he'd tried to locate her for another talk, but she'd left the Sherry-Netherland and hadn't left a forwarding address. He assumed she'd returned to Los Angeles. Now he'd catch her, either here or at the cemetery, and ask more questions.

Several minutes passed, and it became clear that there would be no more attendees than were present now. Another long pause while the organ music swirled, and at last the minister got things under way.

Fortunately, the ceremony was brief. A few psalms, and a cliché-filled oratory that sounded as if it could have applied to any woman, just fill in the name. Listening to the man drone on, Barker wondered if the minister had ever known Delure. It sounded as though he hadn't. More psalms, and then it was over.

As the pallbearers lifted the casket and carried it out to the waiting hearse, people rose from the pews and followed, led by the threesome in the front pew. Barker tried to catch Dana's eye, but she kept her head down and was out the door before he could speak to her.

When he emerged from the church and went down the steps to the street, the casket had already been loaded and she was getting into a car. The couple she'd been sitting with was in a limousine directly behind the hearse. The crowd seemed larger than when he'd arrived earlier, and the TV camera people were busy shooting this part of the event as well. They even panned shots of the hearse pulling away.

Rain was falling again. Barker got back into his car, and when there was an opening in the slow-moving procession he pulled in and joined it. It took only a few minutes to reach the cemetery, which was on a tree-lined side street.

He parked and took a raincoat out of the car and shrugged into it as he walked to the entrance, where a cop was admitting only those with invitations. As at the church, many other officers were on hand, and this crowd seemed even bigger. The media were already here, red lights glowing atop their video cameras.

When he showed his pass and went through the ornate iron gates, Barker saw that many of the headstones were ancient, some so old he couldn't read the inscriptions. There were also elaborate statues here and there, and they too seemed very old. In some of the plots, bouquets of flowers lay near the graves, wilted and bedraggled by the rain.

Dana Laramie and the couple from the church were standing beside Delure's casket, which was suspended over an open grave. Barker again took a position that was on the edge of the crowd, one that would give him a good view of the goings-on. It would also enable him to keep an eye on Miss Laramie.

Like most of the others, she was wearing a raincoat, and it was buttoned up to her neck. But she was holding a small umbrella and wore no hat, and he was able to see her clearly. She really looked beautiful, he thought, even in these circumstances.

Next he swung his gaze to the couple and studied them. The man was tall and somber faced, his hands deep in the pockets of his raincoat. He had on a gray fedora, so Barker couldn't make out his features all that well. The woman was also bundled up against the drizzle, and she too wore a hat. He could see that she had black hair and pale skin, and that was as much of an impression as he could get.

When the mourners were assembled, the minister reappeared and conducted a service that was only half as long as the one in the church had been. He read the Twenty-Third Psalm, said a few more words, and that was it. Maybe he was mindful that some of the women were quietly weeping and wanted to spare them further pain. Or maybe he just wanted to get out of the rain.

Afterward, Barker moved closer to the gates, so he could catch Dana on her way out. She said something to the couple and shook hands with them, and as people offering condolences surrounded them, she collapsed her umbrella and joined those who were leaving.

As she approached, Barker raised his hand in greeting and smiled at her. The reaction he got was not at all what he'd expected.

Dana looked at him and seemed stunned, as if she were seeing a ghost. Before he could explain that he only wanted to spend a few minutes speaking with her, she rushed past him and hurried through the gates. From there she ran down to where a large black car was parked. She ducked into the backseat and the car drove away.

10.

Barker was nonplussed. Dana Laramie had been completely cooperative when he'd seen her at the hotel after the homicide, and she'd expressed willingness to help the investigation in any way she could. He knew she'd even assisted the forensics cops in creating a likeness of the perp.

Now she couldn't get away from him fast enough. What had happened to change her attitude?

Whatever it was, he couldn't sort through it at this stage. Instead, he'd concentrate on his initial purpose in attending the funeral. He walked back to where the couple was standing, and as they too began moving toward the entrance, he introduced himself and showed them his ID.

"I'm Roger Delaney," the man said. "And this is my wife, Sarah. Catherine was my sister. How can we help you?"

Barker spoke quietly, so that the conversation would be private. "First," he said, "I'm sorry about your loss. I know what it's like to lose a family member, and I can understand how you must feel."

"Thank you," Delaney said. "But you didn't come here just to tell us that, did you?"

"No sir, I didn't. As you've probably seen, the stories in the newspapers and on TV have all suggested that the killer's motive was to steal your sister's jewelry."

"Yes, we've seen the stories."

"It might be true, or it might not be. I'm trying to learn if there was another reason for her death."

"Such as whether she had enemies who'd want to harm her?"

"Exactly. Can you comment on that, or give me any information that might shed some light?"

Delaney hesitated before answering. "I'm not sure. But there might be something. In any event, I'd prefer not to discuss it here."

"Anywhere you say," Barker said.

"We were about to go back to our family home, the place where Catherine and I grew up. My father still lives there, although he's in very poor health. For that reason, we're not having people in after the funeral. We've been staying with him during his illness. If you wish, you can follow us, and I'll try to give you whatever help I can."

"You sure that would be okay? I wouldn't want to upset your father."

"No, it's quite all right. One person won't disturb him. You see, he doesn't know Catherine is dead."

Barker thanked him and went to his car. The TV people were busy once again, and he resisted an urge to tell them to turn off their damned cameras and beat it. Not that it would have done much good, but they did remind him of vultures. And now that he noticed, several of the onlookers were snapping shots with their cell phones. What would you call them, amateur vultures?

He got into his car and waited, and when the long black limousine eased past, he pulled out and swung in behind it. They went back through the center of town and then turned toward the Sound. Eventually they came to a private road with an entrance between two stone pillars and a booth for a security guard. A plate on one of the pillars announced that the area was Belle Haven.

The limo stopped, and Delaney apparently spoke to the guard before driving on. The guard then waved Barker through.

Barker continued to follow, ogling the homes as he tooled along the streets. The houses were all immense, and much of the architecture was Victorian. Some places appeared to have been built more recently, but they were no less elaborate, with wings off the main sections, and with cupolas and towers and dormers. Shade was provided by tall trees, mostly oaks and maples.

Somehow the name of the area seemed familiar, and after a moment Barker realized why it did. Belle Haven was where the Moxley murder had taken place. But he doubted that would discourage a prospective buyer. You'd have to be rich to afford a place here, with many millions to spend. And who cared what might have happened years ago?

When they reached the Delaney estate, Barker thought the structure looked more like a castle than somebody's home. Three stories high, it was built of stone and had a steep slate roof. Four chimneys rose from the central part, one at each corner.

A long, tree-shaded circular drive led up to the house, and a guy wearing a windbreaker and a Yankees cap was standing near it. He touched a finger to his cap as the limo approached, and Barker realized he was another security guard.

The limo stopped in a porte-cochère that shielded the occupants from the rain. Delaney and his wife got out and the chauffeur went on, probably to where the garages were, behind the house.

Before Barker could pull closer the guard approached his car. Barker rolled down the window and the guard said, "Who are you?"

"Name's Barker," Barker said. "The Delaneys invited me here."

The guy still seemed suspicious. Barker noticed he had a boxer's nose, a misshapen blob of tissue in the middle of his face. He was about to say something else when Delaney called out, "It's okay, Carl. He's with us."

The guard nodded and signaled to Barker to pull up and park his car in the porte-cochère. After doing so, Barker got out and followed the couple into the house.

Once inside, they guided him to a parlor that struck him as about the size of a basketball court. Table lamps provided light, and there were various groupings of sofas and chairs. Persian rugs covered the floor, and the walls were decorated with oil paintings of landscapes and sailing ships and horses. Although it was summertime, logs were burning in a massive stone fireplace.

A maid took his raincoat, and those of his hosts. The maid also took the Delaneys' hats, and now that he could see her, Barker thought Sarah Delaney was fairly attractive, in a brittle, too-thin way. She ran a hand through her hair and said, "I want to change out of these wet clothes. Please excuse me." She left the room.

Delaney asked whether Barker would care for something to drink. He said he'd like coffee, and Delaney said he'd have some as well. A maid hurried to get it for them.

"I apologize for intruding," Barker said. "On this of all days."

Delaney shrugged. "You're doing what you have to do. And I hope what I can tell you will be useful. This has been a terrible shock, and frankly, the worst part for me has been to control my anger. Catherine was a wonderful person."

Barker was about to reply when the French doors at the far end of the parlor opened, and a woman in a white nurse's uniform pushed a wheelchair into the room. Sitting in it was a wizened man who wore pajamas and a bathrobe and had oxygen tubes stuck up his nose. His head was as bald as a peeled egg.

"Hello, Father," Delaney said. "Come and meet our guest."

The nurse pushed the wheelchair closer, and Delaney said, "This is Mr. Barker, from New York."

There was no response. The old man's eyes were rheumy and unfocused and he showed not the slightest sign that he'd understood. Delaney might as well have been talking to a statue.

"He's not doing too well today," the nurse said. "I thought seeing you might make him more alert." A drop of saliva appeared at a corner of the old man's mouth, and she wiped it away with a tissue.

"Thank you for trying," Delaney said.

"I'll take him to his room." She turned the wheelchair around and pushed it back out through the French doors.

A moment later the maid returned with their coffee. Delaney told her they'd have it in the library, and the two men followed her to a room just off the parlor.

The walls in there were paneled in dark wood, and two of them contained bookcases that ran from the floor to the ceiling. A large mahogany desk stood near the window, and leather chairs were grouped before a fireplace. As in the parlor, logs were burning, filling the room with a pleasant fragrance.

A portrait of a beautiful blonde woman hung above the mantel. Delaney gestured toward it. "My mother," he said.

To Barker, it was like looking at a picture of Catherine Delure. Same high cheekbones and full lips, same blue eyes. He could also see the resemblance between her and her son, although it wasn't as pronounced. Delaney's hair was darker, and it was thinning. In time, Barker thought, he'd be as bald as his father.

The maid placed the tray on a table and left the room. Delaney poured for them, and both took their coffee black.

"Please sit down," Delaney said.

Barker sank into one of the leather chairs and sipped coffee. "You thought there might be something," he said, "that could help our investigation."

Delaney put his cup down and went to the desk. He opened a drawer and took out a sheet of blue paper, returning with it and sitting opposite Barker.

He held up the paper and said, "This is a letter Catherine sent me a short time ago. I've thought about going to the authorities with it, but I hesitated because I didn't know how significant it might be. I also thought it could cause more trouble needlessly. Especially if it were leaked and the media got hold of it. Please read it, and tell me what you think." He handed it over.

Barker saw that the letter was handwritten, in the style taught in fashionable schools, a combination of cursive and printing. It said:

Dear Roger,

I don't want to burden you with my troubles, but I feel I should tell you about a problem. I've run across something that I think is highly illegal, and it frightens me that I know about it. I think Ron knows about it too and may even be involved.

But I'm afraid to speak out publicly, not only because it could ruin my career, but also because I think it would put me in danger. As I've told you, I'll be in New York in a couple of weeks, promoting my new movie. I'll call you, and we can discuss it further. I wish I could come out to Greenwich to see Dad, especially because he's so sick. But you know how he feels about me.

Lots of love to you and Sarah,
Cat

Barker looked at Delaney. "Did you reply to this?"

"Yes. I wrote back and said I'd look forward to seeing her. I told her whatever her problem was, not to worry. I said we'd figure out a way to handle it."

"So did she call when she came to New York?"

"She did, the night she arrived. I tried to get her to tell me more about what was troubling her, but she refused to discuss it over the phone. Whatever it was, she was very tense. We agreed to get together after she'd made some publicity appearances. She said she'd tell me everything then. That was the last time we spoke."

Barker read the letter again. "Ron is her ex-husband?"

"Yes. He's a financier in Los Angeles."

"He didn't come to the funeral?"

"No. He called, after Cat's death, to express condolences, but I didn't have much to say to him. We weren't at all close."

"What did she mean, she wished she could come out to Greenwich to see her father? Why couldn't she?"

"She and Father were estranged, I guess you'd say. Had been for years. Father never forgave her for becoming an actress."

"Why was he against that?"

"You'd have to understand Father. He's always been as strait-laced as it's possible to be. He said actresses were nothing but whores, and if she insisted in pursuing such a career, he wanted nothing more to do with her."

"And you didn't agree with his views?"

"Certainly not. I was always very proud of her. I tried to bring him around, make him see there was nothing wrong with acting, and that she'd become very successful. But that only made him furious with me. Finally, I simply stayed clear of the subject. I had enough to worry about, running the business after he went down-hill."

"That's the family business?"

"Correct. Delaney Industries. We own bauxite mines in Jamaica and Australia. Bauxite is aluminum ore. We produce aluminum from the bauxite and then import it into the United States. Manu-facturers of everything from aircraft to automobiles buy aluminum from us."

"Did your father found the company?"

"No, my grandfather did. He was the one who had this house built."

"And you and Catherine grew up here, went to school in Green-wich?"

"Yes. I was two years ahead of her at Greenwich Country Day. Then I went on to Choate, and when she graduated, she went to Beau Soleil in Switzerland. That's where she got the acting bug."

"And from there to Hollywood?"

"Eventually. She had parts in some forgettable movies that were produced in Paris, but one of them was shown at the Cannes fes-tival, and an American director saw her there. He took her to Los Angeles, and her first picture was a hit. You may have seen it. It's called *Love Me Now*. Runs on late-night television every so often."

"Afraid I missed that one," Barker said. "Did she keep up friendships with other people here in Greenwich? Any of the people at the funeral, for example?"

"Not that I know of. The ones who came today were all family friends. Some of them had known her when she was a child, but I don't think any of them were her contemporaries."

"And the pallbearers?"

"Same thing. They were family friends too."

"Okay," Barker said. He held up the letter. "May I keep this?"

"Yes, of course. But I want to make a copy." Delaney took the letter to a machine on the desk and copied it, then returned the original.

Barker slipped the sheet of paper into the inside pocket of his blazer. "How I can reach you, if I need to?"

Delaney took a card from his wallet and wrote on it, then handed the card to Barker. "That's my office in New York. The number I wrote on the back is the number here at the house."

"You said you're only staying here while your father's ill?"

"Yes, I commute to the city every day. Ordinarily we live there. We have an apartment on Fifth Avenue at Seventy-Ninth Street. And also a summer house in the Hamptons. Sometimes we go out there for a few days, because Sarah gets a little stir-crazy being here."

"Is she also a native of Greenwich?"

"No, she grew up in New York."

"Is that where you met?"

"Yes, a mutual friend introduced us."

"Children?"

"No, unfortunately. Sarah can't bear a child. We're thinking about adopting one."

Barker put the card into his pocket and rose to his feet. He took out a card of his own and gave it to Delaney. "Thanks for your cooperation. If there's anything else you think of, anything at all, be sure to call me."

"I'll certainly do that," Delaney said. "And I realize you must be terribly busy, but could you let me know if there's any progress? I'd really appreciate it."

"I'll do that," Barker said.

Delaney rang for the maid and had her bring Barker's raincoat. The two men shook hands, and Delaney showed him to the door that led out to the porte-cochère. Barker got into the Mustang and backed out onto the driveway.

The rain had stopped and the sun's rays were piercing the clouds, reflecting from the raindrops on the grass. Without the gloom, it was a different world.

As he went down the drive to the street, Barker passed both the security guard and a gardener who was trimming a hedge. He wondered how many in help the Delaneys had. Counting the chauffeur, the maid, the old man's nurse, the cook, the guard, and the guy with the clippers, at least six. And possibly more.

Would he want to live this way? Instead of in his one-room loft apartment in SoHo? Thanks, but no thanks. Life was complicated enough as it was.

Such thoughts aside, this had been a worthwhile trip. In fact, he'd got far more than he'd hoped for. The letter from Catherine Delure could be solid gold. Provided he could follow up on it without having to contend with Hogan.

He'd figure that part out later. And he'd keep trying to contact Delure's secretary. As he pulled onto westbound I-95 his optimism continued to mount. He swung into the far-left lane and gunned it.

11.

When the car bearing Dana Laramie deposited her in front of the entrance to the Regency, she hurried past the doorman and went up to her room. Once there, she got out Len Zarkov's number and called it.

A woman answered, and Dana told her who she was and said she had to talk with Mr. Zarkov, it was important. A moment later he came to the phone.

"I'm sorry to bother you," she said.

"No bother at all. What is it?"

"You were right. About the authorities trying to keep me in New York. I've just come from Catherine's funeral, and there was a detective there who must have followed me, and—"

"Hey, take it easy, okay? Are you at your hotel?"

"Yes, the Regency."

"Stay where you are, and I'll come over. I'll be there in just a few minutes."

Dana closed her phone. She'd worried that by calling him she might seem like just some ditzy female, but he had seen the situation as serious, obviously. And he was right, she had to calm down and get hold of herself.

She took off her raincoat and hung it in the closet, then turned on the TV. As she'd expected, CNN, Fox, and MSNBC were all showing the funeral. She watched as the church doors opened and the pallbearers carried the casket down the steps and put it into the back of a hearse. A female commentator was chattering away, but Dana paid no attention to what she was saying.

Next came a shot of mourners leaving the church, and seeing herself among them was unsettling. The police were holding back the crowd, and a few of the onlookers waved at the camera. From there, the coverage picked up shots of the action at the gates of the cemetery. At least the videotape had nothing of her running from the entrance to the car.

She turned off the set and went into the bathroom, where she washed her hands and face and brushed her hair. Her skin was still tan from exposure to the California sun, and as usual she wore no makeup. She thought her eyes looked puffy, but maybe she was imagining that.

A wall-mounted telephone rang, and the sound made her jump. She picked up. "Yes?"

Zarkov said, "I'm in the Library Bar. I'll wait here for you."

She hung up and made one more brief inspection of her image in the mirror. Then she left the room and took an elevator back down to the lobby.

As its name suggested, the Regency's bar was tricked up to look like the reading room of a library, complete with shelves of books and with newspapers laid out on many of the tables. A little hokey, Dana thought. It reminded her of a movie set.

Zarkov rose from one of the tables. He took her hand and steered her to a seat next to his. He asked if she'd like a drink, and when she said she would, he called a waiter over and they both ordered scotch on the rocks.

"So," he said, "what's this about a detective?"

"He was one of the ones who questioned me at the Sherry-Netherland after Catherine's murder. He was at the cemetery, and as I was leaving he tried to stop me. But I ran past him and got into the car and we drove away."

"We? Was someone else with you?"

"No, just the driver. I hired the car to drive me up there and back. I realize I shouldn't have run, but I was really scared, especially after what you told me about the authorities wanting to keep me here in New York. Now I feel like a criminal."

"You're no such thing," Zarkov said. "And frankly, the police were overreaching. Anyone in your position would have done the same thing."

"I hope that's true."

"Of course it is. At the funeral, did you talk to anyone?"

"Yes, with Catherine's brother and his wife. They knew I thought a great deal of her personally. And that she'd always treated me very well. Almost like a kid sister."

"Did they question you?"

"About what?"

"About anything. Catherine's life in LA, for example. Any of her contacts there."

"We talked about her career a little. And how she'd been holding up under the constant badgering by the paparazzi and having to deal with the media."

"Anything else?"

"They asked about her former husband, Ron Apperson."

"What did you tell them?"

"As much as I could. I knew Cat's marriage had been rocky. He and Catherine spoke on the phone now and then, and afterward she'd be tense and angry."

The waiter returned and served their drinks. Zarkov raised his glass and said, "Good luck."

"To you too," Dana said. They touched rims and drank.

At first, the scotch seemed very strong, but as soon as it made its way down, it produced a welcome warmth. And it also relaxed her.

"This detective," Zarkov said. "What was his name, do you know?"

"Yes. It's Barker. He also has a partner, whose name is Spinelli. But I think he was alone today."

"Did he manage to speak to you at all?"

"No, I didn't give him a chance."

"Good for you."

"Now I just want to get out of here and go back to Los Angeles. You said you could arrange to have the studio send a plane. I hate to ask for that big a favor, but I'm afraid if I tried to take a commercial flight, the police might stop me at the airport."

"I'm sure they would. As far as the plane is concerned, don't worry about it. Diggs is also still here, and the plane will take you both back to California just as soon as I can arrange it. Probably no later than tomorrow." He smiled. "I do have a little clout, you know."

"I'm sure you do."

"Have you thought more about what we discussed, the last time we talked? About going through Catherine's papers, and her files?"

"Yes. As soon as I'm back in LA I'll start going through everything I have."

"As I said, I'll be happy to help you with it. I had another talk with my lawyer, and he said it was vital that it be done as soon as possible."

"All right. I'll let you know."

"By the way, there's something I've been meaning to ask you. What are your plans, now that Catherine is gone?"

"I'll be looking for a job, I guess."

"How would you like to work for me?"

The question surprised her. "Doing what?"

"I need an assistant. And from everything I've seen, you're a very competent person. You learned quite a bit about the business while you were with Catherine, wouldn't you say?"

"I think so, yes."

"And becoming an assistant producer would be a nice step up for you, wouldn't it?"

"It certainly would."

"So what about it?"

"I'm a little bit awed. I need to think about it."

"Okay, do that. We can talk further when I return to LA."

"Sure."

So now, she thought, he not only wants to get into my pants, he has an even bigger treat for me. He wants to hire me. I can imagine what that would be like. I'd probably be the assistant producer in charge of giving him blow jobs. Meanwhile, he's hell-bent on getting those files.

"Another drink?" he asked.

"No thanks, Len. But believe me, I appreciate your help. And thanks for the offer."

"My pleasure."

12.

The newsstand at the Crystal Palace Hotel in Las Vegas carried papers from cities all over America. Each day Mongo made it a point to buy copies of *USA Today* and the *New York Times* and look for stories on the Catherine Delure murder case.

The newspapers usually carried them, saying the police were continuing to investigate various leads, which of course was a bullshit way of admitting they were getting nowhere.

He also checked out what the *Los Angeles Times* was reporting. That paper tended to have more on Delure's career, because its readers ate up anything on people in the movie business, and even the editors were starstruck. But the essence of today's story was the same: the cops had zilch.

Same with TV. In fact, the case was given more exposure on the tube than in print. The cable channels loved wallowing in the story. Night after night, Greta and Anderson and the other news geeks talked about it at length.

At first, they'd babbled about how a daring thief killed both

Delure and her assistant and stole the star's jewels. How a massive manhunt was under way, with detectives sifting a number of clues. Mongo liked being described as daring, but he thought the rest of it was so much asswipe.

For a while, both the TV and newspaper stories also featured a composite drawing of the killer, and it was so far off base it made him laugh. The character in the drawing looked like the Frankenstein monster with a mustache. Not only did Mongo see no resemblance to his regular features, but one of the first things he'd done after the hit was put the wig away and shave his upper lip.

So the job had worked out just as he'd planned. He'd pulled it off and vanished in a puff of smoke, and now the police were chasing their tails and the media were scrambling to come up with something new. And not succeeding.

The supermarket tabloids, however, weren't about to leave it at that. If a new angle hadn't come to light, they'd invent one. Mongo picked up a copy of the *National Enquirer* one night, and there was a photo of Delure on the front page. The headline screamed, "Star Snuffed by Former Lover!"

Seeing that gave him another laugh. The story said the *Enquirer* had learned from an impeccable source that the killer was a famous movie actor who'd had an affair with Delure. She'd dumped him after becoming involved with somebody else, and jealousy had driven the actor mad. He followed her to New York and shot her, and then he shot Penny Ellis as well because Ellis was Delure's new love.

The story went on to say the police were close to making an arrest, and that when the killer's identity was revealed, the shock would be felt around the world. He was a top star.

Sure he was, Mongo thought. And his name was Elvis.

One thing was interesting, though. This was the first time anybody had suggested that robbery wasn't the motive. But so what? Nobody read rags like the *Enquirer* but a bunch of sex-starved housewives. Before long, the papers would move on to other scandals, and the story would be deader than Kelsey's nuts.

So there was really nothing to worry about. From here out, he could relax and have a good time, and there was no better place than Vegas to have it.

In fact, he considered this the best good-time town in the United States. Maybe in the world, for all he knew. The glitz, the glamour, the gambling, the women, the anything-you-want-anytime-you-want-it made for nonstop excitement like nowhere else.

Of course, some of the other cities weren't bad. Miami, for instance, which he'd gotten to know while on an assignment for the Cubans. They were very good at hits themselves, but they'd wanted an outsider for that particular job, so that there wouldn't be so much as a rumor that they were involved. He'd done the work with a pearl-handled stiletto to make it look like payback from an enraged woman, and that's how it was reported. He'd collected a bundle for that one.

Miami also had beautiful women and good dope, and you could bet on anything from the ponies and the dogs to cockfights. The Spanish was a little different from what he was used to hearing from the Mexicans in LA, although expressions like *Chinga tu* were the same in both places.

Chicago was okay, too. Except for the winters, when the wind coming off Lake Michigan would freeze your balls to solid ice. On one job there, the guy he wanted had panicked when he saw Mongo moving in on him, and he'd tried to escape by running up onto the roof of his apartment house. Made no sense, but it was all right with Mongo. He threw the guy off the roof and got a big kick out of watching him spin like a leaf in the wind until he burst apart on the sidewalk. The coroner concluded it was suicide.

Branson was mixed. Some good action, although the town government was filled with assholes who jumped all over any enterprise you might find more entertaining than watching a bunch of clowns beat on guitars and wail country songs.

The mark there was an unfaithful wife, which struck Mongo as ridiculous. Any guy dumb enough to get married got what he deserved.

But some people had weird ideas, and there was a heavy fee. He carried out the hit by following the wife to a supermarket parking lot in a rented pickup truck. When she got out of her Mercedes roadster, he ran over her with the truck. And just to make sure, he went back over her several times, which felt like driving over a speed bump. He celebrated with a hooker who had tits as big as Dolly Parton's, and then it was *hasta la vista*, Branson.

But the town he liked most next to Vegas was probably New Orleans. The Big Easy was wide open, and you could buy whatever turned you on. Even the cops were selling. And the food was sensational, especially the crab gumbo.

He'd gone there on a contract to hit a Cajun hustler who spoke with a French accent. Mongo took him out with a .22 during Mardi Gras. With all the noise from the revelers and the bands and the fireworks, the small pistol's report was just one more pop. Mongo wore a goofy mask and played drunk, shot the guy in the back of the head right on Bourbon Street and slipped away in the crowd. Nothing to it.

But Las Vegas was still the best, in his opinion. The city ran a campaign that said whatever happened in Vegas stayed in Vegas, and for once there was truth in advertising. When Mongo got in touch with Silas Bechel, the owner of several pawnshops, he was confident he could dispose of the Delure jewels with no fuss, no muss.

And he was right: Bechel made the deal without comment, assessing the entire lot piece by piece. Naturally, the amount Mongo was paid for each item was a fraction of what it was worth. But that was simply the cost of doing business. With his round eyeglasses and his thin lips, Bechel looked more like an accountant than the most reliable fence in the city. Nevertheless, he was fair and would guard secrets as if his life depended on it. Which, of course, it did.

So here Mongo was, with a pile of money from both the jewels and the fee paid by the weasel, and an ID that made him born again—although sure as hell no Christian—enjoying himself as a man without a rap sheet anywhere, not even a record of a speeding ticket. The ID said he was Don Quinn, and that he'd been born in Lake Charles, Louisiana.

The Crystal Palace Hotel was still his favorite, despite being a little old-fashioned compared with some of the newer places. The Venetian, for instance, or the Mandarin Oriental.

On the plus side, the Crystal charged him nothing for his two-room suite. Choice digs, too, with a huge bed and mirrors on the walls and ceiling so you could watch yourself doing it from every angle, and a bath with a heart-shaped tub, and a balcony with a great view of the city.

And why wouldn't he be comped, after the load of money he'd dropped in the casino last time he was here?

One thing he'd noticed, though: Las Vegas had changed. In the old days, the wiseguys ran it, and there was no pretending about what they offered and what you were there for.

But now the hotels were mostly corporate owned, and the management stood on their heads to convince tourists the town had turned into a church with babysitters and was all about families having good clean fun.

The truth was that you still could enjoy yourself. Coke was as easy to come by as a pack of cigarettes, and you could also score horse or blow, if you wanted. There was plenty of ecstasy available too, but that was for kids. Like meth, it was bad for your health.

As for the gambling, it was as good as ever, even though today some of the casinos catered more to bluehairs who dumped their chips into the machines like robots, hour after hour, than they did to high rollers.

And Mongo was a high roller. He loved betting big, especially on craps and blackjack, and wouldn't be caught dead playing the slots. Hell, the one-armed bandits didn't even have arms anymore. Instead you pushed buttons, for Christ's sake.

But the tables were a whole different scene. When you tried to beat dealers at twenty-one, you were up against other human beings. You were *taking* from them, and that's what it was all about. Not just winning, but beating somebody.

Of course, they often beat him too, and it pissed him off when they did. It wouldn't take long for him to go through most of his money. But there was plenty more where that came from. When he ran out, he'd just go back to work.

In the meantime, life was a ball. Another great thing about Vegas was how the casinos had no windows, so there was no difference between night and day. You played as long as you wanted and slept occasionally and ate now and then and snorted a few lines and had a few drinks and kept going until you fell down.

He usually started at the Crystal, and from there drifted over to Caesar's and then to the Sahara or the Tropicana, and at each place if his luck was good he stayed till it changed.

His best run was when he was shooting craps at the Flamingo and threw four naturals in a row on top of what he'd already won. But then he bet the whole pile on the next roll and lost it all. Nevertheless, the thrill was tremendous. Later on at Circus Circus, he'd had another streak that was almost as good, so it worked out fine.

Of course, it would have been a lot better if he'd been able to cheat. Especially at blackjack. But the casinos had long since put a lock on that with their eye in the sky, and they were highly skilled at spotting card counters. Still, the gambling gave you a rush that was like nothing else.

And then there were the girls. Jesus, what girls. Most of the high-priced ones were knockouts, and they came in all colors and all flavors, like in a candy store. You could find them in any bar, or you just picked up the phone and ordered one. Or two or three, depending on your mood. Talk about room service.

Almost as much as humping them, Mongo liked listening to their stories. Every hooker had one, but some were more original than others. One told him she was from a rich ranching family in Texas. The men in the family were all bible thumpers who wouldn't say shit if they had a mouthful, but they loved going to Dallas and Houston on business, and while there they could patronize the whorehouses. So why shouldn't she slip away to Vegas now and then, and do this just for kicks? Not bad, although he'd heard variations on it before.

Another said she was working to pay for tuition at UNLV, where she was studying to become a doctor. That story had become a cliché too. The redhead in New York had also claimed she was a student.

A much better tale was told to him by a cute blonde who said she was the illegitimate daughter of a former governor of Nevada. And that tragically, her daddy refused to recognize her.

Mongo liked that one enough to play along. "He sounds like a mean bastard."

"Oh, he is," the blonde replied. "He lives in Tahoe now, in this huge mansion on the waterfront. Him and his wife have got a daughter of their own, send her to all the best schools. He treats her like a princess, but far as he's concerned, I don't even exist. I went to see him there once, and he sicced his dog on me."

"No shit?"

"God's truth. It was the biggest fucking dog I ever saw in my life. A bloodhound, or something. I had to run like hell."

"So how about your mother? Where's she?"

The blonde blinked back a tear. "She died when I was little. But before she did, she told me who my father was."

"Was she beautiful, like you?" Making her feel good.

"Yeah, she was a ballerina. Very famous."

"Damn, that's the saddest story I ever heard," Mongo said. Actually he'd rate it a B-plus.

One tale he found fascinating was told to him by a girl who said the cops had caught her in a sting. The reason they set it up was because prostitution was legal in most counties in Nevada but not in Vegas, if you could imagine anything so stupid.

She told him the cops had dressed up one of their own to look like an Arab and put him in a suite that was rigged with a hidden TV camera. Then they watched a monitor in the next room while he phoned for two hookers.

"So we went to his suite," the girl said, "and you should have seen this guy. He had dark skin and a goatee and one of those things they wear on their head?"

"A turban?"

"Yeah, that's it. He talked broken English and had on sunglasses. You'd think he was the fucking Sheik of Araby."

"And what happened?"

"We told him we wanted fifteen hundred apiece. He gave us the money and we both stripped, and then *boom!* In came a bunch of cops and busted us. Was that lousy, or what?"

Mongo shook his head. "Stinks. But that's cops for you."

Two nights after that, he tied into some interesting action of his own. He'd gambled around the clock, visiting all his usual haunts, and eventually wound up back at the casino in the Crystal. He was ahead a few grand and was about to pack it in. The buzz had worn off long ago, and he was so tired he couldn't see straight.

But first he'd put a few chips on roulette. That was a game he rarely played, because it was nothing but dumb luck, and on top of that the odds gave the house a three percent edge. He placed stacks on a red straddle and hit, but he was almost too exhausted to care.

As he swept up his winnings he noticed a pretty girl who was standing alone on the other side of the table. She had dark, wavy hair and a good body in a low-cut dress. She also wore very little makeup, and when he caught her eye she looked away, so he knew she wasn't a hooker. He moved around beside her.

"You brought me luck," he said.

She glanced at him, not smiling. "I doubt it." She turned and walked off.

As a rule Mongo didn't bother with amateurs; they weren't worth the effort. And this one wasn't responding to his approach. But that made it challenging.

He followed her and tried again. "Speaking of luck, maybe I could change yours."

She kept going. "I doubt that, too."

"Hey, is it that bad? What happened?"

"I had a fight with my boyfriend."

"Why don't we have a drink, and you can tell me about it."

She stopped and this time looked him straight in the eye, and he felt a spark.

"I've already told you all there is to tell," she said. "But I guess I could use a drink."

They went to the bar, and Mongo ordered Chivas for both of them. After a swallow or two, she seemed to loosen up.

"Better?" he asked.

"Yes, but I've had enough of Las Vegas. I'm ready to go home."

"Where is that?"

"Kansas City."

"And your boyfriend?"

"I've had enough of him, too. I should never have let him drag me out here. This is a really crazy town."

"Isn't it, though."

"What about you? And what's your name, by the way?"

"Don Quinn. Yours?"

"Marcia Slade."

"Nice name. Goes with you." One thing about women, you could never flatter them too much.

"Thanks."

"What do you do in Kansas City? You have a career?"

"I guess you could call it that. I'm a fashion consultant for a ladies' clothing store."

"You consult with customers?"

"Yes. When they need advice on what to buy, or how to plan their wardrobe, I help them."

"So I was right. I could tell you had good taste soon as I saw you."

She smiled. "I try. But you should see what I have to work with. You know the expression, lipstick on a pig? I put dresses on them."

Mongo laughed uproariously. As if it was the funniest thing he'd ever heard. When he caught his breath, he said, "And you have a beautiful smile, too."

The smile widened. "What do you do, Don? For a living, I mean."

"I'm a headhunter."

"That means you search out people?"

"Exactly."

"So you must travel a lot."

"Yeah, I do."

"Is the work interesting?"

"Let's say it's never boring."

"You always get the one you want?"

"Never miss. I nail him, or her sometimes, get paid, and move on to the next one."

"That sounds great."

"Has its moments."

"But that's not why you're here now, is it?"

"No, I just came to have a good time."

She drained her glass.

"Another drink?"

"Well . . . okay."

"Good. We'll have it in my suite."

Her eyebrows arched. "Hey, that's moving pretty fast, don't you think?"

"Sure it is." He took her arm and guided her toward the elevators. "But maybe that's what makes it good. For both of us."

She continued to have that look of disbelief on her face, but he sensed she was getting into it. He led her to an elevator and up they went.

Once in the living room he poured them each another scotch. After a quick swallow, he put his glass down and pulled her close and mashed his mouth on hers.

Her response was immediate, and the heat was equal to his. In no time, he had her in the bedroom with her clothes off, and in the next instant his were off too and they were in bed.

It was, he thought, terrific. She was tautly muscled and enthusiastic, a dynamite combination. And she made great noises, gasping and squealing and telling him to give it to her. *Harder*, she kept saying.

He lasted quite a while, considering. But afterward he was so wiped out he couldn't move a muscle. He was determined that this wouldn't be the end of it, though; he'd rest awhile and have another go. And then despite his good intentions, he drifted off.

He had no idea how long he was out. When he regained consciousness, he found himself alone in the bed. With an effort he opened his eyes and was startled by what he saw.

His new friend was fully dressed and standing near the door to the bathroom. The light was on in there, and she'd apparently opened the door just a crack, so she could see what she was doing. It took a few more seconds for Mongo's weary brain to grasp what was going on, but when he got it, he felt a surge of anger.

The damn woman had his pants in her hands, and she was slipping his wallet out of a pocket. Her handbag was sitting on the dresser and as he watched, she put his pants aside and went through the wallet. When she finished, she dropped the wallet into her bag. He'd had some cash and chips in his jacket, and the jacket was draped over a chair, so she'd probably already rifled it. Next, she opened the top drawer of the dresser and began rummaging around.

Jesus God—how could he have been such a fool?

Moving as quietly as possible, he slipped out of bed. But he wasn't quiet enough. She turned and looked at him, and then she made a dive for the door.

Mongo got there just as she did. He grabbed her by the hair and slammed a fist into her belly. The blow knocked the wind out of her, and a second punch caught her on the point of the jaw. She went down as if she'd been shot, her eyes rolling back in her head.

Still furious, he picked up her handbag and retrieved his wallet, tossing it into the dresser drawer. He also found a fat pack of bills in the bag, along with a bunch of chips. He took out all of the cash and the chips and put them in the drawer as well.

The handbag contained her own wallet. He removed everything from it, and as he added her cash to the pile in the drawer, he saw that she'd come around and was rubbing her jaw.

For a few seconds he thought seriously about throwing her off the balcony. But then he decided that was not a good idea. A woman splattered all over the driveway in front of the entrance would bring a gang of cops to the hotel, and they'd go through all the rooms.

"Get up," he said.

She did, slowly and unsteadily. Her face was red and swollen, and her eyes were showing fear.

"Take your clothes off," he ordered.

Her expression turned to one of puzzlement. "You want more?"

"I want you to do what I'm telling you. Now do it. Or else I'll beat the living shit out of you."

"All right, all right." She pulled her dress up over her head and laid it on top of his jacket on the chair. "Listen," she said, "I know what you thought, but it wasn't what it looked like. Actually I was—"

"Shut the fuck up. And take off the rest of it. Now!"

She unhooked her bra and dropped it onto her dress, then kicked off her pumps. Last, she removed her panties and added them to the other things.

She stood there, showing the same baffled expression. "What are you—"

He cocked a fist menacingly, and she shut her mouth again.

Next he picked up his pants and pulled them on, making sure the passcard to the suite was still in one of the pockets. He slipped into his shoes and put on his shirt, leaving it unbuttoned.

He grabbed the girl's wrist and pulled her with him into the living room, where he opened the door and peered out. Satisfied no one was there, he stepped out of the suite, taking her along.

A short distance down the corridor was the door that led into the stairway. Continuing to hold her arm, he walked to the door and opened it. Then he pushed her past him onto the landing and kicked her in the ass as hard as he could. She let out a shriek and tumbled headfirst down the flight of stairs.

For several seconds, he could hear her bumping and banging on the treads, and after that there was silence.

Mongo stepped back and slammed the door. He knew that in

compliance with fire and security rules, the doors from the stairway on each floor had one-way locks, so they could only be opened from the corridors. Even if she survived the fall, she wouldn't be able to get back in. She'd have to go down to the ground floor and make a big appearance, stark-ass naked. Serve her right, the bitch.

Returning to the suite, he emptied her handbag onto the dresser. Then he gathered the handbag and her clothing and carried them out onto the balcony. The predawn sky was turning gray, but the multicolored lights of Vegas were still shining brightly and traffic was streaming through the streets.

First, he slung the handbag over the rail. Next, he threw the other things as well, watching as the breeze caught them and sent them sailing. He returned to the bedroom and got back into bed.

Face it, he told himself. I was just too damn careless. Maybe I'm losing my grip.

As tired as he was, he couldn't get back to sleep. He tossed and turned and finally got up and went into the living room, where he poured himself a fresh drink.

Sitting on the sofa, he sipped the whiskey. He was still seething when the phone rang.

Jesus, now what? He let several more rings go by, and then he picked up. "Yeah?"

The voice on the other end had that hollow mechanical sound, as if it were coming from a machine. "Get back here," it said.

"You got something for me?"

"Not at the moment. But if something comes up, I don't want to have to chase you around Vegas. So come on back."

For a moment Mongo was tempted to tell him to stick it up his ass. But then he thought better of it. "Yeah, okay."

There was a click, and then the dial tone.

Mongo put the phone down. He got up and went into the bathroom and stepped into the shower, turning on the cold water full blast.

13.

Manhattan assistant district attorney David Beilin stood at his desk, silhouetted against a window that gave a view of an airshaft. He was tall and thin, and his gray flannel suit hung loosely from his bony shoulders. His paralegal, a middle-aged black woman, was taking notes.

Vaughn Harriman, the ADA's supervisor, sat off to one side. Gray templed and somber, he was high up in the Investigation Division. For him to be here told you that of all the thousands of active cases in the docket, this one was right at the top of the pile.

Arrayed before Beilin were a number of cops from the Delure task force, among them Dan Hogan and Charley Coyle, along with other members of Hogan's Homicide crew. Jeb Barker and Joe Spinelli were also on hand, as were detectives who'd been drawn from various precinct squads.

As for the ADA, Barker had never heard of him before this. But there were more than five hundred prosecutors in the Manhattan district attorney's office, so that wasn't surprising. Beilin had to be pretty sharp, to be given an assignment as important as this one.

"I hope you men understand," Beilin began, "how much attention is focused on this case. The media are howling that there's been no progress in the investigation, and the public's demanding action. Catherine Delure was a celebrity, and people want to see her murder solved as soon as possible. So does the district attorney, and so do the mayor and our congressmen and senators. The governor has also weighed in. Do you guys realize that?"

Barker exhaled. What the hell did Beilin think, that the cops weren't aware of the shitstorm the case had kicked up? Or that there was no pressure on the cops? The PC was demanding action, and so were all the other top brass. There was a fire under everybody.

"And do you know why there's so much heat?" Beilin went on. "It's not just because the victim was famous. It's also because this is an election year." He paused to let that sink in. "So what have you got for us?"

"We've developed a mountain of leads," Hogan said, "and we're hoping to get a break soon. We've put out an APB with a good composite of the perp, and the FBI is looking for matching MOs. We're also combing our files and hunting for thieves that fit the description, and we're working street contacts. We have to follow up on every tip, but that takes time."

"NDIS give you anything?" That was the national DNA database that contained more than eight million offender profiles.

"No, it didn't. The CSI couldn't get any of the guy's DNA in the hotel."

"How many men do you have on the case?"

"A hundred and ten detectives. And I've been asking the chief to assign more."

"What about suspects? You said you had leads."

Coyle said, "We've interviewed dozens of people, but no luck so far. Either they don't fit, or they have a solid alibi."

"I've seen the security tape," Beilin said. "Not very clear."

"That's why we made the composite," Hogan said.

"I've seen that too. At least it's better than the tape. But I wasn't able to speak to the principal witnesses, the secretary and the bodyguard. They both left town and went back to California. Although according to the DD5s, you got nothing really substantial from them. Is that right?"

"Just their help making the composite. They also explained how the guy conned his way into Delure's suite."

"What did Forensics give you? Anything useful?"

"Only one thing. There was a hair in the bedroom they said came from a wig. It was reddish blond, the color of the perp's hair. So probably it came from him."

"If he was wearing a wig, he could take it off afterward. And that would undermine the accuracy of your composite, wouldn't it?"

"It might. But the witnesses said the face in the drawing looks just like him. So we're making another version that shows him with no hair. We'll send that one out too. Also we're getting information on wig makers and retailers."

"I read the pathologist's report on the post," Beilin said. "According to him, the killer shot each woman with a two-inch-long fléchette."

"That's correct," Hogan said. "*Fléchette* is French for little arrow."

Barker rolled his eyes.

"How could he shoot such a thing?" Beilin asked. "Wouldn't it take a pretty big gun? And wouldn't it make a lot of noise? Yet nobody heard a gunshot. And the bodyguard frisked the guy before he let him in."

"He must've had the weapon hidden someplace," Coyle said. "Strapped to his leg or something. And a silencer would cut down the noise."

Hogan said, "Our ballistics people are still trying to figure out what it was, but so far they haven't come up with the answer."

The ADA looked past Hogan and Coyle at the detectives who were standing shoulder to shoulder in the crowded office. "Anybody have anything to add?"

Barker said, "A lot of us have been checking pawnshops and known fences, trying to find out how the killer disposed of the jewelry. That's what my partner and I have been doing. But I think we may be on the wrong track."

Beilin frowned. "Meaning?"

"Meaning the perp might not have tried to unload the jewels at all. In fact, robbery might not have been the primary motive. He might have deliberately targeted Delure. Stealing the jewelry could have been an afterthought, or else a way of covering his true objective."

"You have anything to back that up?"

"Not at this point. But I certainly think we should be looking into Delure's personal life, especially her contacts in Los Angeles."

"I'm way ahead of you there," Hogan said. "I already called the chief of detectives in LA. He agreed to run a check on possible suspects, both jewel thieves and people who might have a grudge of some kind against either Delure or her manager."

Barker felt rising frustration. "You call that an investigation? Making a phone call?"

Hogan's face turned beet red. "I call it covering all angles, Barker."

"So you made contact," Beilin said. "And LA agreed to cooperate."

"Exactly." Hogan shot a fierce glance at Barker.

"Very good," Beilin said. "I'll be interested to know if they come up with anything."

Barker couldn't believe it. He opened his mouth, and then he thought of Frank Kelly's advice. Do not blow your cork. He clenched his teeth.

Beilin's gaze swung back to him. "You said you were checking on disposition of the victim's jewelry. Do you have an accurate description of what the various pieces were, and what they were worth?"

"No. Delure's secretary made up a list, but most of it was just guesses. We also got another list from the insurance company that issued her a policy. That one wasn't complete, either."

Spinelli said, "Also the descriptions of the pieces were too general. Nothing specific that would tie them to the victim."

"Even so, did you distribute copies of the lists?"

"Yes, we did."

"Okay, be sure to give me copies as well. Judging from what you have, can you estimate the overall value?"

Barker shrugged. "Somewhere around a million dollars."

"If that's true," Beilin said, "it tends to contradict your conjecture about his motive. A million dollars' worth of jewels would be a strong lure for a robber."

"Damn right it would," Hogan said. "Strong enough for him to kill two people. He knew what he was after. The secretary said Delure always traveled with a lot of jewelry."

"How would the thief have known that?"

"She liked to show the stuff off. Every time she went out in public she wore diamonds and emeralds and so on. All he'd have to do was see her in a TV interview. Or in a photo by a paparazzo. "

"So what do we have on him? What have the descriptions and the videotape told us?"

Coyle said, "We know he's fairly young. He's tall and wears nice clothes. Speaks well. And he's got a friendly personality."

"He's also very ballsy," Hogan added. "Willing to take chances. Knowing that much about him, we'd expect someone to come up with a suspect." He shot another glance at Barker.

It was harder, this time, for Barker to stay cool. So now he and Spinelli hadn't been doing their job? Hogan was an expert at offloading responsibility.

"What it comes down to," Beilin said, "is that we've made very little progress. Anybody care to dispute that?"

There was some muttering in the room, and shuffling of feet. But none of the detectives made a protest against the ADA's remark. And then for the first time since the meeting began, Beilin's supervisor spoke up.

"What's needed here," Harriman said, "is a break in the case. It doesn't matter whether it comes from a tip, or from tracing some of the victim's jewelry, or from some other development."

He paused. "But I can tell you this. I've talked with Chief Morrison. And you can be sure that he won't hesitate to shake up the department. If none of you can do the job, he'll assign someone who can. So don't be surprised if he calls in a whole new team."

14.

"How did the meeting go?" Kelly asked.

"It stunk," Barker said.

"Why, what happened?"

Barker gave him a quick rundown on what had transpired in the ADA's office.

Kelly tilted back in his chair. "Doesn't sound so bad to me."

"Maybe not to you, but this guy Harriman said if we don't get a break soon, the chief'll dump us all and put somebody else on it."

"Uh-huh. You always hear that when the pressure's on to clear a big case. Don't let it bother you."

"It's not only that," Barker said. "I've had it up to here with Hogan. He keeps insisting the motive was robbery, and he won't even consider any other possibility. He's got the ADA convinced, too."

"He's just covering his ass. Robbery is the only thing he can point to as a motive, so he has to play it out."

"That might be. But it's no way to run the case."

"Maybe not. But that's the way it is. You got anything else?"

"Yeah, I do. After I went to Delure's funeral, I spent time with her brother at the family's house in Connecticut. He told me she was in some kind of trouble. And to prove it, he gave me this."

Barker took the letter from his blazer pocket and handed it to Kelly. "Delure sent it to him from Los Angeles, a couple weeks before she came to New York."

The lieutenant read through it. When he finished, he put the letter down on his desk and looked at Barker. "Her brother tell you what she was getting at? What she'd seen that was illegal, and why that put her in danger?"

"He didn't know any more than what the letter says. But it's clear to me that this bears out my theory. The murder was not part of a jewel robbery. It was a hit."

"Might have been, at that."

"Might have been? Come on, Lieu."

"Okay, there's a chance it was. Did you show the letter to Beilin? Or Hogan?"

"No. I figured I had to get more evidence first. Otherwise Hogan would just fuck it up."

"How do you propose to get more evidence?"

"I want to go to LA and run it down. That's where this thing must have originated. How else would the perp have known so much about Delure's trip to promote her movie? How would he know who her PR contact was at the studio, or that she'd be staying at the Sherry-Netherland?"

"I don't know. But if that's what you want to do, you better talk to Hogan."

"He'd never agree. Better if I just went."

"Are you serious?"

"Damn right I am."

"You'd be asking for a whole lot of trouble. Keep in mind, you're on loan to Homicide. As long as you are, you answer to Hogan. And whether you like it or not, giving him that letter would be proper procedure."

Barker waited a moment. Then he said, "Let me ask you something, Lieu. Suppose I cleared the case. We'd both get the credit, right? Not just me, but you too, because you're my boss. You're the one who supervises my work, and all Hogan did was obstruct us. You'd make captain, wouldn't you?"

Kelly laughed. "Don't try to con me, young man."

"But you would, wouldn't you?"

"Possibly."

"Then wouldn't it be worth it to let me have a crack at it?"

"No, it wouldn't. Because there's an even better chance I'd get busted all the way down to clerk."

"All right, so how about this. I go out there, and maybe I clear the case, and maybe I don't. But either way, it was just me going off on my own and you didn't know anything about it."

Kelly seemed to consider that idea. "What about Spinelli?"

"Joe stays here, in Hogan's dog-and-pony."

Another moment went by, and Barker wondered whether Kelly might be thinking about showing his old partner's son that he too had cajones.

The lieutenant was silent for few more seconds. Then he sighed and said, "All right, here's what I'll do. I'll authorize you to draw expense money. After that you're on your own."

15.

The following morning Barker drove to the American Airlines terminal at JFK and left his car in long-term parking. At the desk he presented his ID and was cleared to take his pistol aboard. Then he checked in for Flight 1, departing New York at 8:40 A.M. He had one carry-on bag.

His seat was in coach. It was narrow and cramped his legs, and the passenger next to him was a fat woman who smelled of sweat and cheap perfume. The flight attendants were lazy, and the food they served was inedible. On top of all that, the flight was a half hour late, and the 747 did not touch down at LAX until noon West Coast time. Barker had never been so glad to get off an airplane.

At the Hertz counter, he rented a Ford Taurus. He drove north on the freeway, and as always traffic was heavy, worse even than in New York. At the Sunset Boulevard exit, he left the freeway and drove east.

He knew LA fairly well, having visited a number of times years earlier, when he was in the Marine Corps and based at Camp Pendleton. It wasn't a bad town, he thought, especially if you could be there in the wintertime when most other cities were ass-deep in snow.

His reservation was at the Sunset Inn Hotel in West Hollywood. For relatively cheap lodging, the hotel wasn't bad, either. There was a gym and a pool, and with luck he might have time to enjoy both of them.

At check-in, the clerk was a striking young Asian woman with almond eyes and a wide smile. Her name tag said she was Lia. As he began filling out the registration form he heard a commotion and turned around.

Coming into the lobby were five young guys who were scruffy and unshaven and had hair down past their shoulders. Tattoos covered their bare arms, and one of them had a likeness of a large black spider on his cheek. Another was wearing a T-shirt that said OH SHIT! in large letters.

For a moment Barker wondered whether he was in Greenwich Village rather than LA. The men were horsing around and jabbering in a strange patois that sounded vaguely like English. Lia leaned close and whispered that they were a band from London and were on tour.

The room she assigned him was standard issue, with a bed and a table and two chairs and a TV. But at least it had a view of the Hollywood hills. He dropped off his bag and telephoned the LAPD, asking for directions to the Detective Bureau. He was told it was in the new LAPD headquarters building, across from City Hall in the civic center.

He left the room and went back down to the lobby, where Lia gave him another smile. He waved to her on his way out to the Ford.

The drive took just under thirty minutes. East again on Sunset, then south on 101, off at the Broadway exit, and from there to the building at 100 West First Street.

And what a building. A soaring slab of metal and concrete and tinted glass, it was said to be the most expensive police headquarters ever built in the United States. Barker could believe it. Certainly, it bore no resemblance to NYPD headquarters. Compared to this, the drab pile of stone in downtown Manhattan was like an oversized blockhouse.

He went into the lobby and presented credentials to the cop at the desk, saying he wanted to see the commander of the Detective Bureau. The cop made a call and then directed him to the sixth floor. On the way, Barker noted that the place was as sleek and clean as a hospital, and in fact more so than most of the ones he'd been in.

Up on six, there were about seventy people: male and female detectives in cubicles, secretaries out on the floor at desks, everything spick-and-span. This area, too, was far neater than what he was used to in New York.

The atmosphere was familiar, however. Detectives were working the phones and making notes, some typing reports, one guy talking to a suspect, two others shooting the shit about the Dodgers' chances for winning the National League pennant.

The CO's glass-walled office was on the opposite side of the floor. A sign on the door said his name was Deputy Chief Charles Swanson. Barker knocked and opened the door.

The occupant was a lanky guy with a thick black mustache. Unlike the detectives in his command, he was wearing a uniform rather than civvies, and there was a row of ribbons on his blouse.

"Afternoon, Chief," Barker said. "My name's Barker. I'm a detective from New York." He reached across Swanson's desk and shook his hand.

"Like to spend a few minutes with you," Barker went on. "If you can spare the time."

Swanson motioned him to a chair and spoke into an intercom. "Hey, Sam. Come on in here. We got a visitor from New York."

Sam turned out to be a female detective. Her sandy hair was swept back, and she wore jeans and a striped shirt. A holster on her belt held a 9mm Glock.

"I'm Samantha Benziger," she said. "What brings you to LA?"

"He wants to visit Disneyland," Swanson said. "And maybe the La Brea tar pits."

Benziger smiled. She sat down next to Barker and said, "This have to do with the Delure homicide?"

"It does. I'm a member of a task force that's working on the case."

"Don't miss the Universal Studios Tour," the CO said. "You'll love it. Knott's Berry Farm is also great."

"How's it going?" Sam asked.

"Slowly," Barker said.

"Probably the biggest case you guys ever handled," Swanson said. "Am I right?"

"One of them, anyway."

"We've had some big ones here, too. O.J., Robert Blake, Phil Spector, just to name a few."

"Yeah, so I understand." Jesus, was Swanson actually playing can-you-top-this?

Benziger said to Barker, "Delure's got everybody in an uproar. As you know, this is a movie town. So the murder of a star is huge. That's made it a bonanza for the media. The cable channels all put out stories on it every night, and the *LA Times* runs at least one piece a day. Even when there's nothing new."

Swanson said, "She means even though you don't seem to be getting anywhere with it. By the way, we already had a call about the case from a lieutenant on the Manhattan Homicide Squad. What was his name, Logan, Hogan?"

"That's Lieutenant Dan Hogan," Barker said. "He's in charge of the task force."

"Sam did some digging for him," Swanson said. "He fill you in on what she found?"

"No."

"A little communications problem there, huh?"

"A lot's been going on," Barker said. "Some things are bound to slip into the cracks."

Swanson turned to Benziger. "Give us a rundown, will you, Sam?"

"There was only one incident where Delure was involved," she said. "A few months back she had a fight with her ex-husband. He's a financial guy, name of Ron Apperson. Seems they were at his house in Coldwater Canyon and had an argument. It got physical, and she left and was driving back to her place. Her Mercedes was weaving all over the road, and a motorcycle cop stopped her. At first he thought she was DUI, but she said Apperson had punched her in the gut and she was nauseated and feeling faint. The cop wanted to follow up on it, but she said she wouldn't press charges, and that she'd deny ever telling him any such thing. The cop escorted her home and wrote it up, and that was the end of it."

"We usually try to keep anything like that low-key when a celebrity's involved," Swanson said. "So the media never got hold of the story. You wouldn't believe some of the stuff that's in our files. Movie stars involved in all kinds of incidents—shoplifting, trespassing, assault, and so on. But the public never hears a word about most of it. There've been exceptions, though. Like with Mel Gibson. Or Nick Nolte."

"What about Apperson," Barker asked. "Anything on him?"

"Couple of lawsuits," Sam said. "But they were settled out of court. Also about four years ago his wife from a former marriage claimed he'd beat her up, but that was settled too."

"You know what domestic violence cases are like," Swanson said. "The only ones that get as far as a prosecutor are when the guy doesn't have any money."

"And even then the woman usually won't testify," Sam said.

"On the one with Delure and Apperson," Barker said, "I assume you gave that to Lieutenant Hogan?"

"Yeah, but he didn't seem to be much impressed. Said it sounded to him like nothing more than a marital squabble."

"Can you do a check for me on a woman named Dana Laramie? She was Delure's secretary."

"That rings a bell," Sam said. "She was a witness, wasn't she? In the hotel?"

"Yes, she was. I want to locate her and talk to her."

"Sure, I can help you there."

Swanson then said to Barker, "Listen, I hope you understand

our situation. We're dealing with a stack of open homicide cases, most of them gang related. More than five hundred so far this year. The gangs rob civilians, prey on civilians, hijack cars, peddle dope, and fight wars with each other. Blacks against blacks, blacks against Latinos, Latinos against Latinos, Latinos against blacks."

"So I've heard."

"The California Department of Justice maintains a database that shows four hundred fifty gangs in LA, with a hundred forty thousand members. So if I seem preoccupied, you can see why."

"I do see."

"We've also got a number of high-profile cases. Last week, a vice president of the Los Angeles Bank and Trust Company was found shot to death in his bed in Brentwood. His wife's our prime suspect, but she's got a sharp lawyer and he won't let her answer our questions. Then there's another one where the vic was a would-be model. A photographer took her on location to Big Bear and strangled her. We're looking for him now. Those are the kind of cases that get the public riled up and put more pressure on us. I'm sure you know what I mean."

"Yeah, I understand."

"Point is, we're overloaded. That's not to say we don't want to cooperate with your department in the Delure case. But I got the impression that Hogan is pretty sure the killer was a New York thief who was after Delure's jewelry. Hogan says he most likely shot the two women to shut them up. We sent him rap sheets on robbers that might fit the profile of your perp, although none of them seemed like they could operate on that level. Compared to the one you want, these guys were nickel-shit."

"Uh-huh."

"Nevertheless, we'll give you all the help we can."

"I appreciate that."

"Sam will be your contact. Anything you need, let her know and we'll do our best to supply it, okay?"

"Thanks," Barker said. He followed Sam out of the office.

She sat at her desk, and Barker sat beside her. She tapped on her computer keyboard, and after a moment said, "Nothing on Laramie in our Compstat files, so she's clean." She tapped some more. "I'll give you her address and phone number."

"Can you check on Apperson too?"

"No problem." She looked it up and said, "Several complaints, but they all seem to be from investors claiming he screwed them. The charges were dismissed." She put together both addresses and phone numbers, printed the information, and handed the sheet to Barker. "Anything else?"

"One thing. The killer shot Delure and her manager, but he didn't use bullets. Instead he hit each of them with a fléchette. How he fired them we're not sure, because the witnesses told us there was no noise. Naturally, we haven't released that information."

"Interesting. Sounds like he was pretty clever."

"I'd say so, yeah. Anyway, our ballistics guys were unable to find a gun that would fire the fléchettes, which were about two inches long and almost half an inch thick. So in their opinion the weapon was probably custom-built."

"That's interesting too. Says the killer did some careful planning. And either built the thing himself or had it built for him."

"That's the way I see it, too," Barker said. "But we don't have information on anybody who could do that. Anyway, I'd appreciate it if you could ask your own ballistics experts whether they have a line on someone who has that kind of skill with weapons. It's a slim chance, I know, but I'll take anything I can get."

"Sure, I'll ask. Where are you staying?"

"The Sunset Inn."

"Okay, I'll call you there."

"Thanks," he said. "I appreciate your help."

"You need anything else, just let me know."

Once he was back in the Ford, Barker looked at the sheet. He decided it would be best to start with Laramie, even though she'd run when she caught sight of him at Delure's funeral. Her address was on Wilshire Boulevard, in Beverly Hills. He fired up the engine and headed north.

16.

Dana Laramie drove her Honda Accord to the Delure house on North Crescent Drive in Beverly Hills. Two stories high with pale yellow siding, the house was set behind tall hedges that made it nearly invisible from the street. It was also surrounded by tall elms and oaks and several Persian silk trees. Snuggled up against the foundation were lush plantings of jacaranda and hibiscus and bougainvillea.

Dana used her remote to open the gate and pulled up to the front entrance. She parked her car and went to the door.

A man wearing a khaki uniform was standing nearby. An embroidered logo on his shirt identified him as security. Dana told him who she was, and he let her pass.

She rang the bell, and after a minute or so she heard footsteps and was aware of being inspected through the peephole. There was the sound of locks being undone, and Anna Sebowski, the housekeeper, swung the door open. She had on a white uniform, and there were tears in her eyes.

"Oh, Miz Laramie," Anna said. "I'm glad to see you, but so sad."

Dana put her arms around her and gave her a hug. It was no small task; Anna was almost as wide as she was tall.

"It's good to see you too," Dana said. "I just wish the circumstances were different."

Anna stepped aside. "Please come in quick, before anybody sees us."

Dana went past her into the foyer. "Who are you talking about? Who's going to see us?"

The housekeeper shut the door and locked it. "Those awful reporters. They've been out there almost every day, taking pictures of the house. The security man tries to keep them away, but they don't pay no attention. One of them got through the gate by riding in a delivery truck. She told me she wanted to come in and look around. I wouldn't let her, of course, the pushy bitch. Excuse my language."

"It's okay," Dana said. "I feel the same way about them."

She and Anna went into the living room, which was furnished in a combination of French antiques and deeply upholstered sofas and chairs. A Matisse landscape hung over the fireplace, and on another wall was a portrait of Catherine Delure.

It was disconcerting for Dana to see the portrait; the painting had the uncanny effect of the subject's gaze following her. As if Catherine were in the room, watching her move about.

A large dog suddenly bounded in from the hallway and began licking Dana's hand. It was a golden retriever that had been much loved by Catherine. Dana scratched the dog behind its ears.

"Lulu!" Anna said. "You get back in the kitchen. You know you're not allowed in here."

The dog obediently left the room, and Dana said, "Is Marie here?" Marie had been Catherine's maid.

"No. After she saw the news about what happened, she grabbed her clothes and left. I haven't heard from her since."

"Has anybody else been here?"

"Just Mr. Haynes."

"The lawyer?"

"Yes. He said there were some documents he needed, to help settle the estate. He went into Miz Delure's study and poked around in the desk drawers."

"Did he take anything?"

"Maybe some papers, but I don't know for sure."

"Did he go in any of the other rooms?"

"No, just that one. He wasn't here very long."

"I'll take a look."

The study was down a hallway, at the rear of the house. Dana made her way to it and stepped inside. This room was decorated in French provincial, more pieces she knew Catherine had bought in Paris. There were impressionist paintings on the walls, one of them a prized Marc Chagall still life of a bouquet of flowers. An ancient Chinese Turkistan rug covered the floor.

The drawers of Catherine's desk were pulled out, and empty. Including the file drawer. Haynes hadn't even bothered to close them after he'd stripped them of their contents.

Dana went back to the front of the house and said to Anna, "I'm going to go up into Miss Delure's bedroom. There are some notes up there that belong to me."

"Can I get you anything? A cold drink or something?"

"No thanks, Anna. I'll only be a few minutes."

There was a curving staircase in the hall. Dana went up the steps two at a time, and at the top landing she turned right and entered the master bedroom.

Inside was a king-size bed, an armoire that contained a TV set, a chaise, and a boudoir chair, and seeing them gave her a twinge. The last time she'd been in the room, Catherine had been in that bed, suffering from a hangover. The actress had dictated a letter to her agent, which Dana had typed on her laptop and later mailed.

There was also a small white desk near the windows, and that was what Dana was interested in. It was where Catherine had kept her most personal things, and someone like Haynes wouldn't have known that. She sat down and began looking through the desk.

What she found was a mess. Letters that Catherine had started and never finished, other letters she'd received from friends and lovers, engraved invitations, notes on scraps of paper and cocktail napkins, store receipts, ticket stubs, and a scattering of old snapshots.

Dana knew at once she wouldn't have time to go through it all. She'd want to take her time and study this stuff, which meant taking it back to her own place. But how to carry it?

She went into the dressing room and rummaged around, yet found nothing suitable. Next she opened one of the mirrored doors that led into a long walk-in closet, and peered at the rows of dresses and pants and suits and coats on hangers, the dozens of pairs of shoes in racks, the shelves crammed with sweaters and tops and countless handbags.

She spotted a Neiman Marcus shopping bag and picked it up. Inside was a blouse, still wrapped in tissue. That was Catherine for you; she not only hadn't worn it, she hadn't even taken it out of the bag.

Dana put the blouse on a hanger and went back to the desk in the bedroom. She shoved everything from the drawers into the bag and carried it back down the stairs.

Anna met her in the foyer. "Miz Laramie?"

"Yes?"

"What should I do? I mean, with Miz Delure gone, am I supposed to stay here, or what? I tried to ask Mr. Haynes, but he didn't say."

"For the time being," Dana said, "you stay right here and keep on guarding the house. Don't let anyone else in, no matter who they are or what they tell you. I'll let the security man know that too. The only exceptions would be Mr. Haynes, and the police. If you have any doubts, or any questions, call me. You have my number, don't you?"

"Yes, it's on the list by the phone in the kitchen."

Dana patted the housekeeper's shoulder. "You're doing fine, Anna. This is a tough time for everyone, but we'll all get through it. Take care now, and I'll see you later."

She stepped out the door and told the security man the same thing she'd said to Anna about not letting anyone in. Then she got back into her car and drove south through Beverly Hills. When she reached Wilshire Boulevard she turned left, and two minutes later pulled into the garage beneath her apartment house.

Her abode was on the fifth floor. It consisted of three rooms and a bath and was mostly furnished in things she'd bought on sale in the Macy's on West Seventh Street. Quite a contrast between her furniture and the pieces in the Delure house, she thought with a rueful smile. But the décor was passably tasteful, and most important, comfortable.

She didn't own a desk; the kitchen table provided the surface she usually used. That had always been adequate, because most of the time she'd done her work at Catherine's house, or while traveling with her, or at a studio, or on location. She emptied the shopping bag onto the table, wondering if she'd find anything that might be considered damaging.

But first she'd get some mineral water out of the fridge. As she drank it, she thought about Zarkov's insistence on seeing whatever material she had. She'd already gone through the files on her computer and was reasonably sure none of it could even be called controversial. But she'd check this stuff with care. She refilled her glass and sat at the table.

Going through the heap of paper was like trying to make sense of a puzzle when you didn't have all the pieces. But she did her best. Letters, both the ones that had been sent to Catherine and the ones she'd begun and abandoned, as well as the scribbled notes, were put into a stack and set aside. The miscellaneous junk—ticket stubs, store receipts, and the like—she shoved to the far end of the table.

Next she looked at the snapshots. Some appeared to be of Catherine when she was a teenager. Boys were with her in each shot, smiling and mugging. Probably they'd been taken when Catherine was a student in France.

But most of the photos were of men. Dana didn't recognize many of them, but a number were famous actors and other people in the movie business. One shot was of Tony Gregarian, who'd directed *Hot Cargo*, Catherine's last movie. In the photo he was standing behind Catherine and had his arms wrapped around her while he leered at the camera.

It didn't take much imagination to figure out why Catherine had collected the snapshots, or what her relationship with the subjects had been.

Of course, Dana had been aware of many of Catherine's liaisons and affairs. But discretion was part of her job, and she'd done her best to protect her employer's privacy. She put the photos with the other junk and got down to the more important material, the notes and letters. Those she sorted out as well.

A few had been sent to Catherine by women friends and were little more than bits of personal news and lines of gossip. But the ones from men were something else. One had been sent by a producer who wanted her to join him at his vacation house in Cabo San Lucas, where they'd spend a few days together. Part of it said, I get hard just thinking about you.

Another, from an actor who'd been the leading man in one of her films, invited her to sail with him on his yacht. Still another actor proposed that they fly to Monaco, where they could gamble all day and make love all night, or vice versa.

There was more, but all of it seemed to be variations on the same theme: let's get together and screw.

Catherine's half-finished responses were also more or less alike. In each of them she said she'd think it over and call. Dana guessed she'd then skipped the writing and picked up a telephone and said sure, why not. Certainly that would explain Catherine's habit of disappearing for a few days every now and then, not letting anyone know where she was or what she was up to.

Some of her affairs had been more public than others, and the gossip columnists had made the most of those. Dana had also been aware of some of the secret relationships, but much of what she read in the letters was a surprise to her.

When she finished, she sat back and thought about whether they were the kind of thing Len Zarkov had said could be damaging. Certainly they would be a treasure trove for the media. The supermarket tabloids, magazines such as *Vanity Fair*, and even supposedly reputable publications, would go ape over them. So would TV programs like *20/20*, which pretended to do serious investigative journalism. Seen from that angle, the letters would be worth a great deal of money.

But damaging to Catherine? They were titillating, even prurient in some cases, and the freaks who got their rocks off on this kind of thing would love reading them. And so would every movie fan in the world.

And yet their contents could hardly do harm or be grounds for any sort of legal action, as far as Dana could tell. She wasn't a lawyer, but common sense told her the letters were nothing but correspondence between horny guys and a woman who relished her freedom. And besides, how could anything hurt Catherine now?

The only things that remained to be examined were the notes. They'd all been written by Catherine, and as Dana glanced through them, she realized it was as if the actress had been talking to herself. The phrases weren't streams of consciousness; they were too disjointed for that. Some were no longer than a few words. But many seemed charged with excitement.

And in those there was a common thread that Dana found shocking. "Be careful. Dangerous!" And, "Ask Alex. Highly illegal! Warn Bart." One said, "Check R!"

As she read the scribbles, Dana felt a growing suspicion that Len Zarkov had lied to her. Just as she'd suspected when he'd talked to her in New York, he wasn't out to help protect Catherine's reputation; he wanted to save his own ass. And what did the scribbled R mean? Did that refer to Catherine's former husband? Had Ron Apperson been involved somehow?

Whatever it was, Catherine had discovered it and felt that could cause her trouble.

Sometimes, Dana thought, you think you know something, and then you find out you're completely wrong. She wondered whether this was one of those times.

Absentmindedly she picked up her glass and found it empty. Going back into the kitchen, she poured the last of the mineral water from the bottle and drank that as well.

What she needed now was fresh air. Needed to get out of here and go for a walk, try to clear her head. She dumped the bottle into the bag containing recyclable materials and rinsed out the glass. Grabbing her bag, she left the apartment.

17.

For Barker, the drive from the LAPD headquarters was another thirty-minute run. He noticed that the farther west he drove, the more refined the environment became. High-rise apartment buildings, fancy boutiques and department stores, swanky restaurants. Something like Fifth Avenue in New York, or maybe upper Madison.

When he reached the address, he saw that it was one of the high-rises on the opposite side of the street. He was in luck finding a parking space, slipping the Ford into one just after a Jaguar sedan left it. He fished for change in his pants pocket, found nothing but a dime and a couple of pennies, and gave up on feeding the meter.

Now for the wait. It was a common part of police work, and he'd done it more times than he could remember. It also was so boring it made his teeth ache, but there was no other option. He settled down behind the wheel, making himself as comfortable as possible, and kept an eye on the entrance of the building.

The people going in and out were in step with the upscale style of the neighborhood. Mostly they were female, because this was a weekday and men who lived there would be at work. Even the oldest of the women were chic, wearing fashionable dresses or pants and tops, high heels, and the inevitable dark glasses.

He'd been there about an hour when a meter maid came along, riding a machine that was like a cross between a moped and a bumper car. She pointed to the meter and said to him, "Time's expired. Move, or I'll give you a ticket."

Barker slipped the wallet out of his pocket and flashed the tin. At the sight of the gold shield, she rode on.

He again adjusted his position and, in an attempt to relieve the boredom, turned on the radio. The station was playing old records, which he thought were far better than the dipshit rap that filled the airways these days. Rappers called their output music, even though there was no melody and in what passed for lyrics the alleged artists spewed lines about bitches and hos and offing the po-lice.

Two more hours went by, and he began to wonder whether he'd be there all day. Or whether this could even turn into an all-nighter. Hell, she might not be there at all. In which event, he could sit in this damn car until he ossified and they'd have to pry him out of it.

And then there she was. He recognized her at first glance, looking as elegant as any of the women he'd seen since he'd camped there. In fact, more than most of them. She emerged from the building's lobby and turned right, striding confidently along the busy sidewalk.

Barker jumped out of the car and ran across the street, dodging traffic and raising his hand to drivers who angrily blew their horns at him. He drew up alongside her and said, "Miss Laramie? Excuse me."

She turned and looked at him, and her jaw dropped. For a moment he thought she might try another sprint to get away from him. Instead she said, "Why are you after me? I haven't done anything wrong."

"I know you haven't," Barker said. "All I want to do is talk to you."

It was obvious that she didn't believe him. "Talk about what?"

"The case, of course." He gestured toward a nearby coffee shop. "Come on, let's duck in there and I'll explain." Before she could protest further, he steered her into the place and they sat at a table.

"Is this legal?" she said. "You're a New York policeman, and we're in LA."

He smiled, hoping to put her at ease. "Of course it's legal. There's no law against conversation, as far as I know. And that's all I'm looking for. So relax, okay?"

"Relax? You tried to keep me from leaving New York because I was a material witness. And now you followed me out here. I'm supposed to relax?"

A waitress approached, and Barker asked Dana if she'd like coffee.

She shrugged resignedly. "I guess so."

Barker ordered coffee for both of them, and when he and Laramie were again alone he said to her, "Let me make a few things clear, okay? First, I didn't follow you out here. I had other reasons for coming to LA. Second, I wasn't trying to keep you in New York. I had no authority to do that. If we wanted to ask you more questions, it would have been entirely up to you to decide whether or not to answer them."

"Is that really true?"

"Absolutely. You wouldn't have to talk to any of us, if you didn't want to. You could just walk away."

"Such as now?"

He grinned. "At least wait until you've had your coffee."

She didn't return the smile. "I still don't know whether to believe you."

"Then just listen. I came here because I think the murders may not have been part of a jewel robbery. Instead, the killer might have deliberately targeted Ms. Delure and her manager, and the robbery was to cover his real purpose. If I'm right, the motive most likely had to do with something in your boss's personal life, most of which was here in LA."

The waitress returned, served their coffee, and again left them.

"I wanted to talk with you," Barker went on, "because I thought you could probably give me more good information than anyone else."

"And you think I'm going to tell you about Catherine's personal life? Forget it."

"Even if it might help solve the case? Don't you think you owe her that?"

The last question stopped her. She drank some of her coffee, obviously thinking over what he'd said. She put her cup down. "What is it you want to know? Not that I'm necessarily going to answer."

"Do you have any reason to believe she was afraid of something, that she might be in danger?"

Once again she seemed taken aback. "Why do you think there was anything like that?"

So I was right, Barker thought. But he was careful not to push too hard.

"After the funeral," he said, "I spoke with Roger Delaney and his wife, and he invited me to his father's house to talk. He said Catherine had told him she'd learned about something that was highly illegal, and she was worried about her safety. In fact, she wrote him a letter saying so. Does that strike a chord with you? And do you have any idea what was troubling her?"

Dana folded her arms and looked away, and it was apparent to Barker that she was confused. Or perhaps reluctant to take this any further. At last she said, "Suppose I did have an impression along those lines. What would happen if I were to tell you about it?"

"Depends on what it was. But if I thought it was relevant, I'd try to track it down."

"Would I have to be involved?"

"No."

"I don't know whether I should go into it or not."

"So I gather. But there is something, isn't there?"

She hesitated. "Maybe."

"Then let's have it. Keep in mind that by helping me, you'd be helping Catherine, too."

"All right. Earlier today I went to her house and took her personal letters and notes from her desk."

"The house is in Beverly Hills?"

"Yes. On North Crescent."

"Did she own any other homes?"

"One. On Lake Geneva, in Switzerland. But all her correspondence and records were here."

"Why did you take them?"

"Because Len Zarkov had told me there might be some things that would hurt her reputation if they got out. He said he and his lawyer wanted me to give them anything I found, so they could protect her. But when I read her notes, I could see that what he wanted to protect was himself."

"Did the notes contain any details?"

"No. But one of them suggested to me that her ex-husband might be mixed up in whatever had frightened her."

"The ex-husband is Ron Apperson."

"Yes."

"How well do you know him?"

"Not very well. They were divorced before I went to work for Catherine. I've only seen him a few times. And except for answering the phone when he called, I hardly ever spoke to him. Catherine stayed in touch with him though."

"How did you get your job, by the way?"

"I was teaching sociology at UCLA and felt bogged down. I wanted to do something more stimulating and exciting, and I was especially interested in the movie business. In fact, I was gathering material for a book about the history of Hollywood. But what I really wanted was to go to work in the industry. A friend knew Catherine and told me she was looking for a personal secretary. The friend put me in touch, and we hit it off from the first meeting."

"How was she to work for?"

"Terrific. Always treated me very well. She knew I was learning as much as I could about the business, and that I'd move on when another opportunity presented itself. But that was okay. In fact, she encouraged me to learn. I really thought a great deal of her."

"About those notes. I'd like to read them."

"I guess that would be all right. But not the letters. They were from her men friends and were more, uh, personal."

"Sure. Just be sure to take good care of them. At some point, it might be necessary to look into the people who wrote them."

"I understand."

"Are all those things at your place?"

"Yes, they are."

"Then if you don't mind, we'll go there."

18.

There wasn't much, he thought. Just a few hastily written words that confirmed what Dana had told him. But they were enough to make him all the more sure that he was onto something, that his suspicion was correct. The man who'd gone to the Sherry-Netherland had very likely been on a mission to kill Catherine Delure. And maybe her manager as well.

Barker sat back and said, "Would you have any idea what this trouble might be about, and why she was afraid?"

"No. None."

They were in Dana's kitchen. She'd brewed more coffee for them, and Barker was on his second cup.

He picked up one of the scraps of paper. "This says, 'Warn Bart.' Who's Bart?"

"That's personal."

"Meaning what, that he was one of her lovers?"

"I told you, I don't want to go into her relationships."

"I'm not asking you to. But I want to know who the guy is, and why she felt she had to warn him. Warn him about what?"

"His name is Bart Hopkins. He was a friend of hers who made a fortune by investing in computer software companies. Catherine told me he owned more than a million shares of Microsoft, and he bought a big chunk of Google when it issued an IPO a few years back. So he has plenty of money, and like a lot of people he wanted to get into the movie business. He wanted to meet Len Zarkov. I imagine she was warning him not to get involved in movies."

"Or warning him about Zarkov?"

"I don't know. But that's possible."

"How much contact have you had with Zarkov?"

"I'd see him occasionally when he visited the set of one of Catherine's pictures. Or once in a while in some social setting, or at a function that was promoting a movie. He gives parties all the time when he's in LA, and a couple of times Catherine took me along. That was about it. But then after the murders he offered to arrange for me and Diggs to fly back to LA in a studio plane. He was the one who told me the authorities would force me to stay in New York. And he kept urging me to give him her personal letters and notes, stuff like this." She waved a hand at the pile of papers on the table. "He said he and his lawyer would look it over and pull out anything that would be hurtful to Catherine's reputation."

"And that's all he said to you?"

"No. The last time I saw him was in the bar at the Regency, after the funeral. He offered me a job as his assistant. Said I'd be making a lot more money working for him, and that it was a great way for me to step up in the business, as he put it."

"Sounds like he figured once you were on his payroll you'd keep your mouth shut. No matter what you might have found in your boss's notes."

"I realize that now. And it makes me damned angry. Whatever it was that had Catherine frightened, I wouldn't be surprised if Zarkov was somehow mixed up in it. And that note that referred to R? Maybe that meant her ex-husband was in it too."

"I understand his work is financial?"

"Yes. He has an office on Sunset Boulevard."

"Lots of opportunities in the money business. To stick it to people."

"No doubt. But the idea that Catherine and Penny were murdered because they knew about something? I have trouble wrapping my head around that."

"I'm not positive about it either. Yet it's the only thing I've found that's worth following, so far. Tell me, was this all of Ms. Delure's notes and correspondence?"

"There are files on my computer. But as soon as I came back here from New York I looked through every one of them. There's nothing personal in them. Copies of letters from Penny to Catherine's agent, letters to her lawyer and her accountant, things like that. Penny Ellis handled almost all those things."

"Who was Miss Delure's lawyer?"

"His name is Alex Haynes."

"And one of her notes said, 'Ask Alex.'"

"Right."

"Of course, that could have referred to other things she might have wanted his advice about."

"I realize that. Which reminds me. When I went to Catherine's house earlier today, her housekeeper told me Haynes had been there. She said she thought he'd taken some papers from Catherine's study. I checked and saw that he had. But I know he didn't find anything like these personal letters and notes. It was all business correspondence."

"You sure of that?"

"Yes. I was the one who kept it all in order. I did the filing, so I knew what was in there."

"And Penny Ellis would have copies as well?"

"Yes, of course."

"Do you think Ellis might have known about whatever it was that had Catherine worried?"

"She might have, but I don't really know."

"I understand Ellis's body was sent back to her family in Missouri."

"That's correct."

"Coming back to Zarkov, he's expecting to hear from you, isn't he? About this material, and about the job he offered you?"

"Yes. He told me to call him."

"Can you string him along?"

"I guess I could. But why?"

"To give me some time. This guy Hopkins. You have a number for him?"

"I do, but I doubt he'd talk to you. Although—"

"Yes?"

"I suppose I could make a call, let him know you're okay. I know I told you I didn't want to be involved, but I can also see how important this is."

"That'd be great. You can give me his number too, and his address."

"All right, it's on my computer." She got up and left the room, returning with the laptop and a notepad. Again she sat at the table and turned on the machine. She tapped the keys and wrote the number down on the pad, tore off the sheet and handed it to Barker.

He looked at what she'd written. "Is this in LA?"

"Yes. He lives in Bel Air. Do you know where that is?"

"Off Sunset, isn't it?"

"Right. Entrance is at Sunset and Bellagio. "I'll call him now, okay?"

"Go right ahead."

She stepped over to a wall phone and made the call. After a moment she got an answer and asked for Mr. Hopkins. She gave her name and mentioned that she'd been Miss Delure's secretary, said thanks, and hung up.

Returning to the table she said, "He was out. That was the butler who answered. He said he'd give Mr. Hopkins the message and have him call me."

"That's fine. I'll try to see him tomorrow."

"Will you let me know what happens?"

"Sure. I'll probably need more help from you as I go along. I'll also want to talk to Ellis's girlfriend. You can give me her address too, if you would."

"All right." She looked it up and jotted that down for him as well. As she gave it to him she said, "I want to apologize."

"What for?"

"For being completely wrong about you. I really should have been grateful."

"No problem."

"Anyway, I appreciate the way you're handling this."

"Just doing my job." How was that for a dumb cliché of an answer?

"Have you seen the movie, by the way? *Hot Cargo*?"

"Not yet, but I plan to."

"I have a copy, if you want to see it."

"The DVD is already out?"

"No, this is one the studio sent me. The commercial DVD won't be out until the movie has had its run in theaters. Shall I put it on?"

"Okay, great."

They went into the living room, and she put the disc into the DVD player. "It won't have the same effect as on the big screen," she said, "but at least you'll know what it's all about."

Barker sat with her on the sofa, looking at the TV as the titles came up. Then for the next two hours he watched Catherine Delure cavort her way through a string of scenes that emphasized her sex appeal.

The plot, such as it was, involved Catherine going by private jet to a fabulous tropical resort, where she turned heads by strutting around the beach in a bikini. Soon she was romanced by handsome leading man Terry Falcon. They danced in the moonlight, made love in her suite, rode the waves on surfboards, all with as much emphasis on T and A as the director could stuff in.

In the film, Falcon pretended to be on vacation, while he was actually an undercover agent who was there to track down a gang of drug smugglers. That led to the bad guys kidnapping Catherine and taking her aboard a ship packed with about a million pounds of drugs, Falcon attempting to rescue her, the smugglers trying to rape her, and Catherine shooting countless adversaries.

There was a chase scene in which the US Coast Guard dueled with the ship's crew, another chase scene featuring a firefight between SUVs and police cars racing along the coast, and a climax in which Catherine saved Falcon's life and triumphed over the evil characters by shooting more of them. From there, the lovers waltzed off into the sunset, end of story.

Barker was glad when it was over. "Very interesting," he said.

"Not exactly serious drama," Dana said, "but it's a good example of the Zarkov formula."

"Where was it shot?"

"Nuevo Vallarta, Mexico. Everything's cheaper there. And as you saw, we had a great location. The hotel is called Grand Velas."

He smiled. "Must have been good for your tan."

"It was. Care for more coffee?"

"No, thanks."

"Maybe just a half a cup?"

"Nope. I'm about to have a caffeine fit as it is. And it's time for me to move along." He rose from the sofa. "I'll be in touch. You still have my cell number? It's on the card I gave you in New York."

"Yes, I have it. Where are you staying?"

"At the Sunset Inn. You can also reach me there, or leave a message."

"Okay." She walked to the front door with him. "Good-bye, Mr. Barker."

"It's Jeb," he said.

She smiled and shook his hand, saying, "Call me Dana."

He left the apartment and walked back to his car. It was early evening now, and the streetlights and the lights in the store windows were on. As he approached the Ford, he saw something stuck under the windshield wiper.

Shit—a traffic ticket.

But that was a minor irritation. The truth was, this had been a good day. He'd picked up some valuable information, and possibly some leads. First he'd call on the woman who'd been Penny Ellis's girlfriend, see what she had to say.

Then there was Ron Apperson, Delure's former husband. He'd call Apperson in the morning, arrange a visit.

Also, Dana had talked about Bart Hopkins, the investor who'd wanted to put money into a Zarkov project. Hopkins could be another source. He'd make a run on Hopkins tomorrow.

And there was one other thing that pleased him. Dana Laramie was not only beautiful; she hadn't wanted him to leave.

19.

The sky was turning from black to gray, and a cool breeze was coming off the sea. Perfect conditions, Mongo thought, for his morning run. He threaded his way between two beach houses and walked down to the water's edge. The sand was wet there, and that would make running tough. Which was also perfect. He knew how important it was to stay in shape, and the more he pushed his muscles, the better.

It was another thing he'd learned in Q. You had to be strong and ready, because you never knew what you might come up against. Especially when you least expected it.

That was why he'd spent time pumping iron while he was in the joint, and why he made it a regular routine to run in Malibu. He also had a barbell and a set of weights back at the cottage, and he used them too. As a result, his body was as taut and fine-tuned as it had ever been.

A few other joggers were already out this morning, most of them male, but one or two women as well. Mongo was dressed more or less the same way they were; he had on an old pair of shorts and a T-shirt, his feet shod in ragged sneakers to protect against sharp stones and the occasional shard of clamshell. As he passed the others, he kept his head down.

Ordinarily, he felt pretty good when he was running. He liked the smell of the salt air as he sucked it into his lungs, liked hearing the *smack-smack* of his footsteps on the wet sand. But this morning he was in a foul mood, and that made it different.

The problem was he hadn't heard a word from Strunk since he'd returned from Vegas. So why the fuck had he gotten the call to come back? He'd had plenty of money left, could still be having a good time at the tables and with the broads.

On the other hand, whenever he was there he did the opposite of what he was doing now. Here in Malibu, he worked hard to stay in good condition, but in Vegas he did his best to destroy himself. Okay, maybe that was an exaggeration, but not by much. The booze, the coke, the sex, seldom stopping to eat or sleep—Jesus, what a way to live.

And what a hell of a lot of fun.

The more he thought about Strunk not contacting him, the more his mood darkened. The weasel acted as though all he had to do was snap his fingers and his pet would jump up and do a jig. Mongo ground his teeth as he went on thinking about it. Maybe he should tell the little shit to go fuck his hat.

But he wouldn't do that, of course. The arrangement he'd worked out with Strunk was the smartest deal he could ask for. It had turned out just as he'd planned it during those nights in San Quentin. He'd be very stupid to screw it up now.

He turned and ran back up the beach, and from there out to the coast highway. Even at this hour there was plenty of traffic, most of the cars and trucks southbound with their headlights on, and he had to wait a full minute before there was a gap and he could sprint across the road.

At the cottage he lifted weights for twenty minutes, doing mostly squats and curls. After that he took a long hot shower and toweled down, put on jeans and loafers and a fresh shirt. He made himself a breakfast of muffins and a pot of coffee, and as he ate he turned on the little Sony TV he kept on the table and tuned in to the local news.

There was the usual blather about the weather, which at this time of year was the same every day: morning fog followed by sunshine, temperatures ranging from the low seventies at the beach to the nineties inland. Then came the ball scores and a string of commercials, and after that an aerial shot of the 405 Freeway, revealing that it was crowded. Was there ever a time when it wasn't?

Next a Latina chippie was on camera, grinning and jiggling as she read some bullshit story about gang violence in East LA. She said members of MS-13, the Mara Salvatrucha, had confronted a bunch of Norteños at around two A.M., and one of the Norteños had been stabbed. He was taken to a nearby hospital where he was pronounced brain dead.

Mongo snickered when he heard that last part. Fucking idiot had been brain dead long before he was stabbed.

There was more, but Mongo had lost interest. Gang warfare in LA was like the weather: same thing, day after day. He looked out the window. The fog was lifting, but it was still a little early for it to clear.

The TV upchucked more commercials. He would have ignored them, but one was the trailer for *Hot Cargo* and that got his rapt attention. He'd seen it before, but he always got a kick out of watching it. In a series of quick cuts it showed Catherine Delure fighting off a bunch of bad guys, kissing the leading man, shooting a gun, drinking champagne, and looking gorgeous in a bikini, all against a thundering hard-rock sound track.

Oddly, seeing the spot induced a sort of perverse pride in him. Catherine Delure had been a movie star, and he'd played an important part in her life. Too bad they couldn't give him a credit on her gravestone.

He was about to turn off the set when the camera cut back to the Latina. "This just in. There is breaking news on the Catherine Delure murder case. The police have developed a new lead."

Mongo sat up straight and increased the volume.

"We take you now to New York," the Latina said, "where the police are describing the latest turn in the case."

Cut to a blonde standing on the steps of some official building in Manhattan. Alongside her was a guy with a nose like a banana. Several other men were grouped just behind them, obviously police brass.

"With me is Detective Lieutenant Dan Hogan," the blonde said. "Lieutenant Hogan has been directing the investigation and has the latest information on the progress police have been making in the case. What's the new development, Lieutenant?"

"We've got a report from the lab," Hogan said, "that reveals key information about the poipitrayta."

The cop had an accent so thick it was hard for Mongo to understand him. A *poipitrayta*? What the fuck was a *poipitrayta*?

Ah, he got it then. Banana Nose meant *perpetrator*. It reminded Mongo of the jabber he'd heard when he was in New York. If you were going to that town, it would be good to take foreign language lessons before you went.

"Can you tell us what the report said?" the blonde asked.

"The lab tested a hair," Hogan replied, "that was found at the scene. The lab report says it came from a wig, and we believe it was left by the killer."

"And you think that could lead you to the man who committed the murders?"

"We think it could, yes. We may be able to trace it. Also, a wig would have given him a different appearance from what we put out in the first composite. And in that one he had a mustache. If he shaved it off, it would further change what he looked like. So we made a new composite of him without the wig and the mustache."

"Can you show it to us?"

"Certainly."

Hogan held up a flyer with the drawing on it, and the camera zoomed in tight. The man it depicted had high cheekbones and a strong jaw. There was no hair on his head, and none on his upper lip. His mouth was wide and full lipped, and his eyes gazed straight ahead in a menacing expression. At the bottom of the drawing were bold letters that said WANTED IN DELURE MURDER CASE. There was also the number of a police hotline.

Hogan spoke over the shot. "If anyone recognizes this man, please call the 800 number. And be careful. He's armed and dangerous."

Cut back to the blonde. "Thank you, Lieutenant. We urge anyone who thinks they may know who the man is to call the hotline at once."

Cut to the Latina in LA. "That's a very encouraging development. Catherine Delure was one of Hollywood's most famous and beloved stars. Learning that the police now have a way to close in on the monster who cut short her life will be good news for her many fans here in Los Angeles as well as around the world. We'll be showing the new composite drawing of the suspected killer frequently, and we hope someone will respond."

Mongo turned off the TV, feeling a little tense. The fucking drawing did resemble him. Banana Nose was smarter than he looked.

But hold on. The composite wasn't perfect, by any means. In fact, the guy it showed could be mistaken for a thousand others. So take it easy, Mongo told himself. Don't lose your cool over some cartoon.

Nevertheless, seeing the drawing was troubling. It sure as hell was a lot better than the cops' first attempt.

For the next hour he puttered around the cottage, tidying up the place, dumping dirty laundry into the washing machine, hanging scattered bits of clothing in the bedroom closet. As he did, the story of the cops' new direction nagged at him.

Hair from the wig? What else could they have found? No fingerprints, he'd seen to that. And no DNA; he hadn't left so much as a drop of saliva anywhere. Fibers from his suit? That might tell them it was an Armani. Big deal. There had to be plenty of those in New York.

So the hair was all they had. And yet it was significant, no question. The new drawing proved that.

He picked up his attaché case and placed it on his bureau, popped open the top. Inside were two objects. One was the tape recorder. The other was the wig.

The recorder would provide solid evidence as to what had fired the fléchettes. He'd have to get rid of it. Should have done it right away, not let it hang around.

And the wig? That was the root of the problem. Even though he'd paid top dollar for it, the damn thing tended to shed a hair now and then. He remembered brushing a few strands off the shoulders of his suit when he was in the restroom at JFK, before boarding the jet for his flight. He'd get rid of the wig, too.

And yet, could they really trace it? Unlikely. One hair couldn't tell them much, even though they were making a big deal out of finding it. But the drawing was another story.

In fact, of all the jobs he'd done, this was the first time cops had ever come anywhere near knowing what he looked like.

The hotel videotape wouldn't have been clear enough to help them, so how had they done it? That was obvious. They'd have had the good-looking secretary and the slug of a bodyguard work with an artist to draw a likeness.

But the hell with it. The hit had gone down like shit from a seagull, and now it was in the past. He could look forward to getting a new assignment, if the weasel would only call him.

One thing, though. He wasn't about to take on anything remotely as big as the Delure hit for the lousy payoff he'd collected for it. He'd let Strunk know that, right up front.

But damn it, where was the call?

20.

Ron Apperson's suite of offices was in a high-rise on the Sunset Strip. It was equipped with a stunning blonde receptionist and a pair of assistants, one male and one female, and a few secretaries. The furniture was ultramodern, and there was an air of urgency about the place. As if there was a lot of money to be made, and they'd have to hurry in order to scoop it all up.

When Barker walked in and gave his name to the receptionist, she treated him to a dazzling smile and said Mr. Apperson was expecting him. "Please be seated," she said. "He'll be with you in just a moment."

He sat and picked up a copy of *Forbes*, began leafing through it. He was a little surprised that Apperson had been so willing to see him. Or maybe like some people when contacted by the cops, he was anxious to demonstrate that he had nothing to hide. When Barker had called, he was told to come right ahead.

After only a few minutes a matronly woman appeared and

introduced herself as Jane Sherman, Apperson's personal secretary. She asked Barker to follow her.

They went past a cubbyhole that had Sherman's name on it, and from there to Apperson's lair. Sherman knocked and opened the door, and when Barker entered she shut it behind him.

He noticed that although this was a typically bright sunny day in Southern California, draperies covered the windows. All illumination came from spotlights in the ceiling. Apperson's desk, a thick sheet of glass supported by chromium legs, was stacked high with papers.

Apperson got up from the desk. He was a big guy, and apparently kept himself in shape. He had wavy brown hair with touches of gray at the temples and wore a nubby white jacket and a white shirt that was open at the throat. He came forward with his hand stuck out. Barker shook it as Apperson said, "Good morning, Detective."

"Morning. I appreciate your giving me some of your time."

"No problem. You probably want to ask about my former wife."

"That's part of why I wanted to see you, yes."

"Horrible thing, that she was murdered. She and Penny."

"Yes, it was."

"I must tell you, though, I'm a little surprised that you've come to Los Angeles on this. According to the news reports, the murders took place in the course of a robbery in the Sherry-Netherland Hotel in New York. Isn't that so?"

"That's correct."

"Killer stole her jewelry?"

"He did, yes."

"And that was why he killed them, according to the stories in the newspapers and on TV. Also correct?"

"Possibly."

Apperson pursed his lips. "Possibly? You suggesting there was something else?"

"I'm not suggesting anything," Barker said. "Just covering all the bases." He smiled. "Besides, it's nice to have a reason to visit LA." Playing the part of the rube, putting Apperson at ease.

"Ah, of course," Apperson said. He returned the smile. "Anything to get out of New York, eh? I can understand that."

"Change of scenery is always welcome," Barker said.

Apperson indicated a pair of deeply upholstered chairs. "Let's sit over here, shall we?"

After they were seated, he asked if Barker would like coffee.

"No thanks. I promise to be as brief as possible." That too was to make the visit seem routine.

"Don't worry about that," Apperson said. "I'm happy to do anything I can to help you. So what can I tell you about Catherine? I suppose you want to know all about her private life."

"Only anything that might give us a direction to look at. Whether she had problems with anyone, whether she had enemies."

"Oh, that's easy. She didn't have an enemy in the world. Unless you count some other actress who was envious of her. But a real enemy? Not as far as I know. And I knew her as well as anyone. We were married almost five years."

"Whose idea was the divorce?"

"It was by mutual agreement. We literally just drifted apart. She had her life, I had mine. Sometimes I wouldn't see her for weeks on end. She was either in a studio or on location, and when she wasn't shooting she was on a publicity tour. That's what took her to New York, wasn't it?"

"Yes, it was. How did you get along, when you were together?"

"Oh, well enough, most of the time. We had our squabbles, too, of course."

"Over what?"

"The usual. She resented it when women found me attractive. And frankly, I didn't like it when men were sniffing around her. Most of them were smarmy creatures."

"So there was jealousy, on both your parts."

"You could say so, yes."

"Any other reason for hostility?"

"Not really. We had some arguments over possessions when we

broke up. California law says everything gets split down the middle, but there are always some gray areas. Nevertheless, we never got to the boiling point."

That last didn't square with what Sam Benziger had told Barker. He said, "When you argued, did you ever push her around? Slap her, anything like that?"

"Certainly not. I don't hit women."

That was a flat lie, but Barker didn't press it. "You say she had no enemies. Did she ever feel she was in danger, or could be?"

"You mean was she threatened by stalkers, that kind of thing? Every actress has to watch her step there. The world is full of nut-cases who develop fixations on famous women. Cameron Diaz, Sandra Bullock—they've both had to contend with that. And look at Jodie Foster. There was what's-his-name, the guy who thought he could impress her by shooting the president."

"John Hinckley, Jr.," Barker said.

"Yeah, that's the one. But as far as some weirdo stalking Catherine is concerned, I don't recall anything like that happening with her."

"But did she ever believe she was in danger?"

"Tell me something, Detective. Do you know any actresses? Know them personally?"

"Can't say I do."

"Then let me explain. An actress lives a life of drama. Not just when she's in front of a camera, or on a stage. But constantly. She always has to be in the middle of a dramatic event. It might be thrilling, or funny, or sad, or a tragedy. But whatever it is, she feeds off it. That's what makes her tick. It also makes her volatile, or else moody. Or both. And most of all, hard as hell to be around. When I think back, it's a wonder Catherine and I were married as long as we were."

"So I take it the answer is no. She never thought she was in any danger."

"I didn't say that. She might have thought it, but I never saw she had any reason to. If you ask me, her idea of danger was the prospect of getting a lousy review, or being afraid she'd lose a choice part to someone else. But real physical danger? I don't think so."

"What about your own career? You're in finance, right? An investment banker?"

"No. An investment banker underwrites ventures, hoping they'll become profitable. What I do is different. I have a select list of clients for whom I find investment opportunities in many different fields. Real estate, oil, new products, companies that need restructuring, and so on. Anything that I believe could be a moneymaker. I analyze the prospects, and if they're favorable, I advise my client to buy in. And I often take a stake myself. More times than not, it works out well for everyone."

"Do the opportunities include movies?"

"Yes, sometimes."

"Ever do business with the producer of Ms. Delure's last movie, Len Zarkov?"

"Yes, as a matter of fact, I have."

"How did that go?"

"There are a number of projects that are in development. It's too soon to know whether they'll be successful."

"You mentioned having a select list of clients. Who are they?"

"That's confidential, for reasons I'm sure you can understand. They're all very powerful, successful people. They wouldn't want their identities revealed, and I've signed an agreement with each of them that I would never disclose who they are."

"I see." Barker rose to his feet. "I guess that'll do it, Mr. Apperson. Thanks for seeing me."

"Hope I've been helpful."

They shook hands once again, and Barker left the office. So Apperson's clients didn't want to be identified? Okay, but Barker already knew the name of one of them. He'd hear what that one had to say.

21.

Massive pillars holding fake wrought-iron gates flanked the entrance to Bel Air. Barker drove on through and followed the winding road.

The area was heavily wooded, with live oak and cedar and poplar and cypress trees rising from behind high walls. This was some of the most expensive real estate in Southern California, and the owners of many of the homes had seen to it that the walls, trees, and plantings would ensure maximum privacy. It occurred to him that probably more movie stars lived here than anywhere else in the world.

When he reached Hopkins's address he drove the Ford up the drive to the main house. It was an enormous Mediterranean, with arches and a tiled roof and pale pink stucco siding. Elaborate gardens surrounded it.

The inevitable security man was on hand, and when Barker identified himself he was told to leave his car in the side courtyard. He parked the Ford next to a white Rolls convertible and went to the front door. He rang the bell and a butler greeted him, saying Mr. Hopkins was out by the pool and to please follow him there.

A hallway led to the rear of the house, where there was a vast flagstone patio and a pool house and urns filled with red and purple bougainvillea. The butler indicated a man and a woman who were sitting on deck chairs at the water's edge. A table between them held tall glasses. The man waved to Barker to join them.

Both people were in swimsuits. At least the man. The woman was in next to nothing. She had on a thong that covered her pubis, and that was it. She also had a great body and deeply tanned skin that glistened under a coating of oil.

The male wasn't nearly as interesting. He was about fifty, Barker guessed, with iron-gray hair and a matching mustache.

"You're Detective Barker?" he asked.

"Yes. Jeb Barker."

"Hi, I'm Bart Hopkins. Dana Laramie told me about you. Pull up a chair and sit down. This is Donna Ferrante."

Barker said hello, and the woman smiled at him. She was a brunette, although he hadn't noticed that part until now. It was hard for him to look away from her.

"You want something to drink?" Hopkins asked him.

"No thanks."

"Oh, go ahead. We're having rum punch, which is good for you. It's got fruit juice in it."

Without waiting for an answer, he raised a hand and called out to the butler to bring his guest one of the same.

Barker sat beside Hopkins and said, "I appreciate your seeing me."

"Don't mention it. Any friend of Dana's, and so on. She said on the phone you're working on Catherine Delure's murder?"

"That's correct."

"I hope you get the rotten bastard who did it. You think he's here in LA, and not in New York?"

"I don't know. But he could be."

"Catherine was a wonderful person."

"I gather you knew her well."

Hopkins grinned. "Well enough not to say any more about it."

"And her manager?"

"Hardly at all. What was her name?"

"Penny Ellis."

"So how can I help you?"

"I understand you were interested in doing a deal with Len Zarkov."

"Dana tell you that?"

"Yes."

"Did she also tell you Catherine warned me to stay away from him?"

"She did, yes."

"And what does that have to do with the murders?"

"I don't know. It's one of the angles I'm checking out."

The butler returned carrying a tray that bore a glass filled with pink liquid. Barker took the glass from him and the butler said to Hopkins, "May I get you or Miss Ferrante anything else?"

"Not right now, Cedric," Hopkins said.

The butler left them, and Barker raised his glass.

"Cheers," Hopkins said, and all three drank.

Stuff tasted good at that, Barker thought. It was cool and tangy, and heavy on the rum.

"What did you want to ask me?" Hopkins asked.

"I want to know more about Zarkov, and why Miss Delure warned you."

Hopkins said to Ferrante, "Sweetie, why don't you go into the pool house and have yourself a shower, okay?"

She got the message. After putting her glass down on the table she rose from her chair and said, "I've enjoyed your company, Jeb."

"And I've enjoyed yours," Barker said. Which certainly was the truth.

She smiled. "Hope I'll see you before you leave."

"I hope so too."

She walked off to the pool house at an easy pace, and both men watched her go.

"Beautiful ass," Hopkins said. "Among other things."

"She your girlfriend?"

"Some of the time."

"You're not married?"

"Not anymore, thank God. Are you?"

"No."

"Word of advice. Keep it that way. It's a lot cheaper."

Back to business, Barker thought. "How did you come to know Zarkov?"

"Ron Apperson introduced us," Hopkins said.

"Catherine Delure's former husband."

"Right. He'd put together a commodities deal for me some time back, and it turned out well. So when he wanted me to meet Zarkov, I said sure. Ron knew I was looking for a way to invest in the movie business."

"And you discussed that with Zarkov?"

"No. That is, I was supposed to get together with him, but before that could take place I mentioned it to Catherine. A few days later I got a call from her, and she told me not to have anything to do with him."

"She tell you why?"

"Nope. I tried to get her to explain, but she wouldn't. She sounded pretty upset, though. Anyway, I never had the meeting, and since then I've regretted it. I'd still like to talk to him."

"Would it be possible for you to set up something with him now?"

"Yeah, I think so."

"And could I tag along, without revealing who I am?"

Hopkins grinned. "Hey, cloak-and-dagger stuff, huh? Sure you could. I'd just say you were a friend of mine."

"When could you arrange it?"

"You're under time pressure, right? So let me see what I can do. Where can I reach you?"

"I'm staying at the Sunset Inn."

"Okay, I'll call you there. Zarkov has a party at his house almost every night he's in LA."

"So Dana told me."

"If he says tomorrow night would be all right, would that work for you?"

"Yes, it would."

Donna was back. She no longer wore the thong, but instead had on a short white skirt that seemed to be made of Kleenex. And still no top.

Barker got to his feet and said to Hopkins, "Thanks for the drink. I'll wait to hear from you."

"I hope you're not leaving on my account," Donna said.

"Believe me, I'm not." He took one more look and made his way back to the house and on out to his car.

On the return trip to the hotel Barker glanced at his watch. He'd be able to grab a few hours of sunshine and a swim. He'd also have a late lunch; he was desperately hungry.

But first he'd call Spinelli and catch up on what was happening in New York.

And he'd call Dana Laramie as well. He wanted to see her again, and soon. She was as bright as she was beautiful. And once she'd decided to trust him, she'd radiated warmth.

He also thought about Donna Ferrante. And forced the image from his mind. Instinct told him that one could be a large package of trouble.

Once in his room, he called Spinelli's cell. When he got an answer he said, "Joe, it's me."

"How's it going?"

"Making progress, I hope. How about you?"

"Still wasting time talking to a bunch of mutts. And Hogan's been busting my balls."

"Over what?"

"He asked me where you were, and I told him you were pursuing leads, but I didn't know what they were, exactly. So he had a shit fit and called Kelly to complain. I don't think he got very far, though."

"Then he doesn't know I'm out here?"

"No, I'm sure Kelly wouldn't tell him."

"Anything else?"

"Yeah, the lab reported the hair found in the suite was human, but it most likely came from a wig. So Hogan has people trying to run that down, calling wig manufacturers to get a line on who made it and so on. He also had a new composite drawn up, showing the perp without the wig and without the mustache."

"That makes sense. Has he released it to the media?"

"Yeah, earlier today. You haven't watched TV?"

"No."

"It's been on there. Hogan made sure he was interviewed about it, so he'd get credit for being a hard charger. I'll send a copy of the drawing to your phone. Or better still, I'll fax it to you at your hotel. And I'll call you if it produces anything."

"Okay, good. Also, at the post they made a photo of the fléchette Robbins dug out of Delure. Fax me a copy of that too, will you?"

"Yeah, will do."

Barker hung up and opened his travel bag, got out a pair of swim trunks. He was stripping off his clothes when the phone rang.

"Yes?"

"Bart Hopkins here. I called Zarkov and he said there's a party scheduled for tomorrow night, and he'd be delighted to have me come. I told him I'd be bringing a friend, and he said that'd be fine. So I'll pick you up tomorrow at, say, eight thirty. Okay?"

"Sure, I'll see you then. And thanks."

Barker next called Dana Laramie's number. She sounded glad to hear from him. He told her about his visit to Bart Hopkins's house.

"And you say his girlfriend was with him?"

"Yes. Her name was Donna Ferrante."

"Ah, the Italian firecracker."

"You know her?"

"I've met her. She's an actress. Catherine couldn't stand her. Said she drew guys like a magnet."

Barker could understand that.

"So was Bart willing to help you?"

"Yeah, he's going to Len Zarkov's place tomorrow night. Zarkov is having one of his parties. And Hopkins is taking me with him."

"Hey, nice going."

"Thanks, I'll fill you in afterward."

Barker hung up and got into his trunks and a T-shirt. He left the room and went down to the poolside patio, where he put on sunglasses and sat at a table. Wouldn't be a bad life living in Southern California, he thought.

A waiter came by, and Barker ordered a shrimp cocktail, a strip steak medium rare, a baked potato, a green salad, and a glass of pinot noir.

As he waited for his food, he looked at the sky. It was a high, hard blue, and there wasn't a cloud in sight. A light breeze was waving the fronds of the palm trees, and two girls in bikinis were frolicking in the pool.

Not a bad life at all.

22.

At eight thirty sharp, Barker went out the front entrance of the hotel. He wore his blazer, and because this was LA, no tie. Bart Hopkins was waiting for him in the white Rolls, the top down and the engine idling. Barker had guessed right about the tie; Hopkins wasn't wearing one. He wasn't wearing a jacket, either.

"Zarkov's house is on Mulholland," Hopkins said as they pulled away. "You ever been up there?"

"I don't think so."

"You'd remember it if you had. At least if the weather was clear."

Tonight it was quite clear, and the air was balmy and redolent with the fragrance of night jasmine. The convertible purred its way west, and then made a right onto Laurel Canyon. As the big car climbed the winding curves it struck Barker that not so long ago he couldn't have envisioned himself riding through Beverly Hills in a Rolls-Royce.

"Nice car," he said.

Hopkins looked over at him and smiled. "Thanks. I like it. Rolls makes good machinery."

"Didn't I read the company was sold a while back?"

"Right. The Germans own it now. BMW bought it. Remember the old expression, dress British, think Yiddish? This is a new wrinkle on that."

When they reached the Zarkov house, Barker saw that it was a prime example of contemporary design, one story high and with walls of glass. A large crowd of people was visible inside, and the sound of their chatter blended with music as it drifted out onto the circular drive.

Attendants wearing white jackets opened the doors of the Rolls and the two men stepped out. One of the attendants handed Hopkins a card with a number on it and then whisked the Rolls away to wherever they were parking guests' cars.

Other attendants were obviously security. Hopkins gave one of them his name and told him to let Mr. Zarkov know he'd arrived. The man hurried off.

Hopkins grabbed Barker's arm and said, "Turn around and look back."

From this height, the view was panoramic. To Barker, it was as if the city were laid out at his feet. Lights were coming on in the dusk, giving the scene a magical appearance.

"Something, isn't it?" Hopkins said. "Tells you why people like Jack Nicholson live up here."

He pointed. "That's Hollywood down there, and beyond that is LA's business district, where you see the tall buildings. Over there is the Palos Verde Peninsula. And those are the San Bernardino Mountains, on the horizon."

"Beautiful."

"We're lucky," Hopkins said. "Tonight there isn't much smog, and unfortunately there usually is. It's caused by an inversion layer that forms over the LA basin. It traps the smoke and gases and makes it a crapshoot to breathe the air. Do it long enough, and it just might kill you."

They went inside, where it was wall-to-wall people, everyone deeply tanned and dressed in casual but elegant clothing. Wait-ers moved through the crowd, offering glasses of champagne from trays.

There was also a bar at one end of the room, and the more serious drinkers were clustered near it. At the other end, a long table held a wide variety of both hot and cold dishes. Two men in chef's hats stood behind the table, serving guests.

"Hey, glad you could make it." A heavyset man in an ivory-colored silk shirt came toward them, smiling broadly. The shirt was unbuttoned halfway down his chest, revealing a gold chain nestled among the hairs.

"Hello, Len," Hopkins said, and shook the man's hand. "This is my friend Jeb."

Zarkov glanced at Barker. "Hi."

"Quite a blowout," Hopkins said. "You really do this often?"

"Damn near every night, when I'm in town. It's a good way for me to keep a finger on what's going on in the business. And to see friends and make contacts. How about a drink?"

"The champagne looks good," Hopkins said. "You too, Jeb?"

"That'd be fine."

Zarkov raised a finger, and one of the tray bearers hurried to them. Hopkins and Barker both took glasses and sipped the sparkling wine.

It was excellent, Barker thought. Although he'd never tasted enough of the stuff to be much of a judge.

"You'll probably recognize the actors and actresses," Zarkov said. He waved in the direction of the crowd. "There's a lot of them here. That's Terry Falcon over there, poor Catherine's costar in *Hot Cargo*. Also Laura Bennett, who's just finishing her new picture. And more'll be coming. Tom Cruise may stop by, and Bob De Niro. Brad might also come." He grinned. "If he does, I hope he'll bring Angelina."

"I hope so too," Hopkins said.

"Do you know Jerry Chu, the cinematographer?"

"Only by reputation. Is he here?"

"Sure is. Let me introduce you." Zarkov beckoned to a small

Asian man who was talking to a tall blonde. "Jerry, come on over here, will you? Want you to meet somebody."

When Chu joined them, Zarkov introduced him to Hopkins. He didn't acknowledge Barker's presence.

"Jerry won an Oscar for his work on *Savage World*," Zarkov said.

"I saw the picture and the photography was wonderful," Hopkins said. "That kind of expertise bowls me over."

Chu said, "The technology is constantly changing. And usually for the better."

"I'm sure that's true, but you deserve your reputation. You're a real artist."

If Chu was pleased by the remark, he didn't show it. "The secret," he said, "is to understand that photography is light. Doesn't matter whether you're shooting thirty-five millimeter or using film lenses with videotape. I can achieve a wide range of moods through different lighting effects. And I train my camera operators to give me exactly what I want."

"I'd love to hear more about that," Hopkins said. "Whenever you might have some time."

"Be a pleasure," Chu said. "But right now I want to get back to my girlfriend. Good to meet you." He hurried over to the blonde, who'd begun talking with another man.

Next Zarkov waved to Terry Falcon, who steered his companion to the producer. Falcon's tan was so dark that when he smiled it made his teeth appear startlingly white. He was also much shorter than he appeared in films.

The companion was another blonde, well built and giggly. Her name was Jean Adair. When Zarkov introduced them, the blonde flashed a smile at Barker. He decided she probably didn't realize he was nobody.

"I've enjoyed seeing your work," Hopkins said to Falcon.

The actor displayed his white teeth. "Thank you. All a matter of getting good roles." He looked at Zarkov. "Isn't that right, Len?"

"It helps," the producer said.

"Nice to meet you," Falcon said. He squeezed the blonde's buttocks and she giggled. "Come on, baby," he said. "I need a new drink."

After they left, Zarkov said to Hopkins, "You still thinking about getting into the business?"

"Yes, as a matter of fact, I am."

"Good. Let me collect my assistant, who keeps track of money matters. We'll go into my office."

23.

The producer moved off and returned moments later with another man in tow. He introduced him to Hopkins as Norman Klein.

With his clean-cut features and smooth manner, Klein could have been one of the actors, Barker thought. Even had the proper toothy smile.

Zarkov led them to the other end of the house. On the way they passed a large patio, where more people were chatting and boozing. Barker noticed that off to one side a couple were crouched over a low table and snorting lines, apparently not caring whether anyone saw them or not.

Zarkov's office was as impressive as the rest of the place. His desk was a slab of zebrawood, and the entire wall behind it was glass. Another wall held a large TV monitor. And hanging on another was a large painting, an abstract burst of reds and greens and yellows.

The view from here was almost as spectacular as the one from the front of the house. The office looked out over the San Fernando Valley, and it was dark now and the valley was a carpet of lights.

Opposite the desk was a grouping of Barcelona chairs, and the men sat in them, with Zarkov and Klein facing Hopkins and Barker.

Zarkov said, "As Ron Apperson explained to you, Bart, producing a movie is a risky proposition. In fact, financial failures are the rule, not the exception. People lose a lot of money in the business. Right, Norman?"

"Yes, that's quite true," Klein said.

"But I have a formula," Zarkov said. "And it's actually quite simple. For one thing, I finance most of my pictures myself. Sometimes I borrow from the banks in New York, but only because I might have more than one project going at the same time. So with my own money on the line, I keep a tight fist on every aspect of production. Behind my back my line producers call me Attila the Hun. They don't think I know that, but I do." He grinned. "And to tell the truth, I like it."

"Explain to Bart why you remain independent," Klein said.

"Simple reason for that, too. It means I don't have to listen to a lot of shit from know-nothing schmucks at the studio while my picture's in production. All studio people do is slow down the work and make everything cost more. But until my movie's a finished product, they can't get their hands on it."

"I see," Hopkins said. "But you do have a relationship with a studio, don't you?"

"Yes, I do," Zarkov said. "With strict limitations. Mainly, I use them to release the picture. By then it's too late for them to fuck it up. I also use them for marketing and promotion. At my direction, of course."

"How many hits have you had?" Hopkins asked.

"Depends on how you define hits," the producer said. "You're talking high grosses, maybe four or five. *Hot Cargo* is turning out to be a big one. It may become my biggest hit ever."

"I hope it does," Hopkins said.

"Thanks. My standard is does a film make money or not. Take a movie like *Out of Body*. Box office was so-so, and the critics said it was dreck. And you know something? They were right. But with the

DVD and foreign distribution, even that made a profit. So the way I see it, the picture was successful. You understand, Bart?"

"Absolutely," Hopkins said.

"Now that's not to say none of my pictures ever lose money," Zarkov went on. "Some of them have bombed, I don't deny it. But those have been few and far between. Anyhow, financial control is only part of my formula when I'm considering whether to make a certain movie. When it comes to the creative aspects, there are two factors I believe are most important. One is the premise, and the other is the stars I think I can get for it. Paul Newman once said a star can't make a movie, but if the story is a good one, then a star can help make it a hit. I couldn't agree more."

"So to sum it up," Klein said, "Len's success is due to good stories featuring top stars, and tight financial control."

"That's about it," Zarkov said.

"Is there a specific opportunity for me?" Hopkins said "One you could talk about?"

"As a matter of fact, there is," Zarkov said. "At the moment, I'm developing a new movie. And from what Ron Apperson has told me, it sounds like you might make a good partner for the project."

Hopkins said, "How far along are you?"

"Just putting the pieces together. Are you familiar with the screenwriter Jonathan Gault?"

"I've heard the name," Hopkins said.

"He's one of the best. Won an Oscar for *The Devil at Dawn*. Anyway, this picture is a thriller, and he's done a first draft of the script."

"What's the premise?" Hopkins asked.

Listen to him, Barker thought. Getting into the lingo.

Zarkov said, "CIA counterintelligence agent tracks down a suspected Russian spy. There's a great reversal when he discovers it may be his wife."

"Wow. That sounds terrific," Hopkins said. "Who'll star?"

"I want Cruise. That's why I hope he'll show up tonight. I told him on the phone I wanted to discuss it with him."

"You think he'll go for it?"

"Good chance he will, yes. It's just the kind of offbeat idea that appeals to him."

"How about the female lead?"

Zarkov laughed. "That's easy. I get Cruise, I can take my pick."

"I assume there'll be plenty of action?"

"Absolutely. Audiences today are mostly kids. Teenagers. What you want to do is get them excited. First, put in enough sex to give 'em a hard-on. Next, show 'em how much fun it'd be to shoot somebody. Then you can't miss." He laughed again.

"You have a title?"

"Yeah, Gault came up with it. Picture'll be called *The Betrayal*."

"Ah, I like that." Hopkins was quiet for a moment. "If I were to invest in the project, would it be strictly financial? Or would I have any involvement with the actual production?"

"That'd be up to you," Zarkov said.

"Suppose I wanted to sit in on some of the creative discussions. With the director and the screenwriter, for instance. Would I be able to do that?"

"Of course. You'd always be welcome."

"Glad to hear it. Even though I've made my money through investments, I have a lot of creative ideas. I've even done a little writing. So contributing to the creative process would be important to me."

Zarkov nodded. "As I said, we'd be delighted to have your input."

"How about going to the set? Would I be welcome there too?"

"Sure. You'd be a partner, wouldn't you?"

"Sounds really interesting. So now comes the delicate part. How much would I have to invest?"

"I can't give you a precise figure, because I haven't finished making projections. There are a lot of variables, such as talent costs."

"How about a ballpark?"

Zarkov puffed out his cheeks and exhaled. "Okay, top of my head, production'll total around a hundred million."

"Isn't that very expensive? More than the average cost of making a movie?"

"Yes. But for an action thriller it's on the low side. Especially when we'll be shooting some sequences on location, places like London and Moscow. That costs money, and you can't cheapshot it."

"I see."

"Then there's another fifty million for marketing and advertising. So for the sake of discussion, a hundred fifty million is a reasonably accurate figure. Therefore if I let you in for say, ten percent, the share would cost you about fifteen million."

"And the profits?"

"Proportionate. Whatever the net, you'd get ten percent."

Hopkins tapped his fingertips together for several seconds. Then he said, "I like what I'm hearing, Len. Can you give me an outline of the deal?"

"Yeah, I can do that." Zarkov turned and picked up a phone from the desk behind him, touched some buttons. When he got an answer he said, "Find Tyler and send him in here. I'm in my office." He put the phone down.

"What happens," Hopkins said, "if you can't get Cruise?"

"Don't repeat this, but I'd go after Pitt. No problem there, he needs the money. Even though Angelina is the highest-paid actress in the business."

"Amazing."

"Isn't it? But then, everything costs more nowadays," Zarkov said, grinning.

He looks like a shark when he does that, Barker thought. Zark the shark.

There was a knock at the door. It opened and a man stuck his head in. "You wanted me, Len?"

"Yeah, come in and say hello to Bart Hopkins. Bart, this is Tyler Sturgis. Tyler's my lawyer."

Hopkins put out his hand without getting up, and Sturgis shook it. The lawyer then looked at Barker and frowned. "Who are you?"

"This is Jeb," Hopkins said. "He's with me."

Sturgis nodded, but the dour expression stayed in place.

"Bart is interested in making an investment in one of my movies," Zarkov said to him. "Specifically, *The Betrayal.* I want you to draw up a letter of agreement based on a share of ten percent of the cost of producing and promoting the picture, which I'm estimating at a total of a hundred fifty million. Profit to Bart would be the same proportion, ten percent of the net."

"You want the letter to include a breakdown of the costs?"

"Yes. Ed Conforti will be line producer. He has a copy of Gault's script. Ed and Norman here will get together and break down a tentative set of numbers. Director, crew, sets, the locations, transportation, and so on. They'll give you what they come up with."

"What about the cast?" Klein asked.

"Figure twenty-five million, depending on who I settle on. But no more than that, because I want to stick to the hundred fifty million total."

Sturgis said, "Timing of the agreement?"

"Give Bart a week after he receives it to decide whether he wants the deal," Zarkov said. "If he does, he's to provide my company, Zarstar, with a bank draft for fifteen million. If he doesn't, no hard feelings. That okay with you, Bart?"

"Yeah, that's fine."

Zarkov said to Sturgis, "Have the letter on my desk soon as you can."

"Will do." Sturgis backed out of the room.

"Where should I send the letter?" Zarkov asked Hopkins.

"Send it to my home." Hopkins took out his wallet, extracted a card, and handed it to the producer.

Zarkov rose to his feet and dropped the card onto his desk. "Hey, this calls for a celebration. Let's go out and get a drink."

24.

When they rejoined the crowd, it seemed to Barker there were even more revelers than before. And with recorded rock pounding above the babbling voices, the sound level had gone up several decibels. He took a glass of champagne from a waiter and raised it in a salute to Hopkins before downing the contents.

Next he moved to the table where the food was. After glancing over the lavish assortment of dishes, he loaded a plate with stuffed mushroom caps and crab fingers and oysters Rockefeller. A waiter refilled his glass, and he looked for a less raucous place to enjoy it all. A small room off the large one seemed promising, and he went in there.

This was apparently a reading nook; there was an long gray leather sofa and matching chairs and bookcases and a TV. On the sofa, a man was locking lips with a young woman and fondling her. They seemed unaware of Barker's presence. Or of anything else.

Barker put his glass down on a bookshelf and began eating.

"So what'd you think?" The speaker was Bart Hopkins, who'd followed him into the room.

Around a mouthful of crabmeat, Barker said, "More or less what I anticipated."

"Meaning?"

"Meaning he wants to con you out of fifteen million bucks."

Hopkins also had a glass of champagne. He drank some of it and said, "That might be. Although I have to tell you, everything he said made sense to me. And he's putting the deal in writing. I could take it or leave it."

Barker did not reply. Instead he tried one of the oysters. The spinach and the butter sauce gave it a wonderful flavor, he thought.

He also thought Hopkins might be losing his mind. Or at least his money, if he wasn't careful. Zarkov had done a pretty good job on him.

"The guy does have quite a track record," Bart went on.

"Yeah, he does that."

"I'm just mulling it over."

"Of course."

"I want to say hello to some people," Hopkins said. He left the room.

Barker took his time, savoring the food and drinking sips of champagne. He had to smile, thinking back to all the deli sandwiches and the cartons of coffee he and Spinelli had consumed. Once again, this was better.

When he finished, he walked out of the room. On the way he noticed that the man on the sofa now had his hand under the young woman's skirt. Making progress, Barker thought.

A waiter relieved him of the plate and glass, and another waiter offered a fresh flute of chilled champagne. Barker took it and wandered slowly through the crowd, keeping an eye out for Dana Laramie and wondering whether she'd actually made it here.

He was about to conclude she hadn't when he spotted her standing near the bar and talking to some guy. He kept watching her until he caught her eye, and when he did she tapped a finger against her ear. Okay, that meant he should call her. But he would have done that anyway.

A few minutes later Hopkins approached him and said, "I'm ready to go, okay?"

"Whatever you say, Bart."

As they made their way toward the front door, Barker noticed a very large man who was talking to a woman. He was so large, in fact, that he seemed about to burst his jacket. Barker recognized him at once, although he hadn't seen him since the day he'd gone to the Sherry-Netherland Hotel. It was Chuck Diggs.

The big man obviously recognized Barker as well. His eyebrows shot up, and then hunkered down again. He turned away.

I'll be damned, Barker thought. All kinds of surprises tonight. He followed Hopkins out the door, and an attendant took the card that identified the Rolls. The attendant sprinted off to fetch it.

Hopkins's mood was expansive. He waved an arm toward the lights below them and said, "We don't often get it this good. Not in the summertime, anyway. That's when the smog is usually the worst."

The Rolls came up alongside them, and attendants held the doors open. Hopkins tipped them, and the two men got into the car.

The trip back down to Sunset was as pleasant as coming up had been. Better, in fact, because in LA's desert climate the nights were much cooler than the days. Nothing like New York, Barker thought, where the humidity kept you sweating around the clock. Even the Rolls's headlight beams seemed cool.

When they reached Barker's hotel, Hopkins said, "Hope this was helpful to you. Although I don't think Zarkov was what you expected."

Barker didn't respond to that. Zarkov was exactly what he'd expected. And he now understood why Catherine Delure was issuing warnings that the producer was somebody to stay away from.

"Thanks for taking me along," Barker said. "And good luck with your investment."

Hopkins laughed. "Hey, all I said was, it sounded interesting. Tell you what. As soon as I get that letter I'll call you, and we can look it over together. Okay?"

"Yeah, that'd be fine." He shut the door, and the Rolls disappeared into the night.

When he reached his room, Barker took a leak and washed his hands and face and brushed his teeth. Next he turned on the TV and tuned in to a cable news station, which was showing damage sustained by a small town in Oklahoma that had been hit by a tornado. The announcer said the town had been battered by twisters many times, but residents had shown great courage by sticking it out.

Courage? Yeah, Barker thought, they sure had plenty of that. But he wondered if they also had rocks in their heads. From time to time they got blown away by a twister, so wouldn't it make sense to move? Instead, they stayed put, waiting to get hit again.

The thought brought to mind Bart Hopkins, and his fascination with the film business. Barker turned off the TV and glanced at his watch. Would Dana be home by now? He had only the number of her landline at her apartment. Should have gotten her cell number as well, but he hadn't. He picked up a phone and called the number she'd given him.

She answered on the second ring.

"Hi," he said. "Didn't know whether I'd catch you or not."

"I saw you leave with Hopkins, and I left right after that. How did it go?"

"Couple of surprises."

"Will you come over and tell me about them?"

"I sure will. Be there in a few minutes."

He put the phone down, thinking his luck was not only holding, it was going strong.

25.

When Barker walked in, Dana was eager to hear what had gone on at Zarkov's house. He told her about the pitch Zarkov had made, and about Hopkins's reaction.

She said, "You mean he might go for it?"

"He claimed he was just mulling it over, but he sure sounded intrigued to me."

"How did they leave it?"

"Zarkov told his lawyer to write up a letter of agreement he could send to Hopkins. Bart would then have a week to decide whether it would be a good idea to piss away fifteen million bucks."

"My God. No wonder Catherine warned him. Although apparently it didn't do much good."

"What about you? Did Zarkov ask you about Catherine's papers again?"

"Yes, the minute I arrived. I told him I didn't run across anything that would be a problem, and that he was welcome to look through the papers himself. Or have his lawyer do it, if that's what he wanted."

"How'd he react?"

"He said he'd have the lawyer get in touch with me. His name is Tyler Sturgis."

"Yeah, I saw Sturgis there tonight. Did Zarkov mention the job he offered you?"

"Yes. I told him it sounded attractive, but that I had to give it more thought."

"Good, you handled it well," Barker said.

"Did you get the impression Catherine was right about her husband's involvement?"

"Yeah, I did. Apperson's the one who first told Hopkins he could arrange an introduction to Zarkov. Recommended he invest in one of Zarkov's movies, in fact. And in the meeting tonight, Zarkov piled it on. By the time he finished, he had Hopkins's tongue hanging out."

"I thought Bart was smarter than that."

"Looks to me as though smart doesn't have much to do with it. When somebody like him wants to get into the movie business, he checks his brain at the door."

"So it seems," Dana said. "And you know something? Zarkov probably does this often. Uses Apperson to send him people who have a lot of money."

She was wide-eyed again, and Barker saw that the eyes were not only blue, they were almost violet.

"That would explain something else," she said. "When you saw me at the party, did you notice the guy I was talking with?"

"Not really. I saw him, but that's about all."

"His name is Tony Carpenter. He's from Texas, where his father made it big by speculating in oil. The old man died recently and left Tony a huge amount of money. Now he's in LA and guess what?"

"He wants to get into the movie business."

"In the worst way."

"And did he tell you who put him in touch with Zarkov and got him invited to the party tonight?"

"No, but I'll bet it was Apperson."

"So you're probably right, the scam is set up to haul in as many fish as possible. Although here's something I don't get. Suppose, just suppose, somebody like Bart Hopkins buys in and the movie does just what Zarkov says it will do. So the guy makes money and everybody's happy, right?"

"Sure, if it ever turned out like that."

Her eyes are definitely violet, he thought.

"Here's something I learned while I was working for Catherine," she said. "Zarkov and the studios work the same way. Each of their films is incorporated as a stand-alone venture. All kinds of expenses are charged off against it, not just the actual costs of talent and production. The result is that the movie does not make a profit. That way the actors and the director and the writer and anyone else who has a share never see anything but a loss. But that loss is based only on the income from box office receipts. Meanwhile the studio, or Zarkov, gets all the money from DVDs and foreign distribution and licensing."

She also smells good, he thought. Maybe she'd put on a touch of perfume when she knew he'd be coming here.

"Go on," he said.

"The point is that if somebody like Hopkins or this guy from Texas or anyone else puts in money and the picture fails, so what? Happens all the time, right?"

She also looked adorable when she was worked up, he thought. As she was now.

"And to fail," she went on, "the movie doesn't even have to be finished and released. It can fail at any time along the way. Production gets held up for some unforeseen reason or other, the talent balks at what they're being paid, the director goes nuts and spends so much unauthorized money he busts the budget, or all of those. Then the so-called investor is informed that Zarstar Productions is terribly sorry, but they ran out of funds and had to shut the project down. And his money? Forgive the pun, but it's gone with the wind. One consolation, he can list it as a loss when he computes his income tax."

Barker smiled. "Sounds as if you've got it pretty well tied down."

She paused. "Yeah, except for one thing. Catherine blowing the whistle wouldn't be enough to put her in danger, would it? To the point that somebody would kill her to shut her up?"

"You don't think that's possible? Let's say it's true that Apperson and Zarkov are running the scam as often as they can, at around fifteen million a pop. You're asking whether they might go to great lengths to protect that kind of money?"

"Um. I guess they might, huh?"

"The first homicide I worked on as a rookie," Barker said, "the victim was a woman in Washington Square Park. A guy tried to mug her but she resisted, so he stabbed her. He grabbed her purse and ran, but we tracked him down the next day and arrested him. The murder netted him eleven dollars and twenty cents."

"Okay, I understand. So it's possible Catherine stumbled onto what they were doing, and they had somebody go after her. I don't know that much about Apperson, but I do have an impression of Zarkov. People are leery of him, and you can see why."

What he saw was that this was his main chance. "Want to know what I think?"

"Of course."

He put his hands on her hips. "I think you're wonderful."

She didn't seem at all surprised. Nor did she move away. He drew her tight against him and brought his lips to hers. She didn't resist, instead opening her mouth and wrapping her arms around his neck and pressing her body even closer.

When she finally came up for air, she took his hand and led him into the bedroom.

26.

In the morning Barker opened his eyes and stretched and found that he was alone in the bed. The sun's rays were streaming through the window.

Last night had been great, he thought. Dana was not only beautiful, she was also extremely warm and responsive. Their lovemaking had gone on for a long time, and just thinking about it now made him feel good all over again.

He got up and went into the bathroom, where he conducted his usual morning routine. He took a long hot shower and then brushed his teeth. He didn't have a toothbrush, however, so he borrowed hers. He hoped she wouldn't mind, but what the hell, he'd had his mouth all over her, so why should she?

There was also a lady's razor in the cabinet, and some sweet-smelling shaving cream. He used those as well.

When he came out, he became aware of the smell of coffee. And then the aroma of bacon and eggs.

Dana called from the kitchen, "Hey, sleepyhead. Come and eat breakfast."

"Be right there."

He didn't have a robe, either, so his shirt would have to do. He pulled it on and went into the kitchen, where Dana was looking fresh and radiant in a lemon-colored silk wrapper. He put his arms around her and kissed her good morning, and then at her bidding he sat down at the table.

She put plates of bacon and fried eggs at both their places, and from the first bite it seemed to him he'd never tasted better. There was also buttered toast and blackberry jam and coffee that was so strong a spoon would have stood straight up in it, and all that was delicious too.

He ate ravenously, and when he finished, she poured more coffee for him. He sat back and said, "What a breakfast. Thank you."

"Glad you liked it."

She put her hand on his. "You must be pretty happy this morning."

He smiled. "I am. You were sensational."

She returned the smile. "So were you. But not just because of that. I meant because you've figured it out. You know what Zarkov and Apperson are doing, and that Catherine may have been in danger, or was even killed, because she knew it too. You've practically got it solved, Jeb."

This time he laughed out loud.

"What's funny?"

"Just that nothing's solved. There's only a theory. It might be on target, might not. But even if it is, it's still a theory and nothing more."

She looked crestfallen. "But—"

"Don't misunderstand. You've been a lot of help to me, and I really appreciate it. The problem is I don't have so much as a scrap of evidence to back up what we've been conjecturing."

"It's something to follow through on, though, isn't it? I mean, it just seems so logical, the way things fit together."

"Yeah, I'll admit that. But then what? At this point I have no basis to charge Zarkov and Apperson or anyone else with Catherine Delure's murder. So what could I charge them with? Fraud? That's not my job, and it's not what I'm after."

"I understand what you're saying. Arresting them for fraud would be up to the authorities here in LA, right?"

"Sure. And they'd have the same problem. What is there for them to go on? What's the basis for an ADA to ask a judge to sign a warrant?"

"What's an ADA?"

"A prosecutor. ADA is for assistant district attorney. Or as they're called here in California, a deputy district attorney. And even if the judge went along, what could the prosecutor take to a grand jury? The accused committed a crime by offering suckers a chance to invest in a movie?"

"That would sound a little thin, wouldn't it?"

"Would to me. According to what you've said, people can't give their money to a hustler like Zarkov fast enough. And not just to him, but to a lot of other operators in the movie business. Isn't that true?"

"So it seems."

"And as you've also pointed out, most movies don't make money, they lose it."

"Right again."

"So where's your case, Counselor?"

She smiled. "Sorry, Your Honor, for wasting the court's time."

"You haven't. I'm just showing you where the holes are. But as I said, you've been a lot of help. My next problem will be gathering some evidence. And also locating a very important missing piece."

"What is that?"

"The killer. The creep who went to the hotel in New York and committed the murders. If I'm right, he was hired to make the hit. So the questions are, who is he and who hired him? Find him and I get the answer to the first part, and maybe the second as well."

"You think he's here in LA?"

"Could be. Or maybe he's still in New York. Or in a few million other places. But if I don't have him, I don't have anything. I have to find him."

She drew in her breath. "That makes my blood run cold."

Barker rose from his chair and drew her to him. He stroked her back, running his hand down below the edge of the wrapper.

"I have to leave soon," he said, "and get back to work. But before that, I'll do my best to make your blood warm again."

She flicked her tongue against his lips. "It's already getting there."

Still holding her close, he guided her back into the bedroom.

27.

Harold Strunk was on his second cup of morning coffee. He was working on a real estate deal, and when the call came in he was annoyed at being interrupted. But when his secretary told him who the caller was, he picked up. "Yeah?"

"Good morning, Harold. How's it going?"

Strunk considered small talk a pain in the ass. "What do you want?"

"I think I might need you to arrange another assignment."

"Somebody should take a vacation?"

"Yes. A permanent one."

"Where is this person?"

"In LA."

"You said you might need this. You don't know whether you do or not?"

"It's not firmed up yet."

"Why not?"

"There's the matter of the fee."

"What about the fee?"

"The last one was very expensive."

"Balls. What you got was a bargain. And besides, I have a feeling that for your client, a couple hundred thousand bucks is bird shit."

"He doesn't see it that way. Especially because this new situation is much simpler."

"The fee is what it is. Like I told you up front, it's a flat rate. You want this other one on the cheap? Hire somebody yourself."

"Harold, I'm only doing what my client wants me to do. And that's negotiate. Surely you can understand that?"

"What I understand is money. And I don't negotiate. So tell your client he'll get what he pays for. That means it goes to a satisfactory conclusion, without fail. And there's no way for anything to be traced back to him. Not ever. So pay the fee and that's it, take it or leave it."

"Yes, but—"

"Let me remind you, the last one most people would've considered impossible. But it got done, didn't it? And even with the biggest police force in America going all out, the cops couldn't come up with doodly-fucking-squat. Now you're trying to hondle? What do you think I'm running, a pants store? You want fifty percent off?"

"Harold, be reasonable, okay? I'm sure my client was just testing the water. I'll let him know the fee is nonnegotiable, and we'll see what he says. I'm confident we'll move ahead."

"Yeah, sure," Strunk said, and hung up.

He went back to the papers on his desk. The real estate deal was complicated, and completing it would require all his legal skills. A location in downtown Beverly Hills would have to be condemned and then sold to the trust Strunk controlled for a fraction of its true worth. For that to happen, not one but several members of the city council would have to be paid off.

But he'd succeed, he was sure of it. No problem was too tough for Harold Strunk. He buzzed his secretary and told her to bring him more coffee.

As he drank it he resolved to cut down on his caffeine intake, which was a resolution he made every day and never acted on, even though the stuff made his nerves as taut as the strings on a banjo. He was finishing the cup when another call came in from the same party.

"I've talked with my client," the caller said. "He continues to think the fee is on the high side. But I pointed out to him the advantages as you outlined them, and he agrees that they're considerable."

"Cut the shit," Strunk said. "Do we have a deal, or don't we?"

"Yes, Harold. We have a deal."

Strunk picked up a pen. "Who's the person who should go away?"

28.

Mongo was bored out of his mind. He'd gone for his usual run on the beach, and after that had run through his exercises. Now he'd spend the rest of the day reading and watching TV. Maybe later he'd go to the supermarket and pick up something for dinner.

It was a dumb way to waste time, and he was itchier than ever. He paced back and forth in his small living room, finally settling down to call up a porn movie on his computer.

The movie didn't do much for him; the girl was a dog compared to the ones he hired. Still, watching her writhe and squirm and hearing her moan aroused him, even though she wasn't very convincing.

For a minute he toyed with the idea of calling a service and having them send someone, but he dismissed that idea as too risky. He'd never had a girl come to the cottage, and it would be stupid to start now.

Maybe he ought to drive into Hollywood, drop in at a place he knew, get himself some action. That would wipe out the boredom. A good piece always did that for him.

Hell, he'd settle for a blow job. Especially one from a beautiful Filipino who worked there. Her name was Danao, and she had a mouth like a vacuum cleaner.

That idea brought to mind the incident that had taken place in Vegas, when he'd been snookered by that lousy bitch who tried to steal from him. The thought made him angry all over again. Although it shouldn't have, because the fault had been his.

He'd known better than to trust a female. You could play with one, do whatever came into your head, but you always had to keep your guard up.

That was a lesson he'd learned early on, when he was just a snot-nosed kid. And it had been delivered to him by his own mother.

One of the things he'd enjoyed was peeking into the bedroom when she was doing what she called entertaining a friend. It was something she did several times a night, and with a different friend each time. It was comical to see some lard-ass huffing and puffing away.

But then on one occasion Mongo became careless and sneezed. His mother jumped out of bed and beat him with a shoe and threw him out of the little dump they lived in.

He stayed away from home for two days, eating whatever he could steal from a neighborhood bodega, sleeping curled up in an alley. When he finally went back he found her in the bedroom, stone cold and with the needle still stuck in her arm.

How could he ever have trusted her? A mother was supposed to take care of you when you were little. But with her, that was a joke.

The truth was, you couldn't trust any of them. Like the broad in Vegas, for instance. Whether he himself had been to blame or not, he shouldn't have let her off with just a kick in the ass. Should have tossed her down the elevator shaft. That would've served the bitch right, and it would have been a hell of a lot more satisfying.

The phone rang, jarring him. He picked up.

"That you?" the garbled voice said.

Mongo tensed. He'd been waiting forever for this, had been angry he hadn't heard. Now at last, here it was. "Yeah, it's me."

"You have work to do," the voice said.

"Okay, fine. But I got news for you. Prices have gone up. And I need an advance."

"Don't worry, you'll get one. And when the job's finished you'll be well taken care of."

The electronic distortion made the words hard to understand. Mongo strained to catch their meaning. "Go on."

"This one you'll like. He's a detective from New York, and he's here in LA. His name is Jeb Barker."

Mongo sat up straight. A dick from New York? Here in LA? And that was the target?

"He's staying at the Sunset Inn," the voice said. "Get it done."

The call ended, and Mongo stared at the phone. He hit the replay button and listened to the call again. As he did, a number of thoughts went through his mind.

Apparently the cops were much further along than they'd let on. Not only had they come up with a lead, they'd known where to send a detective. The son of a bitch was right here in the city.

But Strunk was right when he said this was one he'd like. Take out a cop? Christ, what a pleasure that would be. The cop had come out here to run him down, but before he could do that, Mongo would wipe the fartbrain off the face of the earth.

29.

First there were a couple of things that had to be taken care of. Mongo wrapped the wig in an old newspaper, stuck it into the fireplace, and set a match to it. He watched it burn, and when it was nothing but a lump of ashes, he opened the trap and shoved the remains into it with a poker.

Next he dealt with the tape recorder. Destroying that required a little more muscle. He took it outside and laid it on the ground and smashed the case to bits with the axe he kept for chopping firewood.

The compressed-air cylinders remained intact, however, so he pushed those aside. He swept up the plastic splinters and dumped them into a plastic bag, and dropped the cylinders in as well before tying the bag shut.

While he was doing this, he thought about the job ahead of him. It wouldn't be easy; a New York detective was a different proposition from the dipshits he usually dealt with.

The cop would most likely be alert and suspicious, and therefore it would be vital to slip up on him. Mongo would have to be gone before the guy ever knew he was in danger.

In his days as a kid in the hood, Mongo had been an accomplished street fighter. His technique had been to size up his opponent, and then give him something he wasn't expecting.

In those days, it was often a quick shot with his homemade sap, a short length of wood with nails driven through it. When the guy bent over in pain, blood streaming down his face, Mongo would whack him again. Surprise, surprise, motherfucker.

That was the kind of thing he had to plan now. Something totally unforeseen. Except that it would have to be much more sophisticated. More along the lines of the way he took out the two bitches in the hotel in New York.

Carefully planned and executed, that one had been his masterpiece. He should have had their heads mounted so he could hang them over the fireplace.

With the detective, the first step would be to identify him, find out what he looked like. That might also reveal some telling characteristics. Was he a big guy, and strong? Look like he had good reflexes?

Important to know those things. Carrying the plastic bag that contained the remains of the tape recorder, Mongo left the cottage and went out to his car.

He drove south on the coast highway, and at a point near Paradise Cove he spotted a dumpster at a construction site. He pulled close to the dumpster and tossed the bag into it.

Continuing on, he turned off onto Sunset and traveled east. As usual the traffic was heavy, and by now the sun had burned off the fog.

He drove at a moderate pace, staying in the right-hand lane. Other drivers overtook him—one in a Mercedes, another in a BMW—and he tried to ignore them as they flashed past.

It wasn't easy; he felt a twinge of resentment. Why should those bastards be driving such cars while he was stuck in this lousy little Oriental shitbox?

He knew why, just as he knew why he was careful to stay within the speed limit. He'd learned not to call attention to himself when on the road. A traffic stop could lead to the cop asking him questions and running his license through a computer, and Mongo did not need that.

Nevertheless, he wished he could be driving the kind of car he felt he deserved. A Porsche, say, or a Ferrari. Top down, a broad by his side, whaling along with the engine screaming. Way to go, man.

For that matter, his whole life needed tuning. Living in a cottage in Malibu wasn't bad. But it was hiding, damn it. And an occasional trip to Vegas wasn't nearly enough to offset that.

So what would he do to turn things around? He already had a plan. Although he needed more money to carry it out. With enough of it, he could get the hell out of the States and live the way he wanted. Strunk sent part of each fee to Mongo's bank account in the Cayman Islands, and settling there would be sensational.

But right now he had a job to do. When he reached the Sunset Inn, he left the Toyota in the parking lot and went into the hotel. In the lobby he picked up a house phone and asked the operator to connect him with Mr. Barker.

A deep male voice answered, and Mongo said, "This is the reception desk, Mr. Barker. There's a man here who wants to see you. He won't give his name, but he says he's got valuable information for you."

"Information about what?"

"He won't say that, either. But he says you'll know what it's about. He'll wait for you here at the desk."

After putting the phone down, Mongo picked up a copy of the *Los Angeles Times* from a table and walked to a chair in the farthest corner of the lobby.

He sat and opened the newspaper, not reading it but holding it so that it obscured his face. From time to time he glanced over the top of the page, keeping an eye on the desk.

A minute went by, and then another. He saw various people walk through the area, saw some of them go to check-in and others stop at the cashier's station, saw still others stroll in and out the front entrance. Men and women, none of them anything like what he was expecting.

And then, there he was. A husky dude wearing a blue button-down. Black hair cut short, square jaw, nose maybe a fraction off-kilter. It had to be the cop.

Mongo watched him go from the elevators to the front desk and speak to the clerk, who shook his head and shrugged. The guy then glanced around and finally returned to the elevators. He stepped into a car along with several other people and the doors closed.

Mongo now had his pursuer pegged, knew exactly what he looked like. He also knew the dick was in good shape and probably quick on his feet. He'd be quick mentally, too. The fact that he'd made detective at a relatively young age indicated that.

Besides, the NYPD would not send some pussy out here. As Mongo had expected, the target would be no pushover.

He began to fold the paper when something caught his eye.

Jesus Christ—there was the fucking drawing!

It took up a quarter of the page. The caption said it was a new composite showing the Delure killer and that it had been created by the police in New York.

He still wasn't sure how much it resembled him. For one thing, he believed he was better looking than that. He stared at the image intently and reluctantly decided the grim face in the drawing was a lot closer than the first attempt. He'd have to be more alert than ever.

Getting to his feet, he walked to the entrance casually and dropped the paper onto the table on his way out to his car.

From the hotel he drove east once again, and then onto 101 South. He turned off at the Alvarado Street exit, which put him in one of the city's poorest neighborhoods.

It was called Pico-Union, because it sprawled outward from the intersection of Pico Boulevard and Union Avenue. To the LAPD it was part of the Rampart Division.

This was an area Mongo knew well. Once affluent, there were

still a number of buildings and homes here that revealed its former prosperity. But now the structures were crumbling and neglected, and many were inhabited by squatters.

The population was nearly all Hispanic. There were people from Mexico, El Salvador, Guatemala, and Honduras, and many of them were in the United States illegally.

The area had the highest crime rates in Los Angeles, with gang-bangers constantly at each other's throats. This was where the Hacienda Village Bloods and the La Mirada Locos and dozens of other gangs had sprung to life.

He continued south, noting that the neighborhood was exactly as he remembered it. Boarded-up stores, small dingy houses, kids roaming the streets looking for something to steal. The asshole of the city.

After making sure he wasn't being followed, he drove into an alley. Slipping between two clapped-out buildings, he stopped before a third.

There he waited, knowing he was being observed. After a few moments a metal door rolled up, and he drove inside the building. He shut off the ignition and got out of the car. As he did, the metal door rolled shut behind him.

A man was standing there. He had close-set eyes and a stubbled jaw and greasy black hair. He was short and muscular and his arms were long and covered with tattoos. More tattoos decorated his neck in a crisscross pattern, and there was a star on his forehead.

"Ay, compadre," he said.

Mongo grinned. "Ay, Culebra. You get uglier every time I see you."

Culebra returned the grin, revealing a mouthful of gold teeth. The two men slapped hands.

Mongo looked around. There were no windows in here; light came from overhead fluorescent bars. As always, he was fascinated by the objects in this place.

Parked just ahead of him was a '54 Chevy coupe. The car had been chopped and channeled and had been given a coat of primer.

Under the hood was a 700-horsepower supercharged marine engine that Culebra had converted and fitted to the drivetrain. He claimed that when he finished, the car would have a top speed close to two hundred miles per hour. Mongo would not doubt it.

Next to the Chevy was the chassis of another old car, that one a sedan. The heads were off its V-8 power plant, and parts and pieces were scattered about on the floor beside it.

Against a wall was a workbench bearing a variety of tools, along with containers of nuts and bolts and other materials. A number of machines were there too, including power saws and shapers and a drill press. Another wall held shelves packed with more equipment, as well as cans of substances ranging from oil and paint to different types of chemicals.

There were also guns, Mongo knew. They were hidden in a cabinet behind the shelves. Among them were rifles and pistols and several automatic weapons such as Uzis and AK-47s.

Beside the gun cabinet was a door that led into a cubbyhole where Culebra sometimes slept on a cot when he'd been working late. There was a sink and a toilet and a hot plate and a refrigerator in there—everything a man could ask for. A man like Culebra, anyway.

"So how you doing?" Mongo asked him. "Keeping busy?"

"I always got work," Culebra said. "If I want it."

"You ever see anybody?" He meant any of the guys from the old days who were still alive.

"No. Chico was around for a while after he came down from Centilena. He was in for armed robbery and did six years in that shithouse."

"He here now?"

"No, man. He got mixed up with another guy's woman. She belonged to a Norteño, but it didn't make no difference to Chico."

"So what happened?"

"The guy caught him in bed with her. Chico was almost out the door and the guy shot him in the back four times. Even with all that lead in him, he still made it halfway down the street before he died. He was a tough motherfucker."

"One of the best," Mongo said. "But not as good as you."

Culebra cocked his head. "Don't shit me, okay? What are you looking for?"

"I got a problem. There is a certain party that needs to go. Trouble is, I have to take him out in a way that nobody could ever tie me to it."

"What way are you talking about?"

"That's the problem. I don't have a way. So I thought, the man to see about it is Culebra. If anybody would have a good idea, you would."

"This party. He in town?"

"Yes."

"He gonna be carrying?"

"For sure."

"If he sees you, would he know what you had in mind?"

"Maybe. Depends."

"How close can you get?"

"Hard to say."

"Mmm. Poison might work."

"Sure. I tell him bend over, and then I stick cyanide up his ass."

Culebra scowled. "Don't get *mordaz*, okay? You want me to help you or not?"

"Sorry. Any other ideas?"

"How about a bomb you could put under his car?"

"Too much exposure. For me, that is. I'd have to go crawling around underneath the car to attach it."

"No you wouldn't. I got Primacord you could use." He swung a shelf aside and opened the gun cabinet. "See? I got a roll of it right here."

"What's Primacord?"

"Fastest-burning fuse there is. Burns around three thousand feet a second. You could connect it to a blasting cap and connect that to the bomb. Then you just roll the bomb under the car and pay out the Primacord. When you got far enough away, you touch a match to it. Pow! No more car, no more problem."

"Too complicated. What else?"

"That tape recorder I built for you. It was a fucking work of art. Why not use that?"

"It's out of commission."

"Too bad."

"It worked great, though."

"Uh-huh. And you screwed me on the price."

"Come on, Culebra. If you weren't happy, I would've paid you more."

"Yeah? You didn't offer to do that at the time. What I recall, you were crying poor-mouth."

"Look. You give me what I need, and you set the price. I'll pay it, no argument."

Culebra gestured toward the gun rack. "I got a Barrett .50 caliber over there."

"A rifle?"

"Sniper rifle, with a scope. Very accurate. You could put one in his eye from a thousand yards. Pop his head like a grape."

Mongo thought about it. "That's a possibility."

"Sure, let me show you." Culebra reached into the cabinet and took out the weapon. It was long and bulky, finished in matte black and equipped with a telescopic sight. "This is the best in the world."

"Where'd you get it?"

"There's a guy from here, he went in the Army. He gets me all kinds of shit. That's how I got the Primacord." He handed the rifle to Mongo.

"Heavy mother."

"Uh-huh."

"And noisy, right?"

"Sure. A fifty is a real cannon. You talk about power? With this you could put a slug through a brick wall."

Mongo passed it back. "Could you fit it with a silencer?"

"You don't want much, do you?"

"I told you it was a problem, didn't I?"

"Yeah, you did. But I guess I could rig one up." He put the rifle back into the cabinet. "How soon you need to do this?"

"I'd do it now, if I could."

"What am I, a fucking magician?"

"In my opinion, yes. That's why I came to you."

One corner of Culebra's mouth twisted upward in a knowing smirk. "You always were some bullshitter, Mongo. I never saw nobody could shovel it like you. Even when you were a kid, you had that."

"So when could you have it ready?"

"Couple days."

"Okay. Just remember, I need it soon as possible."

"I'll do what I can. But don't try to fuck with my head when I say what it costs."

"I told you, set the price, and I'll pay it."

"Fine. Fifteen grand."

"What? Jesus, Culebra."

"Just like I figured. More bullshit, huh? See you around."

"No, no. I'll pay it. Couple days, you said?"

"Right."

"You're my man."

30.

In his room at the Sunset Inn, Barker looked at the faxes from Joe Spinelli that Lia had held for him at the desk. One was the photo of the fléchette, the other was the new composite.

The face bore only a faint resemblance to the one in the first drawing. Without the hair and the mustache, the guy had a much harder appearance, and his expression was intimidating. Looked like a different man.

Next Barker leafed through a stack of phone messages. One was from Dana, and that one couldn't wait; he really wanted to see her. He called her number and got an answering machine. He said, "I miss you," and added that he'd try again later.

Another call had come from his partner. When Barker returned it, Spinelli said, "You get the faxes?"

"Yeah, thanks."

"What'd you think of the new composite?"

"It's great. In fact, the guy looks a little like you, Joe."

"Very funny. But you should see what happened after it was

distributed. Now Hogan's up to his ass in leads, and from what I can tell, they're all bullshit. Mostly guys trying to make trouble for somebody they got a beef with. And also women pissed off at their husbands or their boyfriends, calling in to say they're the one we're looking for. But we have to run all of them down, which could keep us busy till Christmas."

"What about the wig?"

"The lab says it's real hair that was dyed blond, and that it most likely was made in China. Seems that most of them come from there nowadays, there and India. Impossible to say where the guy might have bought it. There's retailers in every city in the country."

"Anything else?"

"Yeah, how about we swap assignments? I'll come to California and work on my tan, you come here and chase wigs and red-hot leads."

Barker laughed. "Keep me posted, Joe."

Still another call had come from Sergeant Sam Benziger. He returned it, and she answered. "I've got something that'll interest you," Sam said. "We've had an arrest warrant out for a hooker named Marcia Slade. At least that's the name she uses most of the time. She was rolling johns in various hotels here in LA, and then she disappeared. We just got a call from the police in Vegas saying they picked her up on the same charges."

"Why would that interest me?"

"She claims she did business with the perp in the Delure case. She wants to make a deal. If charges on both ends are dropped, she'll give him up."

"You wouldn't agree to that, would you?"

"No, we wouldn't. But we could offer to negotiate. And that might flush out whatever she's got."

"Are you going there?"

"Yes. I thought you might want to come along. No guarantee, of course, that she's telling the truth about your case."

"What time is your flight?"

"Southwest has one every hour. You don't need a reservation. I'm leaving for LAX in a few minutes."

"Okay, I'll meet you in the waiting area."

Barker left the hotel and jumped into his rented Ford. He hurried down 405 as fast as the traffic would permit, which was not very fast. That was the trouble with LA: more cars than people, and not enough roads to handle them. New York was bad enough. This was worse.

Nevertheless, he reached the airport before Benziger. At Southwest he had to go through the rigmarole of presenting his ID and filling out the form that would enable him to take his pistol aboard. It would've been simpler not to carry it, but NYPD regs required him to have it with him at all times.

When Sam showed up, they took the 6 P.M. flight. Barker asked her whether she had more details on the hooker.

"Native of San Diego, twenty-seven years old," Benziger said. "Her sheet shows six arrests in LA, charged with loitering for purposes of prostitution. Which is no big deal. Under California law, prostitution is defined as disorderly conduct. It's the other charges we want her for."

"As I recall, prostitution is legal in Nevada, right?"

"Yeah, but not in Vegas. Although that's a joke. The cops there try to keep the city clean, but they're pissing into the wind."

"So how come you're on this, Sam, instead of Vice handling it?"

"Because of the robberies. Also, we may be able to tie her to a homicide. A year ago a guy was found dead in the Beverly Hilton. He had a plastic bag over his head. So either it was part of some erotic stunt, or she killed him before robbing him. Security tape showed him entering the room with a female. We think she resembled Slade's mug shot."

"She roll him too?"

"Probably, but we can't say for sure. Her MO is to take a john's cash, but not his credit cards. She's smart enough to know using them would leave a trail. The Vegas authorities should let us have her, because our warrant predates their arrest. And also because what we want her for is more serious."

"Good luck with that."

"Thanks. She'll probably try to fight extradition, but Nevada's very cooperative with California. Still, it might take some doing."

"I hope she's right about the guy in the Delure case. That'd be a nice break. Incidentally, here's something you might be able to help me with."

He took the fax showing the fléchette from his blazer pocket and handed it to her. "Here's what the killer used to take out Delure and her manager."

She looked at the fax. "This is the fléchette you told me about?"

"Right. He shot each of them with one of these. Hit them right in the heart. Naturally we haven't released that information to the public. I wonder if any of your people might have some idea where it came from."

"Okay if I keep this to show them?"

"Sure."

31.

Fifty-five minutes after takeoff they landed at McCarran Airport. It was still daylight, but the city was ablaze with neon, reminding Barker of a gigantic jukebox. A cab took them to police headquarters, which was on East Lake Mead Boulevard in North Las Vegas.

The department was a fairly large operation. Both the male and female cops wore crisp tan uniforms with Metropolitan Police patches on the left shoulder. The place was busy, and from what Barker could see, most of the people who'd been arrested were drunk. What's more, many of them had cuts and bruises and were disheveled. No surprise, since Vegas was America's greatest party town.

Benziger's contact was Chief Milford Ingram, who oversaw all functions of the department, including the Investigative Command. A big, gruff cop who'd obviously spent years climbing the ranks, Ingram was relaxed and cordial. He poured them all mugs of coffee from an urn that sat on a bookcase near his desk.

Benziger said, "So how's your girlfriend, Chief?"

"She's a real sweetheart. Never did anything wrong in her life. Or so she says."

"She ask for a lawyer?"

"Not so far. Probably thinks she can talk her way out of the charges."

"From what you told me, she was doing guys here the same way as in LA."

"That she was. First she rocked 'em, then she rolled 'em."

Barker smiled. It was probably one of Ingram's favorite lines.

"How many?" Sam asked.

"Hard to say," the chief said. "Could be dozens for all we know. But we only got two complaints, and one of them refused to press. Most guys don't want anybody to find out what happened."

"How'd you get her?"

"The john who complained said he could identify her. He claimed he'd seen her before in a couple of casinos. So we had him make the rounds with a female detective, and sure enough, they spotted her at the bar in the Mirage. When the officer told her she was under arrest she tried to run, but Lori coldcocked her."

"Lori's the female detective?"

"Yeah, Lori Schmitt. She's one of the best. Lot of times when we run a street sting, she plays the bait."

"Can we have a chat with the suspect?"

"Sure. I'll have Lori get her."

Ingram picked up a phone and asked that Marcia Slade be brought from a holding cell to one of the interview rooms. Then he led Benziger and Barker to the room.

When the two women entered, Ingram introduced them to his visitors and had them sit on the other side of the table.

To Barker, Lori Schmitt didn't seem much like a cop. She was slender and blonde and wore a pink sweater and a gray skirt. But then he caught a steely glint in her eye that said she was nobody to mess with.

Marcia Slade wasn't what he'd expected either. He wouldn't call her refined, exactly, but she was a long way from what most working girls looked like. Dark haired and with large hazel eyes, she had on a close-fitting azure dress that revealed a well-sculpted body. When Ingram asked her if she'd like some coffee, she politely declined.

She looked at Barker. "So you're from New York?"

"That's correct."

"Then you know what I have is valuable."

"It might be."

Sam Benziger said, "And it might not be."

"If you don't think so," Slade said, "why'd you come out here?"

"You know why. There are charges against you in LA as well as here."

"And like I told the chief, I'm willing to make a trade. In both places the charges amount to nothing but misdemeanors. Drop them and I'll give you what I know about the guy who did Delure and the other one."

"They're more than misdemeanors," Ingram said. "Stealing is against the law. And you stole from a client."

The courtesy act came to an abrupt halt. In a flat tone, Slade said, "What the fuck is this? I admit I turned a trick, but I never touched a cent of that fool's money except what he paid me. I just left the room, and that was that."

Ingram said, "Sure, Marcia. But the gentleman told us he paid you a thousand dollars, and afterward he fell asleep. When he woke up, he was out three thousand more. Three thousand one hundred and twenty, to be exact."

"So maybe he walks in his sleep, and he flushed it down the john. Or maybe he's just a liar. Where's the proof he's telling you the truth?" She shot an acidulous glance at Lori Schmitt. "And what gave this bitch the right to muscle me?"

Schmitt's expression was calm. In a soft voice she said, "How'd you like another shot in the teeth, pussy-face?"

Ingram held up his hands. "Ladies, ladies. Let's remain civil, shall we?"

"Listen, Marcia," Benziger said. "Here's what we might be able to do. Give us enough so we can put a value on what you have, and we'll consider it. If it's as good as you claim, we'll do our best to make a deal with you. Okay?"

Slade was quiet for a moment, obviously thinking it over. Finally she said, "All right. A couple weeks back there was this guy. He thought I was an amateur and he hustled me. I went along, and he took me up to his room."

"Where was that?" Ingram asked.

"The Crystal Palace."

"What room?"

"I'm not sure. Best I can remember, I think it was 512."

"Go on."

"We had a drink and after that we made it. I didn't charge him anything. But later when I was putting my clothes on, I noticed some things on the dresser. There was a plane ticket, and the name on it was different from what he told me. Also his driver's license was lying there and that had the same name as the ticket."

"So?"

"So I know his real name and the city where he lives."

Barker said, "How do you know he's the man we want?"

"I saw the new drawing you guys made in New York. It was on TV, and I recognized him right away. In the drawing he was bald, but he wasn't really. While I was with him I noticed his hair was just fuzz, so it must have been growing back in again. That made sense, because the stories in the paper said he was wearing a wig and a mustache when he did those women. He must've shaved the mustache, too."

"What else did you notice about him?"

"He had a tattoo on his left shoulder. It looked like it was home-made. Like the ones guys do in prison."

"Can you describe it?"

"Yeah, it was a fishhook. About two inches long."

Ingram said, "He treat you okay?"

Her eyes flashed. "No, the son of a bitch. He punched me out and took my clothes. Then he dragged me out of the room and kicked me down the stairs. He did all that for no reason at all. He was one mean prick."

"You say you didn't charge him. Why not?"

"I don't know. Just found him attractive, I guess."

"Bullshit. What you wanted was to get him to pass out so you could roll him."

"That's a lie. I never rolled anybody."

"So what was the name," Barker asked, "on the ticket and the license?"

"That mean we've got a deal?"

"Not up to me. Chief Ingram has to decide that. And Detective Benziger."

"Decide, then."

Ingram said, "We'll need to discuss it. I don't want to speak for the others, but it sounds like it's a possibility. Lori, take Miss Slade back to the cell, please."

"Oh, shit," Slade said. "Make up your minds."

Schmitt rose to her feet. "Let's go."

Slade's mouth twisted into a grimace, but she got up and the blonde cop steered her out of the room.

Ingram looked at his visitors. "So what do you think?"

"There any way," Sam asked, "to check out the story about the Crystal Palace?"

"Could be," Ingram said. "The manager over there is a bum, but I can get him to cooperate. Let's take a ride."

32.

They made the trip in a police cruiser. It had become dark by now, and the city's lights were not merely bright, but dazzling. Everywhere Barker looked, he saw red and white and orange and yellow and green neon. The lights flashed and pulsed and whirled, and he thought if you paid enough attention to them you could go nuts. Or at least come down with vertigo.

The group's progress was slow, because of the crawling traffic. As he drove south, Ingram passed the Venetian and the Casino Royale and Harrah's. The Crystal Palace was not on the strip. To reach it, he turned off onto Flamingo Road.

When they approached the hotel it was apparent to Barker that this was not one of the fabled superglitz places, such as the Bellagio or Mandalay Bay. Instead it was smaller and a little out of the way.

If Marcia Slade was right about her identification of the guy, he must have had a reason for staying here. Maybe he'd thought it would be better cover. Or maybe it was cheaper.

Smaller hotel or not, its casino was running full-bore when they walked in. There was a crowd around each of the blackjack tables, and people were also jammed close to the craps games. At the slot machines, players were putting in chips with a steady rhythm that made them seem as though they were part of the same mechanism. Nearly all those playing the slots were women, and older women at that.

Ingram and his visitors stopped to survey the scene. Barker noted that the air was thick with tobacco smoke. Most of it was from cigarettes, but a few cigars were also adding to the haze, the smokers nonchalantly puffing away. That was a major difference from public places in New York, he thought, where the mayor considered smoking to be as antisocial as child rape.

Benziger coughed, and Ingram said, "Lousy air, huh? The town's been trying to ban smoking for years, but without much progress. Some of the newer hotels have got smoke-free areas, like the MGM Grand, for instance, and the Monte Carlo. But mostly this is what you get."

"Maybe it has to do with the players' psychological makeup," Sam said. "They figure they might as well go for broke, gamble with their lungs too."

As they stood there, no one paid any attention to them, although Ingram was in full uniform: cap, shield, shoulder patch, holstered pistol, boots.

They were even welcomed, in a way, as a young woman in spike heels and shorts and a low-cut blouse approached them. She was holding a tray of drinks and asked if they'd like one. Ingram waved her away.

"Hey, Chief," someone said. "Nice to see you here." This was a guy wearing a tuxedo, and he had hair that was greased back and parted in the middle. He was smiling broadly as he drew near.

"Hello, Harry," Ingram said.

"Anything we can get you?"

"No, thanks."

The guy stuck out his hand to Benziger. "Hi, I'm Harry Holloway. I'm the manager of our little inn."

Sam shook the hand, and then so did Barker.

The manager turned his attention back to Ingram. "So what brings you here, Chief? Come to see the show? We got a great one starting in about twenty minutes."

"We came to see your tapes," Ingram said.

The smile never left Holloway's face. To Barker it looked as though it had been put there permanently, through plastic surgery.

"Glad to show them to you," Holloway said. "But this really isn't a good time."

He waved a hand toward the action in the casino. "We have to keep watch on what's going on. And as you can see, we're busy. How about tomorrow morning?"

"How about now?" Ingram said. "Or do I have to find reasons to issue citations?"

"No, no, you don't have to do that. I guess we could accommodate you. If it won't take too long. Is there something in particular you're looking for?"

"Yeah, there is. So let's go."

For a moment Holloway hesitated, as if he was trying to come up with another reason to stall, but then he led Ingram and the others to the rear of the main floor, where the private management offices were located. He unlocked a door, and they stepped inside.

As Barker looked around, he thought of the security center in the Sherry-Netherland in New York. That one was primitive compared with this. Here, there was a much larger control console, and stacked banks of monitors showing every gambling pit in the hotel, as well as every inch of open space.

Three men were at the console, studying the monitors. Barker saw that the cameras covering the pits showed images of the action from any angle the operators wanted. By touching keys, they could view what the eye-in-the-sky was seeing, or look at the players, or even zoom in on the dealer's hands.

Holloway called one of the men over and introduced him as Fred Mitchell, head of security. Like his associates, he wore a short-sleeved sport shirt.

"Our friends here need to look at something we might have on tape," the manager said.

Mitchell said, "Oh?"

"It's okay, Fred," Holloway said. "Naturally we want to cooperate." He turned to Ingram. "Can you tell us what it is you're interested in?"

"We want to see what happened one night about two weeks ago," the chief said. "Outside room 512."

Both Holloway and Mitchell seemed to relax a little. Holloway said, "We should be able to find that. Right, Fred?"

"Uh, yes. I think so."

Again Holloway turned to Ingram. "I'm sure you know, Chief, some of what goes on is a little crude. But we can't help that, it's just that at times our guests aren't exactly what you'd call well mannered."

"Yeah, I know," Ingram said. "But I'm not here to give you any trouble."

Mitchell pointed. "We'll use this monitor. About two weeks ago, right?" He went to the console and began pressing buttons.

For almost an hour Barker and the others stared at the monitor as Mitchell called up what seemed like miles of tape. Most of what they saw was innocuous enough, although many of the people going into or leaving rooms on the fifth floor were clearly drunk.

And as Holloway had warned, some of the guests were indeed crude. In more than a few instances the tape showed couples staggering along the corridor, the men groping the women and the women laughing or doing some groping of their own before the pair disappeared into a room.

Several times, single women could be seen knocking on a door and being admitted, and those were obviously hookers on their way to do business. Once a guy lurched from the elevator and got halfway down the hall before falling to his knees and vomiting into a sand urn. Undaunted, he got up and tottered into a room.

Barker was starting to become bleary eyed when still another couple was shown walking down the hall. But when he took a good look, he said, "Hold it!"

Mitchell froze the tape, and Barker and Benziger and Ingram leaned closer to the monitor. The woman they were seeing was dark haired and slim and wore a tight-fitting dress.

"That's Slade," Sam said. "No doubt about it."

Barker agreed. But he was more interested in the man. This one was tall and trim and although he was almost bald and had no mustache, there was something about the way he carried himself that was familiar.

Seen from above by the security camera, his features were hard to make out, but Barker had looked at the tape in New York often enough to be sure he recognized him. "I believe," he said, "we've found our boy."

Mitchell reran the sequence several times, and each time he saw it Barker became more convinced.

So did Benziger. "If the guy looks like the one you want, maybe Slade's got something."

"What about the rest of what she claimed?" Ingram said. "Let's keep going."

It took Mitchell several more minutes to find that part. And when he did, there was no longer any question that what Slade had told them was true.

The image showed the man emerging from the room, dragging the woman along. He was dressed, and she was stark naked. He pulled her to the stairway door, opened it, and delivered a vicious kick to her backside. Then he closed the door and returned to his room.

"I want copies of those tapes," Barker said.

Ingram said, "So do I. Make copies for each of us. And also, give us the name of the man who was registered in that room."

For once Holloway's expression changed, to one of earnest concern. "Oh hey, Chief. You know we'd need a court order to do all that. Not our idea, of course. We do our best to follow the rules."

"Sure you do. So I'll just take another look around, see what other rules you're following. Or not following."

"Okay, okay. Jeez, I'm not trying to be difficult."

"Then don't be."

Holloway exhaled. "Mitch, make copies for them."

"In fact," Ingram said, "make 'em as CDs."

It took only a few minutes for the security man to comply and to give each of the trio a disc.

"And now let's have the name," Ingram said.

For a moment, Holloway looked as though he might put up another argument. But then he stepped to a computer and began working the keys. It took him less than five minutes to find the information.

"Name's Morris Wagner," he said. "Address is 341 Chambers Street, Houston, Texas."

"You mean that's what he gave the desk," Ingram said.

"He had a credit card and a driver's license, so we had no reason to doubt him."

Barker made a note of the information, and he and Sam and the chief walked out of the room and back through the crowds at the tables on the casino floor.

Holloway tagged along, the corners of his mouth again curled upward. "I hope," he said, "you'll remember how cooperative we've been."

"Depends," Ingram said.

He and the others left the hotel and got back into the cruiser. As the car crept bumper-to-bumper up the strip, they discussed what they'd seen and how they'd handle the next move.

33.

Twenty minutes later, the chief and his visitors were once more in the station's interview room. Ingram again called Lori Schmitt, and the blond cop escorted Marcia Slade into the room.

Ingram led off. "We've talked it over, Marcia, and we decided there's no way for us to know whether you're telling us the truth. Or even if you are, what value it has."

Slade's eyes glittered. "And that's it?"

"Afraid so."

She shook her head. "I don't believe this." She looked at Barker. "I can give you the guy you want, and you're turning me down?"

"No," Barker said. "We're not doing that. It's just that you haven't told us enough so we can be sure. We need something more."

"Like what?"

"Like the name you saw on that plane ticket, and on the driver's license."

Benziger said, "At least then we'd have something to go on.

Something we could check. If that pans out, I guarantee we'll do our best to throw out the misdemeanor charges."

"And what about the charges here?"

"Same thing," Ingram said.

"All right, I'll go along," Slade said. "The name he told me was Don Quinn. But the one on the ticket and the license was Morris Wagner."

"And where was he from?" Barker asked.

"Los Angeles."

"Not Houston?"

"No, LA."

"What address?"

"I didn't get that."

"Okay," Sam said. "What you've given us will help with the other charges, too. Show that you were trying to cooperate."

"Wait a minute," Slade said. "What other charges?"

"Homicide and robbery, in Los Angeles."

"What? What the hell are you talking about?"

"In the Beverly Hilton one night last year. You were in a room there with a john. In the morning, he was found dead and his money was gone."

Slade turned pale. For a moment she said nothing. Then her voice rose. "I want a lawyer!"

"Certainly," Ingram said. "You can call one, if you want. Or we'll have one appointed for you."

"You lousy bastards."

The chief had Lori Schmitt take Slade from the room. As she left she spat invectives about stinking, lying cops.

Barker and Benziger thanked Ingram for his help.

"Been a pleasure," he said. "But now comes the battle. Some of the lawyers here have done a good job fighting extradition. They lose in the end, of course, but meantime they run up the tab. Which the state pays. Or I should say, the taxpayer."

"All for the cause of justice," Benziger said. "But this has been a worthwhile trip for me."

"And for me," Barker said. "I hope. No telling whether the name is genuine, but at least I know he went back to LA. It's something to chase down. Same with that business about the fishhook tattoo."

Ingram smiled. "You don't think anybody can ID that for you, do you? Every guy in prison's got tattoos. Some of 'em look like they got more tattoos than skin."

"The fishhook might be a gang symbol, though."

"Yeah, maybe. Say, you folks gonna stay over for a bit? There's lots to do in our fair city."

"Not me," Sam said. "I want to get back tonight."

"Me too," Barker said.

"Okay, I understand. But let me give you a lift back to the airport."

Once more they piled into the police cruiser, and Ingram drove them to McCarran Field. They thanked him again, and after registering their weapons caught the next Southwest flight to LA.

Sitting next to Benziger in the airplane, Barker said, "I really appreciate your taking me along, Sam. This might turn out to be a good break."

"Hope it does. Like I told Chief Ingram, it was good for me, too. I wasn't sure Slade was the one we wanted on the robbery charges until tonight. Now I don't have any question. Proving she did the guy in the Beverly Hilton is another story, but the prosecutor can help us sort that out. Once we get her back in LA, we'll have enough to put her before a grand jury."

"You'll also check out this Morris Wagner in LA?"

"Yeah, I'll let you know what that turns up."

When the flight landed it was past midnight. Walking through the terminal, Sam promised to set up a meeting between Barker and a ballistics expert at the forensic lab. She said the tech might be able to supply some good information on the fléchettes.

Sam would also see what could be done about identifying the man they'd seen on the Crystal Palace videotape. The two cops wished each other good night and Barker walked to his car.

He thought Dana most likely would be asleep by now. So she

wouldn't be happy to have him pop in on her. Or have him call and say he wanted to see her.

On the other hand, maybe she would. He got out his cell and called her number.

When she answered, her voice didn't sound at all sleepy. "I was hoping you'd call," she said.

His spirits took a decided upward bounce. "I'll be there as soon as I can."

"Wonderful. Can't wait to see you."

He put the cell back into his pocket and walked faster.

34.

The Hertzberg-Davis Forensic Science Center was on the campus of the California State University at Los Angeles. The crime lab was the largest and best equipped in the United States and served both the LAPD and the Sheriff's Department.

Sam Benziger called Barker to tell him she'd contacted a ballistics expert there who could help him.

"His name is Deke Edwards," she said. "If anybody can answer questions about those fléchettes, he can." She then gave Barker directions to the college.

To get there he drove eight miles east on Route 10. When he reached the campus he saw that it sprawled over many acres.

There were more than twenty academic and administrative buildings, plus a library and a theater and athletic facilities. The Forensic Center was at the south end, a large five-story building that was said to have cost over a hundred million dollars to construct. As he walked in, Barker could believe it.

At the desk in the lobby he showed his ID and said Deke

Edwards was expecting him. He was directed to take an elevator up to the floor where Edwards's workstation was located.

The ballistics expert was a lanky guy with a gray buzz cut. He had on a white lab coat, jeans, and cowboy boots. When Barker approached, Edwards was crouched over an electron microscope. He got up and the two shook hands.

The first question he asked was the usual one: "I just made coffee. You want some?"

"Thanks," Barker said. "That sounds good."

"How do you take it?"

"Black."

There was an assured manner about Edwards that reminded Barker of some of the lifers he'd known in the Marine Corps. Edwards stepped over to a table on which a large urn rested and poured two mugs full. He handed one to his visitor.

Barker had expected the coffee to be strong, but this stuff was downright powerful. And bitter. As he sipped it he took in the activity in the area.

Like Edwards, most of the techs wore white coats. They were using various pieces of equipment, including a magnaprobe and a centrifuge and chemical processors and a number of other devices Barker couldn't identify.

"Looks like you're busy," he said.

"Yeah, we always are. Big as this place is, it still ain't big enough for all the work that needs to get done."

Edwards led the way to a corner where there was a small desk and two chairs. The desk was piled with folders and papers and held a computer terminal.

"So how are things in New York?" he asked.

"We're busy too," Barker said. "The Delure case has us all scrambling."

"I expect it would. I never been to New York. Hope I never have to go." He picked up a fax that showed a fléchette with a ruler alongside it. "Sam Benziger sent me this. Said you wanted to ask me if I could tell you anything about it."

"I hope you can," Barker said. "The perp used two of them to kill Delure and her manager."

Edwards looked at the fax. "I can tell you right off, it's not like any fléchette I ever saw before. I spent twenty years in the Army before I came on the job here. I was in Ordnance, and we developed artillery shells that could scatter thousands of fléchettes when they hit. We called the shells 'beehives.' They were effective against infantry and were used in Afghanistan. We also bundled them in shotgun shells, twenty fléchettes to a shell. But all those were much thinner than this one."

"I was in the Marines," Barker said. "We had some of them too."

"Then you probably know we're the only country that ever used the small-bore type in combat. They produce serious wounds, but they're only good at short range. After that they go off course pretty quick. You saying this was fired by itself?"

"Right."

"In the Army we experimented with shooting a single fléchette from a shotgun, but it didn't work too good. We found out a round ball was more accurate. So the idea of firing one fléchette at a time was abandoned."

"Okay, but this photo was taken right after the ME performed the post. He took a fléchette like that out of Delure's heart."

"So it was probably fired from up close. Then accuracy wouldn't be a problem. The stories in the papers and on TV just said both women had been shot. Didn't say anything about fléchettes."

"No, we didn't release any information about the killer using them. We've kept that under wraps, for obvious reasons. I think I know why he used them, but I'd like to hear your opinion."

Edwards drank the last of his coffee. "First off, the perp had to know putting one in somebody's heart would kill them in a hurry. Second, he probably had a way of firing them so it wouldn't make a lot of noise. A loud report would've caused an uproar, and then he would've had a tough time getting away with the jewelry."

"Assuming robbery was the motive."

"That's what you guys think too, isn't it? I saw your boss on TV, and that's what he was saying."

"I'm not so sure. But what could the killer have used to propel this if he didn't fire it with gunpowder? Would compressed air work?"

"Sure. A really heavy charge of compressed air could shoot it with plenty of power. That would make some noise too, but not as much. And just like the beehives, it'd be accurate for only a short distance."

"Anything else occur to you about it?"

"Yeah. From what I can see, this thing is homemade."

"Why do you think so?"

Edwards opened a drawer and took out a magnifying glass. He held it over the fax. "Take a look here. See how the fins aren't exactly the same size? How one of 'em's just a hair bigger than the others? Also, the way they're joined looks to me like a spot weld. So this thing wasn't manufactured, it was hand-built."

"That's interesting," Barker said.

"Another thing. A fléchette is usually encased in a sabot to make the propellant more efficient. Soon as the fléchette leaves the gun, the sabot falls away. I don't see any mark on this that would indicate it was in a sabot. That's another way this one is crude."

"Okay, I'm with you," Barker said. "But here's the key question: Is there anybody you know of who could make this? Anybody in LA?"

"Oh, I suppose there's gunsmiths or machine shop operators who could do it. But they wouldn't, because fléchettes are against the law in California."

"That's probably true in a lot of places, isn't it?"

"No, only in Illinois and Florida, besides here. Every place else they're legal and available. You can even buy 'em by mail. They're nothing like this one, though."

"So who are the people who could have made it?"

"Well, we know of a few gun dealers that buy and sell weapons illegally. Just haven't been able to catch 'em doing it."

"Would any of them have the capability to make a fléchette like this? And provide a weapon that could fire it?"

"Hard to say. Mostly they're just dealers. But there's a few who can repair and modify guns, and some of 'em are pretty good at it. So it's possible one of them could make fléchettes along these lines, if somebody waved enough money at 'em."

"Wouldn't somebody in a machine shop do it too, for the money? Or a gunsmith?"

"Maybe. But you want to look at guys who've got a rep for smuggling firearms and doing conversions. Somebody who takes semi-automatics and turns 'em into full automatics, things like that. They're the ones to look at."

"Can you give me names, and addresses?"

"Yeah, I can do that. Just have to take a few minutes to see what I can come up with."

"Sure, go right ahead."

Edwards sat back and stroked his jaw for a moment, then began tapping his computer keyboard.

Barker had given up on the coffee. He resumed watching the activity in the lab. If anything, the place was busier than when he arrived.

As he sat there, a uniformed cop and a young woman wearing a business suit came in and began talking with one of the techs. The woman was probably a DDA, he thought, and she and the cop would be looking for information on a case. Just like what you'd see in New York, except that this lab was a hell of a lot bigger. And no doubt better equipped.

"Okay," Edwards said. "Here's the ones I'd suggest you look into. There's four of 'em, and if there's any more I think of I'll let you know. Or I'll let Sam Benziger know and she can pass the word on to you."

"That's great," Barker said.

"Let me send this to the printer." Edwards hit the keys again, and then he led Barker over to a large Xerox machine.

Someone else was using it and they had to wait a few minutes, but then Edwards had the machine spit out a sheet of paper. He handed it to Barker.

"Thanks, Deke. Hope to return the favor. Maybe when you come to New York."

For the first time, Edwards's face split in a grin. "Fat chance. Good luck with those guys."

35.

Dana's phone rang, and she was quick to pick up, hoping the caller was Barker.

It wasn't. But the voice was familiar. "Dana Laramie?"

"Yes?"

"This is Alex Haynes. I was Miss Delure's lawyer."

"Yes, I know. Hello, Alex."

"I hope you're holding up well under the strain. I'm sure her loss was a terrible experience for you. I understand you were with her when she was shot."

Hearing it put that way was like having her nerves sandpapered. "I was in the suite, yes."

"You have my sympathy. Reason I'm calling, besides that, has to do with settling her estate. Ironically, her manager had her sign a will. I say ironically because poor Penny was killed too."

"It was all very sad."

"The will is fairly simple. Leaves proceeds to her family, and her brother, Roger, is the executor. I'm handling the details here, and

I'm busy inventorying her possessions. It's quite a task, as you can imagine."

"I'm sure it is."

"Catherine was a dear person," Haynes said, "but she wasn't very careful about keeping track of transactions, or of what she owned. Even though Penny tried to help her with that, too. I went to her house recently and took some of her papers. I've been going through them, but how complete they are, I have no way of knowing. You have some of her records as well, don't you?"

"Yes, although I doubt that what I have is any different from what you found. What I have are just copies of business correspondence. The same as what was in her files at the house."

"And perhaps some personal items? Notes, and things like that?"

"Only a few bits and pieces that don't amount to anything."

"Fine, but I have to be sure. I wouldn't want to overlook anything. So I'd like to get together with you, and we can go over whatever you have."

"I guess that would be all right." It wouldn't be, but she could hardly refuse.

"How about lunch today? Are you free?"

"Yes, I am."

"Good. Let's say one o'clock at Mario's, on Rodeo Drive."

"Okay, I'll be there."

"Incidentally, you'll be pleased to know Roger has instructed me to tell you that you won't have to worry about your income being cut off. He'll continue paying your salary until you decide what you want to do next."

"That's very kind of him."

"He's a kind man. And he loved his sister. He's aware that Catherine and you were close."

"We were. I was very fond of her."

"I'm sure you were. So I'll see you at Mario's. Bring any and all papers that relate to Catherine."

"I'll bring anything I can find."

"See you then."

After putting the phone down, Dana went into her bedroom and opened the drawer in her dresser where she'd stored the material she found in Catherine's bedroom.

She'd be damned if she'd share this stuff with Haynes. Most of it was just too personal. Although she'd shown almost everything to Barker, so what was the difference?

Haynes was a lawyer, that's what. And she'd learned not to trust lawyers. So except for a few really innocuous receipts and letters from Catherine's women friends, it would all stay right where it was. Everything else was stored on her laptop, and as she'd told Haynes, that material was all business correspondence.

She sat on the bed and wondered if she was being silly.

She wouldn't trust a lawyer, but she'd trusted a cop. For that matter, if anybody had told her a few days ago that she'd be having a red-hot relationship with a police detective from New York, she'd have said they were crazy.

And now? Maybe she was the crazy one. She'd rarely felt the way she did about Barker with anyone else, although some of her lovers had been pretty nice guys.

She still had fond memories of the first one, a kid she'd known in high school who had long blond hair and played the guitar. His name was Christopher and he claimed that someday he'd become a famous musician. He'd been accepted at the Berklee College of Music in Boston and had gone there to study. She had no idea what had happened to him after that.

There were others she'd thought a lot of too: a fellow student when she was an undergrad at UCLA, a French instructor who was working on his PhD, a poet who could recite Shakespeare's sonnets by the hour. Thinking of the men now called up pleasant memories.

There'd also been some creeps, of course. Including her most recent boyfriend, the actor. What could she ever have seen in him?

Okay, so he was good-looking and could make her laugh. But after she'd discovered he was also busy screwing other people, she couldn't stand to be near him.

And he wasn't the worst, either. There had been a few she could hardly believe she'd had anything to do with. Including one who was another actor, a guy who'd played guard for the 49ers before picking up bit parts in movies. At first she'd been captivated by his raw strength, his tremendous sex drive. But after only a couple of nights with him, she'd concluded it was like sleeping with a bear. A horny bear with a huge, smelly, hairy body. Whereupon that relationship had come to an abrupt end.

Seemed funny now, but it hadn't at the time.

Jeb Barker, on the other hand, was different from anyone she'd known before. He had an easygoing manner, and a direct, open way of addressing any subject, regardless of how complicated it might be. She felt that he never tried to mislead her.

What it came down to, she supposed, was that there was nothing phony about him. And she'd been around the movie business long enough to encounter phoniness on a grand scale. In fact, she could write a book about it.

But that wasn't all she found appealing. Barker was strongly masculine and had great confidence in himself. He didn't parade any of it, but to her it was almost palpable.

And she had to admit it: in bed he was wonderful. Never rushed, knew how to take her as high as she'd ever been, and seemed to care more about pleasing her than himself.

So what was the bottom line? It always came back to the same thing: she trusted him. That might appear a little nutty too, when she considered how suspicious she'd been at first, and how brief a time she'd known him.

But nutty or not, her instincts told her he was rock-solid dependable.

She took one more look at the pile of scraps Catherine had left behind and closed the drawer. She'd pick out the ones she'd show Haynes later.

One thing the lawyer had told her was a welcome bit of news. Roger Delaney would continue paying her salary. That was really very good of him. As Haynes had said, Roger was a kind man. She'd have to thank him.

She looked up the number of his office and called it. A secretary said he wasn't in, but when Dana explained who she was, the woman said he could be reached at his home in Connecticut.

Dana had that number as well, and when she called it, a maid answered. Again Dana explained, and at last Roger came to the phone.

"Dana! How nice to hear your voice. I have a note here to call you, but you beat me to it. How are you?"

"I'm well, thanks. And you and Mrs. Delaney?"

"Oh, we're all in reasonably good shape."

"I'm glad to know that. Alex Haynes told me you'd continue paying my salary until I decide where I'll go from here. I wanted to thank you. I really appreciate that."

"Don't mention it. If there's anything else I can do for you, just let me know. Catherine thought highly of you, and that makes you special as far as we're concerned. Alex is handling the legal matters out there, probate and so forth. At the moment he's making an inventory of Cat's things."

"Yes, he told me. He asked me to have lunch with him today, and to bring any of her papers I might have."

"Fine. I've been trying to tot up everything I know about, although I'm sure he has much more complete information. He said he has the deeds to her house in Beverly Hills and the one in Switzerland, as well as the titles for her cars, and so on. He's also been in touch with her accountant concerning her tax records. Seems the IRS is already sniffing around. You said you'll be seeing him today?"

"Yes."

"One thing I'd like you to do, if you would. Knowing Cat, I'm sure she saved a lot of personal notes and letters and things like that. Do you have access to them?"

"I do, yes."

"Then please don't include them in the material you'll be taking to Alex. I have faith in him, but sometimes things of that nature have a way of winding up in the wrong hands, if you know what I mean."

"Of course I do."

"Good, I thought you would. And one other point. It's rather sensitive, so I want you to be very discreet. Did Cat ever tell you she was in danger? Or is there anything in her personal notes that would suggest she thought she was?"

Dana hesitated. "There are a few notes along those lines. But I don't know how serious she was when she wrote them. They're really little more than fragments. Nothing is actually explained."

"I see. Did you know she wrote to me, describing her fears? In the letter she made it clear that she'd discovered something illegal that was going on. And apparently she believed that simply knowing about it put her in danger. As you're aware, the police are going on the theory that the murders were committed because the killer wanted to steal Cat's jewelry."

"Yes, I know. That's what they said when they had me help with the composite drawing."

"And yet a detective came to see me on the day of her funeral. I took him into my confidence and gave him a copy of the letter. Obviously what it contained could send the investigation in a whole new direction. But I think the police may be keeping it a secret while they try to determine the murderer's real objective. Do you follow?"

"Yes, I do."

"So here's why I'm telling you all this. I wouldn't be surprised if the detective were to contact you. If he does, my advice is to cooperate with him as much as possible. If anything could help solve the murders, it would bring closure to this whole terrible incident. And more important, it would provide some bit of justice to Cat and Penny. I'm sure you want that too."

"Of course I do."

"And one last thing. When you see Alex Haynes today, please don't mention any of this to him. He's a perfectly fine lawyer, but this aspect of the situation is none of his business. He just might try to contribute, and by doing so he could muck up the works. Okay?"

"Yes, okay."

"Very well. All best wishes to you."

She put the phone down, her head whirling.

So Roger Delaney didn't trust lawyers either. Including the one who'd been his sister's personal attorney. The reason he'd given for keeping Haynes out of the loop had been vague. What was it he knew about Alex Haynes?

But she'd do as he asked. If he didn't want her to tell Haynes what she knew about the investigation, then she'd keep her mouth shut about it. And she'd also follow Delaney's advice about cooperating with the detective.

As far as that last part was concerned, she was already cooperating with him. In fact, she was cooperating with Barker as much as one person could cooperate with another.

36.

Barker kept his right hand on the steering wheel of the Ford as he drove south on the Santa Ana freeway. His other hand held the cell phone to his ear.

"We got a suspect," Spinelli said. "And this time he's a live one. When Hogan got the word, he was jumping up and down."

"Who is he?"

"Street name is Danny the Dip. Or just 'the Dip.' Ever hear of him?"

"Don't think so."

"He's a jewel thief with a sheet down to the floor. His real name is Daniel Ennis, but when he's working, he gives himself fancier ones. Last night he claimed he was Reginald Montgomery, a British citizen. He looked the part, too. In fact, he looks a lot like Prince what's-his-name."

"What prince is that, Joe?"

"The one who's married to Queen Elizabeth."

"Philip?"

"Yeah, him."

"So how'd it go down?"

"There was the Governor's Ball at the Waldorf. Very formal, with the women in gowns and the men in white tie and tails. How exactly the Dip got in we don't know, but apparently he has ways of getting himself invited to society events. Once he's there, he snags whatever he can."

"Go on."

"At the ball, he asked a woman to dance. While he had her in his arms, he took off her diamond necklace, so smooth she didn't even know it. But before he could put it in his pocket, it slipped out of his fingers and slid down her back. He grabbed it, and at first she thought he was just copping a feel. But then she caught on and screamed her head off."

"Then what?"

"The Dip dropped the necklace and tried to run, but a guy in the security detail cut him off and the two of them started slugging each other. More security piled on, and the Dip was taken into custody. Right now he's at the precinct house and is still being questioned. Says the woman was confused, and he did nothing wrong."

"Has he been questioned about Delure?"

"Yeah, for hours. He says all he knows about that is what he saw on TV. But Hogan is already telling the media we may have our man. And get this, the Dip was packing. Had a .22 in his waistband."

"A .22? That's a popgun."

"Not as far as Hogan's concerned. To him, it's like he had a howitzer. Hogan's saying he was armed and dangerous."

"What about the composite? Does this guy resemble the one in the drawing?"

"Maybe if you squint."

"Okay, what else?"

"That's it for the moment. You having a good time?"

"Wonderful, Joe."

"Don't suppose I should ask if you're making any progress?"

"I might be. If I do make any, I'll be sure to let you know." Barker ended the call.

A few minutes later he turned onto Third Street and reached his destination. A sign over the door said LUKE'S GUN SHOP. He parked the Ford and went into the store.

A guy with a short black beard was behind the counter, talking to a customer. In the display case under the counter there were dozens of pistols of various makes and calibers. Apparently the bearded one was Luke, the owner.

One other person was in the shop, a man who was looking at rifles that were held on wall racks. Barker stood by, waiting his turn to talk to the owner.

"I want something real powerful," the customer at the counter said. He had a beer belly and wore a vest over a checked shirt. "Maybe a .44 Magnum."

"I've got one more powerful that that," the beard said. "In fact, it's the most powerful handgun in the world."

"Yeah? What is it?"

"A Pfeifer-Zeliska .600 Nitro Express Magnum."

"Hey, show it to me!"

The owner unlocked the display case and took out an enormous revolver. He held it up, using both hands.

Barker had never seen anything like it. The pistol had a long barrel and a wooden grip. It resembled the guns made famous in the Old West, except that it was much larger. He guessed the length to be close to two feet.

"Jesus," the customer said. He stared at the pistol with reverence. "That is some piece."

"It sure is," Luke said. "Has to be this big so it can accept the cartridges. See, they were originally made for rifles by Purdey in England. Hunters used the cartridges to shoot elephants in Africa. You asked about a .44? This one's eight times more powerful. Got a muzzle velocity of 1,950 feet per second. More than four tons of energy."

"Jesus," the customer said again.

Barker thought of the conversation he'd had earlier with Joe Spinelli. So the suspect in New York had been armed with a .22? Compared to this, a .22 was indeed a popgun.

But for that matter Barker's own sidearm was no rival for the huge pistol, either. His was a compact 7.65 Mauser automatic held snugly in an ankle holster on the inside of his left leg. That was where he always carried it and had for so long he was hardly conscious it was there.

Luke continued his description of the revolver. "It's made of superhard tungsten steel. And as you can see, the hammer, the extractor, and the knockout cylinder bar are all gold plated."

The guy who'd been looking at rifles came over to the counter. He wore a sweatshirt with the Harley-Davidson logo on the back. "Must have a hell of a kick," he said.

"Actually, it's not too bad," Luke said. "Gun weighs just over thirteen pounds, and that's partly to handle the recoil." He handed the pistol to the first customer.

"Man, you're right about the weight," the customer said. He peered at the cylinder. "I see there's five shots."

"Yeah, and single action," Luke said. "For added strength."

"Where's it made?"

"Austria. You want one, you have to order it. I only have this one for display."

"Goddamn," the customer said. "I do believe I'd like to have one. How long would it take to get it?"

"Couple months. Every one of 'em's custom built."

"Worth the wait."

"No question."

"How much?"

"Eighteen thousand dollars. Cartridges are forty bucks apiece."

The customer's eyebrows arched. There was a pause, and then he handed the pistol back to the owner. "Have to think about it."

"Fine, just let me know."

The customer left the shop, and Luke returned the weapon to the display case.

The second customer laughed and said, "When he found out how much it cost, he about shit."

"Yeah, they're a little pricey for the average guy. What can I do for you?"

"Need some twenty-gauge, number six shot. Going pheasant hunting. Better give me two boxes."

Luke got out the boxes of shells and placed them on the counter. "Need anything else?"

"No, that'll do it."

Barker looked at the pistols in the display case, noting that nothing came close to the Pfeifer-Zeliska .600 Nitro in size. He waited patiently while the customer paid for his shotgun shells and left the store.

"Yes, sir," Luke said. "Help you?"

"You're a gunsmith, right? Do gun repairs?"

"Yep. Got a problem with a gun?"

"No, no problem. I have a sort of unusual request."

"Yeah? For what?"

"I want some fléchettes, but not the ordinary kind. I want ones that are a lot heavier. I'd shoot them one at a time."

"Can't help you there, mister. Don't have anything like that. Besides, fléchettes are illegal in this state."

"I realize that. But I'm willing to pay anything for them. You could probably make the kind I'm looking for, right?"

A few seconds went by, and then the shop owner said, "You a cop?"

Barker smiled. "Don't worry. I'm not from the LAPD, or the FBI, or the ATF. And I don't want to kill anybody."

"Then what do you want the fléchettes for?"

"I guess you'd call it an experiment. I'd also need some advice on what to shoot them with. At first I was thinking maybe I could take the bullets out of heavy-caliber rifle cartridges and replace them with the fléchettes."

"Uh-huh."

"But then I realized that wasn't practical. So maybe you'd have another idea. Maybe rig an air pistol to fire them. Would that work?"

"Might. If the air pistol had enough power."

"Would you be willing to try it? And make some fléchettes for that purpose?"

"I don't think so."

"Like I said, I'd be willing to pay whatever you ask."

"That's not it. I can repair just about any problem with pistols or rifles, but making something like what you want is out of my league."

"Then maybe you'd have some idea as to where I could buy the type of fléchettes I'm looking for. Or maybe you know somebody who'd be able to make them?"

"Not offhand. You might try contacting gunsmiths in Montana, or Idaho, where they're legal. There's some good people in those places."

"Okay, I'll do that. Thanks for the advice."

Barker left the shop and returned to his car. He looked at the list of four possibilities Deke Edwards had given him and felt rising frustration. Luke had been number three on the list, and like the first two, a strikeout. There was one more, not too far from where he was now.

This time he'd drop the pretense of looking for someone to construct fléchettes for him at any price. It hadn't worked so far, although he couldn't be sure the dealers he'd talked to had leveled with him. Instead, he'd try identifying himself as a cop. See if he couldn't shake the next guy up, get him to reveal something.

He looked at the list again. The name was Culebra.

37.

Mongo had thought long and hard about using a sniper's rifle to take out the cop. He decided Culebra was right. It would be a good solution, for a number of reasons.

Leading off was the rifle's power. He wouldn't want to take a chance on just wounding the guy, and with a .50, one shot would be enough. A rifle like that could stop a train.

Then there was the range. Unlike most of his previous jobs, he'd probably have a tough time getting close to the target. With the .50 he wouldn't have to. Which was good, because from what he'd seen of the cop, the guy was sharp and alert. Much better to whack him from a distance.

A drawback was the noise, but Culebra was rigging up a silencer. That was important. Without one, the .50 would sound like a clap of thunder when it went off.

He'd want to be careful, though, about picking the place to take his shot. It would have to be a location where he could hide, so he wouldn't be seen lining up on the guy. And he'd need a good escape route.

The rifle should be ready by now. Culebra wanted to gouge him on the price, but what the hell. Seen in the light of what he'd be paid for the hit, fifteen grand was chump change.

He went into the bedroom closet and took down the large steel lockbox from the shelf. Lugging the box to the kitchen table, he unlocked it and swung back the cover.

Inside were packets of hundred-dollar bills. He counted out fifteen thousand dollars and put the bills into his attaché case. After locking the box, he took it back to the closet.

Driving to Culebra's place would be a drag. It was late afternoon, and traffic would be even worse than usual, if that were possible. He left the cottage and got into the Toyota, placing the case on the floor by the passenger's seat.

Even pulling out onto Route 1 was a problem. He had to wait several minutes before he could squeeze into the stream of cars and trucks. And when he finally did, it was bumper to bumper moving south.

He told himself to cool down, but that was hard to do. When would this goddamn state build more roads or revoke the licenses of at least half the idiot drivers who clogged the highways? Jesus, if he were governor, instead of that jerk in Sacramento, he'd straighten out the mess in a hurry.

As he'd expected, the drive took almost an hour. When he reached the old neighborhood, he felt the inevitable mixture of contempt and nostalgia. Litter and filth in the streets; junky old cars squatting at curbside; shabby, falling-down houses marked with graffiti; ragged kids chasing one another and shouting curses. Hadn't changed, never would.

And yet, seeing it tugged at his emotions. In some ways his boyhood days seemed long ago. But at times such as this, it was as if they'd happened yesterday.

He was approaching the alley that would take him to Culebra's shop when he noticed a car about fifty yards ahead of him. The car was a gray Ford sedan, and the driver was inching along, as if he was unfamiliar with the area and was looking for something. As the car drew near the mouth of the alley, it slowed further. Finally, it turned into the narrow gap between the buildings.

Mongo drew to a stop and watched intently. This must be one of Culebra's patrons, he conjectured. Some gangbanger who needed a weapon, or maybe expert help with a mechanical problem. But if that were true, why the cautious approach? Didn't make sense.

And another thing. The car was wrong.

Nobody with cojones would be caught dead driving such a piece of shit. That was a grandmother's car, or one for a maricón.

But somebody doing business with Culebra? Forget it. A gangster's ride would be a Cadillac, or a Lincoln, with the suspension lowered and the body jacked up with pearlescent paint and extra chrome.

So who was this guy, and why was he here?

Mongo continued on, and as he passed the Ford he got a good look at the driver. He took in the short black hair and the set of the jaw and felt his gut muscles clench.

Christ, it was the cop!

But hold on. Could he be mistaken? No, there was no question it was the dick from New York, the detective named Barker. The man he'd been assigned to kill.

As Mongo went by, he saw the metal door begin to roll up. So Culebra was letting him in. Somehow the cop had learned of the connection, and here he was.

But how had he done it? How had he figured it out? Or stumbled onto it? Was he here to get more information?

Or did it go beyond that? Had Culebra ratted? That couldn't be. Or could it?

Mongo went on down the street, and when he was close to the intersection he swung the Toyota into a U-turn. He drove back to a point where he could park among the clapped-out junkers and slipped into the space. Settling down low in the seat, he kept an eye on the alley.

For a few seconds Barker thought perhaps he'd gotten the address wrong. Or maybe Edwards had. The alley appeared to be blind, leading to nothing but a metal wall that was brown with rust.

But then he caught sight of a flicker off to one side of the wall and realized he was being watched through a peephole. Okay, he'd decided earlier how he'd play this one. He took out his shield and held it up to the windshield.

He'd guessed right; the wall began lifting. When it was all the way up, a man was revealed standing in the space. The man gestured, and Barker pulled forward. At another gesture he stopped, and the wall rolled down behind the Ford.

Light in here was dim. But when the wall was once again in place, overhead fluorescent bars went on and the space became brightly illuminated. The air smelled of grease, with a top note of marijuana smoke.

This was obviously a repair shop. There were two older cars that were being rebuilt and highly modified. A long workbench ran across the rear wall, and there were power tools and hand tools of all kinds on the bench and hanging from hooks.

More tools were lying on the floor near the cars, along with auto parts. Shelves held cans and boxes and glass containers.

Barker got out of his car and approached the man. He was short and husky, with long arms covered in tattoos. His hair was a greasy tangle, and more tattoos decorated his face and neck. There was a crudely drawn star in the center of his forehead.

"You Culebra?" Barker asked him.

"That's me. What do you want?"

"Need to ask you some questions."

"Yeah? I got no answers. I told you guys, I got a clean business. So why are you fucking with me now?"

"I'm here because we got a tip."

The man grinned, showing gold teeth. "A tip? On what, a horse race?"

"No, a tip that says you're a pretty good gunsmith."

The grin disappeared. "What gunsmith? What is this about?"

"It's about what you do for a living."

Culebra pointed to the pair of vehicles and then to the tools and parts lying on the floor. "You see this? What I do is fix cars."

"That's not all you fix."

"That's true. I also fix machines that don't work." He waved an arm toward the bench. "Sanders, drills, shit like that."

"And guns," Barker said.

"I don't know nothing about no guns."

"That's not what I hear. In fact, I hear you're an expert. Anybody needs a conversion to fully automatic, or wants to make serial numbers disappear, you're the man to see."

"It's a lie."

"What's more, you deal in guns, too. Most of them smuggled."

"I deal in cars," Culebra said. "I buy them, fix them up, and sell them. You want me to buy that piece of shit you got there?"

"No, I want you to tell me how you made the fléchettes that killed two women in New York."

Culebra's close-set eyes showed a glimmer of fear. An instant later the reaction was gone, but Barker had caught it.

"You're demente," Culebra said.

"Am I? The women were Catherine Delure, the movie star, and Penny Ellis, her manager."

"I don't know nothing about that."

"No? How did you make the fléchettes? Probably turned them on your metal lathe and spot-welded the fins, right? Then you buffed them till they were nice and smooth."

"I never made no fléchettes."

"Yes, you did. You made two of them, right over there on that bench. Who'd you make them for?"

"Nobody."

"What kind of gun was used to fire them?"

"Listen, I told you I got a clean business. I don't deal in no fléchettes, and no guns, either. Now why don't you get the fuck out of my shop?"

"Okay, I'll go. But one other thing. You did time, right?" It was a shot in the dark, just to see what it might evoke.

"That was years ago," Culebra said. "I'm not even on parole no more."

"No, but you're an ex-con. You realize what would happen to you now if you were convicted on a charge of aiding in a felony? Especially when the felony was murder?"

This time Culebra did not respond. Instead he stared straight ahead.

"On the other hand," Barker said, "if you give up the killer, the DA will make you a very good deal. You might even walk. Better than going back in for life, huh?"

"Get out."

"Sure. But think it over. And have a nice day."

Barker climbed into the Ford, and when the door rattled upward, he backed out onto the street.

As he began retracing his route, he felt a surge of excitement. He didn't have so much as a scrap of evidence, had nothing to go on but a lot of guesses, yet he felt sure he'd faked his way into a very good lead.

Mongo sat in the Toyota and thought about what his next move should be. He didn't want to confront Culebra too soon, wanted to space this out enough so that Culebra wouldn't guess that he'd seen the detective go into the shop. Mongo wanted him to relax.

The big question was, how much did the cops know? Plenty, probably. Otherwise they wouldn't have sent the dick here. The fact that he'd shown up was proof they already had at least some of the answers.

The worst possibility was that Culebra had admitted he made the fléchettes and converted the tape recorder to fire them.

If so, what was the cops' plan? Were they setting a trap, using

Culebra as bait?

Or maybe they had some other scheme. Maybe they'd wired the shop, so that any conversation he'd have with Culebra would become evidence.

No, if they'd already wired the place they wouldn't come back here until they thought they had something.

Then what were they up to?

He continued to spin out different scenarios, checking his watch every few minutes and growing more antsy each time he did.

A full hour passed, and then he started the Toyota and drove slowly back up the street.

When he turned into the alley he had to wait again, until the metal door rolled up at last.

Once he was inside and the door was shut behind him, he picked up his attaché case and got out of the car. He waved a casual greeting. "Ay, Culebra. How you doing?"

"Doing fine."

"I came to get the rifle," Mongo said. "And I'll pay your price, even though you're a ladrón to charge me that much." He laid the attaché case on the workbench and opened it, revealing the packets of hundred-dollar bills.

Culebra looked at the money. "The rifle's worth it."

"I agree with you. That's why I brought you the cash, okay? So let's have it."

"It ain't ready."

"Not ready?"

"No, man. I'm still working on the silencer."

"Yeah? Let me see it."

Culebra hesitated, but then he opened the hidden gun cabinet and lifted out the Barrett M107. A foot-long cylindrical device was now attached to the end of the barrel.

Mongo took the rifle from him and studied the newly added part. He saw that Culebra had cut threads into the barrel so the silencer could be screwed on.

"Hey, looks okay to me," Mongo said. "You did a nice job, like you always do. So why do you say it's not ready?"

"The way it is, I don't think it'll stop the sound. I need to test it."

"That so? Then what are you waiting for? Give me some bullets."

"Not now, man. Like I said, I'll need to do some more work on the gun."

"Sure. But give me some anyway. I want to see how to load them."

Reluctantly, Culebra again reached into the cabinet. He got out the magazine and handed it over.

Mongo saw that it was packed with ten rounds. He shoved it into the opening on the underside of the breech. There was a sharp click as it went home, and another click as the weapon's action automatically inserted a cartridge into the chamber.

"Hey, be careful with that," Culebra said.

Mongo hefted the heavy weapon. "There any way the cops could trace this? I see it's still got the serial number."

"All they could find out is it came from the Army, like I told you."

"Yeah, but you know cops. They might figure out how it got from the Army to you. And then how it got from you to me. See what I mean?"

"That would never happen."

"Why not? The cops ever come sniffing around here?"

"Sometimes. But I never tell them nothing. I never would."

Mongo raised the rifle and swung it toward him. "You don't think you would. But they got ways to make you."

"Bullshit. And don't point that at me."

"When was the last time a cop was here?"

Culebra's mouth dropped open. "Listen, I can explain—"

"You don't have to," Mongo said. He pulled the trigger.

The rifle fired with a horrendously loud noise, and the .50-caliber projectile blew Culebra's head apart. The impact slammed his body against the workbench and he fell to the floor, his shattered skull gushing blood.

"You were right," Mongo said. "Silencer's not worth a shit." He unscrewed the device and tossed it back into the cabinet. "So you can keep it."

Returning to his car, he put the rifle inside on the passenger side. Even without the silencer it was so long he had to rest the stock on the floor and lean the barrel against the seat back. He retrieved his attaché case and put that in the car as well.

The door of the shop was controlled by a remote that was lying on the workbench. He went over there and grabbed it.

Now what? Was there something here that could help the cops? Something that would prove there was a tie between him and Culebra? The place was such a mess it would take him hours to root around in it. Better if he could just make sure there was nothing for them to find.

Stepping to the cabinet, he slipped the remote into his pocket and picked up the roll of Primacord. Apparently, the roll contained many yards of the stuff. It looked like thin nylon rope and seemed harmless enough. But if it did what Culebra claimed, it could be just what he needed.

A can of gasoline stood on the floor, near the vehicles Culebra had been working on. He opened it, pulled out a length of the Primacord, and stuck the end into the can. Walking backward, he made his way to the Toyota, paying out the Primacord as he went.

He got into the car, started it, and used the remote to raise the door. Slowly he backed out of the shop, holding the roll out the window and continuing to pay out the ropelike material.

When he reached the mouth of the alley, he again fingered the remote. The door came down, and he hoped it wouldn't sever the Primacord as it did.

From there, he eased the car down the street, stopping a short distance from the alley. He got out his pocketknife and cut the Primacord. He held on to the severed end and put the roll on the floor of the car. Then he pressed the cigarette lighter.

"Hey, man. Whatcha doin'?"

He looked up and saw that two kids were watching him. They were teenagers, both wearing grubby shirts and pants many sizes too big. Their feet, however, were shod in sneakers that appeared to be brand new.

"Beat it," Mongo said.

One of them seemed a little bolder than the other. He stepped closer to the car. "Hey, mothafucka, who you tellin' beat it? I axed you whatcha doin'? What's that rope for?"

"It's magic," Mongo said. He dropped the end of the Primacord onto the street.

The kid looked at the Primacord and said, "Magic? You fulla shit."

"Yeah? Watch this."

Mongo took out the lighter, opened the car door, and leaned down. He touched the lighter to the end of the Primacord, and the result was a shock, even to him.

The Primacord exploded into a sizzling, white-hot snake that shot its way back to Culebra's shop, moving so fast it seemed instantaneous. There was a violent boom, and seconds later, flames and black smoke rose above the dilapidated buildings.

The two kids looked at the fiery scene and then at Mongo, their eyes bugging out. The bold one said, "Holy Jesus."

"Told you," Mongo said. He pulled away as fast as the crummy little car would take him.

38.

Rodeo Drive was the most famous street in Beverly Hills, and as usual it was bustling. People, mostly women, were going in and out of boutiques with illustrious designers' names, such as Gucci, Christian Dior, and Chanel, showcased above the doors. Tiffany had a store there, and so did Cartier and Bulgari, and all of them were thronged with shoppers.

Dana arrived at Mario's at 1 P.M. on the dot. The restaurant was also busy, with customers waiting for tables both inside and on the tree-shaded rear patio. She asked the maître d' for Alex Haynes's table, and he led her out back to where Haynes was waiting for her.

The lawyer rose as she took her seat. He was carefully groomed, his dark hair complementing his tan, his beige linen jacket fashionably casual. He smiled and said, "Dana, I'm glad to see you. You're looking lovely, as always."

"Thanks, Alex. You seem fit too. Been out in the sunshine, I see."

"Oh, I try to get in a round of golf as often as I can. Which isn't easy, with so much going on. I've belonged to the Riviera for years and never seem to spend as much time there as I'd like."

She got the message. He was letting her know that he was a member of one of the area's most exclusive country clubs. How subtle.

A waiter appeared and asked if they'd like something to drink.

"I think some wine would go well," Haynes said. "For you too, Dana?"

"Yes, a glass of white, please."

"White it is." He told the waiter they'd have a bottle of Montrachet. The man bowed and hurried off.

Turning back to Dana, Haynes asked, "Did you bring the material I asked for?"

"Yes, I have it right here." She opened her bag and took out a manila envelope that contained only the most innocuous items she could find among Dana's notes. She handed it to him.

"Thank you." He picked up a briefcase from the floor beside his chair and slipped the envelope into it. "I appreciate your help. This is a rather complicated situation, and sorting it out is proving difficult."

"I can understand that."

"On top of everything else, Penny Ellis's records are gone. The woman she lived with threw them out after Penny's funeral. That was really unfortunate."

Maybe it was, Dana thought. But I almost wish I'd done the same thing.

The waiter was back, with a bottle and a bucket of ice on a stand. He opened the bottle and poured some of the wine for Haynes to taste.

The lawyer made a production of it, sniffing the cork and inhaling the wine's bouquet before swallowing a little. He nodded approval, and the waiter filled their glasses. The waiter then plunged the bottle into the ice and left them.

"To your good health," Haynes said, raising his glass.

Dana raised hers as well. "And to yours."

They both drank, and Haynes said, "I must confess that as much as I enjoy our California wines, they can't touch the ones from France. The Montrachets are the finest white wines in the world. Don't you agree?"

"I haven't tried them all," Dana said. Christ, he was a wine snob too?

Undeterred, he went off on a riff about how California whites were perfectly good wines, but even the best of them didn't have the quality of those from the Côte d'Or. The whites produced here, he said, were more like the lesser French wines, such as those produced in the Loire. They were all made from Chardonnay grapes, but the end results were quite different.

This is going to be a drag, Dana thought. Next he'll be telling me about English antiques. But she had to admit the wine was splendid. She sipped it, savoring the depth and the robust flavor, until at last the waiter returned to take their lunch order.

They glanced through menus, and Dana said, "I think I'll just have a salad. Mixed greens, please."

"I'd like a salad as well," Haynes said. "But I want the one made with crabmeat."

The waiter poured more wine for them and moved away.

"I love crab," Haynes said. "Whenever I'm in Washington, I can't get enough. There is nothing like the crabs from Chesapeake Bay."

Dana drank some of her wine and looked at him. He was a pompous jerk, she decided, and he was boring the hell out of her.

"Have you been following the box office results of *Hot Cargo*?" he asked. "It's become a really big hit."

"Apparently it has."

"Over two hundred million in domestic grosses so far. Simply amazing. Especially when you consider how negative the reviews were." He smiled. "But in the movie business, the only review that counts is the one that shows the bottom line. And when you look at it that way, the picture's a winner."

That was right out of the Zarkov lexicon, she thought. Expressed so often it had become a cliché.

"Speaking of *Hot Cargo*," Haynes went on, "I was talking with Tyler Sturgis the other day. You know him, don't you? He's Len Zarkov's lawyer."

"I've met him."

"Tyler was remarking that it would be a shame if anything were to come out now that soiled Catherine's reputation."

A caution sign went on in Dana's head. "Yes, it would."

"And yet the rumor mill is grinding away. You've heard about that, haven't you?"

"If you mean rumors about Catherine's love life, nothing could be worse than what's printed in the supermarket magazines. Rational people know it's all crap."

"That's not what I was talking about."

"Then what were you talking about?"

He lowered his tone, as if he were letting her in on a dark secret. "Anything I say you must hold in complete confidence. Is that understood?"

"Sure."

Before he could continue, their lunch arrived. The waiter fussed about, filling their glasses again and offering fresh pepper, which they refused.

When they were alone once more, Haynes said, "Before she died, Catherine was planting stories about Ron Apperson, claiming he and Zarkov were involved in a fraudulent business conspiracy. There wasn't a shred of truth in the stories, of course. Her real motivation was to damage her former husband. Were you aware of that?"

"No, I wasn't. And what's more, I don't believe it."

"Oh, come on, now. You must have known she hated Apperson, working with her as closely as you did."

"Sorry, Alex. I didn't know any such thing."

She took a bite of her salad. So this was the new strategy, she thought. Cover anything that might come out about Zarkov's scheme by attacking Catherine, who was dead and unable to defend herself. Why would Sturgis tell Haynes about it? So it would get to me, of course.

Around a mouthful of crabmeat, the lawyer said, "There's also another subject I wanted to discuss with you. It's a bit distasteful, but I have to do it, because it's part of tying up the loose ends of Catherine's estate."

"Okay, go ahead."

"This came to light during a conversation with her accountant, Julia Brecht. According to Julia, there was always a large amount of cash in the house. Sometimes as much as fifty thousand dollars. Were you aware of that?"

"I was aware there was cash, but I had no idea how much. That sounds like a lot to me."

"It did to me too. Although when you consider it in terms of the total value of the estate, it's a pittance. Nevertheless, I have to run it down. So I went back to the house yesterday and asked Anna about it. She confirmed that cash was doled out to her whenever she needed it for small household expenses. I asked Anna if she knew where the money was kept, and she said all she knew was that it was in Ms. Delure's bedroom. She thought in the desk."

"I have no idea where it was kept," Dana said. "Anything to do with money was in Penny's bailiwick."

"Yes, Julia said the same thing. But what troubled me was that I also found out that the only person besides Catherine who had keys to that desk was you."

For a moment, Dana was speechless. Then she said, "Is that an accusation, Alex?"

Haynes put his fork down. "Not at all. I'm just trying to locate the money. I thought you could help me with that."

"Afraid I can't. The only reason I went into the desk the last time I was in the house was to get Catherine's notes."

"Which you've given to me."

"Right."

"All of them, of course."

"Do you doubt that?"

"Just making sure. And as far as the money is concerned, frankly I'd prefer not to pursue that at all. It could become messy, as you can imagine."

"Yes, I can imagine that, Alex. And now I have to move along. Thank you for lunch." She grabbed her bag and left the table.

On the way out to the street, her face was flushed with anger. She was also a little woozy from the wine. But not so much that she couldn't think clearly.

What Haynes had conveyed was a warning, no matter how subtly put. Subtly? Hell, it was as if he'd run over her with a truck. The miserable son of a bitch was telling her to back off. Keep her mouth shut, and if she'd held out on any of Catherine's notes, she'd better destroy them. If she didn't, she'd be hit with an investigation about cash missing from Catherine's desk.

But why was he doing this? Was he tied in to Zarkov's scheme? His discussion with Tyler Sturgis about smearing Catherine certainly suggested he was.

Lawyers were charming, weren't they? They smiled while they stuck knives into you.

39.

On his way to Dana's apartment, Barker stopped off at a supermarket and bought vodka and vermouth. This had been a good day, and his plan was to have drinks with her and then take her out to dinner. Not a celebration, exactly, but close.

When she opened her door, however, he found her distraught. She tried to explain why she was upset, but her words tumbled over one another.

He kissed her and told her to relax until he could mix a couple of martinis. He made stiff ones for both of them, and when they'd taken long swallows, she seemed to calm down a little.

She then told him about her lunch with Alex Haynes.

"Nothing to worry about," he said.

"Nothing? How can you say that? He practically came right out and accused me of stealing money from Catherine's desk. Maybe as much as fifty thousand dollars. And I shouldn't worry?"

"Of course not. Who's to say Catherine kept money in that desk? And if she did, that only you and Catherine had a key to it?

The housekeeper might have had one. And didn't you tell me the maid took off? She could've had a key as well. Haynes was just trying to scare you."

"But what if he wasn't? What if he went to the police and reported it?"

"Reported what? That maybe there was money in the desk? Maybe as much as fifty thousand dollars? And maybe you were the only one beside Catherine who had a key? And maybe you went into the desk and stole the money that maybe was there? First the cops would say that's a lot of maybes, and then they'd ask what evidence he had to back up the charge. When he couldn't produce any, they'd laugh at him."

Dana paused. "I see what you mean."

"And here's another thing. Penny Ellis took care of money matters for Catherine, isn't that right?"

"Yes. That was part of her job. She screened all the bills, and she had the authority to sign checks. Also she and the accountant regularly reviewed everything so the tax returns could be prepared properly."

"Then how much cash did Catherine usually have on hand?"

"Come to think of it, only a little. I mean, she spent plenty of money, but she never paid cash for anything, as far as I could see. Whenever she went shopping, she paid with credit cards."

"So whatever cash was in the house was provided by Penny. True?"

"Yes, it would have been."

"And therefore it wasn't Catherine who gave Anna cash to use for household expenses, it was Penny. Also true?"

"Yes."

"Then why would Catherine have kept money in that desk? And not just some money, but as much as fifty thousand bucks? Sounds to me as though your friend Haynes was stirring up a big pot of bullshit."

"He's not my friend."

"No, I'm sure he's not. But the bullshit part is correct, wouldn't you say?"

"Apparently it is."

"So just as you thought, his objective was to convince you that revealing anything to do with Catherine's suspicions would be a very bad idea."

"I believe so, yes."

"Okay, and now let me bring up another question. Why don't you go to the DA's office and tell them what you know? Why not tell them there's a good possibility Zarkov and Catherine's former husband are involved in a scheme to defraud investors?"

"For the same reason you just talked about. I have nothing but a bunch of maybes."

"Yeah, but with the DA people it would be different. It would encourage them to do some investigating of their own. And by going to them you'd be doing one other thing. You'd be protecting yourself. So go, okay?"

"I don't know, Jeb. Everything you say makes sense, but I have this fear of becoming involved."

"All right, I understand that. But will you at least think about it?"

"Yes, I will."

"Good. And for now, let's put it aside. We'll drive out to the beach and have dinner."

"No. That is, it's very nice of you, but I'd rather not go out. I've had enough of restaurants for one day. We could have something here."

"Like what?"

"Well, I don't have much."

"What do you have?"

"A package of spaghetti."

"Hey, pasta's my favorite food. Got any tomatoes?"

"Yes, in a can."

"What kind?"

"Italian."

"Perfect. How about bacon?"

"A few strips."

"And an onion?"

"Yes."

"Garlic?"

"Sure."

"Parmesan cheese?"

"I have some of that, too."

"Then we're in business. I'll make the best damn sauce you ever tasted. Your job will be to cook the spaghetti. Can you boil water?"

For the first time that evening, she laughed. "I think I can handle that."

"Great."

"I also have a bottle of cabernet sauvignon."

"Sensational."

"Nothing for hors d'oeuvres, though."

"Yes, you do."

"I do?"

"Sure. Come with me, and I'll show you." He took her arm and led her into the bedroom.

"What about dinner?" she said.

"We'll do that later. First things first."

As it turned out, Barker thought the evening was wonderful. Good food, good wine, and good love. What more could you ask?

40.

In the morning Dana made breakfast for them, and Barker was pleased to see that her confidence had returned. But when he again brought up the idea of her going to the DA, she stubbornly refused. He had a second cup of coffee, kissed her, and left the apartment.

This promised to be another productive day. He was looking forward to enlisting Sam Benziger's help in putting more pressure on the mechanic. For one thing, Sam could get a warrant to search the guy's shop.

When he reached his room in the Sunset Inn, he changed into fresh clothing. As he was pulling on his pants his phone rang. He answered: "Barker."

"Jeb, it's Sam Benziger."

"Hey, I was just going to call you."

"One of the names Deke Edwards gave you was a guy named Culebra, right?"

"Yeah, I went to his shop yesterday. I think he's the one who made the fléchettes the killer used. At least he's somebody to check out."

"Not anymore he's not. Late yesterday, the shop burned down, and apparently he was in it. Firefighters put out the fire, but they found a body in what was left."

"Oh, shit."

"My sentiments exactly. I'm going down there now."

"Okay, I'll meet you there."

Once he was dressed he got back in his car and retraced his route of the day before. One of the problems with LA, he thought for the dozenth time, was that it was so damn spread out. Took forever to get from one place to another.

When at last he arrived at the scene, he found it blocked off by police barricades. A fire engine was there, along with an LAFD sedan, an LAFD van, two LAPD patrol cars, an ambulance, a Chevy sedan, and Benziger's Honda. Barker parked and clipped his shield to his shirt pocket as he stepped closer.

Culebra's shop, and both the adjoining buildings, had been reduced to smoldering piles of ashes. The framing around the metal door had burned and the door had collapsed. Some of the exterior walls were still standing, probably because they were built of brick, but the interiors were mostly rubble. The usual crowd of rubbernecks were gaping at the wreckage, while two cops kept them behind the barricades.

Looking weary, a half-dozen firefighters were packing up their equipment. Several others, wearing protective gear and heavy boots, were poking around in the ruins. The cars Culebra was working on had burned until little remained but blackened shells. Twisted and melted chunks of metal were also strewn about, apparently what was left of the mechanic's tools.

Two men in civilian clothes were standing near the Chevy, no doubt detectives who were part of the division squad. One was making notes, the other was on his cell phone.

Benziger was in the driveway, talking to a firefighter whose helmet insignia identified him as a lieutenant. Barker joined them.

"We were lucky," the lieutenant said. "Got here early enough so we could keep the fire from spreading. If we hadn't, the whole neighborhood could've gone up."

"The shop must've burned fast," Sam said.

"It did, and it looked to us like a set fire. Which would make the death a homicide. So we waited for the medical examiner to get here and examine the body. He said the guy had been shot."

Sam asked him if he'd told that to the division detectives.

"Yeah, and they weren't much surprised. They get at least one a day, sometimes more."

"Where's the ME now?" Barker asked.

"Over there with the ambulance guys."

"What made you think it was a set fire?" Sam asked.

The lieutenant pointed. "See that long scorch mark there on the ground? Runs from the fire all the way out to the street. It was most likely made by a high-speed fuse."

Barker said, "Such as Primacord?"

"Right. You familiar with the stuff?"

"Yeah, we used it in the Marine Corps. It's actually a form of explosive."

"That's why it burns so fast. An ordinary fuse wouldn't leave a mark like that. I think whoever set the fire used Primacord to get it going. That made it possible for him to be far enough away to be safe when he lit the fuse."

The detective who'd been making notes came over to them.

Benziger asked him whether he'd found anything else that would help the investigation.

"Besides the tools," he said, "there's a lot of guns in the place. Firefighters found them in a hidden cabinet, and they didn't get burned as bad as the other things."

"Did you know the dead man?"

"Yeah, name's Culebra. We questioned him a few times but could never pin anything on him."

Barker left them and went over to where the ME was watching two members of the ambulance crew put a body bag into the vehicle. Barker asked the ME what he'd found when he inspected the victim.

Unlike the guy who'd examined Delure's body, this one had no problem answering. "Burned to a crisp," he said. "And his head was gone. Or mostly gone, anyway. Looked to me like it was blown apart by a high-caliber bullet, probably from a rifle. A very big rifle. Entry was in front, and the slug shattered the skull. It went on through and carried away the parietal and occipital bones. Then the fire fried what was left."

"So he was shot before the fire started."

"No question. Probably the fire was to cover it up, don't you think?"

"Could be," Barker said. "You notice anything else?"

The ME smiled. "Wasn't much left to notice."

Barker returned to where Benziger continued to talk with the lieutenant and the detective. He asked if he could borrow some boots.

"Yeah, I can fix you up with a pair," the lieutenant said. "But if you want to walk around in there, be damn careful."

"Thanks, I will."

The lieutenant went to the fire engine and got a pair of heavy boots. He handed them to Barker, who took off his shoes and pulled on the boots. The lieutenant also gave him a pair of gloves with cuffs that ran almost to the elbow.

Stepping cautiously, Barker went over to the firefighters who were in what remained of the shop. "Good morning," he said. "I hear you found some guns."

"Yeah, they were in a cabinet over near that wall," one of them said. "Seems like there was a layer of wood on the outside, and then behind that was metal. The wood burned away, but the metal protected the guns. Come on, I'll show you."

The firefighter was carrying a short pry bar. He went to the place he'd indicated and pulled back a blackened metal panel with the bar. "Some collection, huh?"

Inside the space were racks holding submachine guns, long

arms, and pistols. By and large they appeared to be intact, although Barker could see cracks in the stocks of some of the weapons, probably caused by the heat. Boxes of ammunition were stacked on the floor, and he was surprised the fire hadn't set them off.

He also noticed a metal cylinder that was lying near the boxes. He picked it up. The cylinder was made of heavy-gauge aluminum, expertly welded and buffed.

He knew at a glance it was a silencer. During his years on the NYPD he'd seen a number of them that had been seized from criminals. All were built on the same principle. When a gun was fired, the violent escape of gas made a loud report. To suppress the noise, a silencer provided a space beyond the muzzle of the weapon that would contain much of the gas and let it escape more slowly.

"What's that thing?" the firefighter asked.

"Silencer," Barker said.

"Huh. So there's no noise when the gun goes off?"

"There's noise," Barker said. "Just less of it. But the higher the caliber of the gun, the bigger the bang. So even with one of these, a .45 would be louder than a .22."

Barker then checked the attachment end of the device and saw that threading had been cut into it. Next he inspected the muzzles of the firearms in the cabinet. None bore threads, so the silencer could not have been attached to any of them. He walked back to Benziger and the lieutenant, carrying the cylinder.

Benziger looked at it curiously. "That what I think it is?"

"If you think it's a silencer, you're right."

"Okay, what about it?"

"This wouldn't fit on any of the guns in that cabinet. But the ME said Culebra was shot in the head with a high-caliber bullet that probably came from a rifle. So the killer might have used this on the rifle. Then he took it off and left it behind."

"And took the rifle with him?"

"If I'm right, yes."

"Wonder why he'd do that."

"Beats me. You have a better idea?"

"Not at the moment," Sam said.

"Then let's concentrate on how we find the shooter."

"That's about where you started, isn't it?"

Barker grinned. "Yeah, but Culebra was killed on your turf. So now it's your case, too."

41.

"Well now," Deke Edwards said, "you got here at the right time. I just made a fresh pot of coffee."

"I've had some of your coffee," Benziger said. "It took the lining out of my throat."

"That's because you gulped it. Have to drink it slower. That way you get to enjoy the flavor."

He filled three mugs, handing one to each of his visitors. Sam dumped milk into hers and stirred the mixture.

They sat at a table and Edwards said to Barker, "I got a feeling this might have to do with one of the gentlemen whose names I gave you. Am I right?"

"Culebra," Barker said.

"Yeah, I thought so. Heard on a police scanner he got shot and his shop burned down."

"You heard correctly. I went to see him yesterday, and we had a talk. I'm pretty sure he's the one who made the fléchettes."

"And now he's in no shape to say whether he did or he didn't."

"No shape at all."

"Which could explain why somebody shot him."

"Seems likely."

"You got anything more to go on?"

Barker produced the metal cylinder, which was wrapped in cotton cloth. He gently laid the device on the table and drew back the cloth.

Edwards peered at it. "Silencer, huh? Was this on the murder weapon?"

"We don't know, because we don't have the weapon. But we think it might have been. And Culebra is almost surely the one who made it."

"Looks like it's a better job than most of the ones we see," Deke said. "And judging from the size of the threaded end, it was made for a high-caliber rifle."

"The ME thinks that's what Culebra was shot with."

"But why would anybody bother to use a silencer in that neighborhood? You got guns going off there all the time. It's drive-by central."

"We don't know that, either. We're hoping there are some prints on it."

"Okay," Edwards said, "let's get an expert opinion on that. Come with me."

He picked up the silencer and led them from ballistics to the center's fingerprint section. That area was busy as well, with technicians in white coats checking prints on everything from knives to various hand tools and even pieces of paper.

Edwards raised a hand and called out to one of the techs. "Hey, Linda. Got a minute?"

A slim brunette came over to them, and Edwards introduced her to Benziger and Barker as Linda Gomez.

"What can I do for you, Deke?" she asked.

"If I told you, you'd say I was a sexist pig."

"You are a sexist pig. Now what do you want?"

He chuckled and held up the cylinder, which was partially

wrapped in the cotton cloth. "These folks are working a homicide. They think maybe the killer used this silencer on his gun. Can you get some prints off it?"

She bent over the device and studied it for a moment. "I don't know. Surface looks smeared. But I can try."

"You're a doll, Linda."

"I know. I'll take it over to my station and see what I can do."

"Good. Just don't drop it."

"If I do, it'll be on your head." She deftly picked up the silencer, taking care to hold the cloth around it, and walked off.

"She's one of the best," Edwards said. "Got a master's in chemistry. We're damn fortunate to have her. In fact, it's hard to get any qualified people nowadays. Meantime, the workload in this place just gets heavier and heavier."

"Wipe away the tears, Deke," Sam said. "Things are tough all over."

"Fair enough. But the crime rate's up, and that dumps more work on the lab. Numbers don't lie, no matter how much the mayor tries to massage 'em. He says the rate's down, while the commissioner says the opposite. Which one are you gonna believe?"

"How does the mayor manipulate the numbers?" Barker asked.

"He throws in every kind of two-bit misdemeanor along with the serious crimes, and because there's fewer misdemeanors than last year, that lowers the overall rate. Then he claims we're making progress."

"So what's the true picture?"

"Murder rate in LA is almost twice the national average, and so are the rates of robbery, felony assault, car theft, and arson."

"The only one that's lower than the average," Sam said, "is rape."

"Burglary's also down a little," Edwards said.

"Yes, although the mayor's trying to treat that as less serious, if you can believe it."

"I don't mean to brag," Barker said, "but over the past few years New York has done a pretty good job of reducing crime. Now it's called the safest of all big cities. The rates of every one of the major crimes are lower, especially homicide."

"Wish we could say the same," Deke said. "Here, it always comes back to the gangs. They spend a lot of their time killing one another."

"We've got gangs in New York, too. And it's a growing problem, just like everywhere else. So far we're keeping it under control, but just barely."

Linda was back. "Okay, I got one readable print," she said. "Best I could do."

Barker's hopes rose. "Hey, good going!"

Edwards said, "That's my girl."

"I'm not your girl," Linda said. "You want me to send the print to the FBI?"

"Just as quick as you can do it."

She returned to her station.

Benziger said, "What would we do without IAFIS?" That was the Integrated Automatic Fingerprint Identification System.

"What we'd do," Deke said, "is operate the way we did before it was invented. 'Course, that was before your time, Sam. But when I think back to how it used to take months to get IDs on prints, that's when I appreciate IAFIS. Now we can get a response in less than an hour."

"I understand the database is the world's largest," Barker said.

"That's true," Edwards said. "The master file holds more than fifty-five million sets of prints and criminal records. Tells you how many bad people are out there. And those are only the ones that got caught."

"Let's watch Linda send the print," Sam said.

The trio went over to her station and stood behind Gomez. She'd dusted the cylinder and had picked out a single well-defined fingerprint. Next, she took close-ups of the light-colored aluminum surface with a digital camera.

Not satisfied with the first few shots, she kept on until she had one that clearly portrayed the subject. She plugged it into her computer, and on the screen the loops, whorls, and arches of the print showed up in sharp detail.

"Surface might cause a problem," she said. "On account of the cylinder not being flat. Naturally, that distorts the image somewhat, so I can only hope the database can read it well enough to produce a match."

"You're doing great," Deke said. "Give it a try."

She called up the IAFIS website and sent a request for ID along with the images, stating that this was a criminal investigation.

From his own experience, Barker knew the designation would elicit the quickest possible response.

"Okay," Linda said. "All we can do now is wait."

"I'm not very good at that," Sam said. "Don't have enough patience."

"Just relax," Deke said. "Have some more of my coffee."

"Thanks, but no thanks."

Barker checked his watch and began looking for ways to pass the time. He and Sam drifted around the lab, watching the techs carry out various forensic procedures. Some were examining hair and cloth samples; others were squinting through microscopes at hair and fibers. Still others were testing blood and bodily fluids, looking for evidence of drugs, alcohol, and poisons. All were making notes as they went along, to be used when writing reports of their findings.

Barker knew he could never work in such a place. Like Benziger, he lacked the patience. Spending his days undertaking examinations like the ones going on here would drive him batty.

He looked at his watch again. Nearly an hour had passed. Maybe Sam was right, and his theory was too much of a reach. Worrying that they were on the wrong path was making his nerves jump. Or maybe that was caused by Edwards's battery-acid coffee.

At last Linda Gomez called them back to her station.

"There we are," she said. "The FBI gave us the goods. Beautiful, huh?"

Barker felt his hopes rise.

Until he looked at the mug shot on the screen. It showed a man with tangled black hair and tattoos, including one of a star in the middle of his forehead. At the bottom of the photo was a number and his name: Alonzo Culebra. Instead of the killer, the print on the silencer had been left there by the victim.

Shit.

Linda hit a key, and another image appeared, showing Culebra's rap sheet. A total of eight arrests, among them two for felonious assault and another for auto theft. That last had got him four years in Corcoran State Prison.

There were a number of other notations on the sheet concerning distinguishing physical features, MO, parole details, and so on. But Culebra's life story wasn't what Barker wanted to see.

Linda caught his expression. "You're disappointed?"

"Yeah. That's the one who made the silencer. Not the one who killed him. But listen, thanks for trying."

"Anytime. Wish I could have been more help."

"Here's something," Edwards said. "While we were waiting for the FBI to come back to Linda, I did some measuring. The weapon the silencer was used on was a .50-caliber. That's a unique rifle."

"Unique how?" Benziger asked.

"It's a sniper rifle. Either an L96A1 made by Accuracy International, or a Barrett M107. My guess is the one that killed Culebra was a Barrett."

"Why?"

"US Armed Forces use the Barrett. The other one's British. I don't know how Culebra got hold of a Barrett, but it's more logical he'd have one of those."

"So what's different about a sniper rifle?"

"The large caliber, to begin with. The only thing a Barrett's good for is killing people."

"But couldn't it be used by a hunter, somebody going after big game?"

"Not likely. A big-game hunter wants power, but he also wants a rifle he can carry in the field without getting himself worn out. A Remington .300 Magnum, say, or a Ruger .375. Either one can kill any animal in North America. Moose, bear, elk, anything. Kill most anything in Africa too, for that matter. But compared with a Barrett, those are relatively lightweight."

"So this Barrett would be too heavy for hunting?"

"Yeah, and too big. But for a sniper it's ideal. There are two things he wants out of his weapon. One is impact. A .50-caliber will likely kill a man regardless of where on the body it hits him. If it hits him in the leg, for instance, it might take the leg off. Same with an arm. Guy would either bleed to death or die from shock."

"What's the other thing a sniper wants?" she asked then.

"Range. He wants to set up and zero in on an enemy even if the target is a great distance away. He'll spot him with a telescopic sight and let go, and with a .50 he can be sure the bullet'll get there."

"There are snipers in the Marine Corps," Barker said, "fighting the Taliban and al Qaeda. They'll shoot from a thousand, even two thousand yards."

"And score hits," Edwards said. "Scratch one raghead."

"So if a sniper rifle is so heavy and clumsy," Benziger said, "why would the guy who shot Culebra be lugging it around?"

"I imagine," Barker said, "it's because he's looking for another target."

42.

Mongo believed the key to making a successful hit was planning ahead. You had to take your time, study the target's habits, decide how you'd get the best opportunity. What you should never do was rush. Going off half cocked was asking for trouble. Or worse, failure.

The immediate problem was the rifle. He wanted it handy when the time came, but if a cop caught sight of it while he had it with him, that could blow the plan before it ever got started. And yet the thing was so damn big there was no way he could hide it. Or was there?

He thought about that, and eventually a light went on. There was a sporting goods store on Santa Monica Boulevard, and that was where he could get what he needed.

He drove there and parked in the lot behind the store, hoping nobody would notice the .50-caliber with the barrel resting against the seat back. Better if he could have put it in the trunk, but it wouldn't fit. So he'd just have to take his chances. He locked the car and went into the store.

Along with the racks of Dodgers and Angels jerseys, and the displays of athletic junk ranging from baseball gloves and bats to scuba gear and tennis rackets, there was a whole section devoted to golf. He bought a cheap bag and a cover for clubs and went back out to his car.

He put the rifle into the golf bag muzzle down, and then dropped the cover over the exposed stock. It was a perfect solution. He could carry the bag wherever he wanted, and anyone who saw him would take him for just another feebleminded schmuck whose idea of a good time was chasing a little white ball.

The next step was to pick his spot. The area surrounding the Sunset Inn was no good. Too many cars and people, no place to hide and get set.

So where? As he thought about it, he recalled that tailing the cop had revealed he often went to a building on Wilshire and spent the night.

Easy to see why he did that. A sexy broad lived in the building, and that was like catnip to a cat. Mongo had seen them together and had recognized her at once. The weird thing was that she'd been Catherine Delure's secretary.

What was her name? Laramie, that was it. Dana Laramie. Mongo remembered her legs and the way her jugs had pushed out the front of her sweater when he saw her that morning in the Sherry-Netherland. No wonder the cop wanted some of it.

But the question for Mongo was how he could be sure of taking him out. He thought there might be a workable location nearby, although that would require some scouting. At first glance, the neighboring buildings didn't look too promising, but he'd check them out anyway.

He parked in the same subterranean public parking garage he'd seen the cop use. Carrying the golf bag with the strap over his shoulder, he made his way up to the sidewalk and stopped in front of various store windows, pretending to study the merchandise on display. His face was obscured by a baseball cap and sunglasses.

A few doors down, he found a building that might suit his purpose. It had the usual row of shops on the ground floor, and at one end there was an entrance for use by residents of the apartments on the floors above. Unlike some of the other places, this one had no doorman.

Was it workable? The best way to find out would be to bluff his way inside.

Again he pretended to be window shopping, and when a woman went into the entrance of the building he followed her. She unlocked the inner door and he pushed it open for her, hoping she'd think he lived there too.

She noticed the golf bag and smiled. "Nice day for it," she said.

"Yes, ma'am. Beautiful."

He stepped with her into a small lobby, and she pressed a button for an elevator. When it arrived they rode up together, continuing to chat about the weather, and fortunately for him she got off at one of the middle floors.

Mongo went on up to the highest, which was the tenth. When he left the elevator, he walked down the hall to the fire exit and opened the door.

As he'd expected, the stairway ran from the ground floor all the way up to the roof. He went out onto the landing and wedged the door with a book of matches so he'd be able to get back in.

From there, he took the stairs up to the heavy metal door that would lead outside. Once more he had to wedge the door open, and this time he used the cover he'd put over the rifle stock. Then he went out onto the roof.

There were a number of structures up there. The largest of them apparently housed machinery of some kind, probably the building's air-conditioning system. Another he supposed was for storage. There were also ventilation ducts, looking like upright metal tubes that curved over at the top.

A low parapet ran all the way around the outer perimeter of the roof. Moving close to the edge and looking down, he found he could see the entrance of the target building quite clearly.

Great, he thought. Plenty of places to hide up here, and at the same time he'd have an unobstructed view when he zeroed in on the cop. Right next to the parapet would be the best spot to fire from.

It'd be risky to sneak a look, but he couldn't resist. He pulled the rifle out of the golf bag and rested it on the parapet.

The weapon was fitted with a Swift telescopic sight. That in combination with its enormous power made it an ideal sniper's rifle, although he hadn't needed the scope when he blew Culebra's head off from a short distance.

Now, however, the range would be roughly a hundred yards, and use of the scope would be vital. When focusing on the cop, he'd get exactly one chance, and he couldn't afford to waste it.

But when would that be? Would the cop show up tonight to call on his sweet little piece? If he did, Mongo would whack him before he made it into the building's entrance.

Night would offer a number of advantages. It would be darker up here then, so it would be even less likely that he'd be observed. Yet there would be plenty of illumination down on the street, where the cop would be.

He pointed the rifle at the sidewalk in front of the target building and squinted through the telescopic sight. At the curb, a woman was getting out coins for a parking meter. He moved the gun a fraction to focus on her, and the image in the scope was so sharp he could see the buttons on her blouse.

Fantastic, he thought. With this rig he couldn't miss, he was sure of it. If he squeezed the trigger now, he'd drill her in the left tit.

And when he had the cop in the scope, it would be just as easy. And just as sure.

But at the moment, he'd stuck his neck out far enough. What he had to do now was stay out of sight and wait for darkness. He lifted the rifle from the parapet and rose to his feet.

"Hey, you! Drop the gun!"

Mongo was so startled he let go of the weapon, and it clattered to the surface.

"Put your hands up! Do it now, or I'll shoot!"

The voice was coming from behind him. He thrust his hands into the air.

"Now turn around."

Mongo complied, slowly turning to face the owner of the voice.

A guy in a dark blue uniform was staring at him. He was training a revolver on Mongo's chest, and at the same time pulling a cell phone from his pocket.

"Don't move," the man said. "You're gonna stay right where you are till I get some backup."

43.

One of the Sunset Inn's amenities was a small gym. When Barker walked in, only one other man was in the place, a fat guy who was pumping iron. His face was as red as a ripe tomato, and he was wheezing loudly as he hoisted the barbell over his head. Barker walked past him and stepped onto a treadmill.

The device was equipped with a small TV set and earphones so that the user could offset the boredom of exercising with the boredom of watching television. Barker put on the earphones and tuned in to a news channel. Then he set the treadmill on a fast pace and began running.

At least today the TV news wasn't about the Delure case, which was a relief. Instead, there was a stream of stories on mayhem, ranging from the latest developments in the war between gangbangers to a double homicide in South Central. As Sam Benziger and Deke Edwards had said, there was no shortage of crime in LA. He switched channels to one that featured country music.

Barker liked country. Mostly it consisted of a singer wailing about an unfaithful lover, but at least you could understand the lyrics and there was an actual melody. Not like the idiot pounding of rap.

He'd clocked about seven miles when his phone rang. He pulled it out of his pocket and went on running. "Barker."

"Hi there," a familiar voice said. "Hopkins here. I thought you'd want to know Zarkov's agreement has arrived. It's complicated, because it's written in lawyerese. I told you I'd call when I got it."

"Thanks. I'd like to see it."

"Fine. Come on over and have a look."

"Okay, when?"

"Whenever you can make it."

Barker said he'd get there as soon as he could. He put the phone away and went on running.

He was due to meet Sam Benziger at the LA County Jail, where Marcia Slade was now being held. According to Sam, Slade was again trying to bargain, claiming she had more information than she'd given up in Las Vegas. But he wasn't to join Sam at the jail until late afternoon, so there was plenty of time.

This was the first chance he'd had to get some exercise, and he hated to cut it short. He ran another five simulated miles before shutting down the machine.

On the way out of the gym he saw that the fat weight lifter was still at it. The guy's red face and loud wheezing suggested he was due for a heart attack any minute now. Strange way to improve his health, Barker thought. Or maybe he just wanted to look good in his casket.

After a shower Barker put on a polo shirt and khakis and headed out. It was another beautiful California day, with warm sunshine and a cloudless sky, and he enjoyed the drive.

Just before he reached Bel Air his phone rang again. For a moment he was tempted to ignore the damn thing. Let it take a message, and he'd decide later whether the call was important. Then he thought better of it and answered: "Barker."

"Jeb, it's Joe."

"How's it going?"

"Not so good. Danny the Dip had a solid alibi for the day Delure and Ellis were shot, and a judge sprang him. So Hogan looked like a horse's ass. The media loved it, of course. The *Post* came out with an editorial that said he should be replaced. The PC gave him a good reaming, said he was an embarrassment to the department."

"And then he canned him?"

"No such luck. He's back to flailing in all directions."

"So stay out of his way."

"I'm trying, but here's the bad part: Hogan called a bunch of us together so he could take his misery out on us, and afterward he pinned me down. He didn't ask where you were, or even ask if I knew. Instead he just told me if you didn't report to him soon, he'd have you suspended."

"Good luck to him. He could take me off the case, but he couldn't suspend me. That'd be up to Kelly."

"Maybe so. But my advice is for you to get back here. Otherwise you'll be in deep shit."

"Can't do it, Joe. Between you and me, I'm close to cracking the case."

"Come on."

"I mean it. The shooter's a hired gun, and I think he's here in LA. The LAPD wants him too, on a separate murder rap. I'm also running down leads on who hired him."

"That's great. So why not let Hogan know? He could even find a way to take the credit if what you're doing pays off."

"You know why."

"You're afraid he'd fuck it up?"

"Of course he would. All I need is another day or two, I'm convinced."

"Okay, I hope you know what you're doing."

"Me too," Barker said and ended the call.

When he arrived at Hopkins's place, Barker nodded to the security man and parked in the side courtyard between a silver Porsche and a green Aston Martin. He got out and looked at the lineup of the three cars. In that company, the Ford put him in mind of a poor relative who'd come to ask for a loan.

For that matter, seeing the huge Mediterranean house had the same effect on him.

He went to the entrance and pressed the buzzer.

The butler opened the door. "Ah, Mr. Barker."

"Hello, Cedric."

"Follow me, sir, if you would, please. Lovely day, isn't it?"

"Couldn't be better."

They traveled the same route as they had the last time Barker was here, winding up on the vast patio at the rear of the house. The area was ablaze with red and purple bougainvillea blossoms.

Hopkins was in swim trunks. He was lounging on a deck chair by the pool, and so was Donna Ferrante. As on Barker's earlier visit, Donna was wearing little more than a coat of suntan oil. Another woman was there as well, similarly attired. This one was a blonde, and like Ferrante, she had a fantastic body.

"Hi, Jeb," Hopkins said. "Welcome. You know Donna, of course." He indicated the blonde. "And this is Audrey Melon."

Barker said hello to the two women, and both gave him brilliant smiles.

"You may have seen Audrey on television," Hopkins said. "She's a regular in *Girls Who Do It*. They wanted someone who had intellectual appeal, and obviously she has quite a bit. In fact, she has two of them."

"Honestly, Bart," the blonde said, "do you have to be so crude?"

Hopkins grinned. "Yeah, it's congenital."

"Part of his charm," Donna said.

"We're drinking piña coladas," Hopkins said to Barker. "You've gotta have one. Most refreshing."

"Thanks," Barker said. "But I'd just as soon—"

Too late. Cedric had reappeared, bearing a full glass on a tray. He proffered it and smiled.

What the hell, Barker thought. He took the glass and drank. Once again he had to admit the drink tasted great.

It was also powerful. When it hit bottom he felt a pleasant suffusion of warmth. And his reservations about being here with two near-naked women began to fade away.

"Bart tells me you're from New York," the blonde said. "I love that city. Don't get there often enough."

"It's an interesting place." He drained his glass and put it down on a table.

"Where do you live?" She linked her arm with his, seeming genuinely interested.

"SoHo."

"Ah, that's a great neighborhood. Do you have a loft apartment?"

"Yeah, as a matter of fact I do." He was aware that her boobs were brushing against him.

"Wonderful," she said. "High ceilings, and views, and all that?"

"Uh-huh, all that." He didn't mention that his apartment was actually one room, with a kitchen area at one end and a bathroom at the other. His bed was a pullout sofa. As for the view, that was nothing to rave about either.

But he hadn't come here to chat about New York real estate. To Hopkins he said, "So how about showing me the agreement?"

"No rush, especially on a day as nice as this one. Tell you what. Why don't you have a swim, and then we'll go over it, okay?"

"Don't have a swimsuit," Barker said.

"Cedric will fix you up with one." He raised a hand, and the butler again materialized.

"Take Mr. Barker to the pool house," Hopkins ordered. "And get him some trunks."

Barker started to protest. "Look, I—"

"Oh, come on," the blonde said. "I'll swim with you. It'll be fun."

So why not, he thought. He followed Cedric and was shown a dressing room in the pool house and given a pair of yellow trunks that came down almost to his knees.

When he returned to the patio, the blonde said, "Wow, you look just like a Malibu surfer." She grabbed his wrist and pulled him into the pool.

The blonde was right, he decided. It was fun. They swam together and splashed each other and generally acted like a couple of kids. Donna jumped in as well, but Hopkins stayed on his chaise and worked on his piña colada.

Later, when Barker and the others had climbed out of the pool and toweled off, he again asked to see the agreement. Hopkins said by all means, but first let's have something to eat.

There was a loggia at one end of the pool house, where Cedric had laid out lobster salad and smoked turkey and ratatouille and warm rolls. He'd also popped a bottle of champagne.

The sunshine and the swim had made Barker ravenously hungry. While he stuffed himself, Hopkins and the women carried on a gossipy conversation about people in the film business.

Audrey was seated next to him, and now her legs were doing the brushing. Barker felt himself respond to her touch and wondered what would happen if he suggested they go into the house and find a secluded bedroom. She'd probably be delighted. Might even make the suggestion herself.

The thought brought him back to his senses. "This has been terrific," he said to Hopkins. "But I'm running out of time. I'll get dressed, and then you can show me the agreement."

"Yes, of course. You girls will excuse us."

"Oh hell, Bart," Donna said. "Can't you forget about business for one day?"

The blonde squeezed Barker's thigh. "Just come back soon, okay?"

Barker went into the dressing room and put his clothes on. Then the two men walked to the house, and Hopkins led the way into a well-stocked library.

There was a refectory table with a lamp on it in the center of the room. A document lay on the table. They drew up chairs, and Barker began to read.

Hopkins was right. This was nothing like the simple agreement

Zarkov had said it would be. Instead, it was page after page of legal babble.

The gist of it was clear enough, however. Hopkins was to invest the tidy sum of fifteen million dollars in a creative venture that might or might not eventually become a profitable movie.

Barker noticed that some of the clauses referred to the movie project specifically, while others were more general and concerned Zarkov's company. One said that the money invested could be used in any way the company chose.

Another said that the investor acknowledged that he would have no claim against the company should the venture fail, inasmuch as development of a motion picture invariably involved a high degree of risk.

Taken in total, everything in the agreement favored Zarkov's company, and nothing protected the investor's interests. Just as Dana had said, if the project tanked, Hopkins would get zilch.

When he finished the perusal Barker said, "May I have a copy of this?"

"Sorry," Hopkins said. "I don't think I should do that. I'm probably stepping out of bounds just by letting you read it."

"Okay, I understand. But thanks for letting me have a look."

"I thought you'd find it fascinating. I don't know, of course, whether Zarkov and Apperson are doing anything that's not on the level. But I intend to hold on to this and study it further."

"What are you going to tell Zarkov?"

Hopkins grinned. "That I'm considering it. Which is the truth. Although after reading this, I keep telling myself to be careful. Very careful."

Barker glanced at his watch. He had to hurry, or he'd be late for his meeting with Sam Benziger at the jail. He thanked Hopkins again and asked him to give the girls his apologies for running off. Then he left the house.

This had been an interesting visit. The agreement could constitute the first piece of hard evidence that showed Zarkov and Apperson were out to commit fraud. A sharp DA could demand to see it, or subpoena it if necessary.

And the possible connection between that scheme and the murder of Delure and Ellis? Okay, that would be a hell of a lot harder to prove.

But if he could prove it, the pieces would fall into place. As he'd told Joe Spinelli, he wasn't there yet, but he was getting close.

44.

It took Mongo less than a second to form an impression of the guy with the gun. The dark blue uniform with the officer's cap and silver badge said he was a guard who worked for a security company. He was older, and obviously very nervous.

He was also dangerous. His hand was shaking, the forefinger pressing on the trigger of the revolver, and his other hand was fumbling with the phone.

Mongo shouted, "Christ, man, what are you doing? You're gonna ruin the whole fucking thing. Are you crazy?"

The guy frowned. "What?"

"Didn't you get the word? We're making a movie!"

"What movie? I don't see any—"

"This setup is for an overhead shot from a helicopter," Mongo yelled. "I was waiting for the chopper to get here. You fuck up the scene and I guarantee you'll find yourself fired. We're making a major motion picture, damn it."

The guard stopped fiddling with the phone. But he kept the

revolver pointed at Mongo. "How do I know you're telling the truth?"

"For one thing, I can show you my ID." Mongo reached into his back pocket for his wallet, hoping the guy wouldn't shoot before he got it out.

Flipping the wallet open he said, "There's my SAG card. See? I'm a member of the Screen Actors Guild."

No such card was visible, because Mongo didn't have one. But the revolver was lowered by a few inches.

A note of uncertainty crept into the guy's voice. "So where's the rest of the crew?"

Mongo returned the wallet to his pocket and pointed. "Right over there. The director's the one waving his arms and having a convulsion."

The security guard hesitated. But he couldn't resist taking a look in the direction Mongo had indicated. "I still don't see—"

Mongo grabbed the hand holding the revolver and twisted it back, so that if the guard pulled the trigger now he'd shoot himself in the face.

"Go ahead, you fucking idiot," Mongo snarled, "kill yourself!"

The guard tried to pull free, but Mongo held him in a tight grip and thrust a leg around behind him, slamming him down onto his back. He struggled, but he was perceptibly weaker. Mongo knelt on his chest and kept on twisting until a sharp crack signaled the wrist was broken.

The guard shrieked in pain, and Mongo snatched the revolver from him. His cap fell off, revealing a bald head, and Mongo used the revolver as a club, smashing it against the top of the head again and again until the skin split open and blood ran down the man's face.

Mongo then seized him by the neck and pressed a thumb against his windpipe. After a few minutes his eyes became glazed and sightless and he no longer showed any sign of life.

Mongo rose to his feet. Breathing hard, he looked at his surroundings. He had to find a place to hide the body, but where? The shed holding the air-conditioning equipment wouldn't do, and neither would the smaller one. They'd almost certainly be locked.

That left the ventilation ducts. There were several of them, each about five feet high and with an opening that was protected by a screen. Mongo judged the openings to be roughly twenty inches in diameter.

That might do it, he thought. He dragged the dead man over to the nearest duct and examined the screen covering the opening. It was fastened with four wingnuts, and they were rusty. He strained to loosen them one by one, and when he had all of them undone, he pulled the screen away from the duct and tossed it aside.

With an effort he lifted the body. The guy was much heavier than he looked, and now that he was lifeless, it was like trying to maneuver a large sack filled with sand. It took a mighty heave to shove him headfirst into the opening, and then more heaving to stuff in the rest of him.

The corpse didn't slide all the way down the ventilation duct, as Mongo had hoped it would. But at least it was out of sight.

Now the question was whether the scuffle with the security asshole had been seen. Even though the roof was higher than the other buildings, some nosy neighbor might have spotted Mongo dropping the guy and called 911. He looked carefully in all directions but saw no one who might be observing him.

Okay, so he was in luck. And after waiting for a time and hearing no police sirens, he was certain he was in the clear.

What's more, it was getting dark. That meant more cover, so much that no one could see him. He went back to the roof's edge and picked up the rifle. Crouching down, he leaned the barrel against the top of the parapet and again took up his vigil.

45.

LA's Twin Towers Correctional Facility was the world's largest jail. The enormous complex was located at 450 Bauchet Street, just off 101 and to the northeast of Union Station.

In addition to the towers, it comprised a medical services building and the Los Angeles County Medical Center Jail Ward. As big as it was, the place was jam-packed with inmates every day of the year.

When Barker arrived, Sam Benziger was waiting for him among a throng of visitors just inside the main entrance. She said a prosecutor would be joining them for their talk with Marcia Slade. Also Slade's lawyer would be on hand.

"So what's she up to now?" Barker asked.

"She claims she didn't give us the whole story when we questioned her in Las Vegas," Sam said. "She's scheduled to go before a grand jury, and she's looking for another bargain."

"You believe her?"

Benziger shrugged. "She knows information is valuable, so it's possible she held something back."

"Yeah, they always do that, if they can. By the way, how did the search for Morris Wagner go?"

"We ran down a bunch of guys with that name, and none of them checked out."

"So either Slade lied about it or the name was another phony."

"Yeah, take your pick."

"And now?"

"She realizes the charges here aren't just ratshit misdemeanors she can walk away from. She's facing murder one with special circumstances, meaning premeditated and committed in the course of a felony. In this state, that can get her the needle. So she's probably desperate. Anyway, it'll be interesting to hear what she has to say."

"Good afternoon." A young black woman wearing a pinstriped business suit and carrying a briefcase approached them.

"Hi, Natalie," Benziger said. "This is Jeb Barker, the detective from New York I told you about. Jeb, say hello to Natalie Adams. Natalie's a deputy DA."

Barker shook her hand. "Glad to know you."

"Same here."

"We were talking about Slade," Benziger said. "And whether she can give us anything worthwhile."

"I think she can," Adams said. "Her lawyer's too smart to let her try to con us. Instead he'll want to trade some chips. You give us this and we'll tell you that."

"Who is he?"

"Mel Torson, a public defender," the DA said. "You know him?"

"I don't think so."

"You're lucky. He's a real worm. When you talk to him, he squirms."

"I'm told we're in room B on the fourth floor," Benziger said. "Let's get our passes and go up."

They presented ID to a sergeant at the desk and were given passes to move about the jail. They took an elevator and then went past a cell block to the assigned room. Marcia Slade and her attorney were already waiting for them. Also present was a large female corrections officer whose nameplate identified her as Marie Santiago.

Slade didn't seem nearly as chic as she had in Las Vegas. Instead of the tight-fitting blue dress she'd worn there, she now had on orange coveralls. Her face was pale, and there were shadows under her eyes.

To Barker, Torson was just as Natalie Adams had described him. He was short and round, with long brown hair covering his ears. He wore a three-piece gray suit, and his patronizing manner revealed what he thought of the DA and the two cops.

After making the introductions, Adams got the meeting under way. She turned to Slade. "So, Marcia, you say you have some additional information for us concerning the perpetrator in the Delure case."

"Yeah, I do," Slade said. "But I want—"

Torson cut her off. "My client is more than willing to be as cooperative and helpful as possible. But I think we need to reach an understanding."

"About what?"

"About giving us something in return for her help. You're putting her before a grand jury on a charge of homicide, which is ridiculous. You may not even get an indictment. And if you do, you won't be able to prove your case in a trial."

"We'll see about that," Adams said.

"We certainly will. Although you know as well as I do that your so-called evidence is extremely thin."

"You think so?"

"Come on, Natalie," the lawyer said. "All you have is a piece of videotape showing Ms. Slade leaving a room in the Beverly Hilton. Do you really believe that amounts to proof that a crime was committed?"

"No, I don't. But you haven't mentioned the other piece of tape. The one that shows her going into the room with a man who later was found dead and with his money gone."

"You call that evidence?"

"Yeah, I do. Especially when the medical examiner said he'd been murdered."

"And also," Benziger said, "when you consider Marcia's history of rolling johns."

Slade's eyes flashed. "Damn it, I never rolled anybody."

"Then what happened to the guy's money?"

"All I did was blow that turkey! What's more, I—"

Again her lawyer interrupted. "Of course that's all you did, Marcia. We know that." He turned back to Adams. "And we also know that any reference to Ms. Slade's history of arrests would be inadmissible. No judge would allow it."

"Is that so?" Adams said. "California law permits priors to come in as long as they show a pattern of similar conduct."

One side of Torson's mouth twisted upward. "Are you lecturing me on the law?"

Adams said, "Just reminding you, Mel."

"Then let me point out that before this my client was never arrested for robbery, and certainly not for murder."

"But the prostitution raps show a pattern, right?"

"Yes, a pattern of arrests for trivial misdemeanors."

"Although the court just might see a connection, don't you think?"

"No," Torson said. "I don't think that at all. So let's stop dancing around. What are you offering us?"

"Just this," Adams said. "If your client gives us something of value, I'll make a favorable recommendation to the judge."

"Not good enough. The very least you can do is request bail."

"Bail? On first-degree murder with special circumstances? You know that's impossible."

"Then what is possible?"

The DA steepled her fingers and looked at the ceiling for a few moments. Then she focused on Torson. "What's possible is that I tell the judge she gave the police valuable help in their investigation of a separate capital crime. Moreover, she would be willing to testify, if and when the perpetrator of that crime is brought to justice.

Therefore, our office believes she is a person who genuinely wishes to redeem herself, and we request that the court take that into consideration as the case moves through the system."

Slade said, "Oh, shit. Are you—"

"Shut up, Marcia," Torson said. He turned back to the DA. "We'll take it."

"Smart move," Adams said. "But before you tell us anything, Marcia, I want to show you something." She opened her briefcase and took out a copy of the composite that showed the killer without a wig or a mustache.

She laid the drawing on the table and said, "Take a good look. Do you swear this is the man you had contact with in Las Vegas, the one you say assaulted you?"

Slade peered at the rendering, and then at Adams. "Yeah, that's him. He looks a little skinnier there, but that's the guy, I'm sure of it."

Barker had been quiet until now. "You said he had a tattoo. Correct?"

"Yes, on his left shoulder."

"You saw it clearly?"

"Of course."

"Then I'd like you to draw it for us."

Slade shrugged. "All right, I can do that."

Adams produced a sheet of paper and a ballpoint and placed them beside the mug shot. Slade laboriously drew her recollection of the tattoo.

Barker took the sheet from her and studied it. The drawing was a simple depiction of a fishhook. Why, he wondered, would the man have worn such a decoration? What was its significance?

Sam said, "Was there anything else? Any other kind of identifying mark on him?"

Slade looked at her with an expression of contempt. "Yeah. He had a picture of the Statue of Liberty on his dick."

Sam grimaced, but before she could say anything, Torson jumped in. "Just answer the question, Marcia. Were there any other marks?"

"No. The tattoo was all I saw."

"Okay," Barker said. "Then can we please hear what the information is that you have for us?"

Slade looked at her lawyer.

"Go ahead," Torson said.

After a dramatic pause, Slade said, "I can tell you the town where the guy lives."

"You already told us," Barker said. "You said Los Angeles."

"I meant the Los Angeles area. But I can do better than that."

"So let's have it."

After another pause, Slade said, "Malibu."

"How do you know that?"

"He had some receipts in his wallet. Two were from a Chevron station on the Pacific Coast Highway in Malibu. And there was another one from Ralphs supermarket, also in Malibu."

Benziger said, "And you think that shows where he lives? Maybe he was just driving through, and he stopped for gas and picked up a few things from the store."

"Not just a few things," Slade said. "The receipt was for a hundred eighty-five bucks. All for groceries and a couple of bottles of wine. Just like what somebody would buy to stock up."

"Okay," Sam said. "What else can you give us?"

Slade glared at her. "What else do you want—his address and phone number? What kind of cops are you, anyhow?"

"That's enough, Marcia," Torson said. He stood up and addressed the others. "I think we've more than fulfilled our end of the bargain here. So that brings our discussion to an end. Have a nice evening."

Barker spoke up. "One more question, Marcia. You claim you never rolled anybody. Is that right?"

"You heard me. Never."

"Then why did you go into the guy's wallet?"

Her mouth dropped open, and Torson said, "Don't answer that. This meeting is over."

Slade shot Barker a fierce look, but she said nothing more. She rose and the CO escorted her from the room. Torson left with them.

Barker said, "What do you think, Sam?"

"Could be nothing, could be a home run. First thing I'll do is ask the Malibu police to help us."

"Do you know that supermarket?"

"Yeah, there's only one Ralphs in Malibu. It's next to the Malibu Colony. I'll show his photo to the staff there."

Barker picked up the sheet of paper with Slade's drawing of the tattoo on it. "And can you get the media to give this some exposure, especially TV? Somebody might recognize it."

"Sure. They're always hungry for anything to do with the Delure case. They wouldn't pay much attention if it only involved Culebra. But Delure? Absolutely. I'll ask our PR people to get out copies to the TV stations and the *LA Times* right away."

"Great. We just might be making progress."

Benziger said, "Thanks for your help, Natalie. Turned out better than I thought it would."

"You're welcome. I hope the Malibu leads and the drawing get you somewhere."

"So do I."

"Natalie, there's one other thing," Barker said. "I've come across a situation here in LA that could be a major case of fraud. If you have a few minutes, I'd like to discuss it with you."

"Not my bailiwick," Adams said. "But we have a section that handles that type of case. As you're probably aware, Congress passed the Fraud Enforcement and Recovery Act in 2009. That gave us more money to work with, and we've got some sharp DAs in the section. You want me to set something up?"

"Yes, I'd appreciate it. It's a little early in the game, but I'd like to hear what they think."

"Sure. Give me a call whenever you're ready."

Barker was looking forward to seeing Dana. They'd have a few drinks, and then he'd take her out to dinner. And this time he'd insist on it.

By and large, the discussion at the jail had been encouraging.

Although whether Marcia Slade's information was any good, who could say? Was the killer actually living in Malibu? Or was that just a smokescreen Slade had used in an attempt to buy herself a better deal?

Same thing applied to her drawing of the tattoo on Mongo's shoulder. And yet, getting the media to put the drawing before the public just might turn up some worthwhile results. Especially if the drawing were shown on TV.

The visit to Bart Hopkins's house might also pay off. The Zarkov agreement could stand as evidence that Zarkov was involved in a widespread scam. And now Natalie Adams would set up a meeting with the people in the DA's office that dealt with fraud.

Still, the toughest part would be to prove there was a connection between that and the murders of Delure and Ellis. He was still thinking about it as he got into the Ford and headed toward Dana's apartment.

Up on the roof darkness had closed in, while the streets below were brightly lit and filled with traffic, and people were going in and out of the stores. With the darkness had come a drop in temperature, and Mongo wished he'd worn something more than a light shirt.

He was also hungry and tired of crouching here like some wild animal that was hoping a meal would come along. This was the part of the arrangement he had with Strunk that pissed him off whenever he thought about it. Here he was, taking all the risks, having to operate in lousy conditions, while the lawyer sat on his ass in his cozy office and counted the money.

And that brought another thing to mind. Mongo was well paid for his services, no question about that. There were plenty of guys in LA who'd be happy to take somebody out for a few bucks, let alone the amounts he got. The difference, of course, was that he handled the toughest contract jobs, and handled them with great skill, never leaving the slightest trace of evidence.

You wanted somebody to go away for good, wanted to be sure the going could never be connected to you? Okay, fine. But be prepared to pay for it. Pay Strunk, that is, who would then dribble out a fraction of the fee to Mongo.

For that matter, Mongo had no way of knowing just how much of a fee the lawyer got for a job. Or what percentage Strunk was passing on to him for doing the actual work. But he was sure the largest part stayed with Strunk.

So what to do about it? He'd given a lot of thought to that, and so far he hadn't come up with a satisfactory answer. But sooner or later he'd figure out a way to get a bigger slice for himself. A lot bigger. And if that meant Strunk would be left with the short end? Tough shit, Counselor.

He looked at his watch. It was getting late, and there had been no sign of Barker. So maybe the cop had other plans for tonight. Mongo would give it one more hour, and if the detective didn't show up, he'd pack it in. Then he'd try again the following night.

But not here. He couldn't take a chance on coming back to this location. The company the security guard had worked for would be wondering why he hadn't checked in, and then they'd start hunting for him. In fact, it was a little surprising they hadn't already sent somebody.

And if they did, then what? Mongo would be forced to deal with yet another turdbrain. He'd wind up having a second body to dispose of, and how many ventilation ducts could he clog up?

The first guy certainly had been a rank amateur. Not a retired cop, as most security guards were. Of course, if he had been, Mongo would have taken care of him anyway, but as it was he'd been almost too easy to overcome.

It was funny, the way he'd gone for the movie gag. *We're shooting a major motion picture* was a magic phrase to most of the shitwits in this town, and Mr. Security couldn't resist the lure.

Mongo glanced at the guard's pistol, which was lying at his feet. It was a .38-caliber six shot Smith & Wesson Police Special, as outmoded as a flintlock. Nowadays, everybody who carried a handgun chose an automatic. Or a semiautomatic, as ladies called them. A Glock, say, or a Beretta, or maybe a Sig. One of those would give you as many as fifteen rounds, fast as you could pull the trigger.

Mongo shivered. The wind had come up, and that made the air even chillier. He again looked at his watch. Be nice to leave this fucking roof and get back out to Malibu.

And come to think of it, he just might stop off in Hollywood. There was nothing like a blow job for lifting your spirits. After that he'd go to the cottage and drink some wine, smoke a joint. There was a steak in the fridge, and that would go good tonight.

Meantime, this place was made even more uncomfortable by the way he had to keep an eye on the entrance to the garage. Squinting down at it, looking for a gray Ford sedan. With a prick at the wheel.

He shifted his position and for about the tenth time peered through the rifle's telescopic sight. Amazing how it brought things up close. You had to keep the rifle perfectly still, though. Any jiggling would throw off the image. So you held steady, while you put the crosshairs on the target.

Come to think of it, there was a windage adjustment on the scope, and with the breeze picking up he probably ought to use it. He estimated the wind at about fifteen miles per hour and twisted the little wheel accordingly.

Again he resumed his wait. And with each passing moment grew more exasperated. Finally he told himself it was time to go. Stuff the rifle into the golf bag and take off.

And then, there was the Ford.

There was no mistaking it, even though there were probably a thousand vehicles like it in Southern California. The car had stopped opposite the garage entrance, the driver waiting for a gap in the traffic so he could make the left turn. And that provided Mongo with an unobstructed view.

He was tempted to take his shot now, instead of waiting for the cop to leave his car in the garage and come out onto the sidewalk.

Looking through the scope, he could make out Barker's face quite clearly.

But then the traffic parted, and the Ford zipped across the opposite lane and disappeared into the garage.

Take your time, Mongo told himself. Let him come out, and make sure. Put the crosshairs on him, and don't just pull the trigger, squeeze it gently.

Seconds passed, and finally the cop emerged. He strode up the sidewalk, his back to Mongo as he made his way past other pedestrians.

Make it a head shot, Mongo thought. As Culebra had said, the heavy slug would pop his head like a grape. Worked with Culebra, didn't it?

So do it now.

Mongo lined up the crosshairs on the black hair just above the cop's shirt collar. He took a deep breath, held steady, and squeezed.

The rifle fired with a thunderous noise and a hard kick against his shoulder. The report was so loud it startled him and made his ears ring, even though he'd anticipated it.

But the big weapon had done its work.

When he reached the public garage Barker took a ticket and parked the Ford, then walked up the ramp to the sidewalk. There was a florist shop along here, he recalled. He'd stop in and buy some flowers for Dana.

He'd taken a half-dozen steps when he saw an older woman coming toward him. She was well dressed and burdened with a large Nordstrom shopping bag and some other bundles, along with her purse. Just as he passed her she struggled to control the load, and instinctively he put out a hand to steady her.

At that instant he heard the unmistakable crack of a high-powered rifle and a bullet whizzed past his ear like an angry hornet. The projectile tore a chunk of concrete out of the sidewalk in front of him and ricocheted off into the night.

The woman cried out, and Barker grabbed her arm and pulled

her with him behind a car that was parked at the curb. Her packages spilled onto the street.

"Help!" she shrieked. "They're trying to kill us! Call the police!"

"Take it easy," Barker said. "Just keep your head down and everything'll be okay."

Mongo couldn't believe it. He'd actually missed! Just as he'd fired, the son of a bitch had turned his head!

And now he couldn't get off another shot because Barker had ducked behind a car, dragging some woman with him. But maybe he should shoot again anyway, put a few more bullets through the car in hopes of hitting him. He raised the rifle and again squinted through the scope.

Hold on, he told himself. Bad enough that you missed with the first one. That shot had made a hell of a lot of noise, and spraying the car with bullets would be like turning a spotlight on yourself.

He lowered the rifle and looked down at the sidewalk. Other pedestrians had gathered and were obviously in an uproar. One guy was pointing up at the roof.

That did it. Mongo shoved the rifle back into the golf bag and dropped the cover over the stock. Crouching low, he scuttled crablike to the door, ran through it, and went down the stairs as the door slammed shut behind him.

Once on the floor below he had to wait for the elevator, standing on one foot and then the other before the damn thing finally arrived. He jumped in and pressed the button for the lobby, hoping the car wouldn't stop on the way.

But it did. On 6 it came to a halt, and a man and a woman got in and seeing the golf bag gave him a funny look. Okay, so going out to play golf on a dark night would strike anybody as loony, but they could mind their own goddamn business. Mongo leaned against the back wall of the elevator car, his baseball cap pulled down to obscure his face, and ignored them.

When they stepped out into the lobby, he heard the sound of

police sirens. He went out onto the street and walked in the opposite direction from the garage. When enough time had passed, he'd go back for his car.

The sound of the sirens grew louder, and he picked up his pace.

Barker waited a few beats and then got to his feet. He continued to reassure the woman and she quieted down. By now she apparently was as humiliated and bewildered as she was fearful. Her packages and her purse were strewn about the sidewalk, and he collected them and returned them to her. She walked off, seeming somewhat dazed.

Meanwhile the onlookers went on buzzing about what had occurred, or what they thought had occurred, ascribing the incident to the war between gang members. One man was pointing up at a building and yelling that he'd seen a muzzle flash on the roof.

Barker stepped around them and walked on up the sidewalk. As he did, he saw that the bullet had torn a fair-sized hole in the concrete. He had no doubt as to what type of weapon had fired it.

Nor who the shooter had been.

The realization jolted him. The murderer must have found out who he was and had tried to kill him, using the same high-powered rifle that had blown Culebra away.

But how had the guy learned his identity? And how did he know Barker would be here tonight?

For that matter, what else did he know? That Barker had come to LA to track the killer of Catherine Delure and her manager? And had learned it was Culebra who built the weapon that fired the fléchettes?

Did he also know Barker had begun to uncover the facts surrounding a scam in the movie business?

Perhaps he did know those things. Certainly any of it would make him determined to kill the cop who was trailing him.

Unless, Barker thought, the cop killed him first.

Once again a familiar picture appeared in his mind. He saw the well-dressed man in the videotape, strolling nonchalantly along the corridor in the Sherry-Netherland Hotel. Flashing his fuck-you grin at the camera.

Remembering that, Barker felt deep loathing. This case, this hunt, this contest, had become intensely personal. And the enemy had come within an inch of winning.

The sound of police sirens reached Barker's ears. Proper procedure called for him to inform the LAPD that someone had just fired a rifle at him.

But the hell with that. He kept going.

46.

Dana was waiting for Barker to arrive. She'd been thinking about him all day and was looking forward to seeing him. In addition to the passion he brought out in her, he made her feel secure, and that in a relationship was a new experience for her. No wonder she'd fallen in love with him.

While she waited, she turned on the TV and surfed channels. There was a discussion on one of the talk shows about an upcoming special on the Delure case. Curious, she turned up the volume.

The interviewer was a vapid blonde who was pretending to be excited. Her interviewee was a TV producer who had the look of an artist, which was probably how he saw himself. Long shaggy hair, a wispy beard, wearing a chambray work shirt.

"The show sounds fascinating," the blonde gushed. "But isn't it a little early to be doing a special on the Delure case when the murders haven't been solved?"

The question was a softball, of course, and the producer caught it deftly. "Oh no," he said. "In fact, that's what makes it so relevant.

Just think about what happened here. A famous star and her manager were shot by a cold-blooded killer so he could steal the star's jewels. And the police haven't any idea as to who he was, or how to find him. I think the case may go down in history as one of the all-time great unsolved mysteries."

"You mean like Jack the Ripper, who killed all those women in London and was never caught?"

"Exactly. Or Lizzie Borden, in Fall River, Massachusetts, in 1892. It's believed Lizzie used an axe to hack both her parents to death, but she was never convicted."

"Amazing."

"And yet as famous as those cases were and still are, they can't compare with Delure. No case can. But the police have failed to produce even one credible suspect."

"So you're saying they haven't done a good job of investigating the case?"

"Obviously they haven't. Swarms of detectives are working on it, and what have they accomplished? Nothing."

"If that's so, what will the audience learn when your show goes on the air?"

"That's the part that makes it so compelling. The audience will hear from experts such as Mark Fuhrman, who was a detective on the O.J. case, and a number of others. They'll describe mistakes the cops have made, and what they should have done to solve the case."

"Sounds intriguing. And by the way, what impact have the murders had on the ordinary citizen? How have they affected the man in the street?"

"That's been simply phenomenal. Not only was Catherine Delure a huge star, but she was loved by millions of fans. Her latest film was released just at the time she met her death. People everywhere are aware of the human drama in that, and they're deeply involved emotionally."

"I'm sure that's true. And of course, *Hot Cargo* has become a big hit."

"One of the biggest. The picture is a favorite to win an Academy

Award, and Catherine Delure is likely to win Best Actress. That's why we expect our show to attract a television audience of the same proportions."

"Another big hit."

"No question about it. Viewers will see and hear comments by people who actually were on hand when the murders took place."

"Who, for example?"

"For one, Ms. Delure's bodyguard, Chuck Diggs. The killer claimed to be from a New York radio station, which was a lie, of course. But Chuck made a careful check and was assured that the man had legitimate business with Ms. Delure. Chuck then went over every inch of him to be sure he wasn't carrying a weapon of any kind."

"And Diggs is sure the killer was unarmed?"

"He's positive. Otherwise he never would have let him into the hotel suite."

"So then how were the murders committed? Both Ms. Delure and her manager were shot, right?"

"Yes, they were. And that's led some observers to think the weapon was already in the suite."

"So the killer knew it was there waiting for him? Does that mean it was an inside job?"

"We'll leave that to the audience to decide."

"But it certainly seems that way, doesn't it?"

"As I say, watch the show, and hear what Chuck and others can tell you."

"Fine, but who else was there? What about Ms. Delure's secretary? Will she appear in the show?"

"We believe she will. As everyone knows by now, her name is Dana Laramie. She's still in a state of shock because of what she witnessed that day, and until now she's declined our invitation to be interviewed."

Oh my God, Dana thought. You mean I wouldn't let myself be used by you and your crappy network.

"But it's really her duty," he said, "to let the world know what she saw. So we're hoping she'll realize that and come around."

Keep hoping, you asshole. Forever.

The TV interviewer pressed on. "And do you also have other members of the movie's cast?"

"Oh, yes. Ms. Delure's costar Terry Falcon has some great insights that he's never revealed till now."

That's enough, Dana thought. The so-called interview was nothing but a massive promo—and a huge con job. She hit the remote and turned off the set.

The buzzer sounded, and she hoped that meant Barker had arrived. When she opened the door, he greeted her with a smile and a bouquet of yellow roses.

"Figured you might like these," he said.

"I love them!"

She took the bouquet from him and inhaled their fragrance. "They're beautiful. And you were very nice to bring them. Thank you!"

"You're welcome." He kissed her and followed her into the kitchen, where she got out a vase and put the roses into them.

She looked at him. "Everything okay, Jeb? You seem a little tense."

"Me? No."

"You sure? No new problems?"

"Not a one. But I could use a drink."

"Coming up. Vodka martini on the rocks?"

"Perfect."

She took bottles and glasses from a cupboard. "I'll join you."

"Okay. After that I'm taking you out to dinner." He smiled. "And no arguments this time."

"Not a peep. Dinner sounds lovely." She filled the glasses with ice from the freezer and went about pouring the vodka and vermouth.

She knew very well what was bothering him. He was frustrated and tired from working on the case. And no doubt this had been one of those tedious days in which nothing significant had happened and no progress had been made. So the day had also been boring, and that could be discouraging as well. It would do him good to relax.

She handed him a glass and said cheers. They touched rims and drank.

"Tomorrow," Dana said, "will be better."

Barker took another long pull on his drink. "I hope so."

47.

Late the following day Barker joined Sam Benziger at LAPD headquarters, and they watched the news on a TV monitor. The program featured overhead shots of the freeways, while a male announcer droned on about how heavy traffic was moving slowly in all directions.

As if you couldn't see it for yourself, Barker thought.

Then came a weather report, the gist of which was that conditions tomorrow would be about the same as today. And the smog would be just as bad.

Barker was getting antsy. "Come on," he said, "let's have it."

"Patience," Sam said. "I've already seen it twice today. They'll show it again, I'm sure."

As if her words were a cue, a female announcer appeared on camera. "We have a new development in the Catherine Delure murder case," she said. "You'll recall that the police are looking for someone they call a person of interest. This is an artist's rendering of him."

Cut to a copy of the composite, the one that showed the killer without the hair and mustache. In a voice-over, the announcer said, "If you recognize this man, please call the police hotline at the number you see at the bottom of the screen."

Cut back to the announcer. "And now here's the latest development. It seems the man has a tattoo on his left shoulder. I'm going to show you a drawing of it, and if you know who wears it, or if it's in any way familiar to you, be sure to call the police hotline at once."

Cut to a close-up of the drawing. Announcer, VO: "This is the tattoo. It's about two inches in height, and as you can see, it's in the shape of a fishhook. The Los Angeles Police Department is asking you for any information you can provide."

Benziger turned off the set. "And there you are. TV's giving it pretty good exposure."

"So maybe we'll get a bite," Barker said.

"Don't get your hopes too high. I've listened to the call-ins, and so far they're worthless. You always expect there'll be some wackos, but these people sound like they're all nuts."

"Nevertheless, I want to hear them."

"Go right ahead," Sam said. "The calls are automatically saved on a dedicated line, and as new ones come in, they're added to the audiotape. Just call 27 on this phone, and you'll get them."

"Okay, I'll do that. And how about your visit to Malibu? You talk to the manager at Ralphs?"

"Yeah, I did. He agreed to distribute the flyers to the clerks in the store, but he didn't seem very optimistic. He said a lot of different people buy groceries there, and the clerks wouldn't pay all that much attention to their appearance. Far as the tattoo was concerned, he just shrugged."

"Maybe he's right. But you never know. What about the Malibu police?"

"I gave them copies of the flyer, and their reaction was the same as the guy at Ralphs. One of them said tattoos are as common as freckles."

"He has a point. But with the media showing the drawing, we might have some luck. Hope they keep on showing it."

"They'll give it a good run. Like I told you, they love anything that has to do with Delure."

A detective in shirtsleeves stopped by Benziger's desk. "Sam, the boss wants to see both of you."

"Now?"

"Yeah, in his office. And just between us, he sounds like he's got a hair up his ass. So watch yourself."

Sam sighed. "Thanks, Walt, I'll do that. Did you give him my message from last night?"

"Uh-huh. I think that's what set him off."

"Okay. Let's go, Jeb."

She led the way to Swanson's office, knocked once, and she and Barker went inside.

The commanding officer of the LAPD Detective Division was standing behind his desk. Flanking him were two other men Barker hadn't seen before. All three wore grim expressions.

Swanson hooked a thumb toward the one on his left. "Barker, this is Sergeant Reardon." The thumb then pointed the other way. "And this is Sergeant Fernandez."

Both stared at Barker.

Swanson said, "Detective Benziger, I understand you're working on a homicide case where the victim was a man named Culebra. That correct?"

"Sure, Captain. I wrote it up in my report."

"I saw that. What I didn't see in the report was anything that put the case in context."

"Put it in what?"

"Anything that would inform me that there was a possible connection between that homicide and the Catherine Delure case."

"Cap, at that point the possibility of a connection was more like speculation. So I didn't write about it, but I did try to talk to you and fill you in."

"I don't recall that."

She made no reply. Obviously she wasn't going to get into an argument with her CO.

"So tell me now," Swanson said.

"We've also been talking to a hooker," Benziger said, "who claimed she could ID the Delure perp. She saw the composite on TV in Vegas and was sure she'd met him a few days earlier. Now she's in the Twin Towers, and from what she could tell us, the guy might be in Malibu. I made up flyers and took them out there. Gave some to a supermarket and some to the Malibu police."

"You also had our people get TV and the *Times* to show a tattoo he has on him."

"Yes, I did. I looked for you last night to tell you about that, but you'd left. So I told Walt and asked him to pass it on to you."

"Not good enough. He gave me the message this morning, but that was pretty late. I should have been informed as soon as you began work on Culebra. Or maybe when you first talked to the hooker."

"But I didn't know—"

"You already have a DA involved. What's her name, Adams?"

"Yes. We met with her and the hooker's lawyer."

"Which is another thing you should have told me about."

Reardon said, "Captain Swanson's right. This never should've gone so far without you bringing him up to date. And if you couldn't reach him, you could have spoken to me."

"Or to me," Fernandez said.

Benziger took a deep breath. "I'm very sorry you don't think I was following proper procedures. I thought I was, and I was doing my best to keep both investigations moving. The reason the hooker's in the Towers is that she's a suspect in the homicide in the Beverly Hilton, where the john was rolled. Her name's Marcia Slade."

"Where does that stand?" Swanson asked.

"Adams plans to put her in front of a grand jury. She's pretty sure she can get her indicted on a charge of murder one."

"Good. I'll want to talk to Adams myself about it."

The captain then swung his attention to Barker. "I'm afraid you've overstepped your bounds, Barker. As a courtesy to your department in New York, I assigned Detective Benziger to give you whatever help you might need in your investigation. But now you've gone and involved yourself in two cases that are the responsibility of the LAPD."

"And you never requested permission," Reardon said.

"How do you explain that?" Swanson said.

Barker replied carefully. "Captain, as Detective Benziger just told you, at first we didn't know whether Culebra or Slade were in fact tied to Delure. That's what we were trying to find out."

"And it's also what you weren't telling us about," Fernandez said.

Barker started to say it was Benziger's job and not his to inform her superiors, but he shut his mouth. The last thing he wanted to do was to undermine Sam. It would also look as if he were trying to shift blame away from himself and onto her. So he said nothing.

Reardon said, "We've always done our best to cooperate with other jurisdictions and departments. That's been a hallmark of Captain Swanson's leadership."

"And, Barker, what you should have done," Fernandez added, "was show him you appreciated the help he was giving you by making sure he was up to the minute on everything you were doing."

Swanson raised a hand. "All right, that's enough. Barker, I probably should register a complaint with your commander in New York about the way you've conducted yourself here. And I promise you I'll do exactly that unless you stick with the rules from now on."

Barker remained silent. He'd begun to suspect there was more to this than the reasons Swanson was giving for tongue-lashing him and Benziger.

"And now let me ask the key question," Swanson said. "Do either of you believe there's a connection between Delure and what you've been turning up here?"

"I certainly do," Benziger said.

"So do I," Barker said.

"How much evidence do you have on that?"

"There's the ID by Slade," Barker said. "And also it looks as though this guy Culebra might have built the Delure murder weapon."

"Might have built it?"

"It's possible."

"But no actual proof?"

"No."

Swanson looked at Benziger. "And now Culebra was murdered and his shop burned down. Correct?"

"Yes."

"You have anything else?"

"Not so far, no."

"It seems pretty flimsy to me."

"We're hoping to get a break soon."

"Fine. But whether you do or not, from this point forward you're to consult with me and with Reardon and Fernandez every step of the way. We'll be giving you direction. Is that clear?"

She nodded, and so did Barker.

"Okay," Swanson said. "That'll be all, for now."

The pair left the office.

Barker was partly mystified, partly angry. When they were again alone, he said, "What the hell was that all about?"

Sam gave him a small, brief smile. "You didn't get it? No, you wouldn't. You'd have to know how our detective bureau operates, and what drives Swanson. See, the investigation of any run-of-the-mill homicide is handled by detectives in the division where it occurred. But if the victim's a VIP, then Detective Headquarters runs the investigation.'

"Okay, so?"

"So until now, Swanson figured Delure was a New York case. And as much as he wished he could be running it, he wasn't and couldn't. In fact, he believed what your department was saying, that the homicides were part of a jewelry heist. That's why he didn't pay much attention to what you and I were doing."

"I'm beginning to see the light. Now with the Culebra homicide and what we've been told by Slade, he thinks there's a chance this could be an LA case and he could take it over. True?"

"If not take it over, at least he'd have reasons to run an investigation of his own. And I don't have to tell you, if he could get the credit for clearing Delure, he'd have struck gold. That'd be so big it'd put him in line for chief of the LAPD."

"I'll bet. So now we have to wait for him and the others to tell us what to do next?"

"You heard the man. And don't take Reardon and Fernandez lightly. They're shrewd politicians too. Both of them have got their noses so far up Swanson's ass they're the same shade of brown."

The detective named Walt was back. "Sam," he said, "Reardon wants you for a meeting in the conference room. Right away."

Benziger shot Barker a look that said, See what I mean? Then she left him.

48.

"Is it done?" the garbled voice said. "Did you get it done?"

"Not yet," Mongo said.

"What do you mean, not yet?"

"Just what I said. I'll do it when I've got it lined up right."

"Listen, you. The client's in a hurry. I told you that, didn't I? That was part of the deal. He wants it done and done fast. So what are you waiting for?"

There were times when Mongo wished he could drag the little shit right out through the phone and beat him to a pulp. This was one of those times.

With an effort, he spoke in an even tone. "I'll do it soon as I can."

"You better. What do you think you get paid for?"

Mongo didn't reply. Rage was bubbling just under the surface, threatening to boil over.

"Did you hear what I said?"

"Yeah, I heard you."

"Then goddamn it, get going." The call ended.

Mongo took several deep breaths and told himself to calm down. When he had his anger under control, he thought about where things stood.

Fortunately, Strunk had no idea that an attempt had already been made to take out the cop, and the attempt had failed. If he found out, the lawyer would go batshit.

The failure in itself was amazing. With all the work Mongo had done, he'd never once had a job go down the toilet.

Until now.

It wasn't just frustrating. It was worse than that. He'd always taken pride in knowing he was the best there was. Smart, with iron nerves, and most of all, effective.

And now he'd fumbled what should have been a simple hit. He'd sat for hours on that lousy roof, chilled by the wind and bug-eyed from watching the street, and then he'd had to deal with the idiot security guard. And after all that, when he finally got his chance, he missed. It was humiliating, and he hated to admit it. Goddamn it.

Okay, so get your thumb out of your mouth, he told himself, and take another cut at it. And this time, be sure it ends the right way. Don't give the weasel another reason to complain.

Although he'd given that some thought, too. Strunk figured he was so clever, using a device that garbled his voice. What the lawyer didn't know was that Mongo had saved the tapes of every phone call. Garbled or not, there was enough in those calls to hang the prick, if it came to that.

But back to the problem. What he needed to do was off the cop for sure, and as soon as possible.

The rifle was out. The fucking thing was awkward to carry around, even in the golf bag, and it made too much noise when fired. And worst of all, he'd missed with it.

So how could he—hey, wait a minute. The answer was right at hand, had been the whole time. In fact, it was in his car, sitting right there on the floor.

Primacord! He still had half a roll of it! The stuff had done a great job on Culebra's dump, and it would do a great job on the cop as well. Why the hell hadn't he thought of that sooner?

No matter. The important thing was that he'd figured out the solution. Now all he had to do was get to the cop. And light him up.

49.

Barker exhaled. He was on thin ice that was getting thinner by the minute. It was apparent to him that he'd been cut out of the loop. Sergeants Reardon and Fernandez now had Sam Benziger working with them, while he was being ignored.

Meanwhile, if he had to keep Swanson's pets informed of his activities, they'd be dictating to him as to what he could do and what he couldn't. And if Swanson were to follow through on his threat and call New York, it would be all over.

Every once in a while, Barker thought, everything turns to shit. But what you have to do when that happens is tough it out and keep going. He picked up the telephone on Sam's desk and dialed 27.

The taped calls were not encouraging. A female caller said the man who had that tattoo was her brother-in-law, and she knew it was him because he was a real dickhead.

Another caller said the tattoo was a drawing of the boss where he worked. The boss had a face like a fishhook.

Still another said it was the mark of a secret force that was part of the CIA. Each member had to have the mark so that the others could identify him.

A woman in Palos Verdes claimed she was clairvoyant. There was no question she could find the man who had the tattoo, she said, and she was willing to do it. For a fee, of course.

Okay, Barker thought, Sam Benziger had warned him. Many of the messages were plain nonsense. But then again, you never knew when one of them might turn out to lead you somewhere. He tried to skip over the nuttiest of them, mostly to avoid growing bored.

A few sounded as though they could be legitimate. He made notes of those on a pad, scribbling the phone numbers the callers had left. Running them down would take time, but there was no other way to check.

He'd heard dozens of messages before one of them brought him up short. A woman's voice said it was Juanita calling. She said she knew the tattoo and knew why the man had it. She'd give him up, so long as the police would promise not to identify her. They'd know why, she said.

That was strange, Barker thought. The cops would know why? What did that mean? And why would she want to remain anonymous?

He could guess the answer. The cops would know why because she was someone they were protecting.

But protecting her for what reason? Was she an informer? Or was there something else?

He dialed the number she'd given.

On the fourth ring, a woman answered. "Yes?"

"Juanita?"

"Who's this?"

"Police," Barker said. "Are you Juanita?"

"Yeah. What do you want?"

"I'm Detective Barker, following up on your call. You said you recognized the tattoo in the drawing we put on TV."

"I recognized it, all right. I know the guy you're looking for. But I want to be sure it never gets out it was me who tipped you. Is that understood?"

"Absolutely. You have my word on it."

"Okay, I'll give you what you want, but not over the phone."

"Fine. Where do you want to meet?"

"You can come to my place."

"When?"

"Now's a good time. Later we get too busy."

"Let me have the address again."

She gave it to him and hung up.

Barker looked at the address he'd jotted down. It was on Ellsworth Drive. He didn't know where that was. And he wasn't about to ask one of the cops here in the room.

Instead, he used Benziger's computer to find it. The address was in the Hollywood Hills, and a map showed him the area. He left LAPD headquarters and went to his car.

Mongo sat in the Toyota and waited as patiently as he could. He was parked on the street near City Hall and diagonally across from the LAPD's new headquarters. Twice a cop had come along and told him to move, and twice he'd circled the block and come back to his perch.

Now he was again waiting. He'd followed Barker here, hoping he'd get a chance tonight, but at the moment he wasn't sure. He certainly couldn't make a move in this neighborhood; it was too public, and the HQ building was swarming with police.

And Jesus, wasn't it some building. He'd seen photos of it on TV when it opened, but they didn't do it justice. The structure was all stone and glass, so modern it looked as though it belonged in some future century. The cops' monument to cops.

But where was Barker? He'd been inside the building for a couple of hours now. Eventually he'd leave, and the question was where he'd go then. Back to his hotel? To the girlfriend's place? Or somewhere else?

Wherever he went, Mongo would follow him. And sooner or later the dick would stop at a suitable spot.

This time, Mongo told himself, he wouldn't miss.

For Barker, the drive was the usual long haul you had to deal with in LA. The traffic was also typical, a thick stream that was occasionally stopped by red lights.

As he drove, he frequently glanced at his rearview mirror, a habit from his earliest days as a cop. There were headlights behind him, and at one point he thought a car might be tailing him. But then it fell back and he lost sight of it.

Nevertheless, he kept taking quick glimpses at the images in the mirror. After being barely missed by a bullet from a high-powered rifle, he wasn't letting his guard down.

When at last he'd climbed up through the hills to the top of Ellsworth Drive, the traffic had become a trickle. He looked back and saw only a few cars, all of them some distance away. The view from up here was much like the one from Mulholland, with the lights of LA seeming to stretch away forever.

He also saw that the neighborhood was old, most of the houses apparently dating from the 1920s. The one at the street number Juanita had given him appeared to be of the same vintage. The place was large, its architectural style faux-English. But it was blacked out, and quiet.

For a moment he wondered whether he'd come to the wrong address, although cars were parked out front, and others were parked nearby. He found a space for the Ford and walked to the house.

Mongo had no idea why the cop had driven up here. Not that it mattered, but he was curious. Maybe he was right about Barker having another girlfriend.

Whatever the reason, for Mongo's purposes the area was perfect. It was shadowy, illuminated by the dim glow of a streetlamp.

When the Ford stopped, he was about fifty yards behind. He

pulled over and turned off his headlights, watching as the cop maneuvered the car into a parking place and then got out and walked to one of the houses.

Although many of the neighboring places had lights showing, the one Barker went into was totally dark. That didn't matter, either. What counted was for the cop to stay inside long enough for Mongo to make his arrangements.

He waited a few minutes, and when Barker didn't reappear he left the Toyota, taking the roll of Primacord with him. There was still plenty of it left, and he was sure that when the cop did return to the Ford, he'd never notice the length of explosive fuse that had been stuck into the gas tank.

50.

As Barker went up the steps to the entrance he heard faint strains of piano music and the babble of conversation coming from inside. He rang the buzzer.

After a few moments a slot in the door opened and a pair of eyes peered out at him. "Who are you?"

"Detective Barker. Juanita's expecting me."

The slot closed, and a minute passed. Then the door opened.

An ape stood there. An ape with a shaved head and wearing a tuxedo. He pointed. "Bar's over there. Have a drink and she'll be with you in a couple minutes."

As Barker entered the room he saw that a party was in progress. Men in California casual, women in slinky gowns. And what women. They were all young, and beautiful.

He got it then. This was a brothel. High class, but a brothel nevertheless.

He made his way through the throng to the bar, which was tended by one of the beauties. She asked what he'd like, and he said a vodka martini on the rocks. When she put the drink in front of him he sipped it and looked around.

The room was furnished in a style that went with the house: early '20s. There were couches and chairs upholstered in various shades of velvet, and light was provided by multicolored Tiffany chandeliers. A black guy wearing a tuxedo was playing an upright piano, banging out Scott Joplin ragtime. The air was hazy with pot smoke.

Several couples were dancing, and as he watched them Barker noticed that the men were much older than the women. In fact, there wasn't a single male who appeared younger than forty. Most of them he'd put at fifty and up.

"Hello, Barker."

He turned to see a woman approach. She had dyed red hair and was wearing a gold lamé evening dress. The skin on her face had the stretched-tight look that came from repeated bouts of plastic surgery. It was a wonder, he thought, she could move her lips.

"I'm Juanita," she said.

"Glad to know you."

"This must be the first time you've been here."

"Yeah, it is."

"You been in the job long?"

"Long enough."

"You guys are always welcome. Just give me a little advance notice."

"Okay, I will." He nodded toward the people in the room. "You seem to be doing a good business."

"We are. It's what we do every night. I run the best house in LA."

"Sorry, when we spoke on the phone I didn't realize—"

"Hey, that's okay. I figured you were a rookie. And I was right, wasn't I? Just moved up to detective?"

He smiled. "Could be."

"That's okay, too. I've got a lot of friends in your department."

Again he glanced at the crowd. "Easy to see why."

"Isn't it, though. You ever seen prettier girls?"

"Can't say I have."

"A lot of them are stars, you know. That's why men go out of their minds to be with them."

"They're movie stars?"

She laughed. "Porn stars, of course. When they're not shooting they spend time here and pick up extra money. A smart girl can make a bundle by playing it both ways."

"So your clients have seen them in porn films?"

"Right. It's a real thrill for a guy. He sees the girl in a film, sees how beautiful she is and how she knows what she's doing. He becomes a fan. And then he can come here and enjoy her himself. It's like he's living a fantasy."

"Interesting."

"They can also try different ones, and that helps give us repeat business. Keeps them coming back. We have lots of regulars."

"Don't some guys hesitate about coming here?"

"You mean because they're public figures, like politicians for instance, and they don't want to be seen? Sure. So a client just calls us, and we send him the girl he wants. We offer a complete service for guys who want to be serviced."

"Very clever. Of you, that is."

"It's the same as everything else today. You need a good idea to start with, and then the rest is marketing. The films are like commercials that show off the girls. A client will buy every film the girl ever made. So it's kind of a cross-promotion, I guess you could say."

"About your call. You said you knew the man who had the tattoo we put on television. We also showed a drawing of his face."

"Yeah, I know him. But first, tell me again that none of this'll ever get connected to me."

"It won't, I promise."

"Okay, good. Because the last thing I'd want is publicity. That'd ruin my business. My clients would have a fit, and then they'd all run and hide. And some smartass DA would try to be a hero at my expense."

"I understand."

She lowered her voice. "The guy you're looking for. His name is Mongo."

"That's his last name?"

"I don't know whether it's his last name or his first name, or even if he's got any other names. I knew him a long time ago. We were together for a while, and then he shot a guy and was sent to San Quentin. I'd mail him packages there, addressed to Mongo in South Block. They always got to him."

"What was he in for?"

"Manslaughter. Should have been murder one, but he had a smart lawyer."

"And you recognized him from TV?"

"Uh-huh. When I saw the drawing of his face I wasn't sure. I thought it looked like him, and then I'd think, maybe not. But the tattoo was a dead giveaway. Soon as I saw that, I knew it was him."

"Does the tattoo mean something?"

"It did when he put it on. Here, let me show you."

She asked the bartender for a pen and a cocktail napkin.

Then she painstakingly drew the tattoo on the napkin. Her rendering matched the one Marcia Slade had drawn.

"Okay, what do you see?" she asked.

"A fishhook," Barker said.

"Right. But it's also a capital J. You see that?"

Barker looked at it. "Yeah, I do."

"The J is for Juanita. I was his girlfriend from before he went in the joint. He did the tattoo with a pin and black ink while he was inside. Then when I went to see him he showed it off to me, saying it was proof that I'd always be his best girl. His true love. The son of a bitch."

"I understand the J part," Barker said, "but why the fishhook?"

"That was his idea of a joke. It represents Juanita the hooker. See, all the time he was in San Quentin, I was walking Hollywood Boulevard, doing fifteen or twenty guys a night. The cons weren't supposed to have money except what they were paid, which was about thirty cents an hour. So I'd send him as much as I could."

"How did you do that?"

"I'd put a hundred-dollar bill in the wrapping and glue some of the paper over it. Then I'd send him a package that had small stuff in it. Candy or cookies, things like that. The prison never caught on, and he was able to use the money to bribe guards. He got a cushy job that way, and he also bribed them to smuggle junk in for him. He'd barter the junk with other cons, and they'd do whatever he wanted."

"Sounds as though he had it pretty good while he was there."

"Good? He lived a life of ease. There were some female guards, and he paid them too, for blow jobs. He had it made."

"And after he got out? Then what?"

"Then he dropped me like I had leprosy. After all I did for him? Didn't mean a thing."

"I can see why you'd be bitter."

"Bitter isn't half of it. I want to dance on his grave."

"Maybe you'll get the chance. If we catch him."

"I hope you do. Man, do I hope you do. Did he really kill Catherine Delure and the other one?"

"I think so, yes."

"I don't know why that would surprise me. There never was a colder guy. Killing somebody wasn't just easy for him. He really enjoyed it."

"You saw that?"

"Up close and personal. When I first met him, there was a guy I was living with, Harry Dusik. Mongo made a move on me and Harry objected. Mongo gutted him with a knife. Just like you would a chicken. Opened him up and pulled his guts out and showed them to him. Watched him die, and then he laughed and walked away. There was nobody colder, ever."

"Then why'd you get mixed up with him?"

"I don't know. Maybe I was afraid not to."

"What did he do after he got out of San Quentin, do you know?"

"I'm not sure. He told me he had an idea where he'd make a lot of money. Something about working with lawyers, but he wouldn't say what it was. After that he just disappeared. I never saw him again. Never heard from him."

"Any idea where he might be now?"

"No. Although I have a feeling he's still in LA. He grew up here. He was an LA kind of guy."

"Okay. I really appreciate your help."

"Wish I could tell you more."

He wrote his cell-phone number on the cocktail napkin. "Call me if you think of anything else."

"I will. And say, Barker?"

"Yes?"

She waved a hand toward the people in the room. "You're welcome to have one of the girls, if you want. No charge, it's on the house."

"Thanks, Juanita. That's very nice of you, but I'm in a hurry. Maybe some other time."

"Sure. Just let me know."

"I will."

"Say hello to Sergeant Reardon for me."

"Um, yeah."

He saluted her with his martini and drank it down. Then he left the house.

Mongo crouched between the Toyota and another car, holding a cigarette lighter. His earlier failure to take out the cop had made him jumpy, and now his nerves were stretched taut. Tonight there could be no fuckup.

When Barker came out of the house, Mongo wondered again what he'd been doing there. Whatever it was, the important thing now was for Barker to get into the Ford without catching sight of the Primacord. Fortunately it was dark, so it was unlikely that he'd noticed the long snakelike fuse that was stretching all the way back to where Mongo waited.

When he reached his car, Barker stopped and looked in both

directions. Come on, Mongo thought. Open the damn door and get in.

Suddenly headlights appeared, to the rear of where Mongo was hiding. A car came toward him, driving slowly along the shadowy street. He ducked so the beams wouldn't pick him up.

The car went on by, and he raised his head just far enough to see what was going on. The car had slowed further, and when it was next to Barker it came to a stop. The driver and the cop seemed to have a conversation.

What the hell was this? Could it be a trap, and the driver was another cop?

But then the strange car moved on, still going slowly. Barker climbed into the Ford.

Now or never, Mongo thought. He produced a flame with the lighter and ignited the Primacord. It burst into a brilliant streak of fire that reached the Ford in less than a second.

BOOM!

The explosion lit the area with a flash that for an instant was as bright as daylight. Pieces of debris flew into the air, and the Ford became a blazing torch, issuing clouds of black, oily smoke.

Mongo didn't wait to see what would happen next. He jumped into the Toyota and pulled out onto the street, swinging the car around and driving away as fast as he could.

51.

Barker heard voices. They seemed to reach his ears from a great distance, and he couldn't make out the words. He tried to see the people who were talking, but that didn't work either. They were only shadows, hovering over him.

He was very tired. And unable to move. When he breathed his throat hurt, and he was conscious of pain in other parts of his body as well.

The voices continued their chattering from someplace far away. He wished whoever was talking would shut the hell up and leave him alone. All he wanted to do was sleep. That might take the pain away.

A few moments later he drifted into a series of strange dreams. He saw images of gunfire, and blood, and torn flesh. He saw the drawing of Mongo's face, but now the mouth was twisted in a devilish grin. He saw Catherine Delure lying naked on a slab in the morgue. He approached the corpse, and as he did she sat up and pointed a finger at him, her eyes wide and staring.

After a time, the dreams faded and he was alone and lost in darkness.

"Hey, you awake?"

It was hard for him to speak. Too hard. His throat was sore, and his tongue was so dry it was stuck to the roof of his mouth. He opened his eyes and blinked against the light. Where was he, and how had he gotten here?

"I said, you awake?"

He mumbled something in reply.

"I figured you were," the other said.

Barker blinked again. He was in bed, and an IV was stuck in his arm. He realized he was in a hospital.

"How you feeling?"

With an effort he turned his head and looked at the owner of the voice. It was a guy with bandages on both arms who was occupying another bed. They were the only ones in the room.

"Not too good, huh?" the guy said.

"Been better."

The other laughed. "I bet. You were out of it when they brought you in here last night."

"What happened to me, do you know?"

"Yeah, from what I heard the docs and the nurses saying, your car's gas tank blew up. Nobody knew why it did."

Barker knew why. Knew it at once. And knew who had caused it.

"But you were lucky," his roommate went on. "Another driver was near you, and he drug you out of the wreck. If he wasn't there, you would've been toast." He laughed at his wit.

Another driver? Ah, Barker remembered then. Someone had stopped to ask directions. The guy was looking for the same address Barker had just left. That must have been the one who pulled him from the car.

But as far as the explosion was concerned, he had no recollection of it. He'd told the driver he was a stranger himself in the neighborhood, and then he got into the Ford. That was all he remembered.

"Sometimes you were talking to yourself," the roommate said, "while you were out. You kept saying now you had his name. What was that about?"

"Beats me," Barker said. To change the subject he asked the guy how he'd injured his arms.

"Fell off a ladder and broke 'em. I'm a house painter, and I was just too goddamn careless. Now I got a problem, 'cause you can't paint much without arms, huh?" He cackled. "By the way, my name's Finnegan. What's yours?"

"Barker. What hospital is this?"

"Hollywood Presbyterian, on Vermont Avenue."

Barker held up his hands and flexed his fingers. They seemed stiff and there were a few burned places on them, but outside of that they were okay. He did the same with his legs, and they too were working, although it hurt when he moved them. And he had a bitch of a headache. He touched his forehead and discovered a dressing had been taped to it.

Continuing to explore his condition, he pulled himself into a sitting position. As he did he felt pain in his back.

"Listen, you better go easy," Finnegan said. "You could make yourself worse."

"Uh-huh." There was a call button attached to the bed. He pressed it.

A moment later the door opened, and a nurse in a green uniform came into the room. She smiled at Barker. "Well, now. For somebody who went through what you did, you're looking pretty chipper. How do you feel?"

"Hard to tell. I hear my car blew up."

"Yes, while you were in it. You were singed, and got a pretty good knock on your head. Would you like something to drink?"

"Just some water, please."

"Sure. And something to eat? There's lunch later on, but I can get you a snack to tide you over."

"Thanks, I'm not hungry."

She filled a glass from a pitcher and handed it to him. Barker swallowed some of the water, grateful for the cool, soothing sensation as it coursed down his throat.

He looked at the IV. "What've you got dripping into me?"

"Just saline solution, and some vitamin B."

He asked how long it would be before he could leave the hospital.

"That's up to the doctor," she said. "He'll be here shortly, and he'll go over all that with you." She handed him a paper cup with two pills in it. "Take these. They're antibiotics."

Dutifully, he downed the pills, chasing them with water.

"Anything else I can do for you just now?"

"Yes, there is," he said. "Do you have my cell phone?"

"I can get it for you. Be right back." She left the room.

He flexed his legs. They continued to hurt, and he lifted the hospital gown and looked at them. The skin was red in places, covered with abrasions.

A few minutes later the nurse returned and handed him the cell. "There's someone here to see you," she said. "A police officer."

Before Barker could reply, a burly uniformed cop walked into the room. He raised a hand in greeting. "Hey, how you doing?"

"I'm okay."

The cop chuckled. "I bet. My name's Jesse Morales. You're Jeb Barker, that right?"

"Yes."

"Glad to know you. When they brought you in here last night, we found your ID and saw you were a detective from New York. Does the department here know that?"

"Yeah, I checked in soon as I got to LA." And Captain Swanson and his merry men will be highly pissed, Barker thought, when they hear about this latest incident.

Morales took out a pad and a ballpoint. "You feel well enough to answer some questions?"

"Sure."

"Do you know your car exploded?"

"I know the gas tank did."

"Any idea why that happened?"

"Nope."

"What do you remember about it?"

"Very little. I was getting into the car, and from that point on I don't recall anything."

Morales scribbled on his pad. Then he said, "The firefighters think it might have been arson."

"That so?"

"Yeah, like somebody put a bomb in the tank."

"Any evidence of that?"

"Not much. They said they'd be back this morning and try to get a better idea of what went on. I'm going over there when I leave here."

"Uh-huh."

"You got any enemies you know about? Probably plenty of 'em, right?"

"Too many," Barker said.

"There anything else you can tell me?"

"Can't think of anything."

Morales scribbled some more. "Okay," he said. "I guess that'll do it for now."

He put the pad and pen away. "If something else turns up, I might want to ask you some more questions."

"Any time," Barker said.

"Take it easy. And feel better." Morales left the room.

Barker looked at the list of calls on his cell. One was from Joe Spinelli. Another was from Lieutenant Kelly. There were also several from NYPD officials, including the chief of detectives, and that struck him as ominous.

There were no calls from Dana Laramie.

Barker would return Joe's first, so he'd know how things stood. He'd also ask if Joe knew what Kelly wanted, before calling the squad commander back. He hadn't heard from Kelly since he'd come out here.

He punched the buttons for Spinelli's number, and when he got an answer he said, "Joe, it's me."

"Oh, man," Spinelli said. "You are truly up shit creek."

"What are you talking about?"

"You don't know? You haven't seen the pictures?"

"What pictures?"

"Turn on TV and look at one of the cable news channels. They've been showing the photos all day. After you've seen them, call me back." Spinelli ended the call.

A TV monitor was mounted on a bracket above the bed. Barker pulled it closer and switched it on. He surfed the channels until he got one that was covering news stories.

For once he didn't have to watch a string of commercials before hearing the report he was after. A grave-faced male announcer was saying, ". . . has added yet another twist to the bizarre Delure murder case. As part of its investigation, the New York Police Department sent a detective to Los Angeles a few days ago. He is Detective Jeb Barker."

What the hell was this? Barker turned up the volume.

The announcer continued: "Supposedly Detective Barker has been working hard on the case. But a collection of photographs has come to light that reveal he's also been involved in other activities. We're going to show you the photos, but we warn you, they might not be suitable for viewing by children. Has Detective Barker been doing his duty? You be the judge."

Cut to a photograph of Barker waist-deep in a swimming pool. He was flanked by two women. One was a blonde, the other a brunette, and both were topless. In the photo he was looking at the blonde and smiling.

"Holy Christ," Barker said.

"These young ladies are movie actresses," the announcer intoned in a voice-over. "The one on the left is Donna Ferrante. And on the right, Audrey Melon. As you see, Detective Barker and the actresses were in a pool and apparently having quite a time of it. But this is only one of the photos. Here are some others."

There followed a number of shots, one after another. They showed Barker swimming with the women, drinking with them, and eating with them at a table lavishly spread with food and wine. In one of the photos, Audrey Melon was leaning close to him with an adoring look on her face. Her breasts were pressed against his arm.

From the next bed Finnegan yelled, "Hey, is that really you? I saw what you were looking at and turned it on. Man, what terrific broads. You're gonna be famous, man."

Barker ignored Finnegan's comments. His attention was riveted to the TV screen.

Cut back to the announcer, who said, "The disclosure of these photographs has shocked the public. And of course the photos have also caused the New York Police Department a great deal of embarrassment. We tried to contact Lieutenant Hogan, who's in charge of the Delure case, so we could ask him to comment. So far he hasn't returned our calls. Now, in other news we have a report from Washington about the latest—"

Barker turned off the TV, his mind whirling.

Who the hell took those pictures? Couldn't have been Hopkins, Barker would have noticed. That fucking butler must have done it, taking the shots on the sly.

Whoever took them, it was clear to Barker that he'd been had. Bart Hopkins had set him up, and then stuck it to him good.

Why did Hopkins do it? Had he been in with Zarkov after all and was playing Barker for a fool?

And what about the agreement Zarkov's lawyer had drafted? That was genuine, Barker would bet on it. So had Hopkins seen an opportunity to ingratiate himself with the producer?

That was a possibility. Then either Hopkins or Zarkov had released the photos to the media.

But however it had gone down, the situation was exactly as Spinelli had described it. Barker was up shit creek. And as the old saying went, with no paddles.

He again called Spinelli.

Joe said, "You saw, huh?"

"Yeah, I saw. And Joe, it wasn't what it looked like, I swear it."

"So it wasn't you in those pictures? Must've been a body double, huh? Some guy who looked like you and was having a ball with a couple of knockout chicks. Give me a break, okay? That's the kind of shit you'd tell your wife, if you had a wife."

"Listen, I'll explain everything when I see you. What's going on there?"

"Just what you'd expect. Hogan's got reporters climbing up his ass, and the whole fucking department's in an uproar. Everybody's been trying to reach you."

"Thanks for letting me know. I'll call Kelly now." He ended the call and punched in the number for the squad commander's direct line.

Kelly's tone was icy. "Detective, I am deeply disturbed by what I've learned of your conduct. You have disgraced this department."

"Lieu, I can—"

"I order you to return to New York and report to me at once. Do you understand?"

"Yes sir."

"Do it." Kelly broke off the call.

Barker shook his head. His boss had been his rabbi forever, but now he was going by the book, treating him as he would a stranger.

And Dana? Had she seen the photos? He hoped to hell she hadn't. He'd have to get to her before she did. He tried her number but reached only her answering machine.

He again looked at the list of calls on his phone. Better if he ignored the ones from the brass. Instead he rang for the nurse.

When she arrived, he said, "Bring me my clothes."

"Sorry, we burned them."

"You what?"

"They were all scorched and filthy."

"And my wallet and my shield, and my pistol?"

"They're okay."

"Get them for me."

She gave him a disapproving look and went out of the room.

Barker pulled the IV out of his arm and swung his legs over the side of the bed, wincing at the soreness in them and in his back. A pair of paper slippers were on the floor, and he slipped his feet into them. He took a few steps, feeling wobbly.

"You gotta be crazy," Finnegan said.

The nurse reappeared. When she handed him his things, he asked her for a robe.

She went to a closet and got out a cotton robe and handed it to him. He put it on and dropped the pistol and the wallet and shield and the cell phone into a pocket.

"I hope you don't think you're going anywhere," the nurse said.

"Just to the can," he lied. He stepped past her and left the room. It was hard to walk, but he refused to give in to the pain.

The elevators were down the hall. He went to them, and when a car arrived he stepped into it and rode it to the ground floor.

From there he hobbled out the front entrance and climbed into a taxi. He told the driver to take him to the Sunset Inn Hotel.

52.

Dana was horrified. She'd seen the photos on CNN twice, and the hurt was no less the second time. If anything, it was worse. The photos were undeniable proof of how Jeb had been spending a good amount of his time.

How could he have done this to her? She'd trusted him, believed in him.

And had fallen in love with him.

He'd claimed he felt the same way about her. Yet all the while he'd been so sweet and tender, he'd been screwing around behind her back. Rutting like a pig, and lying about it.

He'd told her about meeting Donna Ferrante after he'd gone to Bart Hopkins's house. But he'd barely mentioned it. And she was damn sure he hadn't said that Ferrante was almost naked at the time.

Apparently he'd made other visits to Hopkins's place, if in fact that was where the pictures had been shot. Although come to think of it, the action shown in them could have occurred somewhere else, for all she knew.

And who was Audrey Melon? The newscaster on TV had described her as a movie actress, although Dana had never heard of her.

But so what? Hollywood was full of cheap bimbos who claimed to be actresses. Whoever she was, in at least one of the photos she was rubbing her boobs on Jeb. And apparently he was enjoying it.

In fact, he was so happily occupied in all the pictures it didn't look as though he even minded being photographed. Maybe he was planning to put the photos in an album, the bastard.

She grew increasingly furious, thinking about it. And then she broke down and cried. She'd really cared about him, and it was agonizing that their relationship had turned out this way. High on a mountain one minute, down in the mud the next.

She was also disgusted with her own conduct. She'd been taken in like some dumb little chippy. And realizing that made her both angry and tearful at the same time.

Stop it, she told herself. Pull yourself together. Stop blubbering.

She blew her nose and went into the kitchen, poured orange juice and vodka into a glass, and gulped it down.

That helped. She made another one and sipped it.

This whole episode has been bizarre, she thought. Starting with the hideous murders of Catherine and Penny.

Since then her life had been filled with people who were out to use her, like that monster Zarkov, and the creeps in the media, and the asshole producer who had tried to shame her into appearing in his lousy documentary.

And even Jeb. Even he had used her.

So what was she going to do about it?

For one thing, maybe the most important thing, she would get the hell out of LA. Go to a place where nobody could find her. Somewhere she could wash away all the LA dirt and make plans for a fresh start.

But where?

There might be one place. And one person who'd understand. This was a Saturday, so he'd most likely be at home. She got out her book and looked up the number. Hoping she wouldn't be thought rude or pushy, she made the call.

A maid answered, and Dana gave her name and asked to speak with Mr. Delaney.

When he came on the line he said, "Dana! I was so worried about you. In fact I was going to call you. I'm sure you've seen those awful photographs on TV. The ones of Detective Barker?"

"Yes, I've seen them. And I was shocked. The pictures were a total surprise to me."

"Have you spoken with him about them?"

"No, I haven't. That's something I don't want to do."

"Ah, I understand. Of course you don't. I can imagine how you feel."

"Seeing the pictures was . . . difficult."

"I'm sure it was. Look, I don't want to intrude, but may I make a suggestion?"

"Of course."

"Why don't you get on a plane and come to New York. I'll have a car meet you at the airport, and you can come up here to Greenwich and get things sorted out. We'd be delighted to have you, and you could stay as long as you like."

"That's very kind of you, Mr. Delaney. I hope I wouldn't be a nuisance."

"You wouldn't be, I assure you. And please call me Roger. As I've told you, we know how Cat felt about you, and that means you're a special friend of ours. So go ahead and make arrangements. Then call me back and let me know what flight you'll be on. Okay?"

"Wonderful. I can't thank you enough."

Dana put the phone down. She was feeling better already. Not a lot, by any means, but much better than she had before making that call. Greenwich would be a breath of fresh air.

But then she thought of Jeb and choked up all over again.

53.

Mongo laughed out loud when he saw the photos on TV. There was the dumbass detective, getting worked over by a couple of bitches. Looked like he loved it, too.

Although who could blame him? Both the blonde and the brunette were obviously great stuff—what the cons in Q used to call table pussy.

So Barker had been having a ball? Sure he had. The photos showed a wet dream come to life. And now his life had ended.

But where was the story on an exploding Ford? Mongo had expected to see something on that as well, yet so far there was nothing. Apparently the geeks who ran TV didn't think the incident was unusual enough to cover. After all, a car fire was no big deal.

And on top of that, they apparently hadn't figured out that there was a connection between the idiot featured in the photos and the burning car up in the Hollywood Hills. Most likely that was because Barker's corpse had been so badly burned they couldn't ID it.

Maybe Mongo ought to be a good citizen and give them a call, let them know who the crispy critter in the Ford was. He wouldn't do it, of course, but the idea was good for another chuckle. Things were finally breaking his way, and that made him happier than he'd been in some time.

Now as a kind of low-key celebration he'd go for a run on the beach. Important to stay in the best shape possible, he thought. Before going back to Vegas for a much larger celebration.

First, however, there'd be the matter of collecting his fee. This whole ratfuck with the detective had been the toughest job he'd ever had to deal with. And the fee had better be in line with that.

If it wasn't, he'd read the weasel the riot act. Once again, all Strunk had to do was pick up the assignment and pass it on, while Mongo was the one whose ass had been hanging out in the wind while he got it done.

But let's not spoil an otherwise fine day, he told himself. He'd made the hit, he'd be paid big, and he had a stay in the Crystal Palace to look forward to.

He went into the bedroom, stripped off his clothes, and put on the old pair of shorts and the frayed T-shirt and the sneakers. And after tugging the faded Dodgers cap down low on his head, he left the cottage.

Outside, the air was cool and fresh, with a light ocean breeze. Sky was overcast, which was good, because that would keep the sun's heat at bay.

He crossed the Pacific Coast Highway and threaded his way between two beach houses, trotting down to where the waves had made the sand soft and wet. Then he turned left and picked up his pace.

54.

When the taxi pulled up in front of the Sunset Inn, a parking attendant opened the passenger door and saluted. Barker paid the driver and stepped out. As he hobbled toward the entrance, the attendant looked at him with distaste.

Barker couldn't blame him. Probably not many people showed up with a bandage on their head and wearing a cotton hospital robe and paper slippers.

But the hell with how he looked. Some guests in the lobby stared at him, and the hell with them, too. Ditto the doorman and the bellmen. At the desk, Lia also seemed taken aback when she saw him.

He went on by and stepped into an elevator that took him up to his floor. As he made his way down the corridor the patches of singed flesh on his legs and his back pained him with each step. He got out a passcard and let himself into his room.

Once inside, he went into the bathroom and peered at his reflection in the mirror. It was the first chance he'd had to check his appearance since he awoke in the hospital, and what he saw now wasn't pretty. His eyes were red-rimmed and there was a burn on his right cheek and he needed a shave. Also, the thick bandage on his forehead had bled through in a couple of places.

A shower might help, he thought—as long as he kept the water only lukewarm. He stepped into the stall and turned on the spray.

Usually he sang when taking a shower. Today he groaned. But he stuck it out, soaping himself down and groaning again as he rinsed off.

Toweling was another problem. The best approach, he found, was to pat himself dry. Next he brushed his teeth, and after that he worked up a faceful of lather and scraped off the whiskers.

At least he was clean now. Although the bandage had to go. He peeled it off gingerly and was relieved that the raw spots on his forehead had stopped bleeding.

Finally he applied antiperspirant and aftershave lotion, and as he did he decided that despite the burns he was feeling somewhat better. Physically, anyway. The thought of the photos shown on TV and his calls to New York were another story. Joe Spinelli had summed up his situation exactly.

And yet at the moment there was nothing he could do about those issues; he'd deal with them when he got back. Right now the problem uppermost in his mind centered on Dana Laramie. He sat at the desk and tried calling her again, and again reached her answering machine.

Okay, so maybe she just wasn't answering her phone. He'd call later. Or else stop by her place on his way to the airport. Somehow he had to talk with her and convince her that Hopkins had sandbagged him with those photos.

Sitting there, trying to think through his problems and not getting very far, he dozed off. When he opened his eyes, he was surprised that he'd been out for a couple of hours. Come on, he told himself, get with it.

He called American Airlines and made a reservation for the 9 P.M. flight, and then he got dressed and packed his bag. He went back down to the lobby and checked out, and a bellman put his luggage into a taxi.

Barker tipped the guy a couple of bucks and eased himself onto a seat. After he gave the driver Dana's address, the taxi hurtled along Sunset and turned down Rodeo to Wilshire.

Once they arrived at her building, he got out and told the driver to wait. He went into the lobby and pressed the buzzer for her apartment, but there was no response from that, either.

As he stood there, a man wearing coveralls emerged from a door at the far end of the lobby and walked past him. "Excuse me," Barker said. "Are you the superintendent?"

"Yep. What can I do for you?"

Barker showed him his shield. "Police officer. I'm looking for one of your residents. Name is Dana Laramie."

"Not here," the guy said. "She left a few hours ago."

"Did you see her leave?"

"Yeah, as a matter of fact, I did. She had a suitcase with her."

"Did you speak to her, ask her where she was going?"

"Nope. Wasn't any of my business. She got in a taxi and off she went."

Barker had been afraid that was what he'd hear. He thanked the super and went back to the waiting cab.

"Okay, pal," the driver said. "Where to now?"

"LAX," Barker said.

The red-eye was a lousy way to travel. Especially with the burns making his skin feel as though a platoon of fire ants were chewing on him. He was wide awake all the way to New York. When the aircraft reached JFK at dawn, he dragged himself into the terminal and retrieved his bag.

A shuttle took him to long-term parking, where he picked up the Mustang. He drove to Manhattan via the Van Wyck and Grand Central Parkways, and finally through the Midtown Tunnel. Even at this time of day there was a heavy stream of traffic flowing into the city.

After parking the car on the street in SoHo he went up to his loft, wanting nothing so much as a good long sleep.

He wouldn't get it. Instead he showered and changed into fresh clothing, including the usual blue button-down and red tie. He carefully shrugged into his blazer and left the loft. It was time to face the music.

First, however, he'd get something to eat. He'd had no food since he'd been blown out of the Ford in LA, and now he was starved. A rock-hard bun and dishwater coffee had been served on the flight, but he'd passed on those.

There was a diner just down the street, filled with early birds who were stoking up before going to work. He sat at the counter and wolfed down a pastrami on rye and a mug of real coffee.

Thus fortified, he got back into his car and drove up to Seventeenth Precinct headquarters.

As on most mornings, Frank Kelly was already at his desk when Barker knocked and entered the glass-walled office.

"Good morning, Lieu," Barker said.

The squad commander didn't offer to shake hands. His face looked as though it had been carved from stone. He spoke slowly. "You know how much trouble you're in?"

"I've got a pretty good idea. But I can explain what happened."

"I'm listening."

"The thing with the photos. I was set up. The guy who put it to me is involved in a fraud scheme in the movie business."

"What kind of scheme?"

"It pulls in suckers who think they're making a legitimate investment in a film project, but they'll only lose their shirts. It's run by the same guy who produced Catherine Delure's last movie. Apparently she caught on and was about to blow the whistle. That made her a target for a hit man."

"You have evidence to back that up?"

"Not yet, but I can help the DA get it. I've also found out the identity of the hit man."

"Who is he?"

"Name's Mongo. He did a stretch in San Quentin for manslaughter, and after he got out he jumped parole. There was a witness I talked to, a guy who made the device Mongo used to kill

Delure and her manager. But Mongo found out I'd contacted him and blew him away."

"Can you prove that?"

"No, but I think Mongo would break down under questioning. He tried to kill me, too. Twice. The first time he took a shot at me. Second time he blew up my car."

"You report those attempts to the LAPD?"

"No."

"Why didn't you?"

"I wanted more evidence."

"Which you don't have."

"I was getting there, Lieu. I swear it."

"Where is this Mongo now?"

"I don't know for sure. But he's most likely in LA."

"How'd you get a line on him?"

"A hooker in Las Vegas claimed he'd had sex with her and then beat her up. She recognized him from seeing the composite on TV. The hooker was wanted for a homicide in LA, and a detective went to Vegas to interrogate her. The detective invited me to go along."

Kelly's eyebrows rose. "You went to Las Vegas too?"

"I was only there a few hours."

"Uh-huh. Go on."

"The hooker told us there was a tattoo on Mongo's shoulder. When she was brought to the county jail in LA we interviewed her again and she made a drawing of the tattoo. The LAPD got it shown on TV and a woman called in and said she used to be Mongo's girlfriend. I went to see her and she told me Mongo's name and gave me a rundown on him."

"What does the girlfriend do?"

"She runs a fancy whorehouse in Hollywood."

"And that's another place you went?"

"Lieu, I only wanted to talk to her."

"Uh-huh."

"I'm convinced what she gave me was solid."

"Would she testify?"

"Not unless forced to. She'd have to be subpoenaed, and even then she'd be a hostile witness."

Kelly looked up at the ceiling for several moments and then returned his gaze to Barker. "How'd you get those cuts on your head?"

"Happened when the car blew up. They're nothing serious."

There was another pause, and then Kelly said, "I had a call yesterday afternoon from Captain Swanson at the LAPD. He talked about you. Said he bent over backward to cooperate, assigned a detective to help you with your investigation. But all you did was stick your nose in cases his division was working. He was so fucking mad I thought he'd bust a gut."

"Listen, Lieu. Swanson's not giving you—"

Kelly raised a hand, palm up. "That's enough, Barker. What all this boils down to is you've put together a large amount of speculation. No evidence, no proof, just some stories from two whores. Meantime, you've made this police department look like the biggest bunch of assholes in creation."

"But—"

"But shit. You ought to know by now that it's bad enough to fuck up, but when you do it in a way that puts a public spotlight on the whole department, you might as well go jump off the Brooklyn Bridge. Swanson wasn't the only one I heard from. I also got calls from Hogan, and the chief, and even one from the PC himself. They all saw those photos of you with a pair of naked broads, and if you think they'll buy your excuse that you were set up, you're crazy. My opinion? You're finished."

"Don't I get a chance to defend myself?"

"Oh, you're gonna get one, all right. But unfortunately for you, it'll be with Internal Affairs. In their view, you ran off unauthorized to LA, you misrepresented yourself to the LAPD and messed with their business, and you wasted a shitload of the taxpayers' money having a good time. You went Hollywood."

Barker could have argued further, but he knew he'd be wasting his breath. He got to his feet, conscious of the pain in his back and legs.

"You'll be notified by IA," Kelly said, "about when you'll go before the board for a hearing. Until then, stay out of this precinct house and do not involve yourself in any of the squad's activities. That clear?"

"It's clear, Lieutenant." Barker forced himself to stand up straight as he walked out of the office and closed the door behind him.

55.

Joe Spinelli said, "You ever had to deal with IA before this?"

Barker shook his head. "No, never." He and Spinelli were sitting at a bar on Second Avenue, working on their third round of vodka on the rocks.

"Not even after you shot the rapist?" Joe asked.

"No. The chief and two inspectors ran that investigation. They finally cleared me, and when they did, the media went crazy. Or crazier, I should say."

"I remember that part. They wanted you roasted on a spit. And now they'll get another shot at you."

"They already did. Jesus, those photos."

"Yeah, those photos. That's what put you in deep shit. IA's got a system, you know. In the hearing they read you the charges, and then they give you a chance to tell your side of the story, and then they declare you guilty."

"Lovely."

"Doesn't stop there. I heard you're not only gonna get canned, but criminal charges will be brought against you. Misuse of public funds is a felony."

"I'm aware of that, Joe. But I was this close to clearing the Delure case. It's damn unfair."

"Fair's got nothing to do with it."

"Very true. You know, I thought Kelly would go to bat for me, but forget it. Not this time."

"Understandable. Last thing he wants is any part of the blame. If he got sent down in grade, it could fuck up his retirement. He wants to go out as a lieutenant, full pension. But he's got nothing to worry about. Kelly's an expert at covering his ass."

"No question."

"As first I was surprised he didn't tell you to turn in your shield and gun. But when you think about it, he probably figured any action against you should be IA's job. That way he's just playing it by the book."

"Also true. I tried to explain to him what happened in LA, but he wasn't listening."

"Isn't there somebody who could verify what you dug up out there? What about Delure's secretary? What's her name?"

"Dana Laramie."

"You said she helped steer you to what was going on, right?"

"Yeah, she did. Wasn't for her, I wouldn't have learned about this guy Hopkins. It was through him that I found out how Zarkov screws people out of large amounts of money."

"Hopkins is also the one who set you up?"

"The same. But Dana couldn't have known he'd do it."

"So why not ask her to help you now? She could at least back up your story."

"I would ask her, if I could locate her. She left LA, and I think she might have gone to Catherine Delure's family in Connecticut, the Delaneys. She told me once they asked her to come stay with them. I'll try to reach her there."

Spinelli finished his drink and signaled the bartender to give them another round. He said to Barker, "You feeling any better?"

"Some."

"Glad to hear it. Vodka is very good for burns, you know. And for everything else."

"It helps."

"About the shooter."

"Mongo."

"Yeah. Did you give that to the cops in LA?"

"No, didn't get the chance. It was right after I found out who he was that he blew up my car."

"Couldn't you still let them know about him?"

"I don't know how far I'd get. He's something else I can't prove."

"And I don't suppose it'd make any sense for you to tell Hogan about him, either."

"You serious?"

"No, I guess it wouldn't. So now what?"

"Now I get some sleep, and tomorrow I'll go at it again. I still have a few ideas."

The bartender placed fresh drinks in front of them.

Barker raised his glass. "But first I need to continue my treatment."

56.

The following morning the burns weren't quite as painful as they had been. But now they itched. So much that Barker thought he'd lose his mind wanting to scratch them. But he knew better than to give in to the urge.

Besides, his head had become a larger source of discomfort. Each pulsebeat felt like the pounding of a bass drum between his ears. He resolved to drink less, which he always did after drinking too much, and took two aspirin. That relieved the pounding a tiny bit. Or maybe he just imagined it did.

What would definitely help was food. He got dressed and walked two blocks to a deli, where he bought potato salad and sliced ham and jack cheese and pickles and sourdough bread and mustard and bananas and grapes and coffee and a six-pack of Corona. After returning to his loft he made himself a hearty brunch and ate it slowly. As he did, the bass drum quieted down to the level of raps on a snare.

While he ate, he thought about what to do next. His problems, he decided, boiled down to three main areas. Number one was how he could contact Dana.

He telephoned the Delaney home in Greenwich and asked to speak with her. There was a long pause before the maid came back on the line and told him she wasn't there. Which told him she was.

Number two was the Zarkov scam and how to put together some solid evidence.

And number three was Mongo.

He'd try Dana again later. At the moment he'd go after the scam. The deputy DA's card was in his wallet. He dug it out and called the number.

"District Attorney's Office. Natalie Adams."

"Natalie, it's Jeb Barker."

"Hello, Jeb. Seems you've become famous. Or maybe I should say infamous."

"You've seen the photos."

"Is there anybody who hasn't? First they were on TV, and now they're on the Internet, where I understand they're getting about a million hits a day. So what can I do for you—recommend a good defense lawyer? And where are you, by the way?"

"New York. I called because I have something that might help you with the Zarkov investigation."

"Okay, let's hear it."

"Does the name Bart Hopkins ring a bell?"

"Not offhand, no."

"Hopkins is a rich investor who's connected to Zarkov. He set me up with those photos."

"You didn't look like you minded too much."

"I do now."

"I bet."

"A few days ago I went to Hopkins's house in Beverly Hills. He let me read a letter of agreement that would commit him to putting fifteen million bucks into producing one of Zarkov's movies. The production's a fake."

"With Zarkov, most of them are. That's what our people have been trying to build a case on. Does the letter go into detail?"

"Yes."

"Why'd Hopkins let you read it?"

"Ego, I suppose. Showing me what a big man he is. But a copy of that agreement would help build the case, wouldn't it?"

"Yeah, it would. But to go after it would mean getting a judge to sign a search warrant. Which wouldn't be easy. Judges here think the Fourth Amendment is the holy grail."

"Worth a try?"

"I'd say so, yes. I'll discuss it with our DAs and see whether they'll apply for the warrant."

"Okay, great."

"Can I reach you if I need to?"

"Yes, here's my cell number." He recited it to her and wished her luck. She thanked him and hung up.

Next he'd try to start some action on Mongo. He called Sam Benziger's number, got no answer, left a message to call him.

One out of three, he thought. Not too good. But what the hell, nowadays anybody with a .333 batting average would be an All-Star.

Which was irrelevant, and no comfort at all. He put his dishes into the dishwasher and cracked a beer. Then he turned on TV and surfed the news channels. A homicide in Crown Heights, a fire in Queens, and the stock market in the sewer. There was also a promo for an upcoming special on the Catherine Delure case. He turned off the set.

Natalie Adams had said the photos were on the Internet. For a moment he was tempted to boot up his machine and have another look at them, but then he quickly abandoned the idea. It would be just another form of self-flagellation.

His phone rang. He answered: "Barker."

"Jeb, it's Sam Benziger. I hope you realize I'm sticking my neck out just by talking to you."

"I know you are, Sam."

"Why in the hell were you posing with those nude women in the photos?"

"I wasn't posing, and they weren't nude. We all had on swimsuits."

"Really? What were they made of—Saran Wrap?"

"I'll explain that some other time. Right now I've got something for you. I know who killed Culebra. Just as we thought, it's the same guy who killed Delure and her manager."

"Who is he?"

"An ex-con named Mongo."

"Where'd you get this?"

"From his former girlfriend. She saw the drawing of the tattoo on TV and called in. I went to see her, and she said she was positive it was him."

"She tell you where he is now?"

"Only that she thinks he's in LA."

"Okay, we'll pay her a visit. Where is she, and what's her name?"

"She has a house in the Hollywood Hills. Her name's Juanita."

"Uh-oh."

"You know about her, huh?"

"I've heard."

"Heard what?"

"It's a sensitive subject."

"So I gather. She made me promise the cops wouldn't identify her in their investigation. She wants to stay under the radar."

"I'm sure she does. What else did she tell you about this guy?"

"She said he enjoyed killing people. He was sent to San Quentin for manslaughter, and when he got out he disappeared. But there's a way you can track him. Juanita said while he was inside, he told her he'd worked out a plan that would make him rich. She didn't know what the plan was, but it involved a lawyer."

"That figures. That it involved a lawyer, I mean. She tell you who he is?"

"No, although I have a hunch it could be the one who defended him and got him a light sentence. That'll be in the court records. Find the lawyer and you find Mongo."

"Mmm."

"Well?"

"I'm not sure I can touch it."

"Why, because of Juanita?"

"No, because of you. On top of everything else, word came in about your car blowing up. And how an ambulance took you to Hollywood Presbyterian and you walked out. The mention of your name sends Swanson into orbit."

"Then don't mention it."

"Where are you now?"

"New York. I was ordered back here. And by the way, the reason the car blew up was because Mongo set off Primacord in the gas tank."

"I'll be damned. Same stuff that torched Culebra's shop."

"You convinced now?"

"I'm getting there."

"Go after him, Sam."

"I think I'll do that."

"Just be careful." He ended the call.

That left taking another run at reaching Dana. He called the Delaney home again, and this time when the maid answered he didn't ask to speak to Ms. Laramie.

Instead he said, "This is Detective Jeb Barker. Please tell Ms. Laramie there are new developments, and it's important that I speak to her. Tell her to please call me. She has my number."

57.

When the maid gave Dana the message from Jeb, it was a jolt to her emotions. She told herself to ignore his request. She'd made a firm commitment to herself that she'd have nothing more to do with him.

Yet the fact that he'd called made her think about him. And no matter how determined she was to forget him, it was impossible. She knew she was reacting to the message like a love-struck schoolgirl, but she couldn't help it.

But call him? No, damn it. If there really were new developments, they wouldn't concern her. She thanked the maid and closed the door to her room.

So far her visit to the Delaneys wasn't turning out as she'd hoped it would. Not because they weren't trying to make her feel welcome. On the contrary, they made a point of treating her with elaborate courtesy.

Then what was troubling her—besides struggling with her feelings about Jeb?

Partly it was the strangeness of her surroundings. This enormous old house was dark and gloomy and most of the time as quiet as a tomb. The Delaneys didn't seem to talk with each other very often.

Even at dinner the conversation had seemed forced. There was the clink of silverware, and an occasional remark by either Roger Delaney or Sarah, and then would come another period of silence. Dana had tried to touch on subjects she thought they'd find interesting, such as books she'd read or stories in the news, but she didn't get much in the way of response.

Roger was the more animated of the pair, although not when his wife was around. Sarah had an odd personality, from what Dana could tell. Her smile was pleasant enough, and yet it seemed contrived, as if she had put on a mask.

Dana wondered whether the Delaneys' relationship was also different from what it appeared on the surface. It struck her as more like an armed truce than a marriage.

And then there was the old man. Roger's father was merely a husk who sat motionless in a wheelchair, his eyes blank, his skin the color of paste. Dana had only seen him once since she'd arrived. His nurse had wiped drool from his chin and pushed the wheelchair out of sight.

A strange house indeed. And a strange family. But such thoughts were nonproductive. It wasn't healthy to brood, which was why Dana rarely did.

Maybe she simply needed some fresh air. She left her room and went down the stairs to the first floor. Following a hallway to the rear of the house, she stepped outside.

There was a large terrace, paved in flagstone and surrounded by a low stone wall. A striped awning shielded chairs and chaise longues and a table from the sun. Bordering the wall were pink and white and purple azaleas, and beyond the terrace were acres of lawn, shaded by towering oaks and maples. A rose garden and a fountain were in the center of the lawn.

She walked down to the garden and admired the bright red and yellow and peach-colored roses. There were at least a dozen different varieties, each blossom wafting a delicate fragrance. Sunlight was reflecting from the water of the fountain, and it occurred to her that the atmosphere out here was a lot more cheerful than the murkiness of the house.

A flicker of movement caught her eye. She looked up to see Carl, the security man, standing near the garage wing, a shotgun in the crook of his arm. He didn't seem to be watching her, but his eyes were hidden by his sunglasses so she couldn't be sure. It was strange, though, that every time she went outside, he was there.

Some distance away the gardener was riding a power mower, its engine clattering. He swung the machine around and began cutting another swath, and as he did Dana heard a crack of thunder. Moments later a black cloud appeared overhead and lightning streaked the sky.

Better get back inside. She ran toward the terrace, but before she reached it fat drops of rain splattered on her blouse. She hurried through the door into the hallway and went from there into the living room.

The interior was darker than ever. Lamps were on in the vast space, creating isolated pools of light. But that did little to cut through the gloom.

She wandered about, finally going into the library. It was furnished with red leather chairs and a large desk, and a cabinet beside the desk bore a computer, a printer, and a fax machine. There were bookcases built into the walls, and at one end of the room was a fireplace. Hanging above the mantel was a portrait of Catherine Delure.

Dana was delighted to see the way the artist had captured Cat's beauty. Her skin looked as dewy fresh as the roses Dana had been admiring a few minutes ago, and there was a sparkle in the blue eyes.

And yet, looking up at the painting, she began to see differences. The lips weren't as full as Cat's had been, and the jaw was a bit more pronounced.

Suddenly she realized that the portrait wasn't of Cat at all. Instead it was of another woman, one who bore an uncanny resemblance to her.

This had to be Catherine's mother. According to Cat, she'd died years ago, of cancer. Seeing the painting made Dana feel she was in the presence of a ghost. She turned away.

The rain was coming down furiously now, the drops lashing the windows behind the desk. She stepped over there and tried to look out, but the streaming water blurred the view.

The storm was also making the room darker. She sat at the desk and turned on the lamp. The light revealed a number of objects, among them a penholder with a marble base, a case that held scissors and a letter opener, an alabaster vase filled with pencils, a container of paper clips, a variety of paperweights, and other odds and ends.

Among the items was a folder bound in dark red leather. Dana knew she shouldn't pry, but she couldn't resist lifting the cover.

Inside was a sheaf of papers. The one on top bore the letterhead of Marshall, Brach, Whitworth and Cohen, LLP, a New York law firm. It was addressed to Roger Delaney at his Manhattan apartment and was from Carter Whitworth, Esq.

As Dana scanned the letter, the hairs stood up on the back of her neck. The language was legal mumbo-jumbo, but she understood what it conveyed. It was so unexpected she thought she must be mistaken and began to read it again slowly, from the top.

"Hello, Dana."

She jumped at the sound of the voice and closed the folder.

Roger Delaney approached the desk and sat opposite her. He was smiling, and his voice had the avuncular tone he always used when he spoke to her. "Quite a storm, isn't it?"

She hoped he couldn't see that getting caught reading his mail was making her blush. "Yes," she managed to say. "A real downpour."

"You probably don't get this much rain at one time in Los Angeles. Isn't that so?"

"Occasionally we do." Perhaps he hadn't realized what she'd been looking at? That was unlikely—he must have seen the open folder. But there was no way to tell that by his manner. If anything, he seemed faintly amused.

"Sometimes in the winter," she said, "we even get floods. And of course that causes mud slides." God, she was babbling like a nitwit.

"Ah, I've seen some of that on TV," he said. "People often lose their homes, don't they?"

"Yes, they do."

"But here the rain doesn't usually do that much damage. And besides, we need it. The thunderstorms give us a brief deluge, and then they move on. It's a good thing, isn't it?"

"I'm sure it is."

"Weather aside," he said, "I hope you're enjoying your visit."

"Thank you, I am."

"Takes a while, you know, to get over an emotional shock. Also the change of scenery will do wonders for you."

"No doubt it will."

"I have an impression that you and Detective Barker had become quite close. Isn't that true?"

"I'm afraid so. We became . . . friends. And I wish we hadn't."

"Has he tried to contact you again?"

"He called and left a message."

"Called here?"

"Yes."

"How did he know where you were?"

"I don't know."

"If you don't mind my asking, what did the message say?"

"That there were new developments, and I should call him."

"New developments? Do you believe that, or do you think he was just trying to get you to call?"

"It's hard to say. But I'm not sure I can trust him."

"Good for you. It's important to stay strong, and not let anyone manipulate you."

"I realize that." She rose from the chair. "And now you'll excuse me, but I want to get back to the book I'm reading."

"Very well. See you at five, for cocktails."

She left and went back up the stairs to her room. After closing the door, she sat on the bed and tried to think.

It wasn't easy. Everything seemed to have turned upside down.

58.

"You fucking moron! You have any idea how goddamn stupid you are?"

Mongo clenched his fists. It was hard enough to understand Strunk's garbled voice in any of his calls, but now the little bastard's rage was making him sound almost incoherent.

"Did you hear me, moron?" Strunk shouted.

Mongo choked back his own anger. "Yeah, I heard you. Now what are you yelling about?"

"He's alive, dummy! You were supposed to take him out, and you fucked up. You hear me? You fucked up!"

"Wait a minute. He's alive? He couldn't be! I blew up his car with him in it. I saw it explode and burn. Nobody could live through that."

"They couldn't, huh? Well, he did. I'm telling you, he's alive!"

"You sure?"

"Of course I'm sure, moron. They pulled him out of the fire and put him in a hospital with only minor injuries. So he left there and went back to New York."

"How do you know that?"

"How do you think? I've got sources, moron. You think I only get information from dummies like you?"

Mongo wished Strunk would stop calling him a moron. Maybe he should go downtown to the weasel's office and strangle him with the phone cord. Then let him see who was the moron.

Strunk wasn't finished. "You think I pay you so you can make a fucking mess of the job? You think this is some kind of goddamn game, where sometimes you win and sometimes you don't? Are you really that stupid?"

"I'm not stupid at all, and it's not over."

"The hell it's not. I'm ready to dump you. I've got a good thing going here, and you're pissing in the punch bowl."

"The good thing was invented by me, Strunk. Don't forget it."

"Jesus Christ! I told you never to say my name. Didn't I tell you that?"

"But it's true. I came up with the plan, not you."

"So what? You got a patent on it? Maybe a copyright? You think you're the only scumball in LA who knows how to use a knife or a gun? Let me tell you, moron, I can hire ten guys as good as you or better for what I've been paying you. Can you get that through your thick skull?"

"Listen, I know you must be mad as hell, but cool down, will you? I said it's not over, and it's not. I can still get this guy, I'm sure I can."

"Yeah? Is that so? You mean you *think* you can. And that's not good enough."

"I said I can, and I will."

"You already tried, and you fucked up."

Actually, Mongo had tried twice. And missed twice. But Strunk didn't have to know that.

"So why should I believe you now?" the weasel asked.

"Because I'm the best there is. And don't hand me that shit about how you can get a great bunch of pistoleros just by snapping your fingers."

"Okay, okay. You've done some good work for me, I'll admit that."

"Then let's start all over, okay? You're saying somehow he got out of that car alive. Fine. It was a miracle, if he did, but I'm willing to take your word for it. So where can I find him in New York?"

"He works out of the Seventeenth Precinct headquarters, which is on Fifty-First Street."

"Yeah, but where does he live?"

"In a part of town called SoHo. Here's the address." Strunk read it off, and Mongo made a note of it.

There was a pause, and then the weasel said, "You told me when you blew up his car he was in the Hollywood Hills. What was he doing up there, anyway?"

"I don't know. I followed him to Ellsworth Drive, and he went in a house."

"Ellsworth Drive? That's where Juanita's place is."

"Juanita's place?"

"Yeah, it's a fancy whorehouse, and a broad named Juanita runs it."

Mongo felt a chill deep in his gut. Could it be?

"So now what?" Strunk said.

"So now I'll go after him again, and this time I'll make sure. When I'm done, I'll mail you his head."

"I don't want his fucking head. All I want is proof you did what you get paid to do. Understand?"

"Yeah, I understand."

"And hurry, will you? Time is money."

"You'll hear from me," Mongo said.

"I better." The call ended.

59.

The executive offices of Delaney Industries occupied four floors of a building on the east side of Park. Barker decided that Roger Delaney would be on the highest of the four, which was the fortieth. He took an elevator up there and stepped into the lobby.

The space was large, but there was nothing flashy about it. Sofas and chairs for visitors, a rack of magazines, a vase containing white lilies. An older woman sat behind the reception desk.

"May I help you?" she said.

Barker displayed his shield. "I'm Detective Barker. I want to see Mr. Roger Delaney."

She looked at the shield and then at him. "One moment, please."

She picked up a phone and spoke into it and after putting it down said, "Someone will be with you shortly."

"Thank you." Barker stepped past her into the waiting area.

Through the windows he could see the tops of other tall buildings and some of Central Park, and in the distance the Hudson

River and the Jersey Palisades. On the wall to his left was a large framed photograph that depicted an industrial site, and on the opposite wall was a portrait of a man with muttonchop whiskers and a big gut.

The guy was probably the founder, Barker decided. That would make him the current CEO's grandfather. Although there wasn't much of a resemblance.

When he'd visited the family home in Greenwich, Roger Delaney had seemed open-minded and reasonable. Barker hoped he'd be reasonable now, and that he'd be willing to talk sense to Dana when he got home tonight. If he did, that might at least get her to answer a phone call.

"Detective Barker?"

He turned to see a second woman approach him, this one with upswept gray hair. "Yes, ma'am," he said.

"I'm Mrs. Oberholz. You wanted to see Mr. Delaney?"

"Correct."

"I'm sorry, he's not here."

"When will he be?"

"I can't say. I don't have his schedule."

"Who does?"

"May I ask what this is about?"

"I'll discuss that with Mr. Delaney. Find out when he's expected."

She hesitated. "Perhaps you should speak with Mr. Norbert, our executive vice president."

"Fine. Where do I find him?"

"Will you follow me, please?"

She led the way through a door and into an area containing cubicles where people were busy on phones and typing at computers. At the far end of the area were more doors. She knocked on one of them, opened it, and put her head in.

"Mr. Norbert," she said, "I have Detective Barker with me. He wanted to see Mr. Roger Delaney. I explained to him that Mr. Delaney isn't here, but he insisted."

A voice said, "Send him in."

The woman stepped aside, and Barker entered the office. She closed the door behind him.

A man rose from his desk. He had thinning black hair and wore rimless glasses. His suit was charcoal gray. "Hello, Detective," he said. "I'm Douglas Norbert. Sorry we can't help you."

"I think you can," Barker said. "When will Mr. Delaney arrive?"

"Why, ah, I really don't know."

"Is he out of town, on a trip or something?"

"I don't know that, either."

What the hell was this—more runaround?

"You don't know? Roger Delaney is head of this company, isn't he?"

"He has the title of president. But it's honorary, you might say."

"Tell you what, Mr. Norbert. Suppose you spell it out for me, okay?"

Norbert cleared his throat. "Mr. Delaney doesn't actually work here. He did, but that was some time ago."

"So who runs the place?"

"I'm in charge of our day-to-day operations. I was given the responsibility by Mr. Delaney's father, George Delaney, who is still the chairman and CEO."

An image appeared in Barker's mind. It was of an old man who was slumped in a wheelchair. His eyes were glazed, and spittle ran from the corners of his mouth and his lower lip.

"I've seen Mr. Delaney's father," Barker said. "He doesn't seem to be in very good health."

"He isn't. That's why I'm in charge."

"And your directors go along with this arrangement?"

"Yes, of course. Ours is not a public company, we're privately owned. Mr. Delaney's father established our administrative structure before he became ill."

"And when was that, when he got sick?"

"It was some months ago. He had a massive stroke and very nearly died. Up until then he was here every day."

"You said Roger Delaney is not active in the management now?"

"No, he's not."

"But he was at one time?"

"Yes."

"So what happened?"

Norbert's gaze shifted.

"Well?"

"I don't want to say anything that could cast our company in a bad light."

"Look," Barker said. "Anything you tell me from this point on will remain confidential. Okay?"

"Can I depend on that?"

"Absolutely. You have my word."

"All right. Roger Delaney was with us for a couple of years. He was being groomed to take over the company someday. But then it came to light that his personal life was, ah, less than exemplary."

"Booze, drugs, women?"

"All of those. He got into one mess after another, some of them quite lurid. And his mistakes became public. People were talking about him, and his picture was in the papers. Can you imagine what that was like?"

Yes, Barker could. In fact, he didn't have to imagine it.

"And then on top of everything else," Norbert said, "some money was, ah, misappropriated."

"A lot of money?"

"Yes. A lot of money. So his father relieved him of all responsibility. To save face, Roger was given the title of president and put on an allowance. He signed an agreement that said if he got into any more trouble, the allowance would be cut off. I'm not sure, but I think his father changed his will, too, so that if there was even one more indiscretion, Roger would be disinherited."

"So how often does he come in here?"

"Hardly ever. His mail is forwarded, and phone messages are passed on to him. He and his third wife have been living with his father in Greenwich ever since Mr. Delaney got sick."

"Okay, I get it. There anything else you want to tell me about him?"

"No. Except that we're all gratified he's no longer active here."

"I'll bet. Thanks for filling me in."

"I hope you'll honor your promise to keep our talk confidential."

"I will." Barker turned to leave.

"Excuse me for asking this," Norbert said, "but does your coming here have to do with the investigation into the death of the sister?"

"Yes, it does."

"Terrible thing. Mr. Delaney was always so proud of her. Mr. Delaney Senior, I mean."

The remark brought Barker up short. "Proud of her?"

"Oh yes. He kept scrapbooks filled with stories of her career, and he owned copies of every film she appeared in. He loved to talk about her."

So Roger had lied about that, too. Everything he'd said about the old man disapproving of Catherine's work in show business was bullshit.

"Her father must have been devastated," Norbert said, "when she was murdered."

If he even knew about it, Barker thought. He thanked Norbert and left the office, and as the elevator took him back down to the street he tried to sort out what he'd learned. Realization of how far he'd been misled produced a spark of anger. And disgust with himself.

He pushed those feelings aside. Somehow he had to get Dana out of that huge old mansion.

Before Internal Affairs put him out of action altogether.

60.

Mongo was booked on a 10 A.M. Delta flight to New York. But first there was a piece of business he had to take care of.

As he approached the house he held the handle of the fish knife in his right hand, keeping the knife low and close to his leg. The blade was a foot long, and he'd honed it to razor sharpness.

Knowing what he was about to do gave his senses an edge as keen as that of the knife. The feeling was sexual, and as always in such a situation he had an erection. His pulse quickened, and he drew breath deep into his lungs.

The house wasn't showing a glimmer of light anywhere. If he didn't know better, he might have thought it was deserted. Other homes in the neighborhood had lamps along the walks leading to the entries, but not this one.

He went up the steps and for a moment stood motionless before the door. The luminous dial on his watch read ten minutes to four, and the sky had not yet begun to turn from black to predawn gray. It was the perfect time for this.

There was an illuminated button in the wall beside the door. He pressed it and heard chimes sound softly from within the house. He waited a beat and pressed the button again. Then he pounded on the door with his left fist.

Now he heard a different sound: footsteps clomping on a floor and coming toward the door. A slot opened, and eyes stared out at him. The owner of the eyes said, "Beat it, we're closed."

Mongo slurred his speech a little, pretending to be drunk. "Hey, open the fucking door, goddamn it!"

The eyes narrowed. "I said we're closed. Now get the hell away before I come out there and kick your ass."

"Fuck you," Mongo said. "You monkey-faced cocksucker!"

It had the desired effect. The slot slammed shut, locks were undone, and the door swung open.

The guy standing there wore nothing but white boxer shorts. He was slope shouldered and husky, and there was hair on every part of his body except his head, which had been shaved completely bald. His teeth were bared in anger. He raised a fist and stepped forward.

Mongo plunged the knife into the man's belly. The blade sank all the way to the handle at a point just below his breastbone, angled upward to pierce his heart. Mongo then twisted the slender steel shaft.

The reaction was one Mongo had seen before, on other victims. This one's mouth popped open and his eyes showed shocked surprise, as if he couldn't believe what was happening to him. He stared down at Mongo's hand, which continued to turn the knife, and a gurgle bubbled from his lips. He shuddered, and the color drained from his face.

Mongo grinned and withdrew the blade, and blood spurted from the wound. The bald man staggered backward, clutching at the hole in his gut, until he bumped into a wall. He slumped slowly to the floor, ending up in a sitting position with blood running down over his hands and creating scarlet blotches on his shorts. After a few moments he stopped breathing and his eyes closed halfway, resembling shards of opaque glass.

Mongo stepped past him and went from the foyer into what apparently was the living room. The only light came from a single small lamp, but there was enough for him to take in his surroundings.

The area was large and elegantly furnished, and yet it had an oddly dated look. There were deeply upholstered sofas and chairs that were covered in different shades of velvet, and a grand piano, light from the lamp reflecting from its ebony surfaces. And at the far end of the room was a bar.

So why not, he thought. He went over there and checked the bottles that were stacked on glass shelves. All of them contained good stuff: Wild Turkey and Jack Daniel's and Johnnie Walker Black and Hennessy VSOP and several single-malt scotch whiskeys, as well as various cordials. He laid the knife on the bar and poured himself a glass of Glenlivet and tossed it down.

From somewhere on an upper floor a woman's voice yelled, "Eddie? What the hell are you doing down there? Was somebody at the door? Tell 'em to go away."

Mongo poured himself another drink. It had been quite a while since he'd heard that voice, but there was no mistaking it.

"Eddie?" the woman yelled again. "Come back to bed, will you? It's four o'clock, for Christ's sake."

The whiskey had great flavor. Mongo leaned his elbows on the bar and sipped it this time, enjoying the distinctive smokiness and the smooth way it slid down his gullet. They said you had to acquire a taste for scotch, especially single-malt, but he'd liked it from the outset.

Again he heard footsteps, coming down a flight of stairs. A moment later the woman appeared in a doorway. She had on a flimsy nightgown, and her eyes were puffy from sleep. When she saw Mongo, she stopped short, peering at him in the dim light.

"Hello, Juanita," he said.

She tensed, and her jaw dropped. "You."

"Yeah, it's me. Come on over and have a drink."

"How'd you get in here?"

"Walked in, obviously."

"Where's Eddie?"

"He's resting." In peace, he thought.

"You bastard."

Mongo could see that she was trembling. "Relax," he said. "Be sociable."

"Sociable my ass. Get the fuck out of this house."

He chuckled. "That any way to act after all this time? I thought you'd be glad to see me."

"I said get out!"

"Sure. After we have a little talk."

"There's nothing to talk about."

"Oh, but there is. A lot, in fact."

She took a step back, her gaze flickering from side to side.

"Don't do anything dumb," he said. "I wouldn't want to have to chase you."

She stopped.

"That's better. Now how about a drink? For old times' sake."

She remained motionless, and he knew she was thinking the situation over. Trying to figure out her best move. After a moment, she came toward him slowly, as if keeping an eye on a rattlesnake that had suddenly appeared in her path.

"What'll you have?" Mongo asked. "I'm drinking some of this good scotch, myself."

"Same for me."

He reached for another glass and poured whiskey into it. As he handed her the drink he saw that she'd caught sight of the fish knife, its blade mottled by streaks of blood. But she didn't flinch.

"Here's to you, baby," Mongo said. He raised his glass and downed more whiskey.

Juanita raised hers as well and swallowed a little of the amber liquid.

He waved a hand. "Nice place you got here. Done all right for yourself, huh?"

Her voice was steady now. "I'm okay."

"Like your hair," he said. "Looks great, red. Used to be black, as I remember. Face looks a little different, though. Nips and tucks, right?"

"What do you want?"

"Since you're flush, how about sharing some of the wealth?"

"So it's money."

"Isn't it always?"

He could see she was thinking that over, too. In fact money wasn't his top priority, but as long as he was here, might as well get what he could. "Well?"

"I can let you have some," she said.

"That's nice. I'll bet you got plenty of cash. On account of your customers wouldn't want to use credit cards, true?"

"No, they wouldn't. So why don't I give you some money, and then you leave, all right? We'll call it square. I'll never report this to anybody."

He finished his drink. "Sounds good to me. Let's go."

She turned and walked back the way she'd come, with Mongo following close behind. They went down a hallway, and she led him into what obviously was her office. Unlike the living room, this space was strictly business: plain metal desk and a swivel chair, filing cabinets, two straight-backed chairs, heavy drapes obscuring the window, a ratty brown rug on the floor.

Hanging on the wall behind the desk was a framed watercolor of a landscape with rolling hills and a stand of eucalyptus trees. Juanita swung the frame aside, revealing a safe. She flipped the dial back and forth rapidly and opened the door. Reaching inside, she withdrew a stack of bills and put it on the desk.

"Keep going," Mongo said.

"Look, this is—"

"You heard me. Keep going."

She hesitated and then went back into the safe. The next stack was larger than the first. She put that one on the desk as well.

"That's all of it," she said. "All the cash I have."

"You got anything to put it in?"

For an answer she opened a drawer in the desk and took out a canvas bag with the Wells Fargo logo on it. She stuffed the money into the bag and handed it to him.

"Now let's go finish our drinks," he said.

They went back to the bar. Mongo laid the bag beside the knife and topped off their glasses. He drank more scotch, relishing the way it spread warmth through his body. Juanita sipped hers, watching him as she did.

"You believe in loyalty?" he asked her.

"Yeah, I guess so."

"Me too."

"Really? That why you dumped me, after I peddled my ass on the street so you'd have money while you were in the joint?"

"You got that all wrong. I was gonna come back to you, after I got a payoff from a business deal."

"Sure you were."

He ignored the sarcasm. "That's what I meant about loyalty. Goes both ways. So I was surprised when you tipped off the cops about me."

Now there was no mistaking her expression. Her eyes were wide and filled with fear. "I didn't," she said.

"No? You never talked to a detective, guy named Barker?"

"He came here asking about you. I told him I didn't know you, didn't know what he was talking about."

"That so?"

"I swear it."

He picked up the knife and looked at the blood-streaked blade, as if he'd never seen it before. "You wouldn't lie to me, would you? If you did, I'd have to cut your throat."

Juanita moved so quickly her hand was a blur. She smashed her glass on the surface of the bar and swung the jagged edge at his face.

He pulled back, and the broken glass missed him by a fraction of an inch. Grabbing her wrist in a powerful grip, Mongo shook the shattered glass loose. Then he spun her around so that he was behind her. He pinned both her hands to her sides with his left arm, his other hand still holding the knife. She struggled and kicked wildly as he lifted her off her feet.

There was a large mirror on the wall opposite the bar. Mongo carried her over to it, chuckling as she screamed and thrashed and tried unsuccessfully to bite him.

He held her up so that she could see their images in the mirror. "You're in for a treat," he said. "Gonna get to watch yourself die."

She went on kicking, but her struggles had no effect. He punched the blade into the left side of her neck and drew it across in one swift motion, the razor-sharp steel slicing through flesh and tendons and severing both her carotid artery and jugular. Jets of blood sprang from her throat and splashed against the mirror.

She stared in horror as her life ran out of her. She gave a final kick, and he surmised that was probably a reflex. Seconds later she grew limp, and he dropped her onto the growing pool of blood on the floor.

Christ, he thought, what a mess. On top of everything else he'd had an orgasm, and his crotch was warm and wet.

It would take him a long time to clean up. Not the house, which he wouldn't bother with, but himself.

He went upstairs and nosed around for a bathroom. The one he found was clad in pink marble and had rows of cosmetics on the counter beside the sink. He stripped and took a shower, and when he finished he toweled down and rubbed his skin with perfumed body lotion.

After tying his blood-soaked clothing into a ball, he looked in closets until he came upon some men's shirts and pants he assumed were Eddie's. He put on one of the shirts and a pair of pants and was amused at how badly they fit. Carrying the sodden bundle of clothes and the bag of cash and his knife, he left the house.

61.

Barker's phone rang. He answered: "Barker."

"Hello, Jeb."

Hearing Dana's voice was a thrill. And a huge relief. He'd been almost desperate to make contact with her. And now here she was.

"I'm very glad you called," he said. "I've tried to reach you on your cell phone, but apparently you'd turned it off."

Her tone was barely above a whisper. "Yes, but I'm on it now."

"How's it going?"

"Not well. I didn't want to call you after I saw those awful photos."

"I don't blame you. But I can explain, if you'll give me a chance. I was set up by Hopkins when I went over there to read the agreement Zarkov had sent him on investing in a movie. I know I was stupid to let myself get into such a situation, but that's what happened."

"I hear what you're saying. Whether I can trust you or not is another story. But at the moment I feel I have to."

"You still at Delaney's place in Greenwich?"

"Yes, and I need to get out of here."

"I know you do. In fact, I may have found out what's been going on. With Delaney, that is."

"I have too. At least I think I have. Are you in New York?"

"Yes."

"Thank God."

"Does Delaney know you're suspicious?"

"Maybe. I'm not sure."

"You feel you're in danger?"

"I might be. But except for you, I can't think of anyone who'd believe me."

"Can you leave the house?"

"I could try, but Delaney might stop me. He has a security man who's been watching me like a hawk. Every time I step outside, he's there."

"Then act as if everything is normal. Just go on as usual."

"But I—"

"Look, I realize you're under a lot of pressure. But it's important that you don't let on you suspect anything. I'll get you out of there just as soon as I can. Okay?"

"Please hurry. I'm scared." She hung up.

When his plane landed at JFK, Mongo claimed his bag and left the terminal. A row of taxis was at the curb, and he got into the one at the head of the line.

The driver was a rough-looking character with a do-rag tied around his head. "Where to?" he said.

Mongo leaned forward and opened the drawer in the bullet-proof window that separated the passenger compartment from the driver's seat. He put a hundred-dollar bill into the drawer.

The driver turned and looked at the bill. "What's that for?"

"I want you to take me where I can buy some heat."

The guy continued to eye the hundred. "You a cop?"

"Fuck no. I need a good piece, and if you help me find one, there's another hundred in it for you on top of your fare."

The cabbie snatched up the money. He activated the meter and pulled away, driving fast and deftly slipping the vehicle in and out of the lanes of traffic.

Mongo didn't know the freeways, or parkways as they called them in New York, but he could see the Manhattan skyline ahead in the distance. A lot had happened since the last time he was here.

Fifteen minutes later the taxi crossed the Triborough Bridge. But instead of turning south toward the center of the city, the driver drove west on 125th Street. After covering several blocks he swung north and wound his way through a maze of side streets.

To Mongo, the neighborhood looked a lot like South Central in LA. The sidewalks and the pavement were just as crowded and just as dirty, and among the junky cars there were a few that were shiny and dripping chrome and putting out thundering bass beats from oversized speakers. People were sitting on doorsteps, and kids were everywhere.

The driver pulled into an alley between two ramshackle buildings and drew to a stop. "Wait here," he said, and got out of the taxi.

Three minutes later he was back. He climbed in behind the wheel and said, "Be cool. A brother be comin' by with what you lookin' for."

True to his word, a second guy soon appeared and approached the cab. He wore a bright blue mohair cap and was pulling a suitcase on rollers. Opening the rear door, he got in and propped the case on his lap.

He smiled widely at Mongo. "How you doin'?"

"Fine. Whatcha got?"

Blue Mohair unzipped the top of the case and swung it back. Then he threw up his hands, like a chef presenting a perfectly prepared soufflé. "Here you go, man! Take yo' pick!"

Nestled inside the case was an array of handguns: a Glock 9 mm, a .40-caliber SIG Sauer, a Ruger .357 Blackhawk, a .45-caliber Taurus, and a stubby submachine gun with a folded-back metal stock.

Mongo pointed at the submachine gun. "What's this one?"

"That's a Scorpion, man. You can use it like a machine pistol, fire it with one hand. Or you can fold out the stock, and what you got then is more like a automatic rifle. Either way it's a mean little motherfucker. Puts out eight hunnert fifty shots a minute. *Pop pop pop!*"

"What caliber?"

"Seven sixty-five."

"Not much power."

"That don' matter, 'cause I got hollow points for it. One make a hole you could stick your fist through. Know what I'm sayin'?"

Mongo picked up the weapon. It was surprisingly light and felt comfortable in his hands. "How much?"

"Let you have it for a special price. Two grand."

"How many rounds does it hold?"

"Twenty."

"Let me see those hollow points."

"Sure thing." Blue Mohair unzipped a second compartment in the case. He pulled out a box of ammunition and handed it to Mongo. "You buy the gun," he said, "I'll throw in the bullets. No extra charge."

Mongo opened the box. He released the weapon's magazine and began fitting cartridges into it. "I'll take it," he said.

"Like I told you, two grand."

"Yeah, I heard you." Mongo went on loading the magazine. When he finished he snapped it back into place. Then he pulled a thick wad from his pants pocket and counted out two thousand dollars. It barely made a dent in the wad.

Blue Mohair's eyes bugged. "Man, you takin' a chance, runnin' around with all that bread on you. Somebody could strip yo' ass bare."

Mongo handed over the money and put the rest back into his pants. He raised the Scorpion and racked the first cartridge into the chamber. "No, they couldn't," he said. "Not while I've got a machine gun. *Pop pop pop.* Know what I'm sayin'?"

The guy looked at Mongo, and then at the muzzle of the Scorpion, which was pointed at him. "Uh, yeah."

"Take your case and get out of the cab."

The guy did as ordered.

"Have a nice evening," Mongo said.

The driver had been watching the transaction in silence. Mongo shut the door and said to him, "Now let's go downtown."

62.

As the taxi jounced along FDR Drive, Mongo asked the driver if he knew where the nearest Hertz office was. On East Fortieth, he was told. Take me there, Mongo said.

When the cab stopped in front of the place, he paid the fare plus the additional fifty. He put the Scorpion and the box of cartridges into his bag and left the taxi. Then he went into the Hertz office.

Using a credit card and a driver's license that identified him as Paul McGill of Clear Lake, Iowa, he rented a Chevy Impala. The young woman at the desk gave him a map of the city, and at his request she traced out the route to Barker's address in SoHo.

The first leg took him a couple of miles down Second Avenue to Houston Street. Following the highlighted line on the map, he hung a right onto Houston and drove west to Greene. Then a left on Greene and there was the address. He drove past it and kept going until he found a parking place for the Impala. He got out and walked back.

It was dark by now, and streetlights were on. Pedestrian traffic was heavy, people hurrying in one direction or another and paying no attention to him as he stood on the sidewalk and sized up the building.

The structure was obviously old and didn't look like most apartment houses he'd seen. It was six stories high and had fire escapes hanging off the front. Although there were many windows, the entrance was simply a large double door. When a couple went inside, he got a glimpse of a shoebox lobby with two elevators.

After a moment he realized what he was looking at. This old hulk had once been a warehouse. Or maybe a factory. And then it must have been converted into apartments that were called lofts.

Mongo remembered seeing a movie on TV where a guy lived in one. He was an artist, a slob who smeared paint on large canvases and slopped it all over himself as well. In the movie, he was portrayed as a genius.

Supposedly, lofts were now fashionable. There were a number of similar buildings in the neighborhood, and Mongo supposed they'd all been converted. Given a choice, he'd take his cottage in Malibu anytime. To him a place like this had all the appeal of an oversized shithouse.

As he considered what his next move should be, he noticed a battered green Mustang coupe that was occupying a space marked NO PARKING. He stepped over to it and saw a police plate on the dash.

Stroke of luck, he thought. The junker had to be Barker's ride, and the fact that it was parked here meant the cop was home. Okay, so sooner or later he'd come out of the building, and when he did, Mongo would blast his ass.

No foolishness this time, either. No long-distance shot with a sniper's rifle, no blowing up the fucker's car. Instead, Mongo would keep an eye on the entrance, and when Barker emerged he'd spray him with the Scorpion at close range. Up yours, peckerhead. *Pop pop pop.*

He returned to the Impala and got a zippered jacket out of his bag. As he put it on, it occurred to him that he was hungry as hell. The food on the airplane had been revolting, so he'd just had a couple of scotches and some peanuts. Drinking the whiskey had helped him sleep for much of the trip.

But that hadn't allayed his hunger. On his drive down here he'd passed a grocery store that was only two blocks away. He'd duck over there and get himself something to eat. Bring it back here and settle down in the Impala to wait. He locked the car and moved out, walking briskly.

The store was run by gooks. It was small and rickety, but the vegetables and fruit all looked fresh. It also offered deli service, and he had the slant-eyed mama at the counter make him up a ham and cheese on rye. He added a can of Bud, paid the tab, and headed back.

As he approached the Impala, he glanced over at Barker's building. And was startled to see the cop come out the front entrance and go to his Mustang.

Goddamn it! Mongo had left the Scorpion in the car. By the time he got it out it might be too late. How could he have been so fucking stupid?

He threw the paper bag containing the sandwich and the beer into the gutter and sprinted to the Chevy. He unlocked it, jumped in, and started the engine, just in time to see the taillights of the Mustang disappear around the corner.

Go!

He gunned the car, peeling rubber and missing some fool on a bike by a hair. Apparently Barker had turned right onto Houston Street, so Mongo swung onto it as well and accelerated. But he couldn't catch the Mustang.

He drove hard, whipping in and out of traffic, ignoring the blast of horns as other drivers let him know they were pissed at being cut off. He had no idea where he was going, was only aware that he was headed in an easterly direction.

It wasn't until he'd covered four or five blocks and run a red light that he caught up to the cop's car. He hung back far enough to keep an eye on it but didn't get close enough to spook him.

Now what? Would Barker stop someplace where it would be

possible to get a clear shot at him? Or had Mongo blown his chance, at least for tonight?

One thing was for sure: the fucking cop truly led a charmed life. Mongo had trailed him up into the Hollywood Hills and that had ended in a spectacular failure. Now here he was trailing him in New York and he still hadn't snuffed the son of a bitch.

Which was a dumb way to look at the situation, he told himself. Stick with him and watch for an opportunity. If you don't get one tonight, there's always another time. Just don't blow it by being too impatient.

Following the Mustang wasn't easy. Mongo could see the green car several cars ahead, but holding his position forced him to take chances. When the cop went through an intersection Mongo cut off a truck to stay with him, and right after that he had to run another red light.

On top of those problems, it seemed to him that drivers here were even nuttier than the ones in LA, if that was possible. They weren't only aggressive, they couldn't drive worth a shit. And while they played doodlebug with their cars and trucks, they leaned on their horns and shouted curses.

At one point some cowboy came flying out of a side street, and Mongo slammed into his left front. The Impala skidded from the impact, but he was able to keep going. In his rearview he could see the driver get out of his car to check the damage. The guy was shaking both fists, and the sight made Mongo laugh.

After covering some distance the Mustang turned onto FDR Drive. Mongo recognized it because he'd been on it in the taxi, although now he was going in the opposite direction. To his right he could see lights reflecting from the waters of the East River. The traffic moved quickly but in a steady flow, and that made it easier to follow the cop.

He still didn't know where Barker was headed, but wherever it was he was eager to get there. They passed the UN building, another familiar landmark, and then drove by a large bridge that a traffic sign identified as the Queensboro, all the while maintaining a high rate of speed.

As they approached the Triborough, Mongo wondered whether the cop was planning to go to the airport. Maybe fly back to LA? Wouldn't that be a bitch.

But Barker sailed on by the entrance, and finally crossed the river on a smaller bridge that took him and Mongo to the Major Deegan Expressway. They went past Yankee Stadium and eventually turned off onto yet another multilane road, and by then Mongo had stopped guessing. He'd simply keep on tailing the cop until they came to a stop, wherever that might be.

At least the drive gave him time to review his plan. After he'd taken care of Barker, he'd retrace his route to the Triborough and from there drive to LaGuardia Airport, which was much closer to the city than JFK. The map he'd been given by the clerk at Hertz showed the way.

When he reached the airport he'd leave the Chevy in long-term parking and drop the Scorpion into a trash can. A worker would be sure to find it while emptying the can, and the gun would soon be sold all over again.

Mongo had checked the airlines before leaving LA. He'd learned that several of them scheduled flights from New York to George Town in the Caymans. So getting a seat on one would be easy. The trip would involve one stop, in Charlotte, and then on to the islands. The only drawback was that total time would be a little over fourteen hours.

But so what? Once in George Town he'd get a room in a luxury hotel and have himself a huge dinner and a hooker. Then he'd chill out. When the bank received his fee from Strunk, he'd have all his money wired to the bank in Costa Rica, where he'd opened another account.

After that was done, he'd fly there himself. The forged passport he'd use to get into the Caymans said he was Marcus Hollaby. He'd ditch it when he reached Costa Rica, where he'd become Darius

Rudd, with credentials to prove it. Tracing him, he was sure, would be impossible.

From what he'd learned in Q, all you had to do was pay a little grease to the Costa Rican officials in San José and you could live in style with nobody giving you any shit. He'd rent a house, and staff it with three or four cute mujeres to handle his every need.

That was exciting to look forward to, sort of like crossing the goal line. To get there you had to play it just as he had. You had to work hard, take pride in doing your job well, make a shitpot full of money. Then you could retire and keep yourself in booze and broads ever after. It was the American dream, wasn't it?

But first he had some business to take care of. According to the road signs he was now entering Connecticut, a state he'd never been in before. It had begun to rain, and the diminished visibility made it harder to stay with the cop.

They drove a short distance on I-95, and then Barker turned off at Exit 3. That took them into the town of Greenwich. Barker seemed oblivious to the Malibu with the crumpled right front fender that had shadowed him all the way from New York.

Mongo had to be more careful now. Not only to keep the Mustang in sight, but also not to violate traffic laws. Small-town fuzz could be a pain in the ass, and the last thing he needed was to be stopped by one of them.

Barker turned left at a stoplight, and shortly after that left again, and as Mongo followed he saw a street sign that said they were on Field Point Road. Why Barker had come to this one-horse burg was a mystery, but he must have had his reasons.

Now the cop was making another left turn, and Mongo eased closer. As he did, he saw that the road Barker was turning into had a booth with a security guard in it. Barker slowed down, spoke to the guy in the booth, and was waved on.

Damn it. Apparently this was some kind of closed community where you needed to identify yourself before they'd let you in. All Barker had to do was show his badge.

Mongo drove on by. A block or so farther on, he realized the area was not actually enclosed. There was no fence or high wall along here, only trees and shrubs. So he could get inside, but he'd have to do his trailing on foot from here on out.

Which wouldn't be easy. Stumbling around in a strange area at night with rain coming down was not a happy prospect. But he had no choice. He parked and took the Scorpion out of his bag, along with a Dodgers cap. The machine gun he covered with his jacket, the cap he put on his head.

He left the Chevy and pushed his way through some shrubbery. As he reached the street on the other side, he saw a lot of big houses. Finding the one Barker had gone to would be tough.

On the other hand, he noticed that the cars he could see were mostly BMWs and Mercedes, along with a Lexus here and there. The beat-up Mustang would stand out like a sore thumb. He pulled the cap lower on his head and began looking for it.

63.

Dana calculated that with Mrs. Delaney off to the Hamptons and the old man's nurse gone for the night, only four people were in the house: she and Roger; Delaney Sr.; and the maid. It was the cook's night off.

Carl, the security man, would also be around, prowling the grounds as usual. She was pretty sure he lived in one of the servants' apartments over the garage. The chauffeur lived there too, but he was driving Roger's wife to Long Island. And the gardener? Most likely he was here only in the daytime.

So there was no one she could turn to for help.

The problem was the same one she'd been wrestling with since she'd talked to Barker: How could she get out of here? If she could think up some excuse to give Delaney as to why she had to leave, she could call a taxi and have the driver take her to the train station.

Or would that tip him off to what he probably suspected anyway, that she'd stumbled onto the truth about him? The letter she'd read was ambiguous enough to be interpreted as entirely innocent. Just a perfectly ordinary communication from a lawyer to his client.

But it could be read another way as well. With his sister gone and his father on his way out, Roger Delaney stood to gain a fortune. Had he conspired to have those events take place?

It was a shocking idea. And maybe she was wrong. Maybe she'd jumped to the wildest kind of conclusion, like some hysterical kid whose nerves had been shattered by Catherine's murder.

Maybe. But she didn't think so.

And Barker? He'd said he'd come for her, but was that possible? For one thing, there was no question that he was in a hell of a lot of trouble himself. Whether or not he deserved to be was another matter. Nevertheless, after the flap about his activities in LA he could very well have been suspended.

For another thing, even if he did come here, then what? She knew enough about the law to know what a cop could do and what he couldn't. And one thing he couldn't do was barge into a private home and start ordering people around. Especially when Greenwich wasn't even in his jurisdiction.

There was a knock at the door, and she tensed. "Come in."

Roger Delaney came into the room. He had on a light gray shirt, and an ascot was tied around his neck. Quite the country gentleman.

"Didn't see you for cocktails," he said. "Come on down and have a drink with me."

She hesitated, but only for a second. Better to go along, as Barker had said, as if nothing was wrong.

"Sure, Roger," she said. "Be right down."

"Good. There's something I want to tell you." He went out the door.

She stepped into her bathroom, where she combed her hair and put on a touch of pale lipstick. Then she left the room and went down the main staircase, thinking, Here goes nothing.

He was in the library again, and she resolved not to show that returning there made her uncomfortable. She straightened her shoulders and marched in.

"Hi," he said. "Have a seat."

She chose one of the red leather chairs and settled into the deep cushions. A piano concerto by Rachmaninoff was coming from hidden speakers, a dreary composition that to her was like a dirge.

Delaney touched a button under the mantelpiece, and one of the bookcases swung around silently, revealing a fully equipped bar. "What would you like?" he asked. "I'm going to have Shanahans. Are you familiar with it?"

"No, what is it?"

"An Irish single-malt whiskey. Care to try some?"

"Okay, but make it light, please."

"Coming right up."

He made the drinks in short crystal glasses and handed her one. He raised his and said, "Good luck."

"Good luck, Roger." She sipped the drink, finding it smooth and pleasant. She hoped it would also steady her nerves.

He sat in one of the chairs near hers and said, "Tell me, have you heard from that detective again? Barker?"

"No." Flat lie, but she wasn't about to admit that she'd spoken with him.

"When you were with him in Los Angeles, was there anything he told you that might shed some light on Catherine's murder?"

"He didn't say much about what he was doing."

"That's because he hasn't actually done anything. I had a talk with my lawyer. I told him about Barker's erratic behavior, and how he's been stalking you."

"Stalking me? I wouldn't put it that way. He tried to call me, and I didn't want to speak with him. That's all there was to it."

"You may think that's all, but it's actually a lot more serious than that. My lawyer says his sources tell him Barker is about to be disciplined by the police department in New York. He'll probably be thrown off the force."

Hearing that was a jolt. Dana made no reply. She drank more of her whiskey.

"The fact is," Delaney went on, "he's a dangerous man. The

report on him says he's not only untrustworthy, but very likely emotionally unstable. Sorry to tell you that, but I felt you should be forewarned. In case he tries to contact you again."

"I see." This was weird.

"If he does try to reach you," Delaney said, "I want you to let me know at once. For your own good, of course. Will you promise me you'll do that?"

She tried to dodge the question. "I'll be very careful, Roger. Thanks for letting me know."

He was about to say something else, but he was interrupted when the maid knocked on the door and entered the room. She was a young black woman who was obviously intimidated by Delaney. "Excuse me, sir," she said. "Dinner is ready."

"Very well, Lucille. We'll be there shortly."

Dana saw this as her opportunity to get off the subject. She finished her drink and rose from her chair. "I'm famished," she said.

Her host seemed a little annoyed, but he too swallowed the remainder of his whiskey and got up. "We can talk further over dinner."

They went into the dining room, and Dana was aware that the depressing stream of Rachmaninoff was being piped in there as well. It seemed to go with the rain that was beating at the windows. Did it ever stop raining in Connecticut?

Delaney took his customary seat at the head of the table, with Dana close by on his right. It was more intimate than she would have liked, but she could hardly move her place setting.

"With the cook off tonight," Delaney said, "we're taking pot-luck. Lucille put this together. Isn't anything much. Hope you find it okay."

God, but the remark was rude. Lucille was standing off to one side, no doubt anxious about how the meal would be received. Delaney's words probably put a further dent in her self-confidence. She left the room.

"Dinner looks lovely," Dana said.

And it did. Cold vichyssoise, asparagus vinaigrette, sliced roast beef, a salad of lettuce and tomatoes. And a bottle of Montrachet.

The only problem was that the wine reminded her of that slimy lawyer in Beverly Hills, Alex Haynes. He'd ordered it when they had lunch at Mario's.

"Coming back to our discussion of the detective," Delaney said. "I think it would be fairly easy for you to get a restraining order against him. Even applying for one would be a good idea. Then you'd be on record."

"Something to think about." She sipped some of her wine. Delaney seemed obsessed with keeping Barker as far away from her as possible. Weirder and weirder.

Lucille returned to the room. "Mr. Delaney, there's a phone call for you. Should I say to call back?"

"Who is it?"

"Mr. Whitworth."

"No, I'll take it." Delaney rose from his chair. "Excuse me, Dana." He hurried from the room.

Speaking of slimy lawyers, Dana thought. Carter Whitworth was the one who'd written the letter she'd seen when she was nosing around Delaney's desk.

She ate a spear of asparagus and picked at her salad. Why would Delaney's lawyer be calling him at night?

She shivered, aware that the room was chilly. And gloomy. The falling rain was competing with the Rachmaninoff, the drops beating on the windows.

Should have worn a sweater, she thought. In fact, better go get one. She got up and went out into the hall, walking toward the main stairway.

Passing the library, she could hear Delaney talking on the phone. The door was slightly ajar, and his end of the conversation was clearly audible. She stopped to listen.

He sounded angry. "Damn it, you told me it would be taken care of, Carter. I can't believe this thing hasn't been wrapped up by now. Especially when I think about the amount of money I'm paying for it. And paying you, for that matter. What? Don't tell me to calm down. Just tell me that fucking cop is gone. He's dug up too much already. I'm trying to get information on that out of the bitch, but it's like pulling teeth."

Dana had heard enough. She felt chilled to the bone now, and it had nothing to do with the rain or the jangling piano music. The truth was, she was terrified.

So the hell with whether Delaney liked or disliked her leaving. She had to get out of here, right now. And if he tried to stop her? She'd handle him, somehow.

As quickly as she could, she went up the stairs and ducked into her room. She'd call a taxi, and when the driver came to the house she'd get to it if she had to fight her way.

She'd left her cell phone on the dresser earlier in the day. She didn't know the number or the name of a taxi company, but information would help her with that.

When she looked for the phone, the bottom dropped out of her stomach. The phone wasn't there.

And she heard footsteps, coming up the stairs.

64.

Barker had trouble finding the house. Last time he was here he'd simply followed Delaney's limo and hadn't paid much attention to where he was going. Now he was on his own, on a dark rainy night, and he made two wrong turns trying to locate the place.

As he drove he thought about Joe Spinelli's reaction when he learned Barker was going to Greenwich to get Dana Laramie out of Delaney's house. Joe said, "Have you lost what's left of your mind?"

It was a fair question. Joe pointed out that Barker had one foot stuck in shit already. Go to a private home in another state and force a confrontation and he'd not only put in the other foot, he'd be up to his neck in it.

But Barker was nothing if not stubborn. And far more important, Dana needed him.

When he finally found the house, he pulled up the circular drive and parked in front of the entrance. As he got out of the Mustang, he saw someone approach.

It was Carl, the security man. He had on a slicker and a

sou'wester, both glistening with raindrops. And he was carrying a pump shotgun.

Might as well try being cordial. "Hello, Carl. Not a very pleasant evening."

But Carl wasn't buying it. He blocked Barker's path. "What are you doing here? What do you want?"

"Came to pay a visit to your boss."

"He expecting you?"

"No. I'm just dropping by."

"Then drop yourself someplace else. You want to see Mr. Delaney, call and ask for an appointment. If he says okay, he'll let me know. For now, get lost."

Barker hauled out his shield and held it up. "Back off, Carl. I'm a cop. And I'm on official business, so don't give me any problems."

That shut him up. Barker stepped around him and strode to the house. He went up the steps to the entrance and rang the bell. As he did he heard muffled voices from inside, one of them that of an angry male.

The door swung open. Delaney looked out at Barker and his jaw fell.

"I know Dana Laramie is here," Barker said. "I want to talk to her."

Delaney's voice was a snarl. "She doesn't want to—"

Before he could say more, Dana cried out from somewhere behind him. "Jeb! Help me!"

That did it. He reached for his pistol.

And felt a hard object prod his back. He didn't have to see it to know it was the barrel of a shotgun.

"Put up your hands," Carl said. "Or I'll blow you away."

Barker slowly raised his hands, cursing himself for being careless.

Delaney said, "Get him in here, and we'll deal with him."

The shotgun jabbed again, and Barker stumbled forward. Carl kicked the door shut behind them.

Barker said to Delaney, "You're making a bad mistake. Things'll only go worse for you."

"For me?" Delaney said. "You dumb shit. We'll see who made a mistake."

Dana tried to step past him, and Delaney backhanded her hard across the face. She would have fallen, but he grabbed her arm. He said to Carl, "We'll take them back this way. Come on."

With Delaney dragging Dana by the arm and Carl prodding Barker with the shotgun, they went down the central hallway to the kitchen. Delaney opened a cupboard and got out a roll of duct tape.

Barker tried again. "Give it up, Delaney. The whole thing's out in the open now. Starting with how you hired a hit man to kill your sister."

Delaney stared at him. "You don't know what you're talking about."

"You had her killed because your father would have left her the bulk of his estate. Now with her dead, and the old man sick, you stand to get the whole pie when he dies."

"He's right, Roger," Dana said. "I not only read your lawyer's letter, I heard you talking with him on the phone."

"Shut up, bitch," Delaney said. He gave her another backhand, harder this time. It staggered her and left her gasping, a bright red mark on her cheek.

"Don't say anything more," Barker said to her. To Delaney he said, "I know the killer's name. It's Mongo. The cops in LA are picking him up, probably have him by now. You think he won't try to save himself by running his mouth? He'll tell them everything. And that'll leave you swimming in the toilet."

Carl said, "You want me to shut this shithead up, Mr. Delaney? Just say the word."

"What I want," Delaney said, "is to get rid of the pair of them."

"I can do that, too," Carl said.

"How?"

"Take 'em to the boat, go out in the Sound. Tie weights on them and dump them over. No more problem with either one of them."

Delaney paused, thinking about it. "Yeah, that'd work. Let's get them trussed up."

He spun Dana around and taped her hands behind her. Then he pushed her to the floor and bound her ankles. Turning to Barker he said, "Now you, asshole."

"I'm telling you—"

The shotgun slammed Barker on the top of his head. He saw a bright flash and felt excruciating pain, as the blow drove him to his knees. Carl kicked him in the back, and he fell onto his face.

He was dazed, and his ears were ringing. He was dimly aware that the Mauser had been ripped out of its holster, and that his hands and legs were being bound with duct tape.

When Delaney finished he stepped to a wall cabinet and opened it, revealing a row of keys on hooks. He took out one of the keys and handed it to Carl.

"Get the Escalade out of the garage," he ordered. "And bring it up here to the back door. We'll use that to take them down to the boat."

He peered into the cabinet. "I don't see the keys to the boat in here. I'll look for them. Meantime, go get the SUV."

Carl went out the door, taking the shotgun with him.

Barker's Mauser was lying on the counter. Delaney picked it up. "Don't try to move," he said to the pair on the floor. "I'll be right back." He left the room.

"Are you okay?" Dana asked.

"Yeah, sure," Barker said. "Just hurting from a case of stupid."

"I have the same problem. Never should have come here."

"No way you'd have known. Can you move your hands at all?"

"No. Can you?"

"I'm trying, but this damn tape is tight."

The swinging door to the dining room opened, and the maid came into the room. She had on a raincoat and was carrying a valise.

Dana said, "Lucille! Can you help us?"

"Yeah, I will. I heard what that man was doing to you. He's a low-down motherfucker. 'Scuse my language, but that's what he is. So's the other one."

She put the valise on the floor and took a knife out of a drawer.

Getting down on her knees, she began sawing on the tape that bound Barker's hands behind his back.

"I feel like I been workin' in a nuthouse," she said. "And praise God I'm leavin'. You don't know what I seen here, but it's crazy. Delaney and his wife, they hate each other. And the old man? The nurse keeps him drugged up so he got no idea what's going on."

Footsteps sounded, and Lucille dropped the knife. "Jesus God, he comin' back." She got up and grabbed her valise and hurried out the way she'd come in, through the door into the dining room.

Mongo was soaking wet, and furious. He'd been wandering around the neighborhood for what seemed like hours, ducking behind trees when headlights approached, rain pounding down on him. Looking for the Mustang and not seeing it.

And he was beginning to have doubts. Was Barker actually in here somewhere? Or was there another entrance, a road out that the cop had taken? Leaving Mongo here in the slop.

Maybe the smart thing to do was cut his losses. Go to his car and drive back to New York. Camp out near Barker's apartment and wait for him to show up. Hell, the cop might already be on his way there.

The more Mongo thought about it, the more retreating made sense. He turned around to retrace his steps.

And spotted the Mustang.

It was parked in front of a huge house, one that looked to him more like some kind of municipal building than a place where people lived. It would have been right at home in Beverly Hills.

He studied it, seeing slivers of light here and there, probably from gaps in the draperies. Except for those, the house was dark. He moved toward it, taking the Scorpion from under his jacket.

When he was only a few yards away from the entrance, someone emerged from the side door under the overhang that covered part of the drive. Mongo froze.

It was a woman. She was carrying a small suitcase and running like hell. What was this? She acted like she was being chased by a pack of dogs. He hoped there were none of those in the place. He wouldn't want to have to contend with a bunch of angry mutts.

But as far as he could tell, nothing was chasing her. And she never saw him. Too caught up in whatever was bothering her, apparently. She kept going.

He waited a few more seconds, to be sure she was out of sight and that no one else was coming from the house. Then he again moved forward, going up the steps and trying the door.

It was locked, of course. So now he'd look for another way in. He tried the side door next, the one the woman had come from. Still no luck.

That left the back. He went around to it and saw that there was a large terrace surrounded by a low stone wall. French doors led from the terrace into the house, but they too were blacked out and locked.

At a point farther on, however, lights were showing. Which meant the windows along there weren't shaded. He crouched down and stepped cautiously toward the lights.

There was another entrance, probably for deliveries, and as he approached he saw that a large black SUV had been backed up to the door. The engine was running, but as far as he could see no one was inside.

He had no way of knowing what was going on in the house, but the one thing he did know was that the cop was in there somewhere. He'd have a good chance now to get him.

He checked the Scorpion and thumbed off the safety. Then he went to the door.

Barker strained at the tape binding his wrists. Lucille hadn't succeeded in cutting it all the way through, but he could feel that it was ready to come apart.

He gave another heave, and at that moment Delaney returned to the room. He was holding the Mauser in one hand, a set of keys in the other. He was obviously nervous, chewing his lip.

Next, Barker heard the growl of an engine as the SUV was backed up near the rear entrance. The car's door slammed and Carl also came into the kitchen.

Delaney shoved the keys into a pants pocket and laid Barker's pistol on the counter. He bent down and grabbed Dana under the arms. "Give me a hand here," he said.

Carl leaned the shotgun against the wall and stepped over to Dana. He seized her ankles and the two men prepared to lift her.

At that moment, the rear door opened.

Barker was astonished. A man was standing in the doorway. He was dripping wet and holding a submachine gun.

There was no mistaking him. It was as if the composite drawing had come to life.

Delaney and Carl were equally startled. For an instant, they were motionless, staring at the man who was brandishing an automatic weapon. But then they let go of Dana, and Carl lunged for the shotgun. At the same time, Delaney reached for the Mauser.

Delaney was a fraction quicker. He snatched up the pistol and fired a shot at the intruder. It missed, the slug passing by Mongo's head and shattering a window in the door.

Mongo snarled and raised the Scorpion. He fired a long burst, the loud reports shaking the room. Bullets tore into Delaney, slamming him back against the counter, his mouth wide open and the front of his shirt red with blood. He fell to the floor, a mass of torn flesh.

Carl made it to the shotgun. He brought it to his shoulder, but before he could aim it, a cascade of bullets ripped into him also. Mongo went on firing as Carl went down, blood spurting from the holes in his body.

Barker gave another heave, and the tape parted. His only chance, he thought, was to get to one of the weapons before Mongo blasted him as well.

The Mauser was closest, lying where Delaney had dropped it when Mongo shot him. Because his feet were still bound with duct tape Barker couldn't stand up. Instead, he dragged himself across the floor toward the pistol, hoping desperately he'd get to it in time.

Mongo saw him. Eyes glittering, he shouted, "Die, you bastard!" And pulled the Scorpion's trigger.

There was a click, and that was all.

Mongo stared at the gun in disbelief. As if he was unable to comprehend that its magazine was empty.

He threw the gun aside and looked around frantically for another weapon. He spotted the shotgun and started for it.

Barker reached up to the counter and his hand closed on the Mauser. He swung the pistol to bear on Mongo and fired.

It was a clean shot. The bullet struck the killer in the head. He staggered a few steps and then dropped like a bag of cement, the life gone out of him.

Barker was breathing hard, and he was clammy with sweat. As he put the pistol down, he felt an almost overwhelming sense of relief.

Looking about, he saw that the room had been turned into a slaughterhouse. Three men lay dead in pools of blood, and bits of hair and bone and flesh were stuck to the walls and counters and cabinets. Empty shell casings littered the floor, and the air stank of gunsmoke and burnt cordite.

He turned to Dana, who was trembling from the shock of witnessing the violence. Her eyes were filled with tears.

"You okay?" he said.

"I . . . I guess so. It was just so ghastly."

"But it's done. Give me a minute, and I'll cut you loose."

First he had to free his own bindings. The knife Lucille had used earlier was lying where she'd dropped it, and he picked it up and cut through the duct tape that was wound tight around his ankles.

Next he repeated the process with Dana. He helped her to her feet, and after he stripped the tape from her arms, he chafed them to restore circulation.

She looked over at Mongo's body. "That's the one who came to the Sherry-Netherland and killed Catherine and Penny. I recognized him right away."

"So did I. Name's Mongo. He was a professional hit man, based in LA."

"But why did he come back here now?"

Barker didn't answer. He knew damn well what Mongo's purpose had been. But he'd explain that at some later time.

Dana shuddered. "I want to get away from this place."

"Sure, of course you do. But we can't leave now. I have to call the police."

A wall phone was mounted beside one of the cabinets. He stepped past Carl's shotgun and picked up the phone. Dialed 911.

A female dispatcher answered.

"This is Detective Barker of the NYPD," Barker said. "I'm calling to report a triple homicide at the home of Roger Delaney in Belle Haven."

"Who'd you say you are?"

"Detective Barker."

"You're not a Greenwich officer?"

"No, New York."

"And there's three homicides?"

"Correct. Three down. Delaney and two others."

"They're all dead?"

"Affirmative. I'm calling you from the house."

"How were they killed?"

"Gunshot wounds."

"When did this happen?"

"A few minutes ago. You'll need to send Homicide detectives. Also patrol officers and CSI and an ambulance."

"What caused the shooting?"

Jesus Christ, where did they get these people? "Send police!" he yelled, and hung up.

A muffled cry sounded from behind him. He turned and took in a nightmarish sight.

Mongo was on his feet. He was standing behind Dana and gripping her tightly, one hand over her mouth. Blood was streaming down his face. Apparently Barker's bullet had only creased his skull.

Barker reached for the Mauser, and at the same time Mongo picked up the knife. As Barker leveled the pistol, Mongo held the point of the knife against the side of Dana's neck.

Barker froze. A number of thoughts flashed through his mind: Shoot him! And this time make sure you kill the bastard. But hold on. If you miss, he'll slice into Dana's neck and she'll bleed to death. What he really wants isn't Dana, it's you.

Barker said, "Hello, Mongo."

He scowled. "How do you know my name?"

"I know a lot about you. So do the cops in LA."

"Yeah? So what? Drop the gun or I'll cut her throat."

Barker kept the Mauser trained on Mongo's face. "You were supposed to make another hit, right? Instead you screwed up. Killed the guy who hired you."

"The fuck you talking about?"

"The first guy you shot. His name is Delaney. He paid to have you kill his sister. She was Catherine Delure."

"Bullshit!"

"It's true. He's the one in the gray shirt."

Mongo glanced at the crumpled corpse.

As a distraction, it was enough. Barker squeezed the trigger, and the pistol bucked in his fist.

The bullet struck Mongo between the eyes. The knife flew out of his hand and he staggered backward before going down again.

Barker wasn't about to take any more chances. He stepped over and looked down at him. The killer's eyes were staring sightlessly, and there was a blue hole between them.

Make sure, Barker thought. Make damn sure. He pointed the Mauser at the center of Mongo's chest and fired twice more.

Dana had turned away and was leaning against the counter. Her eyes were shut tight, and she was holding her hands over her ears.

Barker went to her and put his arms around her. "It's over now," he said. "It's really over."

From outside the house came the sound of police sirens. They were coming their way and growing louder.

65.

For the media, it was a bonanza. The broadcast TV networks devoted their evening news shows to the story, and the cable channels featured it for hours on end. It was front page in the *Post* and the *Daily News* and even the *Times* and the *Wall Street Journal*, and newspapers in every city in the country ran accounts fed to them by the wire services.

According to the story, law enforcement authorities had identified the killer of Catherine Delure and her manager as a jewel thief and ex-convict from Los Angeles named Mongo. In the most recent occurrence Mongo had broken into the Connecticut home of Roger Delaney, Ms. Delure's brother, and killed him and his security guard. Mongo was then shot to death by a Detective Jeb Barker of the NYPD. It was unclear why Mongo had gone to the Delaney home, and a further investigation of his motive was being conducted.

New York's police commissioner held a press conference, at which he and the chief of police and the chief of detectives spoke of how the tireless efforts of the NYPD had cleared the case. Detective Barker was praised by them for his courage and dedication to duty. They also lauded Lieutenant Dan Hogan for his leadership of the task force.

Barker was then besieged by the media for interviews and was decorated by the mayor of New York in a ceremony at City Hall.

Sam Benziger was commended by the LAPD for her work in clearing the Culebra homicide.

Captain Swanson said the investigation he and his detectives had directed was instrumental in bringing the Delure case to a close.

The murders of Juanita Romero and Eddie Latanzi remained unsolved.

No connection between Mongo and Harold Strunk was ever established. Strunk continued to enjoy a successful career as an attorney and steadily added to his client roster and his billing.

Variety reported that *Hot Cargo* was the highest-grossing movie yet produced by Zarstar Productions. It also said Catherine Delure was a sure bet to be nominated posthumously for an Academy Award as Best Actress.

The LA district attorney's office brought fraud charges against Len Zarkov and Ron Apperson. The charges were dismissed by the Los Angeles Superior Court for lack of evidence.

Dana Laramie was offered book and movie deals. She was also offered a job by Paramount as an assistant producer.

While excitement over the case continued to mount, Jeb Barker slipped away for a week's vacation. He rented a small cottage at Montauk, on the eastern tip of Long Island, and took Dana with him.

They spent each day the same way. Long walks on the beach, swimming in the surf, dozing in the sun, and making love. They went to a different restaurant each night and ate clam chowder and broiled lobster and drank beer. Later in the cottage, he built a roaring fire, and when it burned down to embers, they went to bed and made love again.

Afterward Dana snuggled up next to him, and they talked until they fell asleep. One night she asked him about his plans for the future.

"Don't have any," he said.

"None at all?"

"Well, I was thinking maybe I'd just stay here with you for the rest of my life."

"Sounds lovely. But not very practical."

"Does it have to be?"

"Afraid so."

"Then how about you? What are your plans?"

"I'm going to write a screenplay."

"About what?"

"About all these terrible things that've happened. About poor Catherine and Penny and Cat's crazy brother and that hideous attack in Greenwich. And how a brave detective rescued his girlfriend and shot the bad guys."

"Huh. You think it'd make a good movie?"

"Absolutely. I think it'd be a big hit."

EBOOKS BY
JAMES NEAL HARVEY

FROM MYSTERIOUSPRESS.COM
AND OPEN ROAD MEDIA

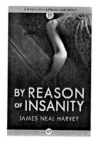

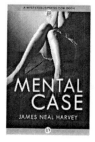

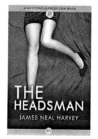

Available wherever ebooks are sold

MYSTERIOUSPRESS.COM

OPEN ROAD
INTEGRATED MEDIA

MYSTERIOUSPRESS.COM

Otto Penzler, owner of the Mysterious Bookshop in Manhattan, founded the Mysterious Press in 1975. Penzler quickly became known for his outstanding selection of mystery, crime, and suspense books, both from his imprint and in his store. The imprint was devoted to printing the best books in these genres, using fine paper and top dust-jacket artists, as well as offering many limited, signed editions.

Now the Mysterious Press has gone digital, publishing ebooks through **MysteriousPress.com**.

MysteriousPress.com offers readers essential noir and suspense fiction, hard-boiled crime novels, and the latest thrillers from both debut authors and mystery masters. Discover classics and new voices, all from one legendary source.

FIND OUT MORE AT

WWW.MYSTERIOUSPRESS.COM

FOLLOW US:

@emysteries and Facebook.com/MysteriousPressCom

MysteriousPress.com is one of a select group of publishing partners of Open Road Integrated Media, Inc.

THE MYSTERIOUS BOOKSHOP, founded in 1979, is located in Manhattan's Tribeca neighborhood. It is the oldest and largest mystery-specialty bookstore in America.

The shop stocks the finest selection of new mystery hardcovers, paperbacks, and periodicals. It also features a superb collection of signed modern first editions, rare and collectable works, and Sherlock Holmes titles. The bookshop issues a free monthly newsletter highlighting its book clubs, new releases, events, and recently acquired books.

58 Warren Street
info@mysteriousbookshop.com
(212) 587-1011
Monday through Saturday
11:00 a.m. to 7:00 p.m.

FIND OUT MORE AT:

www.mysteriousbookshop.com

FOLLOW US:

@TheMysterious and Facebook.com/MysteriousBookshop

OPEN ROAD
INTEGRATED MEDIA

Open Road Integrated Media is a digital publisher and multimedia content company. Open Road creates connections between authors and their audiences by marketing its ebooks through a new proprietary online platform, which uses premium video content and social media.